Night Visions

Melissa Alvarez

writing as

Ariana Dupré

Adrema Press

To dreams that come true.

NIGHT VISIONS REVIEWS

Winner of the CataRomance.com Reviewer's Choice Award for Best Single Title Paranormal Romance

ForeWord Magazine's Book Of The Year Award Finalist
Category: Romance

4 STARS - This book is brisk and entertaining, with someone attempting to sabotage the construction of the hotel, kill Angie and even hurt Jared. The road to the end is exciting! This is a marvelous story about developing trust and a sensuous expression of love, despite the fear that is reinforced by unexpected forces. The secondary characters are interesting, and their roles occasionally draw on their connection to the early inhabitants of the property. ~ Romantic Times

5 STARS - This first installment of the Visions Trilogy has me pulled so far in I couldn't dig my way out. I am salivating for more. I need to read the next book more than I need my next breath. Ariana Dupré has written a mystical story of characters so real they can reach out and grab you. FIVE stars for a lovely story. ~ Paula Beaty, The Romance Review Spot

5 STARS - Ariana Dupré has masterfully created a scintillating romantic suspense story with eerie paranormal elements and roller coaster episodes that compel you to hold your breath with fright and then sigh with desire in NIGHT VISIONS, the first story in THE VISIONS TRILOGY. . . . Things that go bump in the night will never seem the same after reading this mystical love story. I whole heartedly recommend Ariana Dupré's NIGHT VISIONS for a thrilling read and I am anxiously awaiting the next installment of THE VISIONS TRILOGY.

~ Donna Zapf, eCataRomance & CataRomance Reviews

TALGORIAN PROPHECY REVIEWS

Winner: Speculative Fiction Romance in the Dream Realm Awards
Finalist in the Colorado Romance Writers Award of Excellence

4 STARS - Dupré's well-plotted and exciting novel grabs the reader. At its center is a wonderful story about lovers reconnecting. This is surrounded by a suspenseful paranormal adventure with several twists that will continually surprise. ~ Romantic Times

5 CUPS - Ms. Dupré has created a mind blowing tale that grabs you right from the start, throwing you into a maelstrom of action and keeping you on the edge of your seat all the time. With superb ingenuity the author pens a breathtaking adventure with some astounding characters and sensual romance. Without missing a beat the author takes you from a normal hunt into a spectacular paranormal world where you learn the key to what is happening. This is one of those stories that at the end the reader feeling like they had just run a marathon. To sum all of it up would be to say one phenomenal read. ~ Wateena, Coffee Time Romance

5 STARS - Talgorian Prophecy is filled with suspense, love, and fantasy. The plot will keep readers on the edge of their seat. The emotions in this story run deep, I was wiping tears several times before I finished reading. The characters are well-defined. Fans of suspense, romance and fantasy will love this one. ~ Ann Boling, ReviewYourBook.com

SRR GRADE: A - "I really loved this book, it had a couple of really great surprises and it was never slow.... One warning, make sure when you start Talgorian Prophecy you have plenty of time to read, you won't want to put it down until you have turned the last page. I can't wait to read more by this very talented author. ~ Lynda, Simply Romance Reviews

Other titles by Melissa Alvarez

365 WAYS TO RAISE YOUR FREQUENCY
YOUR PSYCHIC SELF
SIMPLY GIVE THANKS
ANALYZE YOUR HANDWRITING
YOUR COLOR POWER
GHOSTS, A SPIRIT GUIDE AND A PAST LIFE
CHAKRA DIVINATION® CARDS & CHARTS ACTIVITY BOOK
THE ESSENTIAL GUIDE TO CHAKRA DIVINATION®
CHAKRA DIVINATION® ULTIMATE BALANCE JOURNAL
THE ELINK DIRECTORY OF PARANORMAL INVESTIGATIVE GROUPS AROUND THE WORLD
HOMEMADE RECIPES FOR HORSE TREATS PLUS FLY SPRAYS & TIPS FOR OWNERS
THE PHOENIX'S GUIDE TO SELF RENEWAL
CHRISTMAS DESSERTS
PENELOPE PANDA'S SHOOTING STAR

Titles by Melissa Alvarez writing as Ariana Dupré

Romantic Suspense

NIGHT VISIONS
TALGORIAN DRAGON
TALGORIAN PROPHECY
PARADISE DESIGNS
BRIAR MOUNTAIN

Websites:

MELISSAA.COM
APSYCHICHAVEN.COM
TOPHATFRIESIANS.COM
BOOKCOVERS.US
BOOKCOVERSGALORE.COM
VOMGRENZPOLIZEIK9.COM

Published by Adrema Press

ISBN: 978-1-59611-107-3

Cover Design © Melissa Alvarez at BookCovers.Us/BookCoversGalore.com
Cover Art ©Depositphotos

PUBLISHING HISTORY
New Age Dimensions trade paperback / June 2004
Adrema Press / May 2013

Third Edition

10 9 8 7 6 5 4

Trademarks Acknowledgement - The author acknowledges the trademarked status and trademark owners of the following wordmarks mentioned in this work of fiction:

Casper the Friendly Ghost: Harvey Entertainment, Inc

Ford: Ford Motor Company

Mustang: Ford Motor Company

THE VISIONS TRILOGY

Night Visions
*Enchanted Visions**
*Celestial Visions**

Two hundred years ago, Mary Slayton witnessed the murder of her husband, Theodore. Pregnant and overcome with grief, Mary revenged Theodore's murder with a curse cast by the local gypsy witch. With her emotions in turmoil, Mary extends the curse to include everyone who ever hurt Theodore during his lifetime. Now, the souls of several families are bound to the Earth for the next 200 years and their descendants are denied true love. There are three in the future, gifted by the gypsy witch with special paranormal abilities, who can break the curse. But if the three fail to find true love and unite as one family, the doomed souls will walk the Earth for eternity.

**Enchanted Visions and Celestial Visions are Adrema Press future publications*

Prologue

Slayton Homestead
Southern Central Virginia
August—early 1800's

THE BLISTERING HEAT OF THE MIDDAY SUN WAS NO match for the fire burning within Theodore Slayton. Thunderheads rose in the crystal blue sky, a sure sign of turbulent storms to come. Not even a driving rain would cool his angry suspicions.

Small puffs of dust rose around the hooves of the dappled gray stallion fidgeting beneath him. Theodore clasped his legs against the horse's body to still the animal as he studied his overseer's house.

He adjusted his wide-brimmed hat and squinted into the sunlight. This two-story home would be his undoing, he was sure of it.

Theodore inhaled the still air, so thick and hot it hung like a weight inside him, adding to the heaviness already in his heart.

Glancing down the dirt road, he saw Mary, his wife of three months, running toward him. He gripped the reins tighter. Why hadn't she listened? He'd told her to stay at the main house while he confronted Clyde. If the rumors he'd heard were true, she was putting herself and their unborn child in danger by coming here.

Her wild impulsive streak would get her into trouble one day. She could be a spitfire, that Mary! She'd always said, "You'll be mine Theodore. One day I'll make you love me as I love you. You'll see." Now she had his heart. No doubt she thought she could protect him. The woman had such daring, such boldness. She was a handmaiden, beneath his status in the eyes of the community, but she had the spirit of a queen. The love she felt for him, the loyalty and devotion—it was a small wonder he felt like a king among men.

A moan escaped through the open window on the second floor, disrupting Theodore's thoughts. His body went rigid and he pressed his lips together. He knew that sound well—a woman in the throes of passion. He glared at the window, his jaw clenched.

He'd talk with Mary later. Right now, there were more urgent matters.

The growl vibrating in his chest threatened to become a full-blown scream of fury, but he pushed his anger down, struggled to remain silent. *I need proof.* There would be hell to pay if he found his younger sister Ruby inside with Clyde.

He glanced down the road at his beloved. He must surprise them before Mary arrived.

Theodore dismounted so quickly his horse shied. He didn't bother to tether the animal before he slipped into the house and began to climb cautiously up the wooden stairs.

When he reached the bedroom door, he stopped. He knew in his heart what he would find. Was he ready to face it?

He gathered his courage, twisted the knob and stared through the partially opened door.

What he saw enraged him.

No woman would ever tarnish the Slayton name again. His grandmother, in her youth, had done that job quite well enough, taking every man she fancied to her bed. It took years for the Slayton name to gain respect again, after the damage she had inflicted on the family reputation. Theodore would not allow his sister to repeat his grandmother's mistakes.

"I love you, Clyde."

His sister's throaty words exploded inside Theodore's head. He slammed the door back against the wall. His voice boomed, deep and ominous, belying his small stature. "You love him, little sister?"

Ruby's eyes widened in shock. "Theodore!" she gasped, pulling up the cotton blanket to cover her nakedness.

Clyde leaped out of bed to face Theodore's rage silently. His eyes, narrowed with contempt, the only indication of his feelings.

"You only love him as Grandmother loved her men!" Theodore's voice pulsed with fury. "Get away from my sister, Clyde, and leave my property at once!"

"No." Clyde's voice was eerily calm. His steady gaze locked with Theodore's even as he grabbed his pants, jerked them on and fastened the buttons. "Ruby and I belong together. You can't make me leave."

"I'm the owner of this estate," the other man snarled, advancing toward Clyde. "You work for me. Now get out."

An insolent smile curved Clyde's lips. He took a step closer to Theodore, stopping the other man in his tracks. "You sold this house to me. I'll quit, but I'll never leave my home."

"Then I'll make you pay for spoiling my sister's reputation and our family name." Theodore charged, fists swinging.

Clyde stepped out of the way to miss the blow. "You'll make me pay?" He laughed derisively, "You're half my size. You've got it wrong—"

Theodore swung again. Clyde pushed him away.

The smaller man crashed against the edge of a table, scattering its contents, before hitting the wall with a loud thump.

Immediately, he doubled over and fell to the floor. His voice, when it came again, was low, "Curse you both!" Then his eyes closed and he became eerily silent.

"Oh, no," Ruby whispered, turning wide-eyed to her lover. "You've killed him!"

"I didn't push him hard enough to kill him," Clyde responded, struggling to keep the worry out of his voice. He looked at Ruby. The shock in her pale face was unbearable, so he turned his gaze back to her brother. "He's out cold, that's all." Pulling on his shirt, Clyde kept an eye on Theodore. *He can't be dead.*

"I'm not a murderer, Ruby," he said, his tone anxious. He walked over to where Theodore lay in a crumpled heap. "Get up," he ordered, pushing the smaller man's shoulder with his foot.

Theodore's limp arm thudded against the wooden floor. Mumbling, he shifted slightly.

Clyde squatted down. "What did you say?" His brow furrowed at the sight of Theodore's pale skin, the slow trickle of blood that oozed from the corner of his mouth.

Theodore turned his head and stared up at him with a look of pure hatred, but Clyde saw the life ebbing from his glazed eyes.

No! Not this... Panic filled him. *Please. Don't die.*

With great effort, Theodore spoke louder. "I'll haunt you—I swear you will pay..." He grimaced in pain as death claimed him.

Clyde stared at the smaller man's chest, waiting for the steady rise and fall that never came. Finally, he pressed his fingers against Theodore's neck. He looked at Ruby. "There's no heartbeat," he said in a choked voice.

"Are you sure?" Ruby shuddered as she got out of bed and quickly stepped into her dress.

Clyde frantically searched for any sign of life in Theodore. Picking up the man's wrist, he pressed his fingers to the pulse point. Nothing. He hung his head. "He's dead, Ruby."

He stood to shove his feet inside his boots, was silent for a long moment, as his mind raced. "We've got to think this through," he said at last. "I could say I found him in the woods, thrown from his horse—an accident." He turned toward her. "When I tell you about it, later, when other people are there, you'll have to act surprised and upset. Do you understand?"

"Yes, I understand," she replied, her voice hollow, tears streaming down her face. Aimlessly she searched for the sleeves of her dress while staring at her brother's body. "He died thinking that I'm like Grammie. I wish we had told him that we got married."

Clyde heard the helplessness in her voice, saw the pain in her eyes and rushed to her side. He ran his hands down her arms to steady them before he twisted the fabric that hung around her waist to reverse it.

Trancelike, Ruby allowed him to dress her, then stepped into her shoes. She stood in silence as Clyde's trembling fingers fumbled with the small buttons on the back of her dress.

"We'll only keep our marriage secret a little longer. You know we didn't tell Theodore because he'd never approve of you marrying me, his employee, even though he did the same. He wanted you to marry into money."

When the last button was in place, he slipped his arms around her waist, pressed his face into the long brown locks that cascaded over her shoulders and held her tight. "Are you all right?"

"No, Clyde, I'm not." Her voice was flat, empty of emotion. "How can I be all right, when my only brother's dead?"

Clyde held her close. "I'm sorry, Ruby. I'm so very sorry. I never meant—" How could I have killed anyone, especially my wife's brother? He took a step away from her. "Go wait for me outside. Please."

Without looking back, Ruby left the room.

Sighing deeply, Clyde lifted Theodore's lifeless body over his shoulder and followed her. Outside, he laid the corpse over the dappled gray stallion. His wife was already halfway down the dirt road that led back to the main house, so he led the heavily laden horse into the forest alone.

When the hoof beats faded, Mary moved from behind the hallway curtains. She had darted behind the thick green fabric just before Ruby entered the hall. *If Clyde could kill Theodore so easily, surely he'd do the same to me and my unborn child. They must never know that I witnessed Theodore's murder.* Her face stained with silent tears Mary caressed her abdomen, the last link to her husband.

"Theodore," she whispered in anguish, then stepped into the bedroom where, just moments before, her one true love had met his end.

Water from a white washbasin dripped down the side of the small table and splattered against the matching pitcher overturned on the floor. The bed was disheveled, the sheets a rumpled mess.

If only I'd arrived a few moments earlier, Mary thought miserably, *I could have done something, anything, to save him.*

"My love, my life," she choked between agonized sobs. She knelt on the floor where Theodore had fallen, murdered in cold blood. Her stomach twisted and curled, threatening to release itself. "Why did this happen?" Her body shook with the depth of her sorrow. "You'll never even know our child, Theodore," she whispered through her tears.

How could this have happened? She had never known her own father and now that joy had been taken from her baby in a manner so horrible she almost couldn't bear it.

Too exhausted to cry any longer, she dropped her head into her hands. What would happen now? Ruby and Clyde were each in their own way cruel, despite what Theodore thought of his younger sister. Separately, they had already hurt her family in ways she could not forgive. Now this. Who knew what other terrible things they would do as husband and wife.

"I'll make them pay," she said to the empty room, her voice forceful and distinct. She raised her head high and wiped her tear-stained cheeks with her fingertips.

I swear…you will pay… Theodore's dying words echoed in her mind.

Only one person could help her now. She stood, walked out of the house and headed for the woods.

The lush greenery of the forest streamed by as she ran. The squirrels twitched their tails and scuttled out of her way. She barely noticed the woody scent of pine or the fragrance of wildflowers in her hurry to reach the cave.

She had approached this clandestine place once before, but fear had made her run for home. She knew the rumors that were whispered everywhere. The gypsy witch would grant you favors, but the price was very high—part of your soul was demanded in return.

Mary paused to catch her breath beside the stream that flowed alongside the cave. In her grief and desperation, she was sure its gurgling song whispered her name.

"Come inside, Mary," a low voice vibrated from the inky blackness.

Mary stiffened in alarm. Thieves were known to hide in the woods. "Who are you?" She stepped back, surprised that her voice sounded strong and clear.

"The one you seek. No thief am I."

A wave of uneasiness washed over her. How had the voice known what she'd been thinking? She hesitated, thought of Theodore and knew that this time she had to go inside. She willed her feet forward and cautiously entered the dank, dark cave.

Cool air caressed her sweaty skin. The cave's musky scent sent a rippling shiver and then a shudder through her. As her vision adjusted to the darkness, she focused on the glimmers of candlelight flickering along the rocky crevices in the walls. A stone table grew upwards from the earth. On top were four unlit candles set apart in an imaginary square. Inside the square were a white candle, a large empty bowl and several small bowls containing what looked like salt and herbs.

Mary stared at the table. Fear struck a chord inside her. She'd made a mistake in coming here. Suddenly, a scratchy hardness bumped against the back of her knees and she whirled around. She saw no one, but a hand-hewn wooden chair sat on the ground behind her.

"I've been waiting for you." The disembodied voice filled the cavern. "Please rest. Running is dangerous for the child you carry."

Mary searched the shadowy depths. Where was the owner of this smooth, measured voice that surrounded her? It was as if the cave itself spoke her innermost thoughts.

"How did you…?" With a slight waver, she sat on the edge of the chair. "Are you the gypsy witch I seek?"

"Yes, I am the one, Mary. I already know your secrets. I know you want to make the lovers pay for killing the father of your child."

Mary's mouth dropped open, her pulse quickened and her gaze darted nervously about. Glancing back at the table, she noticed a double-edged knife lying beside the bowls. Had it been there a moment ago? At the sight of it, she fought against the desperate feeling to flee this evil place.

No, no! Clyde and Ruby must pay. She grasped the edges of the chair with both hands in anger and called out, "Show yourself!"

"Say what it is you ask of me."

"A curse. A curse on those who killed Theodore Slayton."

"There is a price, Mary."

Her head dropped. Her pockets were empty. "If it's money you want, I have none with me," she said. Sighing heavily, she stood to leave.

"It isn't money I require."

The rumors came flooding back and Mary's heart quaked. Did she dare ask? "Then… What?"

The gypsy witch stepped from the shadows into the light and stood insolently in front of her.

Mary gasped. Her hands flew to her mouth to silence the scream that threatened to burst from her. She scrambled backward into the darkness, to hide. "You're…a…" Her mind whirled. This couldn't be right.

Candles flamed to life around her.

Speechless, Mary gazed up at the gypsy seer.

He was gorgeous. His long hair, the color of a raven, fell across his shoulders. His white shirt hung open to expose a tanned and muscular chest. His unblinking smoky gray eyes scorched into hers, as if he could look right into her soul. The candlelight danced over his handsome features. Opening his mouth slightly, he ran the tip of his tongue sensuously across his full lips.

Mary stared in disbelief. "But… You're a man!"

Hadn't others who visited this cave told her she would find a woman here? She searched the recesses of her memory, suddenly realizing that she'd never heard anyone describe the gypsy witch.

"Surprised?" The seer's tone was arched.

Mary ignored his question. She had already experienced so many terrible things today and now this…

It was too much. Her emotions were spinning out of control still Theodore must have his revenge.

Stay strong, Mary. Fearing for her soul she asked, "What do you require in payment?"

"A kiss."

A kiss? A wave of dizziness buckled her knees, her body swayed. Kiss the devil himself? Kisses were the last thing on her mind. How could she kiss someone else? Her kisses were only for

Theodore. But this was for him—she must do this for her husband, whose dying words still echoed in her ears.

"Is there no other way?" she asked, lifting her chin in defiance. "Do you not wish to take my soul instead?"

Mary's body burned under the gypsy witch's intense inspection, as he slowly looked her over until his gaze finally locked with hers. "A kiss is what I require." He took a strand of her hair, curling it around his fingers, awaiting her reply.

Revulsion grabbed at the pit of her stomach at the thought of kissing something so evil. Could she bring herself to do it to revenge her beloved husband? Yet, he hadn't asked for her soul or her child, only a kiss. "In return, you will curse all those who hurt Theodore Slayton?"

He stilled and scrutinized her face. "Are you sure of what you ask?"

In her mind's eye Mary saw her sister's mangled body, broken and violated by a group of rogues the day after Ruby had banished her from the farm because she had flirted with Clyde. She saw her mother's stooped shoulders, weighed down by years of overwork under Clyde's rule. Then Theodore's brilliant smile nearly broke her heart.

"Yes, I'm sure."

"You understand this affects several families?"

"Yes."

He released her hair, slid his hands across her shoulders and down her arms until he grasped her hands. "You must be certain."

Her body trembled at his touch. "I want them all to pay." A tear inched down her cheek still she stood tall. "I'm positive."

The gypsy witch blinked and all four candles on the table burst into flames, drenching the cave in a bright light. He moved quickly, pulling Mary near. With his free hand, he grabbed some salt from a bowl and sprinkled it on the ground around the table, enclosing them inside a circle. Releasing her, he took herbs from the smaller bowls and dropped them into the large one, chanting words she didn't understand.

"What language are you speaking?" she asked.

"The Romany of my ancestors." The white candle flickered to life. He turned to face her, a mocking smile played on his sensuous lips. "Now…payment."

Mary closed her eyes for a brief moment. "Forgive me, Theodore," she whispered.

She went to him, stood on tiptoe to reach his mouth. As she lightly held his shoulders for balance, she felt hard muscles ripple beneath her hands. A brush of her lips against his and she stepped back, releasing him.

His eyebrows lifted. "That's it?"

Mary nodded. "It was a kiss, as you required."

"That's not payment." He grabbed her around the waist, pulled her hard against his body, held her tight as he crushed his lips to hers.

Mary struggled against the fire inside him, pushing at his shoulders, but it was no use. He filled her with his unholy passion, until she surrendered beneath him, relinquishing with a deep shudder all the goodness left in her soul.

He broke the kiss and then stared at her. "That's payment."

Seizing her hand, he ran the knife blade across her spread palm. She screamed in pain. When did he grab the knife? She tried to wrestle free but his grip was relentless. He held her hand above the bowl. Three drops of her blood dripped onto the herbs inside. Only then did he release her.

She pressed her bleeding hand against her breast, her pulse throbbing through the wound. The gypsy witch reached over and in one deft movement sliced off a lock of her hair.

"What are you doing?" She cried out, grabbing at the shortened strand.

"This is the curse you place on all who harmed the one you

love. You are the main ingredient. One drop of blood for each of the three who can break the curse, a lock of hair and spit bind the potion together. Now spit."

"What?"

"Spit in the bowl, Mary."

She did as he commanded, then wiped her chin with a sleeve, her gaze glued to his blazing eyes.

Once more, he took her bloody hand into his own and placed the mixing stick in her palm. Wrapping his fingers around hers, he slowly stirred the potion. He closed his eyes and spoke in a soft songlike lilt.

In answer to harm done to you,
I put a curse on love that's true.
Never shall the lovers gain,
Instead to them comes only pain.
Until the three shall meet as one,
All joined by family once unknown,
The souls of those who live today
Shall walk the lands and never stray.

Mesmerized, Mary watched his eyelids flutter open. He lifted the stick from the bowl and laid it on the table. Taking a handful of potion, he sprinkled it over the candle flames and closed his eyes again.

The gifts of sight I now bestow,
The virgin shall dream, the sister shall know.
To the secret one I give,
Visits from others who might have lived.
Two hundred years, no more, shall pass,
Before these three find true love at last.
When the three bind blood to blood,

The curse I place shall turn to love.
The souls I capture by my hand
Will then be free to leave the land.
But if true love is never found,
The souls will ever walk the ground.
When at last the time's at hand,
They will meet in the circle of trees you plant.
Then they shall see all that is true,
Why love was lost, avenged by you.

The gypsy witch raised his eyelids to look at Mary. His smoky gray eyes were now pitch black. The four candles on the table dimmed then went out. He reached over, snuffed out the white candle and picked up the double edge blade.

Mary cringed.

He whispered more words of his ancestors, then, bending down, he placed the blade into the earth and cut through the salt, breaking the circle. Straightening, he turned to Mary, then reaching out, he ran the pad of his thumb across her cheek, removing a single tear.

"It is done," he whispered.

Mary blinked and, in the next moment, she was standing in her kitchen, a knife in one hand, the palm of the other cut and bloody.

How did this happen? She dropped the knife, grabbed a cloth and pressed it to the open wound. As she did so, she recalled the details of the curse and that she must plant a circle of trees deep in the forest.

She stood for a moment searching her thoughts. She frowned, then shook her head. No matter how hard she tried, she could not remember what the gypsy witch looked like. What difference did it make? She'd carried out Theodore's dying wish.

Suddenly overwhelmed from the pain of the loss of her

husband, the emotional turmoil of the day and the pain in her hand, Mary collapsed on the floor. Lying there, brokenhearted, she buried her head in the bend of her elbow and let the emotions pour from her, mourning her loss with sobs and tears. *Oh, Theodore! You're gone. You're really gone.*

Without Theodore, all that was left in her life was sorrow and despair. Not even the thought of her unborn child could console her.

ONE

Old Slayton Homestead
Present day

THERE WAS NOWHERE TO HIDE.

Angie Benton watched the young woman running through the forest. As she fought the brush and bramble, her torn clothes ripped even more.

She tripped over a tree root and fell to the ground. Quickly, she struggled to her feet while leaves caught in her hair and briars slashed her arms, drawing blood.

Angie could feel the woman's terror—like a knife slicing through her own heart.

Just then a man appeared. Angie, watching from a high perch in the trees, trembled. What now?

Jaw clenched, eyes narrowed, the man opened and closed his fists repeatedly as he tramped toward the frightened woman. His shirt was unbuttoned, revealing the sweat glistening on his heaving chest. He looked so angry, so hostile. She could even hear the fury in his strong, deliberate footsteps.

The woman heard him too and looked over her shoulder.

Angie gasped. The woman's face was her own!

Horrified, Angie watched the woman who could be her twin run into a clearing, then pause and look frantically around. She could feel her desperation and when the other woman sprinted across the meadow toward an old shack, Angie experienced a jolt of hope and a burst of energy as she mentally followed her twin.

Arriving breathless at the cabin, the woman jumped onto the porch, pushed through the broken door and ran into the first room on her left.

Angie spotted an exit at the back of the shack. She willed her twin to find it and escape that way. Instead, the woman ran wildly through the house in terror, searching for a place to hide.

Entering the kitchen at last, she didn't run out the back door as Angie willed. Instead, she crouched in the corner behind an antique hutch.

The old pine floors creaked as if under a heavy weight.

Angie screamed, "Run! Run!" But the twin didn't move.

The man's footsteps moved methodically through the dilapidated old shack, searching, slowly, room by room.

Still her twin waited motionless, until, at last, the footsteps left the house.

Tentatively, the young woman stood up and glanced around. Inching toward the back door, she looked through the screen and out the side windows, surveying the yard with wide, frightened eyes.

All clear.

Cautiously, she opened the door and slipped out. With her back to the yard, she quietly closed the door behind her, then spun around to make a run for it.

And crashed right into her pursuer.

A loud whistle pierced Angie's hearing. What on earth was happening?

Someone was pulling her from her perch. Someone had a grip

on her biceps and searing stabs of pain were shooting through her arms.

She looked up and stared into the angriest blue eyes she had ever seen.

Eyes belonging to the man she'd just seen outside the cabin door.

Her heart pounded. *How had she become the woman she'd been watching?*

The man's sandy brown hair hung over his face in wet strands, its blond highlights still noticeable. Sweat beaded across his brow. He clenched his jaw against chiseled cheeks and he tightened his grip by digging his fingers deeper into the soft flesh of her arms.

Angie jerked her body violently, but could not break his hold. Wave after wave of terror crashed through her. She had to escape!

"Angie!" he growled.

She snapped her head back to look up at his angry face.

A flash of light in her peripheral vision caught her attention and she turned to see someone, shadowed by trees, leveling a gun at them.

Angie froze. As if in slow motion, the muzzle of the gun moved until it was pointing straight at her. She heard a booming blast, so loud it hurt her ears. *Oh God, I'm going to die, she thought in terror.*

The man with the sandy hair whirled her around, using his body to shield her from the oncoming bullet. Suddenly, his face contorted, his back arched and his grip on her arms loosened, then released, as he fell to the ground.

Angie watched him land in a crumpled heap at her feet. She'd barely had time to take this in before she felt something hard and cold jab into her back and an arm clench around her neck, forcing her to look skyward. She heard a deep, raspy, laugh behind her as a man dragged her backward, knocking her off her feet with a quick pull, his laughter intensifying.

Angie struggled frantically with the gunman. She was so desperate, so frightened, that several seconds passed before she noticed that the man who had come between her and the bullet was no longer there.

Where had he gone?

The pressure increased against her throat.

Angie twisted and turned, trying to break free, trying to find the man who had saved her before.

But it was useless. He'd disappeared and the more she struggled, the more her assailant tightened his hold.

Then the realization hit her. The sandy haired man was dragging her across the yard. Somehow, he'd captured her.

A gunshot rang out.

Fire burned through her chest. The man pushed her and she sank to the ground, feeling her life ebbing away.

ANGIE'S EYES FLEW OPEN. She didn't dare move as she peered into the inky blackness.

Where was he?

Who was he?

Propping herself up on one elbow, she covered her racing heart with her hand. Her nightgown, wet with sweat, stuck to her chest. Even the sheets were soaked.

The dream terrified her.

He terrified her.

Those angry blue eyes, crystal clear and light as the sky, still seemed to be staring at her, so full of intense emotion she couldn't look away. She tried to swallow but her parched throat tightened until she thought she might choke.

Shaking her head to clear it, she slipped out of bed and headed through the darkness to the kitchen for something to drink.

It isn't real, she reminded herself. *It's just a dream.*

A dream that followed her, tormented her, caused so many sleepless nights, more lately than ever before. And it was always the same. She was an outsider looking in, unable to do anything to help.

Except this time, for the first time, she had watched herself. That worried her. She didn't have a twin.

She reached for a glass, filled it with cold orange juice from the fridge. She drank deeply, then set the glass down on the counter with a thud.

It would not be like the other times when she had been a dream observer. She simply wouldn't let it.

When she dreamed of Aunt Martha's death before it happened, she'd told herself that it was only a coincidence. And her dream about the accident that left her great-uncle paralyzed? Same thing. And the time when—

"No!" The sound of her own voice startled her. She hadn't meant to speak aloud.

Angie knew the truth in the depths of her soul, but she would not, could not, admit that her "observer dreams" came true. Aunt Martha called them prophetic. But she was wrong. She had to be.

Angie licked the juice from her lips and glanced at the stove clock. Five a.m. There was no way she would ever fall back to sleep now.

"Might as well start the day," she said with a sigh. She went into the bathroom, turned on the shower and peeled off the clammy gown. The scent of lavender soap mixed with the silky warmth of the hot spray had a calming affect, but still the dream haunted her.

Stepping out to dry off, she tried hard to think of something, anything, other than the nightmare but it consumed her thoughts. Still unsettled, she selected her clothes and dressed, then checked the mirror to make sure everything matched.

The store doesn't open until ten, she reminded herself, dabbing lavender perfume behind her ears and on her wrists. I could complete the jewelry inventory and submit reorders.

The house creaked and she jumped in fear.

"All right, that's it!" she yelled at the walls. *No way is this stupid dream going to take over my life!*

She wasn't about to screw up after all the years of hard work she and Aunt Martha had put into The Variety Vine. She would not lose her focus now. Together, she and her aunt had made the store one of Dansburg's most successful gift shops. She'd practically grown up in the store, until she decided to become an interior decorator—a job she'd given up the moment Aunt Martha willed the business to her.

Angie picked up a scrunchie, pulled her hair into a ponytail and went into the kitchen. Still thinking about all the work she needed to do at the store—and the dream—she toasted a bagel, then spread cream cheese inside.

I better go in early, she thought, pushing the dream to the recesses of her mind.

Grabbing her breakfast and briefcase, she headed out the door.

ANGIE PARKED HER sport utility vehicle in front of The Variety Vine at exactly six a.m.

The store had been converted from a family home years ago. "The old Randall house", people used to call it. Sitting off the road with no other buildings in sight it looked eerie with the sun dawning behind it. A misty fog surrounded the wisteria vines that covered the front porch banister and crept up the round columns to the roof.

Angie climbed out of the SUV and brushed the breakfast crumbs off her shirt. Grabbing her briefcase, she locked the vehicle and headed toward the store.

She saw the web, shimmering with sunlight through droplets of dew, just before it touched her face. Too late, she dropped her briefcase, jumped off the steps and frantically pulled the web from her eyelashes and hair.

"Uugghh!" She shuddered, spotting the spider. "Nasty little creatures."

Using a long branch, she removed the remaining web, including the spider and tossed the stick under the tree.

Aunt Martha's favorite rocking chair sat on the front porch, gently swaying back and forth.

That's odd, thought Angie. *How is it moving? There's no breeze.*

Dismissing the chair, she sorted through her keys for the one to the store, but before she could place it in the lock she heard a voice behind her.

"Angelina."

She froze, feeling a cold chill quake through her body. Impossible!

"Angelina, sweetie," the voice said again.

She forced herself to turn around.

There in front of her stood Aunt Martha. She was smiling at her as though her ghostly appearance were the most ordinary thing in the world.

Oh God! Oh God! Breathe Angie!

She pressed her back against the door and inhaled deeply. *Good. Breathing's good.*

Sweat broke out on her forehead and her stomach clenched.

Aunt Martha looked beautiful. Her long dark hair flowed unrestrained around her shoulders.

She never wore her hair like that in life. Well, maybe when she was young, but she always worn it in a bun around me.

The apparition seemed to be waiting for her to speak, but

Angie, her throat tight with fear, couldn't form any words. *Geez...what do you say to a ghost anyway?*

She cleared her throat. "H-Hi." The word was a mere whisper.

"Oh, honey, I scared you," her aunt smiled but made no move to hold or comfort her as she had always done when she was alive.

"Yes, you did," Angie said, finding her shaky voice, struggling to remain calm. She couldn't take her eyes off the woman in front of her, the woman she'd loved like a mother.

"I'm so sorry. Look, sweetie, I don't have much time." Martha's smiling face darkened. "You must be careful, Angelina. Danger is near."

"What do you mean, Aunt Martha?" Angie said frantically, losing the battle for calmness. Why would she, of all people, receive a warning from the dead?

"Remember your dream and be careful," Martha replied, her face still serious, her voice low. "Things happen in threes, Angelina. You must be aware of what's going on around you. That's all I can say. I love you, sweetheart."

"I don't understand, Aunt Martha."

Angie blinked. In that split second, her aunt disappeared.

She looked to either side of the porch. Nothing. Her feet were frozen in place. Inside she shook with fear. What would come next?

But no more apparitions appeared and no strange sounds met her ears. The air around her was unusually still.

Then the realization hit her full force. A real ghost had just visited her!

Angie turned around quickly and tried to unlock the door. The keys fell from her trembling hands, clanking onto the wooden porch. Scooping them up, she used both hands to steady the key as she placed it into the lock. When it turned she scooted inside, slammed the door behind her and leaned against it.

Her heart hammered against her chest. She took several deep

breaths in a desperate attempt to calm herself.

Exhaustion. That must be it. Her beloved aunt had died three months ago and since then she had taken on so many new responsibilities. All those late nights and long hours were finally affecting her, causing hallucinations.

Bewildered, she walked down the hallway. Dropping the briefcase on her desk, she fell into the leather executive chair and then rubbed her eyes.

"It must be Friday the thirteenth or something," she muttered, looking at her desk calendar for any reason not to believe in Aunt Martha's visitation. Monday the eleventh of June. She shook her head to clear it.

No, she couldn't dismiss this as easily as she'd dismissed the rocking chair. Aunt Martha had returned to warn her that she was in danger. Angie knew in her heart it was true. What kind of danger would bring her aunt back from the dead?

Pull it together girl, she thought after several minutes. *You have work to do.*

She got up, went behind the register and began taking jewelry out of the storage bins.

After spreading the pieces across the floor behind the counter, she started counting. At first she jumped at every little noise, but the work was exacting and soon she was immersed in it.

Slow, deliberate steps thudding against the wooden floor brought her back to the present with a jolt. Had she been so engrossed that she hadn't heard someone come in? She glanced at the clock on the wall behind the register. Eight-thirty.

She still had an hour and a half before the store opened and no morning meetings were scheduled. Her brow knit into a frown of concentration as she tried to remember if she had locked the front door.

She heard the footsteps again, closer now, as though someone were approaching the counter. My God, they sound like the ones in my dream. Angie put her hands over her ears for a moment. *Stop it. Stop it!* she admonished herself. *Don't be so silly. This has nothing to do with the dream.* She closed the storage bins, certain now that she had forgotten to lock the door and would find a customer waiting at the counter. Wanting to look her best, she pulled the scrunchie from her hair and laid it on a shelf under the register.

"How can I help you?" she asked, as she stood then turned around, wearing her most welcoming smile.

She was alone in the room.

"Hello?" she called. "Is anyone in here?"

She ventured into the hallway of the old house. Her heart beat faster—her palms began to sweat.

When she saw the man in the art room, his back to her, she froze and held her breath. His build reminded her of the stalker in the dream. He was admiring one of the paintings on display.

God, Angie, now you're really getting paranoid. She let out her breath as the panic ebbed. He's just an early customer. She had left the door unlocked after all.

"Good morning. Welcome to The Variety Vine. If I can help you find anything just let me know," she said to the man's back.

"This is an exquisite piece," he replied, admiring an oil painting of a winding river bordered by large trees. The magnificent colors of the changing leaves were captured in the glistening hues of the artist's paint.

"I think so too. That part of the Dan River, with those large stones, is near the bypass and Memorial Park. Are you familiar with that area?"

She waited, but the man didn't respond. *Must be the quiet type,* she thought, taking in his broad shoulders and narrow waist. His white tailored shirt was tucked into tight blue jeans that hugged his round behind and long, muscular legs. He stood about six inches taller than her five-foot-nine-inch frame.

Great body, she thought. Wonder if his face is as striking?

"Local artists made all the pieces in this room," she said in hopes that he would look at her. "I like to showcase their work and of course, offer them the supplies they need to do it."

He wandered over to one of the tables and, with his back still to her, picked up a picture of Angie, taken by a local photographer. "Interesting," he muttered.

Was he responding to her statement or the photo? As he studied it, her stomach gave an odd flutter.

"Are you looking for anything special?" she asked, rearranging the paints and brushes behind him. Why hadn't he looked at her yet? Maybe he was just rude. The way he held the framed picture made her uneasy and she really wanted to finish the jewelry inventory before opening the store.

I'll just tell him we're closed and to come back after ten, she thought. Taylor, her assistant manager, would be in then and Angie wouldn't be alone with this man.

"No, but I think I'll take this," he said, turning to her.

Angie gasped. The paintbrushes slid from her hands and crashed onto the floor.

Aunt Martha was right. Everything always happened in threes. The dream, Aunt Martha's spirit and now—this.

The blue eyes weren't angry now, but sparkled with humor as a grin inched toward those chiseled cheekbones. His sandy hair was dry, not wet from sweat, the blond highlights were even more noticeable as strands slipped across his forehead toward his eyes. His lips were full, his nose straight. She hadn't noticed either of them in her dream.

Unable to move or speak, Angie just stared at him.

"You're the woman in the picture." It was more of a statement than a question.

She nodded her head, tried to take a breath and couldn't. She would suffocate before he could kill her. Her eyes felt like they were going to pop out of her head at any second. Ripping her gaze from his face, she bent down to pick up the paintbrushes only to drop some again.

He walked to her side and knelt to help her. "I must say, you're more beautiful in person."

Angie used her hair as a shield against him. Her hands trembled, betraying her fear. Maybe he didn't notice, she thought. When she gathered the last of the brushes, she forced herself to look at him and smile.

He's a customer handing me paintbrushes, nothing more.

"Thank you," she said, more calmly than she felt, as she accepted the items he held out to her.

The slow innocent brush of his fingers against hers made her stomach tighten but it wasn't in fear. Not this time. Never in her twenty-six years had such a slight touch confused her so.

Oh, no. Am I attracted to him? The sudden thought made Angie cringe. *I must be out of my mind! How could I be attracted to someone who stalks me, terrorizes me, night after night, in my dreams?* Sure, the nightmare man had saved her from a bullet, but he'd shot her himself at the end, hadn't he?

Hadn't he?

"Did you want the picture?" she asked abruptly, standing up.

"Do you come with it?" He stood too and smiled, revealing brilliantly white straight teeth. He moved toward her.

"Uh, no." She took two steps backward. He is handsome.

Stop it, Angie, stop it! a voice inside her said. *Stay away from him! He's dangerous!*

Through her renewed terror, Angie heard the man say, "Then I guess, for now, I'll just take the picture. Perhaps it will be different some other time. Unless, of course, you're married."

"I'm not," she said and then instantly regretted revealing anything about herself. She shoved the paintbrushes into a mug, took the picture from him—making sure their hands didn't touch again—and walked down the hall to the register.

"Boyfriend?" he persisted, following her.

"Maybe."

"My name's Jared Maxwell."

"Angie," she replied, stepping behind the counter to ring up the picture. She collected his money and then folded the top of the bag. Holding it out to him by a corner, she forced yet another smile. "Thank you, Mr. Maxwell."

Jared wrapped his large hand over hers as he took the bag. Their gazes locked and, suddenly, against her will, against her fear, Angie felt drawn to him. Those ocean blue eyes smoldered. Her gaze dropped to his full lips.

Wonder if he's a good kisser? she thought, her pulse quickening. Oh, no, stop it, Angie.

Jared reached out with his free hand to caress her cheek lightly. Angie stilled at his touch. Then he ran the pad of his thumb over her bottom lip. A festival of butterflies danced inside her as she watched Jared's blue eyes darken even more.

What was wrong with me? Fantasizing about the man who attacks me nightly in my dreams.

Jared leaned toward her.

He's going to kiss me!

No, this cannot happen. Angie jerked back, pulled her hand from underneath his, releasing the bag, ending the moment and breaking the spell.

The clock ticked. Time hadn't stopped after all.

Jared grinned as he picked up a business card from the counter. "Angelina Benton, Proprietor of The Variety Vine. Well, thank you, Ms. Benton. I hope we'll meet again soon."

"Angie," she spoke on a breath, "everyone calls me Angie."

"Until next time, Angie." He smiled, lightly running his fingers down her forearm. Then turning away, he walked down the hall and out the door.

As soon as he left, Angie ran over and turned the lock. She sank into a nearby chair, one hand absentmindedly caressing the place where his fingers had trailed down her arm, the other to her lips. A soft smile briefly lifted the corners of her mouth before a frown took its place.

She didn't know what to think. Every night, she ran in terror from this man and she certainly never expected to see him in her store.

Who am I kidding? She sat back hard in the chair. *I've always known he'd come after me one day.*

The electric current of his touch. His smoldering blue eyes. She had to put these things right out of her mind. Because they drew her to him—to the one person in the world who absolutely terrified her.

If she had anything to do with it, Angie decided, the "next time" he had mentioned would be never.

Two

JARED MAXWELL JUMPED INTO HIS RED MUSTANG convertible, slammed it in reverse and backed out of the driveway.

What in the hell just happened back there? He had never been so entranced by a woman before, especially one he'd just met. God, he'd wanted to taste her lips and almost did before she'd pulled away. *What were you thinking, Maxwell? You, Mr. Confirmed Bachelor, put those playboy ways behind you a long time ago.*

It was her eyes. They captured him, connecting him to a long-lost friend. Could this be the woman he had searched for his entire life?

Had he even been searching?

A boisterous laugh exploded from him, full and unrestrained. *Love at first sight? Nah, it couldn't be, could it?* He'd never believed in it before, but now he was certain that this was another secret he'd have to keep.

When he'd spoken with Alan Harland, the attorney in charge of the estate, the lawyer had said the property wasn't for sale because the new owner was in mourning. Out of respect, Jared had kept his distance, even though he remained determined to purchase the twenty acres someway, somehow.

If only he had stopped by three months ago when he'd first inquired about The Variety Vine, he could have gotten to know Angie and convinced her to sell by now.

Jared chuckled again thinking about it and shifted into third gear. Spotting the silver SUV in front of the old converted house and finding the door unlocked had been pure luck.

Only now he wanted more. Not only did he need the property, he also wanted the woman who owned it.

Why did she stare at me in absolute horror? He frowned as he shifted gears again. Her reaction was one of fearful recognition, but he was certain they'd never met before.

Many times women reacted to his looks with surprise or desire. There was a time when he'd been flattered, now he found it irritating. Until today, he'd never come across a woman who'd been afraid of him. He realized Angie's fear was genuine and he just couldn't figure out why.

Angelina Benton in the flesh sure had complicated his plans. He hadn't even considered that he might find her attractive, from the silkiness of her hair, the fullness of her body when it tugged against her shirt, to the gentle curve of slim hips flowing into lean, long legs. Or that he would want her more than he'd ever wanted another woman in his life.

It's more than just a physical attraction you know, a small voice murmured in his mind.

Jared shook his head to clear away the thought. In a brief moment, this woman had stirred up feelings he'd never experienced before but he would have to deal with them later.

Picking up his cell phone, he dialed the office. He couldn't afford to let a woman, even such an intriguing one, distract him from his work. Not now.

"Maxwell Development and Realty," said a chipper voice.

"Good morning, Sandi," Jared said to his secretary. "Do I have any messages?"

"Let me check. How did your meeting with Tom McNichols go?"

"I listed the farm and already have a buyer in mind."

His half sister, Terri Logan, had always talked about owning land near a small town like Dansburg, away from the hustle and bustle of Richmond. Since McNichols' acreage was eight miles from his own farm, Jared had decided to convince Terri to buy it, but if she refused, he'd just give it to her as a birthday present. He could afford to, after all, thanks to both his shrewdness in business and an enormous inheritance from his grandfather. Then, once he'd bought the two properties that bordered his land from the current owners, Sam Slayton and Angelina Benton, he would have accomplished all he set out to do when he moved to Dansburg. He'd own the original Slayton estate and he'd have his sister nearby.

"That's great news. Let's see, you have two messages from your sister, the bank called and Mr. Harland wants to reschedule your meeting until nine tomorrow morning."

"Okay. Will you contact Harland and tell him I'll be there?" He glanced at the clock on the dash. Eight-fifty. "What time did Terri call?"

"Consider it done. Um… She spoke with the answering service around ten last night and again at seven this morning."

"Thanks, Sandi," Jared said, steering the car from the hard surface road onto the mile long dirt driveway to his house. "I'm mending fences on the farm today and you know the cell doesn't work out there. I'll check in when I get back to the house. If Terri calls again make sure you ask her if everything is okay."

"No problem, we'll hold down the fort."

"I know you will," Jared said. "Talk to you later."

After Sandi said goodbye, Jared pressed the off button and

gripped the wheel tighter with his left hand.

This wasn't like Terri. He couldn't remember the last time she'd called him that late—or that early. Something must be wrong. She had struggled too much since her husband divorced her unexpectedly, then left town a year ago.

He dialed Terri's number again. If only she'd quit being so stubborn and accept his help. This time he wouldn't give her a choice. That farm was a done deal whether she liked it or not. Besides, he would enjoy having her and the kids close by again.

Jared listened to Terri's phone ring as he drove between rows of large oak trees. Their intertwined branches created a canopy that shaded the road from the sun.

Where the heck is she? Four rings and she still hadn't answered. He rounded the gentle curve to see his two-story home tucked between large oak and maple trees. The deep green shutters blended well with the natural setting and the rocking chairs on the open veranda seemed to preserve it in an earlier time.

He left a message and disconnected as he drove to the back of the house, parked and put the convertible top up.

He noticed three of his prized Angus calves in one of the paddocks. They'd escaped through some damaged fencing yesterday. Luckily old man Carson down the road had housed them in the barn after they'd wandered onto his property. Otherwise, he would have lost them for sure. The inspection and repairs he'd put off couldn't wait any longer and would take all day to complete.

Inside the house, Jared snatched the portable phone off its stand in the kitchen and dialed Terri again as he headed upstairs.

Again, no answer. *Dammit, Terri! Where are you?*

Jared changed into a work shirt and old jeans, then went back to the kitchen for something to eat. Maybe he should take a road trip instead of working. It was only a two-hour drive to Richmond and he was starting to get worried. It wasn't like Terri to call and then vanish. He slapped two sides of a sandwich together as the phone rang.

"Hello? Terri?"

"Hey, handsome," said a southern drawl.

"Terri, where in the hell have you been?"

"At the grocery store."

"What?" he said, pouring a glass of milk. "I'm over here, worried sick because you called last night and at seven this morning and you're *grocery shopping*?"

"Don't get your pants in a wad, bro, I'm fine. I called your work number because you didn't answer any of your other phones."

He let out a sigh of relief. "I sat out on the porch late last night, thinking. I didn't hear the phones."

"You mean scheming, right?"

"Ah, you know me so well," he teased. "What's up? Why didn't you leave a message?"

"I did. Anyway, guess what? Devin lost his first tooth."

"No kidding?"

"No kidding. Kevin's sooo jealous, he's wiggling his tooth to make it looser." She laughed, hesitated, "And... I was lonely and wanted to talk to you."

"Have you heard from Paul?"

"No. He's vanished without a trace since the divorce. It's just that, well, since you moved to Dansburg, I've missed you. So have the twins."

"Yeah, it's been six months. Time flies, huh?" Jared leaned against the kitchen counter. He'd been so busy relocating the company that he hadn't even been back to Richmond. It took dedication and a constant effort to keep his edge against the local competition. "I think I should take a week off and come visit."

"I've got a better idea since I know you'll feel guilty about leaving your business. I'm taking vacation the week of July Fourth.

Maybe we could spend it with you?"

"Just in time for your birthday..." Jared grinned, then purposefully blocked all thoughts of the farm. "Sounds great. Squeeze the boys for me."

"Okay."

"And don't scare me like that anymore."

"Of course I will. What's a sister for if she can't scare her brother every now and again?"

"Well then, since you're fine, I guess I'll talk to you later," Jared said, thinking of her birthday present. Remembering his sister's telepathic abilities, he quickly imaged a big brick wall between them.

"Jared, is something wrong?" asked Terri. "I feel like you're hiding something from me, blocking me out."

Jared quickly said his goodbyes without answering her question and put the portable back in its stand.

Whew! He'd almost slipped up. "I'll keep blocking you, sis," he muttered as he left the house, "until I surprise you with the deed to your new farm."

After gathering his fence-fixing tools and readying Thunder, Jared rode his horse down the dirt road.

There were still places he had yet to see on his two-hundred-and-eighty-acre farm. If he had time later, maybe he'd do some exploring.

Beginning with the perimeter, he rode until he found the two sections that needed mending.

Hours later, when the work of repairing the damage the calves had caused was finally done, Jared switched his sights to the interior, tracking along one barbed wire fence until the spiked metal cornered on a tree.

He looked up to see that he was on the edge of a meadow. Far across the field, he spotted what looked like a tired old shack. *I haven't seen this before.*

He trotted the stallion across the field, tethered him and went inside.

The dank mustiness of dust and cornhusks filled the air. In one room an old armchair served as a home for field mice. A broken bookshelf lay across the middle of the floor. Torn, faded drapes clung against the windows.

In the second room, a stained, old mattress leaned against a decrepit chest of drawers. Rain had dripped through a large hole in the roof, warping the old wood. Cornstalks, stored for cow feed, filled the entire left side.

Jared walked down the hall and opened the door into what looked like an old kitchen. An icebox, its bottom hinge broken, door ajar, stood beside a handmade table. In the opposite corner was an antique hutch, remarkably well persevered.

I can restore that hutch, he thought as he went through the back door and down the three concrete steps and *use those cornstalks as feed.*

A small building, painted red, stood at the forest's edge behind the house. An unusual noise came from inside, like glasses clinking together. Jared tried to open the door but it wouldn't budge. Finding no other way inside, he made a mental note to bring something to break the door open when he returned.

This little house, shack and meadow were a great discovery. A few repairs and they'd be perfect for storage of the fescue or corn he would plant in the meadow next spring.

Someone had stored the corn in there recently, he thought as he untied the reins. He'd ask around to find out who was using the old house. Jumping astride his horse, he rode across the meadow to finish his fence inspection.

As Thunder's hooves plodded out their monotonous rhythm, Jared's thoughts once again turned to Angelina Benton.

. . .

"ANGIE, I JUST don't know what's gotten into you," said the town gossip, hands on her hips.

"I'm fine, Mrs. Turner." Angie smiled at her customer. "How's Kimmie? I haven't seen her in a while."

"Oh, you can't evade the question by asking about my daughter." Mrs. Turner adjusted her glasses, allowing her to look over them at Angie. "I swear you're just a-shakin'. Now, tell me what's wrong, sugar."

"Really, I'm fine." Angie had learned to keep her thoughts secret when she and Kimmie were still in middle school. Mrs. Turner meant well, but she could spread a rumor faster than a rocket could burn fuel. She could also irritate Angie faster than most. Angie had learned to control her temper over the years, at Aunt Martha's insistence, but some people could still set her off like a wild fire.

"Well, now that's got to be the biggest lie you've ever told. What would Martha say?" Mrs. Turner took Angie's chin, twisting her head from side to side. "Just look at those circles under your eyes. It's not natural I tell you, not natural at all."

"I'm closing up in five minutes," Angie said, pulling free of the older woman's grasp, while picturing a calming scene of the beach in her mind. She'd gotten stuck working alone all day. Now all she wanted was a good long soak in the tub, away from the memories of today's events, without losing her temper on top of it all. "What can I help you with?"

"You can confide in me, Angie. I know you don't have anyone to talk to since Martha passed, bless her soul."

Angie stared at her. Damn it if the woman wasn't right. She hadn't had anyone to talk to since Aunt Martha died.

But before she said anything, she remembered the time when Kimmie had a crush on her best friend, Eddie Harland. When Eddie had turned down Kimmie's advances, Mrs. Turner told everyone that Angie had stolen Kimmie's boyfriend. What a mess.

She'd barely survived that one without losing a lot of friends.

Wonder what Eddie's up to? He hadn't written or called in months, since the winter semester started at Virginia Tech. But then again, neither had she.

Angie clenched her teeth, forcing a smile. She was worn out. Sales had been slow, but the customers demanding. "You know, Mrs. Turner, I just received these cool paintbrushes. I know how much you love to paint. Would you try them out for me? Let me know what you think of them before I purchase more?"

"Oh, I'd love to, dear. This store always carries such unique merchandise. Made Martha a celebrity, you know." Mrs. Turner dug in her oversized purse, pulled out a picture and shoved it in Angie's hands. "Have I shown you my grandson's graduation picture? How much do I owe you for the brushes?"

Angie glanced at the picture. A young man with blue eyes stared back at her.

The memory of Jared Maxwell's icy blue eyes flashed through her mind for the hundredth time that day. How could the monster of her nightmares have come to life in the body of a gorgeous man? Was he somehow connected to the appearance of Aunt Martha's spirit and the warning she'd given?

I really need to get out of here. "Your grandson is very handsome," Angie said, handing the picture back to Mrs. Turner. "Why don't you just let me know how the brushes work out? No charge."

"Oh, thank you! He is a cutie pie, isn't he?" She put the picture back in her purse then folded her arms across her chest. "You go ahead and lock up, dear. I'm going to wait for you to finish. A pretty girl like you shouldn't be walking out alone at night you know." Mrs. Turner looked Angie in the eye. "And neither should I."

Angie couldn't help the grin that spread across her face. "Just let me count the drawer and we'll leave. But I only have to walk as far as my car, Mrs. Turner."

"I know that," answered the older woman. "But you can't be too careful."

So the two left the store together. Angie shivered as they walked across the porch where Aunt Martha had stood early that morning.

Reaching her SUV, she waited for Mrs. Turner to get into her car before climbing inside. She waved goodbye through the window, let the older woman pull out of the driveway first, then followed but turned in the opposite direction.

When she passed Sam Slayton's farm that bordered her property, her car lights flashed over the red "Sold" sticker on the real estate agent's sign.

How odd. Property never sells that fast around here.

Sam had just passed away yesterday. She'd never expected his property to go on the market and sell within twenty-four hours. She'd thought about buying the farm herself when she'd seen the For Sale sign go up yesterday. An additional two hundred acres would substantially increase the value of her place but the expense had made her hesitate and now it had sold.

She would ask long-time friend and attorney, Alan Harland, if he knew who'd bought it during their meeting the next morning.

When she arrived at home exhaustion settled over her. Going into the bathroom, she ran hot water for a bath, praying that when she went to sleep that night, her dreams would not be filled with Jared Maxwell.

Now her attacker had a name and that name spelled fear.

An uncontrollable shudder ripped through her body. It wasn't like her to be so edgy all the time and she worried it was already affecting her work.

As the steamy water filled the tub, she poured in the lavender-scented bubble bath.

It was time to put this dream in the past. If Jared Maxwell

wanted to harm her, she couldn't stop him. She would just make sure that she stayed well away from him, that's all.

She stripped down and put her feet in the hot water. With a sigh, she lowered her body into the tub, letting the calming effect of the heat and fragrance wash over her.

Ah! Exactly what I needed.

Soaking in the bath, she closed her eyes and tried to forget the day for a while. But images of Jared's blue eyes and the way she felt absorbed in them kept invading her thoughts.

He's a playboy, she thought, remembering his flirtatious actions in the store. Well, maybe he hadn't given her any real reason to think that, but after the way he'd touched her lip, he *must* be a man who'd use and then leave a woman with a broken heart.

And she wanted a man who didn't play games—someone loyal, kind and strong. Jared didn't seem to be that kind of a man, despite the swarm of butterflies he'd set loose in her.

She wondered yet again if she would ever meet a man who would sweep her off her feet. Maybe she'd set her standards too high and it was just her destiny to die a virgin.

But Jared had looked at her so intensely. With a fire she could see in his eyes and feel in his touch.

Despite herself, she imagined Jared gathering her in his arms and placing a passionate kiss on her lips. As she fantasized how her own lips would part beneath his, emotions stirred within her that had nothing to do with fear.

"I must be insane," she whispered before sinking under the water, trying to wash the images from her mind.

THREE

JARED ROUNDED A CORNER IN THE HALLWAY THEN slowed his steps to enjoy the incredible view in front of him. Angelina Benton stood in front of Alan Harland's dark-glassed office door, where gold lettering proclaimed him Attorney and Counselor-at-Law. She twisted the handle, glanced at the silver watch on her wrist, then, cupping her hands beside her eyes, she peered inside. Her jeans hugged her hips as she bent over. Her thick dark hair, pulled into a ponytail by a blue scrunchie, lay down the middle of her back and then slipped over to one side, its silky highlights reminding him of moonlight shimmering on the Dan River at midnight.

This is a welcomed surprise, he thought as he stopped behind her. "Good morning, Angelina."

Angie, obviously startled by his voice, jerked around to face him.

"And how are you this fine day?" he added, watching her bright smile fade and brows knit together.

"What are you doing here?" Angie snapped. Crossing her arms, she set her mouth in a straight line of indifference. Her big brown eyes, slightly widened, betrayed her fear.

"I have a meeting with Mr. Harland," Jared said casually, walking closer to her. "And you?"

Angie stepped back, tripping against her briefcase on the hall floor.

Jared studied her. He had to think of some way to set her mind at ease about him, to convince her that he could be trusted, or he'd never persuade her to sell him her property. Before he could do that, he had to figure out why she seemed afraid of him.

"I'm meeting with Alan too." Her firm tone surprised him, belied the emotions in her eyes.

Jared raised an eyebrow and smiled at the tall, lithe woman. *Interesting, she's fighting her fear. She's also looking very intriguing in those tight jeans and sleeveless, scooped necked blouse.* The shirt's top button had popped loose, allowing him a glimpse of the tempting flesh underneath. He felt his reaction to her stirring in places that were better left alone.

Seconds later, her slender fingers pushed the pearl button through the buttonhole.

He lifted his gaze to find her glaring at him. Turning away, she crossed her arms under her breasts, which made them lift and swell in the dip of her shirt.

Damn!

It was obvious she wanted to be left alone, but didn't she realize the effect she had on him?

He didn't consider himself an impulsive man, but he wasn't about to let this moment, or this woman, pass him by again.

I'm probably going to regret this later. Jared reached out and took her hand in his. "Angie," he whispered, the softness of her palm warmed his hand. The silence in the hallway was deafening as he looked into her eyes. He couldn't help but wonder what was going on behind those wide brown orbs.

Angie could only stare at Jared. The touch of his hand had

sparked up her arm like an electrical current, catching her breath. She'd never imagined Jared would touch her.

Again.

She glanced down at his large, strong hand engulfing her smaller one, his tanned skin sharply contrasting her fair complexion. She allowed her gaze to travel up his arm, his suit unable to hide the muscles underneath. The cut of the jacket made his shoulders and chest look even broader and tailored down to his narrow waist.

When she realized the direction her eyes wanted to travel, she looked back up at him. His eyes were smoky blue, deep, dark and full of desire. His full lips beckoned to her.

The images she'd envisioned during last night's bath came rushing back. As much as she wanted to fight him, run from him, the desire to feel his lips touch hers was overwhelming.

Are you crazy, Angie? Get a grip. He's a stalker! This isn't a dream!

She couldn't move as Jared cupped his free hand under her chin, lifting her face closer to his. The blue of his eyes was deeper still and she saw the danger flicker through them, like the eyes in her dream.

She trembled at the memory.

The pad of his thumb slid over her lips, parting them ever-so slightly. His head tilted toward her.

Angie, realizing that he intended to kiss her, jerked her hand from his grasp. Pressing both palms firmly against his chest, she pushed him away. "Don't ever attempt that again, Mr. Maxwell."

"I just—" he began, then his eyebrows furrowed together.

"I am not a piece of meat," Angie interrupted, "to be ogled by some playboy used to getting his way with women."

Glaring at him, Angie noticed that his still-lustful gaze held a hint of embarrassment. *Good,* she thought, *maybe standing up to him had set Jared Maxwell straight.*

At the sound of fast approaching footsteps, Angie moved further away from Jared, picked up her briefcase and looked toward the sound.

"Sorry, I'm late," Alan Harland said as he walked up to them, shook Jared's hand and then kissed Angie on the cheek. "I see the two of you have met."

Angie looked to Alan, raised an eyebrow. "What happened, Alan? I've never known you to be late for an appointment."

A grin plastered to his face, mischievous glint in his eye, Alan unlocked the door and let them into his office.

Had he been late on purpose? Angie thought, holding the door for the older man as he went into the office. "It looks like I'm underdressed but I've got to go into work after our meeting, Alan."

"You look beautiful in anything, besides you didn't need to get all fancied up for me." Alan grinned, flipping on the light switch to illuminate the room. "I'm sorry to keep you both waiting. I had to stop by the post office. I swear, the lines there just get longer and longer."

"Where should I wait while you meet with Ms. Benton?" Jared asked, closing the door behind them.

"I need to speak with both of you." Alan entered an office attached to the reception area, took off his jacket and hung it on a wooden coat rack.

"Both of us?" Angie glanced at Jared then stared through the open door at Alan. *Was her long-time friend playing matchmaker or was this another of his projects?* "Together?"

"That's right. Come on in, have a seat." Alan motioned toward the maroon high-backed chairs facing his desk and then busied himself gathering paperwork and laying it across his large mahogany desk. "Oh, Angie, before I forget, Eddie called last night. He said to tell you hello."

"Tell him hi when you talk to him again, since he never calls me anymore." Angie scooted back in the huge chair. Her belt squeaked against the leather as she settled into it. She tilted her briefcase against the chair leg.

She thought about all the times Alan had tried to involve her in some project or another over the years, while fixing her up with a "nice man" who was also helping out. She'd been more than willing to help him in the past, putting up with his attempts at playing Cupid, since she loved him like a father. But this time, she'd have to pass, especially if it involved Jared. From the sound of it, that was exactly what he had in mind.

"So what's going on, Alan? I thought we were just rescheduling the meeting I missed yesterday. This doesn't involve Mr. Maxwell."

"There were some other developments yesterday afternoon. I needed you both here so I could do this once and get it over with."

"This sounds interesting," Jared said, as he took the window seat beside Angie.

Angie glowered at Jared but he just grinned in response, so she turned to Alan, who was now sitting behind his desk. "Well, whatever it is, I don't have time to take on any additional projects right now. You know how busy I've been with the store."

"Yes, I know, but this involves The Variety Vine."

"What do you mean?" she asked.

"The Slayton estate bordering each of your properties sold yesterday," Alan said.

"I noticed that," she said, studying Alan.

"I've heard the rumors about that farm being haunted," Jared said. "Do you think they have a factual basis?"

Alan nodded. "I have a letter Ruby wrote to her son that proves how Theodore died."

Most of Dansburg's residents knew the tale of Ruby and Theodore, but Angie wondered why Jared was so interested in those old stories. "What does this have to do with us, Alan?" she asked impatiently, her voice strained.

Alan tapped a pencil on the desk and leaned back in his chair. "Did you know that Sam Slayton passed away the day before yesterday?"

"Yes, I heard," Angie said, "and I thought it strange that his estate was sold within twenty-four hours of his death. I mean his funeral's tomorrow."

"I didn't know," Jared said.

Alan nodded. "Well, the sale went exactly as Sam willed it."

"Which was?" Angie asked.

"The original plantation totaled five hundred acres and included your farm, Jared and Angie's twenty acres." Alan set the pencil aside. "The Slayton's went through some hard times and sold your properties off from the original estate. But, they included a clause, which followed all future sales."

"Is this the clause to ensure the unity of the original estate?" asked Jared.

Alan nodded and pulled out a sheet of paper, yellowed with age. "In the clause, it states that if the last Slayton died without an heir, the main estate would be combined with the other two farms to unite the original property."

Angie took the paper from Alan. The hand written part at the bottom grabbed her attention so she started reading it.

Alan continued, "The owners of the other two farms would inherit fifty percent ownership of the union of all three properties. Sam knew that he wouldn't have an heir and added to this clause three years ago."

"Oh God!" gasped Angie. Her hand flew to cover her mouth. "Alan, please tell me this isn't true."

Leaning forward to prop his elbows on the desk, Alan watched Angie. "Yes, it's true but this is a good thing, Angie. Now each of you owns half of the original estate. That's two hundred and fifty acres each. You just have to complete all of the requirements."

"I don't think I remember all of the details," Jared said. His hand stopped beside Angie's. "May I?"

Trembling, Angie gave him the document, "You knew about this?" she confronted Jared.

"Yes, didn't you?"

Angie shook her head. "Is this even legal? Can someone sell property with conditions attached?"

"Yes it is. The buyers knew about and accepted the Slayton's conditions when they purchased the property," Alan said. "Would you read the clause aloud, Jared?"

"Sure. Mr. Slayton's addition states—" he looked down to read the clause, .Upon my death, all three farms which made up the original Slayton estate will be deeded as one property. The current owners of the two separate farms must live in the homestead located on the main property while it is renovated into a bed and breakfast inn that will honor the Slayton name. Should the parties succeed in creating a fully functional inn, they will each retain fifty percent ownership in the land, buildings and businesses associated with all three properties. However, if either party refuses to participate, then both parties forfeit their original investments. The original five hundred acre Slayton estate will then be sold at private auction to the highest bidder who agrees to the creation and continued success of the Slayton Bed and Breakfast Inn."

Angie stared at Jared in disbelief.

He looked up. "This works for me."

Panicking, her breathing becoming ragged, Angie turned to Alan. "No, this isn't possible, Alan. You never mentioned this to me before today."

Alan looked alarmed. "Angie, I'm so sorry. Martha knew about this clause. I just assumed she'd told you at some point." Concerned, he stood and came to her side.

"No, she never said a word. Why do we have to live there? Why would Sam concoct such a ridiculous situation for all the owners? I just don't understand," she whispered, searching his face for some sign that this was all a big, bad joke.

"Sam was eccentric. Who knows why he came up with this? But he did and it's legal and binding. You have to follow his instructions exactly or lose your property and the business." Alan crouched down. "Angie, are you okay?" He took her smooth hands in his wrinkled ones and looked at her intently. "You look pale. Would you like some water?"

Angie nodded, then took a deep breath while Alan went to get the drink. She looked at her hands shaking in her lap. "I can't believe Aunt Martha didn't tell me," she whispered.

"I knew this was always a possibility," Jared put in. "It really is a good investment if you think about it. We can each have our homes, you can still run your store and now we'll both own more property and have a new business to share."

Angie was sure her eyes were going to pop out of her head from staring at Jared so much. There was no way she could live in the homestead alone with him. It was the entire summer, when one day would be far too long to be confined with the man who terrorized her nightly in dreams.

Alan came in and Angie took the glass of water he offered and sipped.

"Better now?" Alan asked.

"A little," she said weakly as Alan returned to his seat behind the desk. *How will I...how can I share a house with this man? Why did the clause say we must live in the homestead? Just my luck.*

"Okay, there's also a trust set up with enough funds in it to finance the renovation and for start-up money for the inn."

"How much?" Jared asked.

"A little over a million dollars."

"*What?*" Angie and Jared said in unison.

"Yes, over a million."

"Why would he do that, Alan?" Angie scooted to the edge of her chair and sat the water glass on Alan's desk. "If Sam had that much money, why not just renovate the place himself while he was alive?"

"I don't know, Angie," Alan answered. "Like I said, Sam was eccentric and very proud. It's unconventional and he never gave me a reason why he wanted the estate handled this way. Maybe he thought this would create a legacy just as the haunting rumors keep up interest in the Slayton place. Whatever his reasons, I'll be working with you to ensure the inn's success. The way I see it, between the three of us, we have the skills to make it work."

"Why would you want to help us?" asked Jared.

"I was Sam's lawyer for many years. He made me the executor of his estate, but not in the traditional sense. I agreed that in lieu of payment as executor, I would be paid when the renovation was complete. I don't collect any money until you open for business. As you can see, I too have a stake in the inn's success."

Angie slid back in her chair, gripping her hands together. She might as well find out all the details if not participating meant losing the store. "What skills are you referring too, Alan?"

"You gave up your interior design career in Roanoke to come back here and run The Variety Vine after Martha's death. You could offer your redecorating expertise and work on the interior of the homestead," Alan said, then turned to Jared, "Your background is in developing subdivisions and selling real estate, Jared. You could contribute your construction and real estate knowledge to aid in the remodeling of the house and other areas of the property. I will handle the marketing to ensure we have guests for the inn."

"I'm sorry, Alan," Angie said, "there's no one I can trust to run The Variety Vine."

"What about Sharon Brady? She used to help Martha run the

store," Alan suggested. "I'm sure she would love to help out."

Angie looked between Alan and Jared, then stared at her quivering hands, all the while tugging on her bottom lip with her teeth. *I'm out of excuses and I can't tell Alan about the nightmare.*

She glanced at Jared. The muscle in his jaw worked as he stared, deep in thought, out the window, rubbing his palms against his knees.

"You know, Angie, it will be interesting to see if you have one of those dreams."

"What do you mean?" Jared asked.

Angie shook her head slightly to quiet Alan. *Don't tell Jared about my dreams.*

"Angie's known in these parts for having dreams that come true," Alan told Jared.

Great. Just great! She glared at Alan but he didn't even look her way.

"She can see in a dream what will happen in the future and she has seen the past too. I'm hoping that, after spending time in the house, she will dream about Theodore Slayton." Alan leaned back in his chair. "Then we'll know if his ghost indeed haunts the place. Local folk know about her dreams and would back up her predictions as true, thus making the Slayton Bed and Breakfast more intriguing to ghost hunting visitors."

"Do you believe her dreams come true?" Jared asked.

Geez! Now they are going to talk about me like I'm not even sitting in the room with them, thought Angie. *God I hate this! Why did Alan have to bring it up?*

"She doesn't flaunt her gift." Alan's gaze settled on her and Angie gave him the *hush* look. "You still have a hard time accepting it, don't you?"

Without waiting for a response, he turned back to Jared. "She has helped many people by telling them about her—what did Martha call them? Oh, yes—prophetic dreams. She helped me and now, my friend…I'm a believer."

"What dreams of yours came true?" Jared asked with genuine interest.

"I just dream and sometimes it happens," she said.

"Is there something in the dream that lets you know it will come true?" Jared pressed.

"I don't know what you mean," she lied. *Like I'd ever tell you about my observer dreams.*

"Do you dream in color or see a symbol that lets you know this dream is different from a normal dream? A sign which means this dream will come true where another one without the sign wouldn't come true."

No way would Jared Maxwell ever know that she watched the dream happen night after night until it came true. That was private. The only person she'd ever told was Aunt Martha. "There's not a sign. Some of them just come true, that's all."

"Hmm, you have a unique gift," Jared said. "My sister, Terri, has a similar ability. It's hard for her to talk about her paranormal experiences too. I bet the two of you will get along great."

Angie studied Jared and tried to figure out if he was teasing her or being truthful. He probably thought she was a freak now. People usually did when they found out about her dreams.

It didn't matter what he thought of her anyway and she doubted if she would ever meet his sister. What she knew for sure was she would never sleep under the same roof with him, especially since the horrific dream continued each and every night. If the past had taught her anything, this would not end until the dream came true in life."

"I've drawn up all the necessary paperwork," Alan said. "All you have to do is sign and we can start today. Both of you can move into the house tomorrow."

"I'm in," Jared said.

"Great!"

Angie looked at the contracts Alan slid across the desk, one for each of them and panicked.

"I'm sorry, Alan. I just can't do it," she said, pushing the contract back toward him. *I can't risk putting my life in jeopardy by living with Jared Maxwell.* After the episode in the hall, her life wasn't the only thing at risk—her virginity was too!

"Why don't you just admit the truth, Angie," taunted Jared as he looked over the contract. "You're just afraid to sleep in a haunted house—with me."

That's only the half of it. "Riiigght," she said, drawing the word out in an attempt to appear unaffected by the whole situation, "haunted houses. Why would I be afraid of staying there with you?"

"My dashing good looks?" Jared teased.

What an ego. "I am not afraid of you, Mr. Maxwell."

"Then prove it," Jared grinned, signing his name across the bottom of his contract and handing it back to Alan. "Take a risk, Angie. Or are you afraid of ghosts?"

"No, Casper doesn't scare me. I just don't have to prove anything to either of you." But, come to think of it, if she said yes but needed time away from him, she'd have five hundred acres at her disposal. There would be workers there during the day that could protect her and she could get people she knew to hang out with her if she felt threatened. It was just the nighttime. How could she sleep in the same house with him at night?

Alan sighed. "Angie, if you don't participate, I'm legally bound to put the property up for auction. You'll lose The Variety Vine. Think of Martha and all the work you two put into that store."

Jared touched her…again. He gently took her chin, trying to turn her toward him, but Angie resisted. He tried again and this time she looked over into those blue eyes.

"No, you don't have to prove anything to either of us but

don't lose your store because of fear. You've barely looked at me since our little fiasco in the hallway. I think you're worried that you wouldn't be able to handle yourself alone with me, away from the world and you know it."

She pulled her chin from his grasp, surprised at Jared's boldness. Then, her anger at the unfairness of everything that had happened in the past three months caught up with her. She narrowed her eyes. "How dare you!"

"Listen you two," Alan interrupted, "the renovation could be completed a week before the new convention center opens, if it's started immediately. We could book guest reservations beginning on September first, if we're on schedule. I know the deadlines are short and you will work long hours each day, but this way you could both meet the conditions of the clause over the summer and move on with your lives."

"You have to be kidding me, Alan." Frustrated and angry, Angie grabbed his desk and leaned forward. "Do you honestly believe the house can be ready before the convention center opens? I just don't see it all coming together that fast."

"I'm game. I think we could do it," Jared told Angie. "If you know how to work hard."

"Are you insinuating I'm not a hard worker, Mr. Maxwell?"

"No, I wasn't insinuating anything. To be quite honest with you, I don't want to lose my property because you're afraid to commit."

Angie's knuckles whitened as she clenched the desk. *How dare he? What an insufferable, arrogant man!* Grinding her teeth together, she glared at Jared. *Control, Angie. Do not let your temper get the better of you.*

I'll show you, thought Angie, looking between the two men. *Dammit! I might be afraid, but I'll hide my fear from you, Mr. I-Wasn't-Insinuating-Anything, so you'll never know. I can handle anything you can dish out and I'll throw it right back at you, tenfold.*

At least I hope I will.

It was a risk. A big risk that could put her in grave danger, especially after the warning Aunt Martha's ghost had given. Angie knew she had to do it. She owed Aunt Martha that much. She couldn't lose her aunt's most prized possession just because she gave up before she'd even tried.

Maybe, if she agreed, she would actually be able to understand Jared's role in her dream. Had he saved her from the bullet or was he the one who stuck the gun in her back?

The mix of emotions that this man and this situation caused in her made her shake inside, made her temper flare. Instead of her usual angry outburst, Angie looked Jared straight in the eyes, accepting his challenge. Then, her gaze still locked with his, she took a deep breath, released the desk and extended her hand toward Alan, palm up.

"Give me the contract, Alan. Where do I sign?"

FOUR

ANGIE PUT HER BAGS DOWN BY THE FRONT DOOR AND took one final walk through her house before leaving. The last thing she needed was an electrical fire while she was away. She began to check the outlets. When she reached the kitchen, she found the coffeepot still plugged in. *There. I knew I should double-check.* She pulled the cord from the wall.

That's it. Everything was in order. She could leave.

Still she hesitated.

How did I get myself into this mess? she thought for the hundredth time. She leaned against the kitchen counter. Her temper always seemed to get the best of her and this time was no exception. Jared's provocation had sent her right over the edge.

Two hours after signing that stupid contract she had begged Alan to let her out of it.

He'd laughed and said, "Nope, you'll just have to make the best of the situation."

Yeah, right. Make the best out of spending the summer living with her worst nightmare.

Angie's head began to throb. Reaching to the shelf above the kitchen sink, she grabbed the bottle of ibuprofen and took two of the white pills.

It was while replacing them that she noticed the silver key to the Slayton house. She'd almost forgotten it. She snatched it up and pocketed it.

After the meeting with Alan, when it finally sank in that she couldn't have a change of heart, she had asked for more time. According to the terms of the contract she and Jared had to move into the Slayton place by the following morning. That left only yesterday to get their personal affairs in order.

She had lucked out with Sharon Brady, Angie thought as she began rifling through her junk drawer to find the pocket flashlight she'd just remembered she needed.

Sharon was bored at home and wanted a part-time summer job. She jumped at the chance to run The Variety Vine full-time, even on such short notice.

Where did I leave that flashlight? Oh, the heck with it. I better get my butt in gear if I'm going to beat Jared to the house and claim that downstairs bedroom. He has his own key and he's sure not going to wait for me to arrive before going in and grabbing the best room.

Angie closed the drawer, grabbed the ibuprofen off the shelf and shoved it into her purse, just in case, walked to the door and picked up her bags.

Making her way to her SUV, she threw her luggage in the back. Outside, it was still pitch black at four in the morning. One last trip back to her house to turn off the porch light and lock up and she was all set to go at last.

As she strapped on her seat belt, she thought about the layout of the Slayton homestead. She'd stopped by late yesterday afternoon and planned a strategy to keep her as far away from Jared as possible.

The enormous two-story house, that some might call a

mansion, had six bedrooms upstairs and one downstairs. Perfect! She'd take the downstairs bedroom and force Jared to sleep upstairs. He'd be alone up there and she'd have a quick escape route it she needed one.

She'd seen so many books in the library that she'd never be in want of reading material. The ballroom with its large domed ceiling had impressed her the most. She knew immediately what she could create in that space—not just a ballroom but a romantic getaway for visitors too.

In the combined kitchen and dining area, Angie was relieved to find a contemporary new stove and refrigerator. Good old Sam Slayton. It seemed he'd installed every modern convenience, including a dishwasher. There was even a washer and dryer inside the screened back porch attached to the kitchen.

A strange place for appliances, she had thought before noticing the courtyard.

She went outside and walked to the center of the square part of the yard, where a hand pump glistened in the sun. Water sloshed out unexpectedly when she moved the handle up and down and she had to jump out of the way before her feet were soaked.

Later, back at her own place, she got out an old ladle and bucket and put them in her SUV. They'd look good on that pump and might even come in handy.

Now, as she drove through the morning darkness, she could hear them clanking together in the back. Perhaps they'd be the first things she unpacked when she arrived at the Slayton place—her new summer home.

She drove cautiously, watching for deer, as the SUV's headlights illuminated the crooked country road. She knew, from growing up in the area, that the animals could leap out of the forest without warning.

Only half her mind was occupied with her driving. The other

part was thinking about Jared. For once she wasn't afraid. In fact, a smile played at the corners of her lips. Jared had provoked her into this project, but she would always stay one step ahead of him. He would arrive around nine, as they'd agreed, to find her already settled into the downstairs bedroom. Surely he wouldn't wake up at four a.m. as she had to be the first to arrive.

Approaching the turn to the dirt road that led to the homestead, she felt her pocket again for the house key.

She braked as a route driver, approaching from the opposite direction, stopped and shoved the Wednesday edition of the *Register & Bee* into the newspaper box. When he pulled away, she stopped her car, got out and went to the newspaper box to retrieve the paper before hopping back into the SUV.

She didn't realize the long dirt road was in need of repair until she hit the washboards. Where the road sloped downward, the rain had eroded the earth, creating small dips that looked like the slats on an old fashioned washboard. Swearing under her breath, Angie slowed the SUV to a crawl. She'd knocked the front end out of alignment before by going over those little dips too quickly. Flicking the headlights to bright, she surveyed the road ahead—potholes everywhere.

Jared should repair the roads first, she thought.

Geez, she was doing it again. Thinking of Jared and what he would be doing around the homestead while she worked on the interior design. At least working on the roads would keep him away from *her*. Now all she had to do was get him out of her mind and dreams. She sighed deeply.

God, how she hated feeling trapped, like a wild animal waiting for the hunter to arrive. Was Jared the hunter? If she could only shake the feeling that death waited for her at his hands.

The headlights shone against the old white house, jolting her out of her reverie. Peeling paint and once black shutters, now gray, made the dwelling look its age.

She parked to the side, took a deep breath and grabbed her things from the front seat. She'd come back later for her clothes.

The downstairs bedroom was near the front entrance, so she went in that way, shutting the door behind her. Sliding her hands over the wall, she felt for a light switch.

Nothing. She should have noted where they were before. She continued to her bedroom, slowly, feeling her way in the dark. Once there, she reached inside the doorframe, groped around for the light switch.

Ah ha! Got it!

It took a moment for her eyes to adjust to the sudden brightness. When they did, she looked in and could barely contain her anger.

Where were the bed, dresser and nightstand?

Someone had converted the room to an office. It must have been Jared.

There were two desks, two computers and two filing cabinets. One of each for each of them, she figured. One desk was already cluttered with files, folders and books. She guessed the other one, free of clutter, was to be her workstation.

"How dare he!" Fury raged within her. "Damn him!"

"Damn who?" said a voice from behind her.

She screamed and practically flew to the opposite wall, her heart beating so fast it threatened to explode. When she turned, anger rose above her fear.

"What is the matter with you?" she shouted at Jared. "What are you doing here this early?"

"I've been here since late yesterday afternoon." Jared propped the baseball bat he was carrying against the doorjamb to rub the sleep from his eyes. "Sorry, I didn't mean to scare you."

She bent forward, her palms against her knees. The long straps of her briefcase and purse fell from her shoulders to the floor. She took several deep, calming, breaths.

Then glanced over at Jared. Twice.

How could she stay mad at him when he stood there rubbing his eyes like that? He looked like a little kid who'd gotten up in the middle of the night for a glass of water.

"It's okay. I'm okay, now," she said to convince herself as much as Jared. "I wasn't expecting anyone to be in the house. I didn't hear you come up behind me."

She also didn't expect him to be half naked.

Her mind whirled as she took in the expanse of his broad shoulders, thick biceps and narrow waist. His muscular chest was covered with a coppery dusting of fine curly hair that tapered across a six-pack stomach before disappearing into blue silk boxers.

Angie swallowed hard.

From the looks of it, he liked to spend time in the gym. Taking a deep breath, she hung her head again. This man was hot! Her blood pounded in her veins, but not from the scare he just gave her.

"Angie, look, I really am sorry. I didn't mean to frighten you. I heard a noise and came down to investigate."

She straightened up to look at him.

Jared offered her a grin, walked over to take her hand in his. "Forgive me?"

His blue eyes were searching hers. He wanted forgiveness but she couldn't trust him.

Or herself for that matter when a nearly naked, hot bodied man stood so close, touching her. She didn't want to start the project in a negative way, either. She never expected to see this compassionate side of him and it put her off balance.

"Fine, I forgive you." Her hand tingled from his touch, so she withdrew it. "Just don't sneak up on me again."

"Done." Jared smiled and she saw his eyes lighten with relief.

"Why did you do this?" she asked, moving away from him,

raising her hands to indicate the room. She needed a little space between them in order to breathe. "I wanted this bedroom, but now you've changed it into an office. Did you ever consider talking to me before altering the rooms?"

"No. This house is very old. It would have taken a lot of time and money to rewire it. It was the easiest room to wire for the phones and computers at a reasonable price. Besides, there are plenty of bedrooms upstairs."

She couldn't argue with that one. "I sure hope you don't plan to make a habit of walking around at night in just your boxers."

Jared looked down at himself. A blush crept to his cheeks. "I…uh…sorry… I'll go dress." With long strides, he moved toward the door, grabbing the bat as he rushed out of the room and up the stairs.

Would wonders never cease? He blushed. The man had actually blushed.

So much for Mr. Cool Sophistication. A smile tugged at the corners of her mouth. She couldn't believe Jared had been at a loss for words.

So he had a bashful streak too. In that moment, he seemed so different, not the womanizer she'd experienced in her store and at Alan's office. And certainly not the angry villain from her dream.

Who was Jared Maxwell? She would find out, one way or another, even if it killed her.

Taking a moment to settle down, she sat at the empty desk and told herself that Jared scaring her half to death was what was making her heart race.

So why did she keep imagining him standing there in his underwear rubbing his eyes? Why wasn't her heart slowing down? No matter how much she wanted to deny it, she was attracted to him.

She rubbed at the dull throb thumping out a hateful melody. It was too early to start work and she had no desire to go upstairs where Jared was either taking a shower or getting dressed.

For a split second she pictured water from the showerhead beating down on all those tanned muscles. She shook her head to clear the image. She had to stop letting the attraction she felt affect her. This was a man who might really hurt her physically, it didn't matter how gorgeous or built he was, she had to remember that.

She picked her belongings up from the floor and put them on her desk. *There's no point in being so wrapped up in a nice body.* Angie grinned at her own thoughts. *Wrapped up indeed.* She went into the kitchen, taking the newspaper with her, praying that the cupboards were stocked.

She needed coffee.

After Jared was safely out of the way, she'd take her clothes upstairs. Once she figured out which bedroom he'd chosen, she'd claim one on the opposite end of the house from his.

THE AROMA OF freshly brewed coffee made Jared breathe in deeply after he emerged from the bathroom showered, shaved and dressed.

Downstairs, he found Angie sitting in the dining room at the round oak table, absorbed in the newspaper with a cup of the dark brew cradled between her palms.

He didn't want to startle her again so he knocked on the doorjamb to get her attention.

"Morning," he said when she tilted her head up at him.

She seemed more annoyed than anything else but sounded pleasant just the same. "Good morning to you." Her eyes scanned him up and down before passing him a knowing look.

"I thought it would be better if I put on some clothes." He crossed the room, then leaned down to whisper in her ear, pressing his cheek against her hair, "But you can feel free to rip them off any time you'd like."

He felt Angie's body stiffen, saw the tiny goose bumps prickling the skin on her arms. He inhaled the lavender fragrance of her shampoo before stepping over to the coffee maker.

"You're something else, Mr. Maxwell."

"So I've been told." He poured a cup of coffee then returned to the table and sat across from her.

Angie looked up, her brown eyes scrutinizing him. "Let's just set the ground rules right now before we start off on the wrong foot, okay?"

"Okay, Angelina. Let's make the first rule that we call each other by our given names," he said, staring at her until she became uncomfortable and glanced at the paper spread out on the table.

"Fine." Folding the paper, she pushed it aside. "Then call me Angie. Only Aunt Martha called me Angelina. And I want you to agree to drop the playboy image with me. No flirting, no come-ons—nothing. I would like for you to keep your womanizing nature out of this business arrangement."

"Let me get this straight. You think I'm a player?"

Angie gazed at him over the rim of her cup before draining the last of her coffee. "Aren't you?"

"I'll leave that one to your imagination." He chuckled. "You know, Angie, you really should get to know a person before judging them."

"You're telling me that you aren't the type of man to 'love 'em and leave 'em'? You don't have a string of broken hearts trailing in your wake?" She rose and went to the sink, purposefully turning her back on him.

Jared laughed. "Like I said, I'll leave that one to your imagination, Angie. I might be the most reliable person you've ever met. You never know, I might already love you."

"You forgot the 'and leave me' part," Angie said, rinsing out her coffee mug in the sink. She dried her hands on a dishtowel and turned to face him. "Now, I think the next rule should be—"

Unbelievable! Where did he go? Yep, that was a pickup line if she'd ever heard one. Why else would a man say something like that and then take off?

Damn him anyway. He was too quick, too quiet. Why did he insist on calling her Angelina? She narrowed her gaze on the empty table and doorway. She had to be more aware of him, especially since he snuck up on her in the dream, then disappeared just as fast.

JARED PLACED THE coffee cup on his desk and sat down in his chair. He rubbed his eyes, shook his head slightly.

Was it possible that he was in love with this woman who thought he'd break hearts without a care in the world? How could she think so little of him?

He'd only been in contact with Angie twice before today. He *had* thought about love at first sight the other day but he'd disregarded it as impossible.

Was that why he acted like a hormonal teenager around her?

Love at first sight. Jared tapped his fingers on his knees and rocked the chair from side to side as he considered his feelings. How in the world did this happen to him?

Get a grip, Jared, you've known you loved Angie from the moment you saw her picture in The Variety Vine.

No, I don't have time for this, he told the little voice in his head that goaded him. *I'm not so sure it's love.*

Lust.

No doubt about *that*. He wanted her in bed but did he love her? He couldn't, could he? It was way too early for that. He didn't even know her.

He jumped when Angie slammed her palms on his desk. He grabbed her wrists like a reflex.

"What planet are you on, Maxwell? You walked out on me in

the middle of a conversation."

Jared glared at her. She'd caught him so deep in thought that she'd taken him by surprise. His mood darkened. "Don't ever do that again." He hated people sneaking up on him.

Angie jerked her arms from his grasp, straightened and backed up a step. She opened her mouth to speak, closed it again and then ran out of the room.

"Perfect," Jared muttered, "just perfect."

THE DARKNESS OF night felt like a blanket covering something sinister within the room. Angie lay still in her bed and stared into the shadows, her heart pounding in her ears. There was something wrong. She'd woken up because of the dream, but this felt different.

Maybe it was just nerves. This was her first night sleeping in the Slayton homestead with Jared right down the hall, after all.

Summoning her courage, she got out of bed and reached for the light switch by the door. She flipped it up. The room remained cloaked in darkness.

That's got to be it. She'd just felt strange because the power went out.

Electricity or not, nature called. The bathroom was at the other end of the hall.

She groped through the darkness for the door handle only to find that the door she had locked before going to bed was now open.

Jared unlocked the door? Her heart pounded a little faster against her ribs. Why would he do that?

She reached into the darkness and groped for the doorjamb opposite her. Sliding her hands down the wall, she maneuvered slowly toward the bathroom.

Three feet down the hallway her fingertips touched the

softness of human flesh.

She froze.

"Jared?" she whispered.

Suddenly she was yanked forward, pulled into the hardness of muscled flesh. The man was shirtless, her face pressed against the smooth, slippery skin of his chest. He smelled of wet dirt, sweat and alcohol.

Unable to scream, barely able to breathe, she scratched at his skin as she tried to get away. She felt the rumble within him before she heard the low, evil laugh.

Panicking, she pushed her hands against his waist and felt a wide belt in the loops of his jeans and the butt of a handgun. She twisted and grabbed for the gun, but he caught her wrist. She moved her head, took a deep breath and plunged her teeth into him. He propelled her across the hallway, into the banister, as her blood-curdling scream filled the silence.

She spit mud out of her mouth. The sounds of footsteps were everywhere—down the steps, in the hall. Just how many people were in the house? Using the banister rails for support, she stood.

"Angie!"

"Jared?"

"Stand still, the lights are out. I'm getting a flashlight."

She stumbled from the banister to the opposite side of the hall. Still unsure who'd attacked her, still suspicious of Jared, she didn't want to give him the opportunity to throw her to her death over the rail.

The flashlight's brilliant beam frantically wobbled around the hallway, until it flashed in her eyes, then lit downward. Jared was immediately at her side.

"What happened?" Too fast, his arms enveloped her. Her body trembled against him. The fuzzy softness of chest hair caressed her face. Her body molded to his, a perfect fit.

Minutes before she had been forced against a much larger

intruder. “There’s a man in the house.”

“What?” Turning her, Jared led her back to her room. “Go inside. Wait for me to come back.”

“No way! I’m going with you!”

“Stay here, Angie,” he ordered as he went downstairs.

“Like hell I will!” she muttered, then, using the wall to guide her, she crept toward the bathroom. Her need to relieve herself had vanished in the excitement but she needed the flashlight she’d seen in the closet earlier.

She retrieved it, slid the on button and light burst forth from the bulb.

At the end of the hallway she turned to go down the steps. There were streaks of dirt marking the walls where the man had touched them. Anger welled up inside her as she ran down the steps searching for Jared.

She found him on the back porch, his flashlight pointed at the fuse box.

“Did you find him?” she asked, shining her light into the box too.

“No, he went out this way. See the mud on the door? I bet he ran into the woods. I searched the yard but there’s no trace of him.”

“We need to call the police.”

Jared flipped the last switch into its “on” position to restore the electricity, then shut the small gray door. “You’re right. Let’s go inside.”

Covered in a film of mud from the intruder, she stood by the window staring into the night.

Jared left to call the sheriff and check out the house.

Was she wrong about Jared? The man who’d broken into the house felt like the attacker in her dream and that laugh—it was a perfect match. In the dream, Jared took a bullet for her. Tonight he’d come to her rescue. For a moment, she’d felt safe in his arms.

Unlike every other time he'd touched her when she'd been afraid.

Angie put the flashlight on the end table, rubbed her eyes. *It's so damn confusing!* Maybe, just maybe, Jared wasn't a threat to her after all.

Ten minutes later, Sheriff Trevor Oakley stood in the living room, taking notes. A tall athletic man in his early thirties, he reminded her more of a professional athlete than a county sheriff.

"You two are lucky I was on patrol near here. Is anything missing?"

"No, I checked the house and nothing's been touched," Turning to Angie, Jared's brows furrowed. "Except Angelina. The intruder manhandled her."

The sheriff scrutinized Angie. Even though she'd known Trevor since grade school, she suddenly felt self-conscious of her silk nightgown, covered in mud, clinging to her body. She hadn't missed Trevor's gaze drifting over her breasts and hips.

She crossed her arms to cover her chest, shifted her weight from one leg to another. The skin on the left side of her face felt tight under the drying mud.

"Tell me what happened, Angie." Trevor raised his pen to the notepad.

"I woke up to go to the bathroom but something felt wrong. When I realized the power was out, I thought that had to be it." She glanced at Jared. "I always lock my door but tonight it was open. I started down the hall, using the wall as a guide and then my hand touched flesh. A large man grabbed me, slammed my face into his chest. I couldn't breathe so I bit him. He threw me against the banister and I screamed—"

"Bloody murder," Jared interrupted. "I found her like this in the hallway. I told her to stay in the bedroom until I searched the house, but she didn't listen and came downstairs anyway." Jared's stare burned through her.

"That's because she's stubborn. Are you hurt, Angie?"

"No, I'm not," she said, staring back at Jared before turning her attention to the sheriff. "Just shaken up a little. He's got a gun. I felt the butt of it sticking out of the top of his pants."

"I'm going to look around outside. Angie, you should get cleaned up." He motioned to Jared. "I'll be back in a few minutes to let you know what I find. Both of you stay inside until I return."

"Okay, Sheriff. I looked around outside before you arrived. I think he may have taken off into the woods."

"I'll check it out." Sheriff Oakley tipped his hat and walked through the porch door.

"What is the matter with you?" Angie snapped at Jared. "Why are you staring at me like that?"

"You should have changed your clothes before he got here. I can almost see through that flimsy piece of fabric you're wearing."

"You can't see through it." Angie said, looking down at herself. "Why do you care anyway?"

"I care because you were attacked tonight. Now go upstairs, take a shower and put on something a little less revealing."

"First of all, Mr. Maxwell, don't tell me what to do. Secondly, I'll wear what I like to sleep in, thank you. In fact, maybe I'll just sleep naked." She rolled her eyes. "Oh, but then again, you're just right down the hall. I wouldn't want you to be my next attacker."

Jared stepped close, nose to nose with her, his eyes darkened with emotion. "Don't press your luck, Angelina Benton," he growled, then turned and stormed out of the house after the sheriff.

His tone was menacing enough to arouse all of her fears about him at once. She peered after him as he walked out the door.

Maybe, just maybe, the dream was right.

FIVE

FOR THE NEXT TWO DAYS, ANGIE MANAGED TO AVOID Jared by diving into work.

Now she stood in an upstairs bedroom, thoughtfully looking around. After much exploration and pondering, she'd decided to decorate the Slayton house in a manner reminiscent of the early 1800s. She'd put all the details—notes and drawings for each room—into her special "Renobook." She'd designed the basic template years ago and created a new book for every job. As the project progressed, swatches and samples would be included within the pages.

She glanced at the Renobook then appraised the room. Because the Slayton's had renovated the house fifty years earlier, it didn't need as much work as they had originally thought. The second floor, especially, had little need of structural changes so she had started there.

Most of Jared's work was on the main level and the grounds. She didn't need to see him much at all, which suited her just fine.

Deeply engrossed in the Renobook, she sketched out chair rail designs for the walls and made remarks about the layout. A loud rap on the door drew her attention from the pages.

She glanced up to see Jared leaning against the doorjamb.

"Oh, hi," she said without enthusiasm.

"Are you at a stopping point?" he asked.

"Just let me finish this note." Angie scribbled a reminder to order blue satin fabric, then turned to Jared. "What's up?"

"Wanna go for a ride?"

"A ride? Where to?"

"I need to check out a small house on the farm. I think we could make it available to the tourists, but I'd like your opinion on some of my ideas. That is, if you have time."

Angie found his distant politeness suspicious but he'd asked for her professional opinion and she owed that much to the project. What harm could there be in going with him? She'd been inside for two days, after all. Fresh air and a change of pace would do her good she reasoned. "Sure, why not?"

"Come on then." Jared stared at her.

She shuddered at the indiscernible look in his eyes, but followed him anyway.

"Hang on a sec," she said, entering the office and picking up the phone. "How long are we going to be gone?"

"An hour or so."

"All right, but I need to phone Alan first. I was waiting for his call about the supplies."

"Okay, I'll wait outside."

She dialed the numbers then told Alan she would be inspecting a house on the farm with Jared and rescheduled their call for an hour and a half later. At least Alan knew she was with Jared and where they were going in case she didn't return.

She walked outside and to her amazement, there stood two horses, saddled and bridled.

"Horses?"

"Don't tell me a country girl like you can't ride."

"Oh, I can ride," she replied with disdain, taking the reins of the horse that appealed to her most, a beautiful Arabian.

"Here, take Thunder," Jared said, holding the Morgan's reins out to Angie. "The Arabian's too fast for you."

"You take Thunder." Angie mounted the white mare. "What's her name?"

"Whisper."

"Where are we going?"

"Clyde Davis' house."

She raised her eyebrows, but said nothing.

They rode through the woods in silence, the air thick with the growing tension between them.

"I can't take this," she said after a while. "Race ya!"

She sped away, her dark hair flying behind her, her thighs clenching the powerful animal beneath her. She grinned when she heard Thunder's hoof beats quicken behind her. She gave Whisper her head and they raced over the earth together for several minutes before Angie finally reined the mare in and pulled up underneath a tall oak tree beside a stream.

She looked back in triumph. She was so far ahead of Jared that she took the time to tether Whisper to a low limb where the mare could drink from the creek.

Angie herself crouched down on some rocks close to the water, then dipped her hands in and sipped from them, before splashing her face and neck.

When Jared finally appeared, she called to him, "What took so long, slowpoke?"

"Thought I'd let you win this time."

She laughed. "Yeah, right. I beat you fair and square. You're just slow."

"Well, get back on that horse," Jared said, riding past her. "We're not there yet."

So much for trying to be friendly. She remounted Whisper and followed. Soon they approached a small two-story house. She noticed the front porch and door were in need of repair and stopped Whisper short.

"What's the matter?" called Jared. "Come on."

Angie closed her eyes for a moment without answering. Just the site of this old house filled her with terror. It was so similar to the one in her dream. She glanced at Jared and her stomach lurched. Was this the day she would die?

She dismounted in a daze, tethered the mare's reins to the porch with trembling hands, then stood at the base of the steps.

"Come on," Jared said, reaching down to take her hand and then pulling her into the house. "I want to show you something."

Inside, Angie stared around. The interior of the house was completely different from the house in her dream. Except for the condition of the porch and front door, the house appeared to be in good repair. She blew out a breath as relief flooded through her.

Jared led her upstairs and stopped in front of a closed door.

"I came by here earlier today and found this room locked," he told her. "I picked the lock and couldn't believe what I found, so I did a little investigating. Paul Davis, a descendant of Clyde, said the family preserved this room the way he left it. Apparently, Clyde closed it off the day after Theodore caught him in here with Ruby. He wouldn't even let members of his family go inside while he was alive. According to Ruby's note, the one Alan has, this is the room where Theodore died." Jared released Angie's hand, pushed the bedroom door open and stepped back to allow her to enter. "No one has lived in the house since Clyde's death but it's cleaned every month."

"Oh my…" Angie stood motionless, allowing herself a moment to take it all in.

A large hand-carved, four-poster bed filled the center of the room. Covering it were thick gingham blankets and two pillows. There was a fireplace toward the outer wall, filled with partially rotted logs. An old hand-hewn chair faced the hearth. On the other wall, near the window, sat an antique chest of drawers with old-fashioned hairbrushes and a delicate hand mirror lay atop of it. Another small table beside the bed held a white washbasin and matching pitcher. Angie could tell the fabric of the window curtains had once been beautiful, but now they were deteriorated from the sun's harsh glare.

"This is like stepping back in time," Angie whispered, as she moved further inside.

"Amazing, isn't it? Paul said the housekeeper was here last week, that's why it's so clean. I thought we could make the few improvements needed to the structure and you could redesign the interior, keeping authenticity in mind. Maybe nothing needs to be done, apart from updating the bedding and window treatments. Then we could market this as the honeymoon suite."

Angie turned to look at Jared. "Even though Theodore died in here?"

"It'll add to the mystique."

"Most honeymooners wouldn't want to stay in a room where the man who haunts these grounds died. Maybe we could market it as a lover's getaway with a haunted twist or something like that, instead of a honeymoon suite." She walked around the four-poster, trailing her fingers on the aged fabric. "Alan once told me that Clyde and Ruby were married. In the note Ruby left to her son she said they met in secret because Theodore wouldn't approve of the marriage." Angie sat on the edge of the bed, spreading her fingers wide against the fabric of the bedspread underneath her. "I wonder how they felt, hidden away in this room, vowing their love for one another."

She glanced over at Jared. He shoved his hands into his pockets, returning her look. Suddenly, her vision tunneled until she felt a million miles away. Intense love washed over her.

Jared watched as Angie closed her eyes and lay down on the bed. Her hair swirled around her.

"I wonder how they felt when Theodore found them here and saw their love." She slid her arms across the fabric then left them above her head, lost in the emotions of the past.

What is she doing? thought Jared. *Is this an invitation?* He'd spent the last few days ignoring Angie, but with her lying across the bed like that…

Man, she's killing me!

He walked over to where she lay. Placing his knees between Angie's, he put his hands on the bed by her waist to support his weight. Leaning over her, he whispered, "Angie, are you okay?"

Her big brown eyes opened slightly, sleepily. A small smile tipped the corners of her mouth as she reached up and touched his cheek, ran her fingertips lightly across his lips.

"Angie?"

"Hmm…?"

"What are you doing?"

"Show me you love me," she said, running her fingers through Jared's hair then clasping her hands behind his neck. She pulled him down, lifted herself up to him and captured his mouth with hers in a demanding kiss.

"Show me now," she breathed against his mouth.

An unknown urgency overtook Jared and he crushed her lips beneath his. God he wanted this. He wanted her.

Angie parted her lips, darted her tongue into his mouth. His body churned with desire and he deepened the kiss. Angie gave herself, totally and completely, until she claimed his tongue, gently tugging it tighter within her mouth.

Jared moaned with pleasure.

Breaking the kiss, his gaze locked with eyes that were now chocolate brown and full of desire. Angie pulled his shirt out of his jeans and ran her hands across the naked skin of his back.

His heart was so full of love for this woman. He'd never known he could feel this much happiness. Yet…

Jared saw love for him reflected in her eyes and felt his heart plunge deeper. Desire pulsed through him in response to her. Lowering his mouth to her neck, he tasted the tempting silkiness of her throat before moving down to the rise of her breasts.

This time it was Angie who moaned. The sound of thick desire made him throb with need. He branded her with another kiss, slid his palm underneath her shirt to cup her breast. "Angie, are you sure about this?" he whispered.

"Clyde, don't stop now, my love."

Jared stilled. "What?"

"Don't stop, I love you, my darling."

Uncertainty filled him. Perhaps he hadn't heard her right? "What did you call me?"

"Why, Clyde, of course." Angie laughed. "Now stop being silly and make sweet love with me."

Jared placed his forehead against hers and groaned. Lifting her from the bed, he carried her out of the house.

Angie showered his face with kisses until he placed her astride Thunder. He untied both horses then mounted behind Angie. She rested her head against his chest while they rode the short distance to the section of creek where Angie had stopped earlier.

He let the reins drop, knowing that neither animal would wander far. Lifting Angie off Thunder, he carried her to the grass beside the rocks.

"Angelina?" Jared's heart was still pounding hard in his chest. The moment she called him Clyde, he'd known.

Hadn't the same thing happened to Terri when they were kids?

She'd scared him half to death when they went to a "haunted" house, by telling him details of all the "real" spirits there. He remembered how his body shook as he'd dragged his sister outside, how it had taken her some time to come out of the trance.

Just like Angie was doing now.

She blinked several times, then looked around. "Why are we by the creek?"

"Don't you remember?"

"Yes, we were in the house, in Ruby and Clyde's room. I told you we shouldn't market it as a honeymoon suite and now we're here." Angie's voice went up an octave. "Why are we here instead of the house, Jared?"

Jared took Angie's hands in his. "That's all you remember?"

"Yes."

His heart plummeted. She'd never wanted him at all. Trying hard to control his bitter disappointment, he kissed the top of her hands, then released them. "I brought you here because you called me Clyde."

"I what?" Her eyes widened in surprise.

"You thought I was Clyde."

"Why on earth would I think that?" Her eyes frantically searched his face. She wanted answers that he couldn't give. Then her brows knit together.

"Unless...oh, no...Jared."

"What is it?" he prodded.

"You have my lipstick all over your face."

He laughed. "No doubt."

"Jared, what did I do in that house? What did *we* do?"

"Let's just say you got a little carried away. You thought I loved you. You seemed strange, like you weren't yourself. *We* didn't do anything."

Angie's face flushed pink as she turned away.

Did he dare press her on this? Most of the time, he saw either fear or indifference in her eyes when she looked at him. She jerked away every time he touched too quickly, as if she thought he would hurt her. It just didn't make any sense. He had to figure out some way to get close if he wanted to convince her to sell. More than that, he wanted to win her love. He was sure of it, now, though not so sure why. Sometimes, he had to admit, *why* didn't matter.

"What happened back there, Angie?"

"It was Ruby's essence," she answered automatically, without thinking.

"I don't understand." Was she telling him she'd become possessed by Ruby?

"I should have told you before," she said, rubbing her face with her hands and taking a deep breath. "You'll think I'm a freak after this, but I don't see where I really have any other choice. I owe you an explanation."

"It's okay, you can tell me."

"I have empathic abilities," said Angie, looking away from his gaze. "That means I feel the emotions of others, especially when they are strong. The love that Ruby and Clyde felt in that room was intense, so powerful that I felt Ruby's love for Clyde as much as Ruby did all those years ago."

She brushed her hands across her jeans. "It's as if the imprint of their emotions lingered in the room. I don't know how else to explain it. From the look of your face and shirt, I'm afraid I acted on those feelings with you." Angie reached up and wiped some of the lipstick off his cheek. "I'm sorry, Jared."

"Sorry? Don't be sorry." He smiled broadly at her. "I thoroughly enjoyed it. But seriously, I guess this means you don't remember kissing me?"

The pinkness crept into Angie's cheeks and she turned away. "No, I just remember feeling Ruby's love for Clyde."

As uncomfortable as it made him, he had to ask. "Were you possessed by Ruby?"

She looked back at him. "I know you think the worst because you don't understand. It's not a possession. I feel the love, pain and fears of the person. A spirit doesn't take over my body."

"Is it always like this? I mean, is the emotion the only thing you ever remember?"

Angie sighed. "No, it's rare for the feelings to overtake me the way they did back there. Usually, I remember everything because I'm feeling it just like I feel my own emotions. I don't know how to explain it so that you'll understand."

She twisted her body toward him. "Once, when I lived in Roanoke, my neighbor's kid fell out of one of those wooden play sets in his backyard and broke his leg. My leg started to hurt and I knew something was wrong. I looked out of my window and saw him lying on the ground so I went over. His baby-sitter was talking on the phone, instead of watching him. When his mother arrived and took over, my pain disappeared."

"But that wasn't a trance like today."

"No, it wasn't. In high school, I went into a trance at a football game and felt a friend's heartbreak, as if she was dying. After I came out of it, I went to her house. She was hysterical because her boyfriend had broken up with her. There have only been a few times when I went into a trance like today."

She put her head on her knees briefly. "It's weird, I know, but I've learned to deal with it. I'm really sorry if I freaked you out back there." *And from now on I'll always block my empathic abilities where you are concerned.*

Jared lifted her chin, brushed her hair from her face. "You're a passionate woman, Angelina. Even if you were acting on Ruby's love for Clyde, I felt your passion."

Angie raised her eyelids to look at him.

"You are Angelina Benton right now, aren't you? Or are you still empathing Ruby?"

Angie shook her head. "No, I'm myself now."

"Then what do you say we try this one more time, because I want you to remember the feelings we shared, you and I. Can you tell me again?"

"Tell you what?"

"Call me your darling and tell me you love me."

The shocked expression on Angie's face was overwhelmed only by her mouth, which fell open. Jared wasted no time but took her lips quickly with his own, caressing them softly until Angie responded and kissed him back.

"I DON'T BELIEVE your arrogance!" Angie stormed through the kitchen, moving a sponge around on the counter, trying hard to control her embarrassment with a show of temper. "I did *not* say that I love you!"

"Yes, you did. And you kissed me back when you were yourself, before you realized what you were doing and bolted away on Whisper." Jared wrapped his arms around her waist from behind and leaned close to her ear. "I'm gonna hold you to both your words and actions, Angelina."

Angie moved out of his grasp and across the room. She turned and glared at him even as he grinned at her. Funny how she lost all fear of this man when he behaved like a typical, arrogant male. But now, the anger she had just pretended was real. She flung the wet sponge at him. Jared ducked and it hit the wall behind him, leaving a dark stain. His boisterous laugh echoed through the room.

"Just drop it, Jared. You're nothing but a womanizer! If and I mean *if* I said those words, they were an expression of Ruby's feelings for Clyde. Not my feelings toward you."

Jared just stood there, grinning at her. She sure was beautiful when her temper got the best of her. "I don't believe you."

"Uugghh! I don't have any feelings for you. Get it through that thick skull of yours. We're here to do a job and we agreed that our relationship, if you want to call it that, is strictly business." Angie backed away, glaring at him. "And with that thought in mind, I suggest you wipe that stupid grin off your face and let's both get back to work."

Angie moved further away, stared at him. She had to increase the distance to settle her stomach, her temper and her heart.

"If that's what you want." Jared rubbed his chin, his features suddenly serious. "We'll see how long it takes you to realize the truth."

"You're impossible. I am *not* having this conversation with you anymore." She turned her back to him in dismissal.

Jared closed the distance to stand right behind Angie. He turned her rigid body to face him, caressed her upper arms. "You, Angelina, are the only one who agreed to keep this relationship strictly business." He had every intention of making this relationship much more personal. Starting now.

He bent down and lightly brushed his lips against hers, then studied her face as anger set her lips into a thin line, drew her brows together and blazed through her narrowed eyes.

"To use your own words, you would do well to remember that from now on." Releasing her, Jared walked out of the kitchen, through the porch and headed toward the stables, whistling "Zip-A-Dee-Doo-Dah".

Angie watched through the window while his sauntering strides carried him across the yard. The mix of emotions this man aroused in her was frightening and confusing. "I'm afraid of what you'll do to me, Jared, so how could I possibly love you?"

SIX

A BEAD OF SWEAT TRICKLED DOWN THE CENTER OF Angie's back. The sun dipped low in the west, but the heat of the day still clung in the air. Even at dusk, it was sweltering hot.

She slipped the bridle off Whisper's nose, releasing the mare into the pasture, where she ran across the field, circled Thunder and raced through the tall pines toward the creek. The stallion reared against the tranquil sky then bolted after her.

Walking back to the stable, Angie wiped her brow with the back of her hand. After placing the bridle back on its hook, she threw a shovel into the wheelbarrow and pushed it to Whisper's stall. She knew she didn't have to clean the small cubicle, but the rhythm of the task would relax her. Maybe she could sort through her conflicting emotions about Jared.

Yes, I like his teasing, she thought as she began mucking out the stall. *But all it takes is a glint in his eye, a curt remark, or an unexpected touch, to remind me of that awful dream.* How could she trust him until the nightmare played itself out?

Confusion made her stomach knot. When he was near she fantasized about touching him, kissing him. She'd always pushed men away, but now the "virtuous Angelina Benton" was thinking about sharing Jared's bed.

Shaking her head ruefully, Angie leaned the shovel against the wooden wall. If Mrs. Turner was to find out that she wanted a man the woman would spread it around town faster than that time she overheard the conversation with Kimmie and dubbed me "Dansburg's oldest virgin." The townspeople sure got a kick out of that one. She'd never lived that nickname down.

She rolled the wheelbarrow out across the field and emptied the soiled bedding into the compost pit. On the way back, she stopped by the hay barn for the three bales of straw needed to bed down Whisper's stall. As she pulled the flat metal bar off the half circle loop, it occurred to her that, after the break-in the other night, she should call Alan and order a lock for the latch.

Leaving the door open, Angie crossed through the dim light to the straw bales at the back of the room. The lack of electricity was a necessity. Should the wiring malfunction, the results would be devastating. The building would go up like a torch.

The low light from the sun streaked in through the open doorway. Angie slid her fingers under the twine rope and lifted a bale. She needed to hurry before it was completely dark outside.

The door slammed shut.

"Damn wind!" She lugged the scratchy bale across the dark room then kicked the door.

It didn't budge.

"Great! Just great!" she muttered, dropping the straw bale on the floor. She pushed against the wooden door. It still didn't move. "What the…"

"Bye-bye, Angie baby," a gravelly voice threatened eerily from outside.

Angie jumped back and then stood motionless. "What's going on? Who are you?"

"You don't remember?" the voice mocked. "Now you'll *never*

forget!"

"Tell me who you are!" she shouted, pounding her fists against the wood. "What do you want with me?"

The only answer was the man's deep guttural laugh. A shiver of fear shot up Angie's spine. "Let me out!"

Suddenly she smelled gasoline. Good God! He wasn't going to set the barn on fire, was he? "No!" she cried out in terror. "No, please! I'll do whatever you want! Let me out!"

She heard a faint crackle and turned around. In the darkness behind her was a small amber glow. "Oh my God!"

Driven by panic, she threw the weight of her body against the door. It didn't budge. "Help! Somebody help me!"

"There's no one to help you this time." The man laughed, shining a flashlight through a knothole in the door.

Angie moved into the light, looked through the hole and begged for her life. "Please…please…let me out!"

"Since you don't remember me, here's a little hint. You can think about this on your way to hell."

Angie stared out of the small opening, but the man was standing so close that she could only see the torch beam of his flashlight as it moved upward and illuminated one blue eye.

"See ya, Bitch Benton." He laughed again and disappeared.

Angie spun around to see flames licking from bale to bale.

She couldn't wait for help to arrive. She'd be a shish kebab by then.

There has to be another way out. Think, Angie, think!

The building used to be a stable. She tried to picture the outside of it. The entrance she'd used was in the center of the building. She'd seen another door to an old stall on one end.

But which end?

Climbing over the stack of bales to the left of her, she felt along the wall for the metal door hinges. She coughed as dense smoke filled her lungs, choking her. The flames were getting hotter…

Pulling the neck of her shirt over her nose, she scooted along the top of the stored hay. There was little more than a crawl space between the hay and the roof. Her fingers moved along the rough edges. No hinges.

Damn! She had the wrong side.

She quickly pushed herself backward to the middle of the barn. The section where the man had started the fire was burning furiously.

She ran across the room to the other side, staying close to the wall and climbed up by grabbing the twine ropes around the hay bales. Maneuvering along, she searched again for hinges.

The eerie glow of the flames lit her way. *Please let it be here, please,* she silently prayed. Coughing, she rubbed at her eyes, which were stinging from the smoke.

Sliding her hand across the wooden wall, she touched the smooth hardness of metal. The hinge! She slid into a narrow space between the hay bales and the old stable door.

And pushed.

"No!" Throwing all of her weight into the door, she pushed repeatedly. Nothing happened.

"I'm going to die." Angie leaned against the door and laid her forehead against the back of her hands. "So this is my fate. To die at the hands of a maniac in a burning building, to never know the wonder of love or the joy of children."

Something tickled her arm and she lifted her head. A spider crawled swiftly across her skin. Knocking the insect to the ground, Angie shuddered. "Now I'm going to die with what, thousands of nasty spiders? Go figure."

Angie slammed her body against the door again. "Let me out! Help! Someone, help me!"

I am not giving up! This isn't the dream. I'm supposed to die by gunshot, not in a fire.

The fragrance of roses and jasmine suddenly filled the air, overpowering the smell of gasoline flames. A brilliant light blue glow shone through the cracks of the door from outside the barn. Angie stared at it.

"Look down, Angelina," a voice whispered.

Angie immediately looked at her feet and the iridescent glow sifted up to her knees. The wood at the bottom of the door was worn away. An animal had dug out the earth underneath.

She could fit. Oh God—she had to fit!

The heat of the fire was right behind her now. The flames licked closer as the fire roared to life.

Dropping to the ground she got down on her belly and stuck her head under the doorway.

"Yes!" She pushed and pulled with every ounce of energy, scrambling to get free. Halfway through, her belt loop caught on something—she couldn't see behind herself and she couldn't get free. "I will not die here."

She kicked off her shoes and maneuvered her hand into the tight fit between her belly and the ground then struggled to unzip her jeans. When she finally got the zipper down enough to fit her hips through she wriggled free of her pants. Crawling a few feet and then standing, she ran across the field toward the safety of the stables.

At the sound of cracking wood she turned to look back at the hay barn. Fully engulfed in a roaring fire, half of it collapsed as the searing flames licked toward the treetops.

I barely made it out alive. If the voice of that blue glow hadn't told me to look down I would be dying a horrible death right now.

Shaking, Angie crumpled to the ground. In a shocked daze, she watched the rest of the barn collapse before her eyes.

JARED AND HIS construction superintendent, Burt Emerson, ran toward the burning barn.

They were too late.

Jared saw the smoke just as Burt had nailed in the last board on the roof of the Davis house. Even driving the tractor at full throttle, the trip still took ten minutes.

"Damn. How could this have happened, Burt?"

"I don't know. Seems strange to me." Burt said. Looking around, he walked past him. "Oh, no. Boss, get over here!"

Jared turned. Burt was already running across the field toward someone lying on the ground. With darkness almost upon them, it was hard to see who it was.

"Angelina?" Jared whispered. Breaking into a sprint he quickly passed the older man.

"Angie!" Jared knelt down beside her. "Come on, baby, talk to me."

No response. She just stared into space, her face darkened with soot.

"Burt, go to the house and call Doc Martin. Get him over here fast."

"I'm on my way, Boss," Burt said then ran in the direction of the house.

"Angie? Are you all right?" What in the hell happened here? Why is she sitting in the middle of the field in just a T-shirt and pink lace panties? How did the hay barn catch on fire?

Jared picked her up and carried her to the house. Answers to his questions would have to wait. Burt held the door open, a blanket in his hand. Jared carried Angie into the living room and laid her on the couch, took the blanket from Burt and wrapped it over her. Easing down to the edge of the sofa, Jared gently took her hand in his.

"Boss, I'll be in the office calling Sheriff Oakley if you need me."

"Thanks," Jared responded, his gaze never leaving Angie's

face.

"Angie, talk to me," he said softly after Burt left. "It's Jared."

Her eyes moved over his face and he saw the faint flicker of recognition. He lifted her hand, turned it upward and kissed her palm. "Angelina, please say something. What happened to you?"

She turned toward him, her eyes lost and vacant.

"Angie, Burt and I found you in the field. The hay barn burned down. Angie, can you hear me?"

She still didn't answer so he watched her, uncertain how to proceed.

His indecision was interrupted by knocks on the front door.

"Burt," he called, "can you get the door?"

"I'm already there." Burt opened the door to Doc Martin and whispered, "She looks bad, Doc."

"What happened to her?" the doctor asked, his tone both professional and concerned.

"We don't know." Burt shook his head. "She hasn't said a word since we found her sitting in the middle of the field in her underwear. The hay barn burnt down."

"She wasn't burned?"

"It doesn't look that way, but Jared can't get a word out of her."

"Where is she?" the doctor asked.

"Right this way."

In the living room, Doc Martin exchanged places with Jared. He checked Angie's pulse, then looked at her pupils. He spoke to her softly, but still she didn't respond.

"She's been through an ordeal," he said to Jared, his eyes still on his patient. "She may be in shock and I don't want to take any chances. I'd feel better if we checked her at the hospital."

"No…no…" Angie's hoarse voice was barely audible.

"I'll get her some water," Burt said, leaving the room.

"Angie?" Jared sat on the coffee table to hold her hand again.

In a few moments, Burt came back and handed the water to the doctor. "Sheriff Oakley just got here," he said as the man in question followed him into the room.

Three men were now standing over Angie, looking down at her while Jared stayed by her side.

Angie stared back at them. Their blurry faces slowly came into focus. Doc Martin held a glass of water to her lips and she sipped the cool liquid. Then, pulling her hand free from Jared's, she grabbed the glass, seeking to drench her parched throat.

"Just a sip, Angie, just a sip." Doc pulled the glass away. "Jared, lift her up a little please."

Jared helped Angie up, wrapping the blanket behind her. Doc Martin again held the glass to her lips, drawing it back when she drank too deeply.

She sipped several times then lay against the pillow. Rubbing her eyes, she looked up at them again.

"You're getting a little color back," Doc said as he rechecked her heart rate.

Angie managed a small grin and saw the relief in the four faces around her. Relief that wouldn't last long. Not after she told them what had happened.

"How are you feeling now?" Doc Martin asked.

"Shaky." Her voice was still hoarse. "I just couldn't stop staring at the barn."

"Can you tell us what happened?" asked Sheriff Oakley in the ensuing silence.

Angie didn't look at him. Instead, she glanced at Jared, saw the strain etched across his face.

Why is he so worried? She took a deep breath and spoke directly to him. "The intruder from the other night came back," she said slowly. "He locked me in the barn, poured gasoline around it and set it on fire."

"What?" was the unanimous response.

"I never even got to bed down Whisper's stall," she murmured and then told them the details of what had happened. "I'd just made it to the field when the barn collapsed. If I'd been just a few seconds later…"

"Don't think about that now," Jared comforted her.

"I'm going to check out the barn," said Sheriff Oakley. "Burt, can you pull your truck around to add some light?"

"Sure. I'll meet you back there."

Angie waited for the two men to leave the room. "Doc, I feel better now. I'd really like to get cleaned up."

"Okay, but someone has to stand outside the door in case you need help."

"Really, that's sweet of you but I'm fine now. I don't need anyone to stand guard."

"I'll carry you up," Jared said, standing to help her.

"That's okay. I can do it." Angie wrapped the blanket around her waist as she stood. "I have to call Alan. I don't want him to have another heart attack. If he hears about this from someone other than me, he might."

"We'll be here if you need us," said Doc Martin.

They watched Angie go upstairs.

"Can you stay here a few minutes, Doc? I want to see if the sheriff found anything."

"I was going to suggest that." Smiling, the doctor patted Jared on the shoulder, his blue eyes glinting. "Go on, get out there."

"Thanks, Doc, I'll be back in a few."

THE HEADLIGHTS OF Burt's red Ford pickup and the police SUV shone across what remained of the hay barn. Burt stood beside his truck and watched Sheriff Oakley poke around the edges of the rubble where the door had been.

"Find anything, Sheriff?" Jared strode over to stand beside

Burt.

"Yeah, I found something." Oakley straightened, turned to Jared and adjusted his hat. "You're not going to like it."

Jared's stomach tightened. "What is it?"

"Whoever trapped Angie in this barn didn't intend for her to escape. Both doors were padlocked. She would have died in there if she hadn't found her way to that stall."

Jared leaned back hard against Burt's truck. "Do you think someone is trying to kill her?"

"After the break-in the other night and now this? I don't just think it, Jared. I'm pretty damn sure of it. Trapping her inside a padlocked hay barn, soaking it with gasoline and setting it on fire is way beyond the boundaries of trying to scare her. This time he meant for her to die."

"Not while I'm around," Jared said angrily. "I'm not letting her out of my sight again." Pacing back and forth, he ran his fingers through his hair in frustration. "Who would want Angie dead?"

"I don't know but I intend to find out." Sheriff Oakley put the evidence he'd collected inside the SUV as car lights lit up the dirt road approaching the house. "My deputies are here. We'll secure the area until tomorrow morning. I'll be back at sunrise with the fire marshal to do a more thorough investigation after the heat has dissipated. The deputies will take everyone's statement tonight."

Sheriff Oakley adjusted his hat. "I have a few more questions for Angie. I'll be at the house if you need me."

When the sheriff was out of earshot, Jared turned to the older man. "I swear, Burt, I'll kill him myself if he hurts her."

"I'll have your back, Boss. I've never seen Angie like that before. She's always been so feisty."

"From now on I want one of us, or someone from the crew, guarding her at all times."

"She's not gonna go for that, Boss." Burt wiped his face with a red bandanna then shoved it in his hip pocket. “Angie’s a stubborn one. Independent too. If she thinks we’re watching out for her, she’ll get mighty upset.”

“Then we won’t let her know, will we? Tomorrow I want you to tell the crew what happened tonight. Make sure someone’s near her at all times. If she sees the men working, she’s less likely to guess what we’re doing.”

“But Angie only saw the guy’s eye color. We don’t know if the intruder and the man who did this are the same person. What if it’s two different men or one of the crew?”

“You’re right, I’m not thinking clearly.” Jared leaned wearily against the truck. “I’ll hire a security team, pay them double time to pretend to be workers and stay near Angie. The regular crew we’ll keep a safe distance away. And we’re changing the locks on the house.”

“And at night, Boss?” Burt grinned, “Are you gonna move into her bedroom?”

Jared looked at Burt in disbelief. “Yeah sure. Like that would ever happen. I’ll hire two uniformed security guards to keep watch outside the house at night until this guy is caught.”

“I hope this works. I don’t want anything to happen to that girl. Martha was like a sister to my wife. I’ve watched Angie grow up. I want to keep her safe.”

“Me too, Burt, me too.”

ANGIE FELT THE warmth on her face even before she opened her eyes. Her bedroom was on the east side of the house. Every morning, without fail, the sun woke her.

Lying on her side, she snuggled deeper into the pillows. Pulling the sheet over her head, pushing the nightmare from her mind, she tried for a few more minutes of rest.

Since she’d been staying in the Slayton house, she’d been able to fall back asleep after the dream woke her, something she'd never done in her own home. True, she had paced the floor in the middle of every night during the three weeks since she moved in. As far as she knew, Jared was unaware of her interrupted sleep.

Although Alan had hoped she would dream of Theodore Slayton, the ghost of Sam's ancestors had yet to occupy her night visions. Instead, the face of Jared Maxwell came night after night to torment—and intrigue—her.

If only the end of the dream was clear. Yes, Jared took the bullet meant for her, but he also disappeared from her sight. That meant he could have snuck up behind her. He could be the man who dragged her away at gunpoint.

So much for sleeping in.

Pulling the covers off her face, Angie rolled onto her back. Usually her premonition dreams were so clear. Why was this one so confusing?

Hearing a steady pounding outside, she pushed the covers back and swung her feet over the side of the bed. She looked out of the window to see Jared already hard at work. A locksmith's truck was parked out front. Good idea to have the locks changed. After rubbing the slumber from her eyes, she quickly made up the bed, grabbed some clothes and her toiletry bag before heading down the hall to the bathroom.

She passed the four center rooms, now empty, then paused at Jared's bedroom. For the first time since they moved in, the door was open.

She glanced down the hall. She was alone.

Curiosity will surely kill this cat, she thought as she ventured inside. What did she hope to find? She only knew she wanted to learn more about Jared.

The room was spotless. He had made the bed—no clothes littered the floor.

A wooden box with intricate designs on the lid caught Angie's attention. It was sitting on top of the chest of drawers. She walked over and looked at it more closely. It was about the size of a cigar box. A deep mahogany offset the lighter shades of several small wooden triangles in the square inset. The hinges and latch were made of a golden metal. She lifted the open lock but left the lid closed, respectfully holding her curiosity in check.

Angie next went to Jared's bed and sat on the edge of it. Soon she was deep in thought.

Two weeks ago she had argued with Jared over what had happened between them in Clyde Davis' bedroom. Her narrow escape from the fire, with Jared showing so much concern and care, had brought them closer again. Since then, Jared had been polite but distant. They ate separately and talked together only about the renovation.

It was exactly what she said she wanted when she moved into the homestead. It suited her just fine.

Didn't it?

It seemed as though confusion were her only friend.

Jared could still terrify her, especially when his eyes would darken over some snide remark she threw his way. All the same, she kept wondering why it was so important to him that she remembered the way they'd kissed.

Lordy could that man kiss!

She'd never forget the day by the stream, when Jared aroused feelings in her she didn't know existed, when her body responded to him in ways she'd never before experienced.

Angie inhaled deeply. The room smelled like Jared, a fresh clean scent with a hint of musk. She noticed it every time he came close to her.

It was all too damn confusing. Thank heavens she only had two more months here with him. At this frantic work pace, they might even complete the project early.

Thinking of him, she felt hot and bothered and that just

wouldn't do.

Time to get in that shower.

She stood to leave, turned and stopped dead in her tracks.

Jared leaned against the doorjamb, quietly watching her. She felt her face flush. *Oh boy. What can I say? Nothing.* So she just stood there, staring at him.

"Find what you were looking for, Ms. Benton?" Jared's eyes were like steel.

Angie drew in a breath at the coldness in his voice. "I wasn't looking for anything. I was just looking."

"Snooping, I'd say."

Her temper flared. He'd watched her, never saying a word. "Call it what you like. If you didn't want anyone coming in here, you shouldn't have left your door open. How long have you been standing there?"

"Long enough."

"I didn't touch anything, I was just looking at your room…uh…thinking how I'm going to redecorate it."

"Are you sure?" Closing and locking the door, Jared stepped toward her.

"What are you doing?" Panic was closing in along with Jared. The air around her grew heavy making it hard to breathe.

His damp hair hung in his eyes and his body glistened with sweat. This was way too familiar. Too much like the dream.

"I'd say I'm taking advantage of a beautiful, scantily dressed woman, snooping around in my bedroom."

Angie glanced at herself in the mirror. The silky fabric of the short pink nightgown was too thin. She saw her nipples pressed against the sheer cloth. Obviously, Jared had seen them too. She lifted the towel against her chest to cover her breasts.

"I told you, Jared, I didn't touch anything. I was just trying to get decorating ideas." He had her cornered now, between the wall and the bedpost. Her breathing became heavier, more labored. She didn't dare tell him what she had really been thinking.

This wasn't fear causing her to tremble.

It was excitement. Anticipation.

He was so close, stroking her hair, looking at her *that way*, his eyes full of passion.

Kiss me, Jared. I know I shouldn't, but I want you to kiss me.

"You know, you're beautiful in the morning, Angelina. Modesty becomes you." He slid the narrow strap of her nightgown off her shoulder and brushed his lips across the flesh beneath.

She drew in a sharp breath and turned her face to him. His lips were just an inch away from hers. Her own trembled with longing.

"Next time ask before you enter my room," he whispered and stepped back. He stripped off the sweat soaked T-shirt, revealing hard muscles and Angie's heart skipped a beat. Tossing it on a chair, he grabbed a clean shirt from a drawer. He walked across the room, pulling the fabric over his head. Then, without as much as a backward glance, he unlocked the door and walked out of the room.

"Uugghh," Angie released the built up tension with the deep guttural sound and headed to the shower.

The water would be cold, ice-cold. Of that, she was sure.

Seven

ANGIE SAT ON THE FLOOR IN THE SLAYTON LIVING room surrounded by catalogues, her back resting against the couch and her legs propped up on the coffee table. She flipped between several new swatch books, looking for a light mauve paint to complement the wallpaper she'd chosen for one of the bedrooms.

When Alan brought her the new books after breakfast that morning, he'd asked if she'd dreamt of Theodore Slayton. She expected him to be disappointed with her reply. Instead, he'd patted her cheek and said, "If he's here, he'll come to you."

Angie turned the page and found a match. Jotting down the color number on her order form, she put the swatch samples aside. Then, turning to that bedroom's page in the Renobook, she wrote the number down again.

The research for the prints and styles of the early eighteen hundred's was complete, most of the supplies were ordered and the plans for the interior would be done in a day or two.

Now she just needed to fax in the remaining orders, hire someone to construct the window treatments she'd designed and then next week it would be hands-on work.

This is my baby, she thought, *I can't wait to get started.* It was the individual care she showed each client and the fact that she did most of the work herself that had made her reputation as an interior designer. This project was no different, except the client was herself. Today Jared and his crew would finish inside the house, then tomorrow, after the cleaners were through, the place would be hers alone.

She stretched, tightening all her muscles at once, luxuriating in the energy that spread through her body. Bringing the interior together, striving for both historical accuracy and modern appeal, had focused and challenged her in these last few days. It had also kept Jared Maxwell in the recesses of her mind, where he belonged.

Until this morning, that is.

She could still see his blue eyes darkening with desire as he'd slipped the strap of her negligee off her shoulder. Oh, he'd wanted her, really wanted her, she was sure of it, even though he was angry to have found her in his room. The way his muscles rippled when he pulled that shirt off—

Nah, she wasn't even going there.

The clank of the knocker drew her from the floor to the entrance hall. She opened the front door a little, expecting a salesman, then flung it wide.

"Oh My God! Ed—die!" Angie threw her arms around the big man's neck, kissed him on the cheek and squeezed him as tightly as she could.

"Glad to see me, are ya?" Eddie grinned at her.

"Of course I'm glad to see you," Angie said, releasing her hold on him. "How did you know I was here?"

"Alan told me." He shoved his hands in his jean pockets. "So you're partners with the old coot now?"

"Eddie Harland, that's no way to talk about your uncle! I'll tell you all about it but first come inside. Let me fix you something to drink. Wow! Look at you! You're huge—been working out, huh?" Linking her arm with his, Angie led him inside the house.

WHEN THE DOOR of the house closed, Burt, outside in the front yard with Jared, jabbed his employer in the arm. "Why don't you go inside? See what it's about, Boss?" Burt spoke over the hum of the electric table saw.

"It's none of my business if Angie has a man in the house." Jared picked up a two-by-four they had just cut.

"Looked more like an overgrown boy to me."

Stacking the lumber on the trailer, Jared turned to Burt. "It's not my concern, nor yours. You just stick to running the crew. Now let's finish this job. The sooner, the better."

"Yes, sir." Burt picked up the next piece of wood. The Boss had it bad for Angie, even if he didn't know it himself yet.

A few minutes later, a loud clank made Burt look up from the table saw. Jared was throwing, not stacking, the wood. Glancing at the house, Burt figured he knew why.

Angie stood in front of the window, lip-locked with the guy she'd invited inside.

Burt smiled when she pushed him away and slapped his face. She was a feisty one, that Angie. He glanced at Jared but the Boss had looked away and missed the most important part.

The hum of the table saw slowed and then stopped.

"What are you doing, Burt? We have four more stacks to cut."

Burt lifted his cap off his head and mopped his face with a red bandanna. "I'm an old man, Mr. Maxwell, and in this heat I have to take time to cool off now and then." He narrowed his blue eyes at Jared. "Seems to me that you should do the same," he said, shoving the cloth in his hip pocket. "I'm gonna get a drink of water and be back in fifteen minutes. If you don't need a break, why don't you go into the house and check the measurements on that last doorframe we need to replace."

"All right, but be back in fifteen, we have to finish today. I'll go take the measurements," he said, then started across the yard.

"Hey, Boss. You're gonna need this." Burt tossed him the measuring tape. He grinned as Jared caught it.

"Thanks," Jared muttered, walking quickly toward the house.

"Yeah, I'll just bet you take some measurements." Burt chuckled. "At least I got you to go inside." He reached down to pick up the water bottle he'd sat by the table saw earlier. He took a long draught of the lukewarm liquid then went back to work.

"WHAT IS THE matter with you, Eddie?" Angie glared at him from across the room. Her lips stung from that forced kiss. He'd probably bruised them.

"Come on, Angie, you've teased me for years."

"What?" She couldn't believe her ears. *Teased Eddie? How?*

"Eddie..." she began but, seeing the fury and agony flashing across his oval face, she bit back her retort.

Eddie's face was red. "Angie, I..." He stopped, as if lost for words. "I...I told myself I had to come here today and speak to you." Taking a red bandanna from his pocket he nervously wrapped it around one palm. "This isn't easy, Angie." Suddenly, the expression on his face hardened and his hands stilled. "But you *know*, Angie, you've always known. It's *you* that's making it difficult," he said with a calm forcefulness.

"What?" she responded. "What have I always known? Eddie, please..."

"Ah, there you go again." The anger was back. "Always teasing me. You know that I love you. That's what you know!" Eddie's voice was an anguished snarl and Angie stared at him in horror.

He approached her, unwrapping the bandanna and captured her hand with his. She stood motionless, unable to imagine what was coming next.

When Eddie fell down on one knee and begged, "Angie, will you marry me? I can't live without you," she had to will herself not to run out of the room.

"Eddie!" she cried. "What in the *world* are you talking about?" Pulling her hand away, she scooted toward the couch.

Eddie had never shown the slightest romantic interest in her. Or had he? They used to share their secret crushes on others, their pains, hopes and dreams.

Had Eddie taken their friendship all wrong?

"Eddie, wait a minute," she said, her mind racing. "I thought you knew that we were just friends. I've never given you any reason to think otherwise, as far as I know. We grew up together, for goodness sake!" Angie paced the floor, bewildered.

She turned to him. "What do you mean you want to marry me? Damn it, Eddie! You've never even *hinted* before today that you had feelings for me."

To her great confusion, Eddie crossed the floor and enfolded her in his large arms. She went as still as a chipmunk caught in an eagle's gaze. *What next?*

"Angie," Eddie murmured into her hair, "I'm leaving in three days to go to Egypt. Won't you come with me?"

Huh? Angie felt as if she'd fallen into some other dimension. She said nothing and didn't move, rigid in Eddie's embrace.

"After all we've shared through the years," he said, pulling back and looking into her eyes, "you didn't know? I've always loved you, Angie. Since I started grad school, I've thought a lot about what I'm going to do with my life." He kissed her forehead. "The one thing I'm sure of is that I want you in it. Please, Angie, say you'll marry me."

Eddie pressed his lips to hers again and Angie thrust her arms between their chests, struggling to break free.

Suddenly, Eddie hit the floor—hard. When he landed a key ring with a small black remote fell out of his pocket.

"If you ever come near the lady again, I'll have you arrested," a low growl threatened. "Now get out."

Eddie swiped up the remote, touched his lip and saw that blood covered his fingertips. He looked at the man who'd just punched him, then at Angie. Jumping up he lunged at Jared, fury raging across his features. "I'll kill you!"

Angie leaped between the two men.

"No! Stop it! Just go, Eddie," Angie screamed, fighting back tears. "In a matter of minutes you have ruined the one friendship I valued most in this entire world. I loved you as a *friend*, Eddie. The best friend I ever had." She pressed her palms against his chest, pushed him away from Jared, memories of shared experiences crowding into her mind.

"Angie, don't do this."

"Eddie, don't *you* do this," she shouted, stepping away.

Jared, Angie noticed, was clenching his fists and advancing toward Eddie who was the bigger of the two.

She grabbed Jared's arm to stop him, worried that if they fought he might get hurt. Angie turned once again to Eddie. "Just leave, Eddie. Please. This is too much for me. I can't handle it. Don't force me to tell Alan what happened today."

"You'll regret this, Angie."

She was shocked to see his scowl, to hear the menace in his voice.

"Eddie, what's happened to you?" she asked.

"Nothing's *happened* to me, Angie," he snarled. "You're just a cruel witch, that's all. And one of these days you'll regret throwing my love away, you'll see." He stormed out of the house, slamming the door behind him.

Jared took a step toward Angie. "Are you all right?" he asked gently, taking her hands to examine her arms. "Damn him! Look what he did to you. Who was that guy anyway?"

Angie looked at the red marks darkening her skin. She licked her swollen, bruised lips. "Alan Harland's nephew," she said faintly. "We grew up together."

"He thinks he owns you?"

Angie gazed up at Jared. His eyes were locked on her lips. *Did he see Eddie kiss me?* "He's got some crazy notion that he loves me and wants to marry me. I've never given him any reason to think that we're more than friends." The whole ordeal made her feel weak. A shiver ran through her body. Without thinking, she rested her forehead against Jared's chest.

"His mother is mentally ill," she said. "Schizophrenic. Now I'm wondering if Eddie isn't too. He's never acted like this before." She looked up. "How awful, Jared. How sad and awful."

"It's over now," he whispered. Encircling her within his arms, he drew her close.

Jared's embrace was so comforting, so warm. For the first time since they'd met, Angie felt completely safe with him. She couldn't imagine being anywhere else but in his arms right now. She bent her head into his chest again.

"Maybe, maybe not," she murmured. "If he does have his mother's disease and if he isn't properly diagnosed and medicated, he could do anything."

Jared continued to hold her tightly, stroking her back with one palm. When the small sobs came he lifted her chin up. Angie saw his surprised look at the tears streaming down her face.

"Angie?"

"I'm sorry. It's just too much. He was my friend—a really close friend. I just hate to see him like this," she said. She backed out of Jared's embrace and wiped her cheeks with her fingertips. "Plus I'm scared. I've seen his mom in one of her rages. She was terrifying. Eddie used to tell me about them too. About what she did to him when she was ill. I feel so sorry for him." She looked down as Jared gently took one of her hands in his.

"Are you going to be okay?" he asked.

She gave him a little smile. "I'll be fine. Honest. I think I should go and freshen up now."

"I'll be here if you need me."

"Thanks," she said, waving him off, "but I'm really okay. Go back to work."

Jared watched her go upstairs then sat on the couch and took a deep breath. He'd never known a man could feel so protective of a woman or experienced it himself until now. He would have killed Eddie to defend Angie.

I'll wait for her to come back down. By God, I'll wait until the end of time for her.

ANGIE PACED ACROSS her bedroom floor, tears once again streaming down her cheeks. Eddie had frightened and upset her. He'd had the same look in his eyes that she'd seen in his mother's right before she deliberately drove her car into the neighbor's house.

But her tears weren't just for her lost friendship. They were also for her lost heart. She flopped down in the overstuffed winged back chair and dried her face with the neckline of her shirt.

It had hit her, while leaning against Jared's muscular chest, feeling and hearing his heartbeat, that this was what she'd been longing for. A strong man's arms, a kind man's acceptance without question, without criticism, without judgment. It was in that moment that she knew she had lost her heart. Lost it to love.

Love for Jared Maxwell.

She went to the window to look for him but Burt still worked alone. She turned, leaned her back against the wall and let the tears flow once again, before sinking to the floor and putting her head on her knees.

What am I going to do? She knew what she wanted, but how could she want it? It was madness, straight and true. Death at the hands of the one she loved. *Could it get any worse?*

"Angie, for God's sake, what's wrong?"

Obviously, it could.

She looked up as Jared closed and locked the door behind him. *He sure has a habit of locking doors,* she thought, as she struggled to get her emotions under control.

Before she could answer, Jared lifted her from the floor and sat her on the bed. "He hurt you, didn't he?"

She shook her head, "No."

"Then what is it?" he said softly. "Are you in love with him?"

"Oh, good lord." She sniffed. "No, I don't love him. I only thought of him as a friend."

"Then why are you crying like this?"

Breathing deeply, Angie wiped away the last of her tears, then looked Jared straight in the eye. What would it hurt? The situation couldn't get much worse.

"Mr. Maxwell," she said, "have you ever wanted something and not known what it was until it smacked you in the face? Then, in that very same instant, known that what you desired was the one thing in the world that you could never, ever, have?"

"I can't say that I have, Angelina." Jared sat beside her, tucked her dark tresses back behind her ear.

She turned away from him, aching from hopeless, impossible love.

Jared touched her chin, turned her face to his. "What is it that you want and can't have?"

You. It's you! Her mind screamed the words but her mouth only parted slightly. "It doesn't matter," she said softly. "It's just the realization hit me hard. I'll be okay."

She rubbed her arm and Jared examined it more closely.

"Bastard! Look what he did to you."

Angie looked at the deep blue marks marring her flesh. "They're just bruises," she said.

She noticed then that Jared's forehead was creased with worry. Here she was carrying on about herself when he had something else on his mind.

"What's wrong? Jared, tell me."

"Angie…" He ran his hand through his hair. "I'm not sure this is the right time."

"Oh, I think it is, Mr. Maxwell. If you know something, spill it. After all, you let *me* gush like a blubbering idiot."

Jared reached into his shirt pocket and took out a folded piece of paper. "I went outside to make sure Eddie really left and found this on the front porch."

She took the paper from his hand and opened it.

Know that I'm watching and waiting. You had better look over your shoulder, Angie Benton…when you least expect it I will have you for my very own.

She stood and moved away, sudden suspicion flaring within her. "Did you write this?"

"No. Why would you think I wrote it?" Jared's tone bordered on indignant.

Angie turned to him. "This letter sounds like it's about sex. After all your innuendos, can you blame me for wondering?"

He raised his eyebrows, reached over and took her hand, gently leading her back to the bed. "As much as I'd like that, I don't need to leave you a note when I can do this."

He brushed his lips lightly against hers, then deepened the kiss. Without hesitation, Angie wrapped her arms around his neck and pressed her body against the hard planes of his chest.

He leaned back to the bed, dragging her with him.

She kissed him passionately, his masculine scent surrounding her, enjoying the feel of him beneath her, she nibbled his lips, tasted him. For the first time in her life she wanted more—much, much more.

Jared rolled her over, his lips moved from her mouth to her neck and back again. Then he broke the kiss, "I don't think a note could ever say that, now could it?"

Angie took a deep breath. "Nope." She stared up at him. "No way."

He sat up, surprising her, then pulled her to a sitting position beside him on the edge of the bed. "I think Eddie wrote that note. I'm amazed you didn't think so too. He was mad as hell because you rejected him." His voice was cold.

I guess the moment is over, Angie thought. *I've made quite the fool of myself.*

Jared held her fingers between his, then raised them to his lips and kissed each tip.

She couldn't take any more. The emotions were too strong. Pulling her hand away, she stood up then walked to the dresser. "It does make sense," she said coolly. "I'm sorry for accusing you, Jared." Her heart was beating so loudly she was surprised he couldn't hear it. "I think we should give the note to Trevor, just in case."

"Don't worry about it. Eddie's obsessed. I'll call the sheriff's department, fill Oakley in and ask him to come by to pick up the note."

"Jared, it's been a rough morning." She looked at him for a few silent moments, assessing the situation. "I'm emotionally wiped out. Would you mind if I stayed here while you called?"

The concern in his eyes belied the smile he gave her. "Of course not. Try to get some rest, Angie."

"Okay," she said.

He got up and unlocked the door.

"Jared?" Angie asked.

"Yeah?" He looked back at her.

"Next time ask before you enter my room."

He grinned. "Yes ma'am."

The door clicked shut behind him.

Anger pushed Jared through the rest of his day. He imagined every possible way he could make Eddie Harland pay for hurting Angie.

When, later that morning, Burt told him that he'd seen Angie smack the daylights out of Eddie, Jared smiled and thanked him for letting him know. When Burt added that he was proud of Angie, that Martha had raised the girl right, Jared could only agree. But when he said Angie was a handful, Jared wasn't sure how to react. Burt had laughed as if he knew something Jared didn't.

The woman drove him crazy.

Angie deserved something special after all she'd been through. He would make sure she got it.

LATER THAT AFTERNOON, Angie dropped several empty boxes on the library floor and scanned the room. Once the books were stored, the crew could replace the shelves.

Taking a large box over to the wall, she began pulling books and packing them. A wide variety of literature passed through her hands—Shakespeare, Edgar Allen Poe, poetry, even woodworking manuals.

She'd just removed the last volumes from a bottom shelf when a loose back panel caught her attention.

She got down on her hands and knees to peer at it.

Something was back there.

She worked her fingers behind the loose board and tugged. It moved a half inch, revealing the edge of a book. She tugged again. A nail squeaked.

"Why would anyone hide a book behind a board?" she

muttered.

Angie braced her feet against the wall, reached in and worked the length of her fingers behind the plank.

"Please don't let spiders live back there."

She took a deep breath and pulled hard. Nothing.

Then, jerking the board with all her might, her hands slipped and she fell flat on her back.

Groaning, she propped herself up on her elbows. "Yes!" The board had loosened halfway. Leaning forward, she pulled on the loose board with her left hand, grabbed the book with her right.

The brown tome was covered with dust. Angie brushed off the leather cover with the palm of her hand. No words graced the cover or the spine.

She opened the book to the first page.

Theodore Slayton—August entries.

"Oh My God!" Her hand trembled as she turned to the next page and saw a handwritten entry.

She read a few sentences and knew. This was Theodore Slayton's personal journal.

A door slammed somewhere in the house. Angie quickly scooted over to the box, grabbed two books and sandwiched the journal between them.

"Angie?" Burt called out.

She kicked the loose board back against the wall then stood up. "I'm in the library."

He poked his head in the doorway. "Working hard I see."

"Hardly working," she joked.

"Just wanted to let you know I'm going home now. I couldn't find the Boss to tell him."

"Okay. See you tomorrow, Burt."

She waited for him to leave then snatched up the journal and ran with it to her room.

EIGHT

IT HAD BEEN HARD TO LEAVE THE JOURNAL BEHIND, but Angie knew that if she had brought it with her the steam from the water might damage it.

Now, in the otherwise dark bathroom, the fragrance of lavender and jasmine permeated the air and glimmers of light flickered from short columns of wax. Angie lay in the hot perfumed water, eyes closed.

She hadn't been able to concentrate after the incident with Eddie. Most of the day she'd sat staring at swatches of material, her mind endlessly replaying the scene with the young man she'd always seen as her friend. The excitement of finding the journal had added to her stress.

Finally, she had given up and ran a bath. Now that her nerves were beginning to calm, she thought about growing up with Eddie. When had his obsession begun?

Everything was fine until that time after he went away to college. Naturally, they had drifted apart. When she moved to Roanoke without telling him, he had shown up on her doorstep one afternoon, mad as a hell.

That was strange, she remembered. *But not strange enough to prepare me for what happened today. He must have inherited his mother's illness, she finally decided. Like I need any more craziness in my life.*

It was sad and it hurt to lose a childhood friend. Maybe she should reach out to him, try to help. The thought made her uncomfortable. He could take that the wrong way too and then what would she do?

Angie sighed and, pulling the plug from the drain with her toe, rinsed the last of the bubbles from her warm reddened skin.

After drying off she wrapped her body in an oversized towel, her hair in a smaller one. Pattering down the hall to her room, she ducked inside, grateful she hadn't run into Jared. She put on a shirt and shorts then towel dried her hair.

As she brushed her still damp locks, her stomach growled.

I'll run downstairs and have a bowl of cereal, then read more of Theodore's diary. Maybe I'll find entries about Clyde and Ruby. There's nothing better than a hot bath, full tummy and snuggling into bed with a book to end a bad day.

When she reached the kitchen, she had to rethink her plans.

In the dim light, Jared leaned against the counter, sipping a glass of what looked like champagne. The khaki slacks, white shirt and dress shoes he wore were a stark contrast to his usual daytime attire of T-shirts, jeans and sneakers.

Angie drew in a sharp breath. He held a glass out to her and her stomach tightened. Speechless, she walked to him and curved her fingers around the narrow stem.

Several tall candles illuminated the room. Soft music emanated from a little clock radio. Fresh flowers, arranged in a water glass, served as a centerpiece for a table set for two.

Jared had removed the ice bin from the refrigerator. Inside was a bottle of champagne, partially covered by a white cloth napkin. A skillet simmered on the stove. Whatever was cooking smelled delicious.

"Jared, what is all of this?"

"After everything you've been through today, I thought you should eat more than a bowl of cereal tonight."

Great! How did he know that? "I like cereal."

"Or you don't like to cook." Grinning, he put down his glass, took her by the hand and led her to the stove. "Take a whiff of this," he said, lifting the skillet's lid.

She did as he asked. "Ummm, what is it?"

"My grandmother called it roasted chicken in garlic mushroom sauce." He scooped a bit of sauce into a spoon, held it out to her. "I call it dinner."

Angie smiled at the mischievous glint in his eyes. She had never expected such a sweet and generous gesture from him. She tasted the sauce, found it delicious. "This is really good. Did your grandmother come over to cook it?"

Jared put his hand to his chest and rocked back on his heels. "You wound me to the heart."

Laughing, Angie leaned against the counter and sipped her champagne. "So, you're a chef too? Because you know, Mr. Maxwell, I believe you could serve this dish at a five-star restaurant."

"And now you give me a wonderful compliment. I don't know what to make of you, Angie."

"I just can't believe you would go to all this trouble for me. Thank you, Jared."

"It's the least I could do. Now let's eat. I'm starved."

Over dinner, they discussed the progress of the renovation. Jared was a week ahead of schedule because of the extra men he'd hired. Angie had to wait for the cleanup crew to finish before she could start the hardest part of her job. Still, she was on schedule.

They did the dishes together, Angie rinsing and Jared stacking them in the dishwasher. After they finished, he refilled their champagne glasses and led her to the courtyard.

The night air was just beginning to cool. They sat down in the lounge chairs and allowed a comfortable silence to fall between them. Quietly, they enjoyed the sound of crickets and cicadas. Occasionally, a breeze played lightly over them and a bobwhite called in the distance.

Angie was aware that Jared was watching her every move. Strangely, this time it didn't make her self-conscious.

In a short while he stood and rubbed her shoulder. "Let's go in. The mosquitoes are out."

"Hmm?" she looked up at him to see his blue eyes darkening with desire. She could feel heat coming from her own eyes and looked down quickly. While he walked to the porch, she stayed in her chair.

"You coming?" he called, turning toward her.

Angie nodded, stood, swayed and steadied herself against the chair.

Whoa, too much champagne! She glanced at Jared. His back was to her now. *Thank goodness, he didn't see me stumble. Time for bed,* she thought, following him inside the house.

She set her glass on the counter, picked it up again and put it in the dishwasher.

Jared had disappeared without saying goodnight, so Angie headed straight for her bedroom.

Halfway up the stairs, Jared came behind her, scooped her into his arms and carried her back down.

"What are you doing?" Angie inhaled the musky scent of his cologne. Lightheaded, she found it hard to focus on anything but his face.

"You'll see. Patience, my dear."

As much as Angie tried to fight it, the champagne wouldn't allow her to do anything but give herself up to this moment, this man. She snuggled against his neck, breathed deeply and then sighed.

How could I have lost my heart to a man who may do me harm?

Right now, it didn't seem to matter.

JARED CARRIED HER into the ballroom and put her down. He turned to an old record player and soon the graceful strains of a waltz filled the air.

"May I have this dance?" he asked, bowing deeply.

"Why, yes you may, kind sir." she curtsied, then smiled broadly when he took her into his arms.

They glided around the room. She looked deeply into the bluest pair of eyes she'd ever seen. She felt no fear now, only longing. So lost in his gaze was she, she didn't even notice when the music stopped.

Jared watched her closely. He wanted to take his time, to treasure the woman in front of him. But those lips… They were just too delicious, too tempting. He lowered his mouth to hers, gently at first, then demanding more as Angie matched his ardor with her own.

I want you, Angie. All of you.

Reaching down, Jared slipped his arm behind her knees and lifted her, cradling her against his chest. This time he carried her up the stairs to his room, laid her across his bed and kissed her deeply.

Kissing Angie was like kissing the wind. Gentle and strong. It engulfed him with a magic he never would have believed possible before this moment.

As his heart whispered her name, he knew it was too late to save himself. He was lost in her. She was the only person in the world who mattered.

Still gently brushing her lips with his own he unbuttoned her shirt and moved it aside. The jasmine scented softness of her flesh intoxicated him as he kissed his way down her neck. When he reached her breasts, he buried his face in their valley while cupping them in his hands. She felt just as he'd imagined she would—silken, warm, firm.

Angie sighed his name.

Moving his mouth to her swollen lips, Jared slipped his hands around her back.

Damn. No hooks.

He rolled over, pulling Angie on top of him, then sat up with her in his lap.

Locking his gaze with hers, he brought one hand up between her breasts. She didn't protest, so he released the front clasp of her bra and drew in a quick breath at the sight of the pale orbs that spilled from the lace. His fingers curved against the soft roundness of her breasts as he stroked her, then teased her nipples between his fingers and thumbs, feeling them harden at his touch.

Angie groaned. Jared's body pulsated with the sound of her desire.

"Angelina, you are so beautiful," he whispered then flicked his tongue quickly across the hardened tip of her right nipple, finally taking it within his mouth, pulling and tugging.

I'VE DIED AND gone to heaven. The sensations Jared ignited turned Angie's insides to lava. She wanted to completely surrender to her own desires. She wanted to know what it felt like to make love to a man. This man.

She'd never gone this far before.

The need to touch…to feel…was so very strong.

Gathering all of her courage, she slipped her hands inside his shirt.

He pressed his hips against her. Angie felt something large

and hard against her thigh.

What was that?

Lost in the surprise of the feel and shape of him, even through clothes, she didn't notice his hand slide up her leg and under the fabric of her knit shorts until he stroked her.

Oh my God! Sweet mother of… "Oh Jared!"

No one had ever touched her there.

Heat scorched through her. She couldn't think, couldn't breathe. She didn't want him to stop. When his fingers dipped, she arched into his hand.

What the…? Her body tightened then exploded. Fireworks had nothing on this. A dizzying whirl of pleasure surrounded her, invaded her.

Jared's mouth covered hers, capturing her moans of ecstasy. Her body rocked with wave after wave of pleasure.

She grabbed his wrist. Sensitivity and embarrassment brought her back to reality. "Jared, stop."

"I want you, Angelina," he whispered. He ran his hand up her hip to her stomach.

"Yes, but this has gone too far." *Way too far!*

She never knew it was like this. So tender, so intense.

He must have been with a lot of women, to know how to make me feel this way.

The sudden thought made her heart sink and she turned away, almost in tears.

This isn't special to him at all, I'll bet.

She was just another conquest. She had to struggle not to let him see how hurt she felt, how disappointed. A fool that's what she was—a damn fool. "I'm sorry Jared, I can't. Please, let me up."

He rolled off her and lay back on the bed. Angie closed her shirt over her exposed chest and sat up, fastening the buttons.

Their labored breathing filled the room. She took a minute to gather herself before she turned to face him. "Look, Jared, I enjoyed the dinner and the conversation, but the situation got out of control. I can't do this with you."

"Why not?" He propped himself up on one elbow. "I don't understand."

"I never—" she muttered, "Oh...you wouldn't understand."

He reached out, caressed a strand of her hair. "Try me."

"I can't do it because...I... I don't love you," she lied and fled the room.

Nine

IT JUST DIDN'T ADD UP.

Jared lay on the bed, staring at the ceiling, his body so tense and tight he thought it would burst.

Since when did a woman turn down sex because of love? This was the twenty-first century, after all.

Try as he might, he couldn't figure out why Angie had run from the room. Was she just a tease? He didn't think so, not really. She'd seemed surprised by the spasms that rocked her body.

And embarrassed.

Almost as if she'd never experienced an orgasm before.

He smiled as he thought of how much she'd enjoyed his touch. Her breathless whispers and the strength of her embrace had told him as much.

If he didn't stop thinking about it, he was going to explode.

Getting off the bed, he went and opened the window. The cool night air chilled his sweaty body, cleared his head a little.

Angie thought he was a womanizer. *That was it!* He'd forgotten. *She probably ran away because she thought I was adding her to my little black book. Or trying for a new notch on my bedpost.*

Of course!

Relieved, he went into the hall. Maybe he should go talk to her.

When he got close to her door, he could hear the sound of stomping inside. Raising his hand to knock, he was stopped by a string of curses.

"Damn him! Damn him! Damn him to hell! Why did I let things get so out of control? I'm such an idiot!

Jared lowered his hand and grinned. Burt had been right. Angie *was* a handful. He'd never heard her this angry. It sounded like she was angrier with herself than with him. She was so mad that she didn't even realize how loud her voice was. He could probably have heard every word from his own room.

"Hell will freeze over before I sleep with a conniving man like him. How could I have been such a fool knowing what he's going to do to me?"

Jared stilled. *She knew that he wanted to buy her out? How did she find out?*

Grinding his teeth together, he stalked angrily back down the hall to his room and shut the door behind him.

His plan was ruined.

ANGIE PLOPPED DOWN across the bed on her stomach. What was her problem anyway? She'd let Jared touch her and damn it all, she wanted to make love with him.

Since when had a good-looking man been able to shatter her resolve? *It must have been the champagne,* she reasoned. *But there is no way I'm giving up my virginity before I'm married. I made that decision years ago after what happened to Kimmie and Jared Maxwell isn't changing my mind. I'll just be more careful, that's all.*

She got up, opened her door and peeked down the hall. *Thank God he didn't hear me ranting like a lunatic.*

Tomorrow she would talk to him, but not tonight. Right now she needed to straighten out all these mixed up emotions she felt.

She got into bed and tossed and turned for what felt like hours before falling asleep.

THANK YOU, CHAMPAGNE, for a dreamless night, Angie thought as she got up the next morning. Smelling a familiar fragrance, she stopped suddenly to look around.

Was that Aunt Martha's rich earthy scent filling the room?

Impossible! Her wild imagination was off and running way too early today.

A car door slammed, startling her. She went to the window and looked out to see a cleaning crew unloading supplies. She'd forgotten all about the cleanup this morning. Jared walked across the yard to meet them.

She couldn't face him yet, not after last night.

What a disaster, she thought, turning from the window.

Theodore Slayton's journal lay on her nightstand. Angie picked up the leather bound volume. It wouldn't hurt to read a little more of it before she went downstairs.

JARED AND BURT, standing on the top of tall ladders, were painting the upper trim of the house when the porch door slammed shut. Jared watched as Angie rushed toward them, holding a book, her face flushed and excited.

"Jared, can you take a break?" she yelled. "I need to talk to you."

He didn't answer.

She called again, louder this time. "Jared! I need to talk to you. Can you please come down for a few minutes?"

"You're being summoned, Boss," said Burt.

"Yeah? So what. I'm busy."

Burt rubbed his forehead with his red bandanna. "You know Boss, if I had a beautiful woman begging me to come to her, I don't think I'd stay busy for long."

"Well, she's not calling *you*, is she?" snapped Jared. Laying down the paintbrush, he looked at the older man. "I'm sorry, Burt. I shouldn't spout off at you when it's her neck I want to break."

Burt laughed. "So you got a taste of the little lady, did ya? And now you're suffering."

"Jared?" Angie called again.

"Hang on, I'll be down in a minute," Jared replied. "What would make you say that, Burt?" Jared considered Angie tapping her toe, waiting for him to descend the ladder.

"She's got a fiery temper, when it erupts," said Burt. "There's been a few men who'd have sold their soul for one night with that charming little lady. But she's not gonna give it up until she finds true love. She's stubborn as a bull."

Jared's eyes widened. "You mean she's still a virgin?"

Burt laughed aloud. "Yep, Boss. Sure as you're born, that's 'Dansburg's Oldest Virgin' standing down there. Rumor is, all she'll do is kiss." He dipped the paintbrush then stroked it across the wood. "My boy dated her about seven years ago, never got past first base. Angie told him that no man would touch her until she found true love and then not until their wedding night. One time they argued and she punched him in the eye. That's the last time they went out."

"Why did they argue?" Jared narrowed his gaze at Burt. "It doesn't sound like Angie to hit someone, unless she was provoked."

"Now don't go getting riled up. He just tried to get in her britches, so she nailed him in the eye. Got himself a girlfriend right after that. They're still together." Burt winked. "I told you she was a feisty little thing. She's got high standards too."

"A twenty-six-year-old virgin?" Jared looked down at Angie in amazement. He couldn't believe it, but Burt's words made last night crystal clear. "That explains a lot."

Burt laughed. "Explains why you didn't sleep last night or why you took a cold shower?"

Surprised, Jared just stared at Burt then started down the ladder.

"It was obvious, Boss. Can't pull the wool over an old man's eyes. You better be careful though or your heart will be next. Or was it first?"

"Shut up, Burt," Jared said, "and get back to work."

Burt howled with laughter.

"What's so funny up there?" Angie asked, "Is Burt telling stories about me again?"

"Are they true?"

"Depends what he's saying, doesn't it? I think I can guess. There's only one rumor he can spread about me without lying. Burt may not be discreet, but he's honest."

She cupped one hand beside her mouth and yelled up at Burt. "A regular motormouth, that's what you are."

Burt waved, laughing harder.

"Oh, very funny, Burt. You know darn well you're proud of me, or you wouldn't keep broadcasting my status to the world at large." Angie, her hand on her hip, turned to face Jared. "But I didn't come out here to talk about me. You're never going to guess what I've found!" Her eyes were dancing with excitement.

Jared lifted an eyebrow. "What now?"

"Yesterday, I was working in the library—"

"Wait." He took her by the hand. "We need to go somewhere more private."

"Why?"

"You'll see."

He led her in silence down to the stable.

Angie glanced nervously around the dim and dusty room as Jared closed the door behind them.

"Before you tell me anything, Angie, I want you to clarify just one point for me."

"Can't that wait?" she said, backing away from him a little. "This is important."

"So is this." He lifted her chin, forcing her to look at him.

"Fine. What do you want to know?" She fidgeted under his scrutiny.

"Burt said it's rumored that you will only kiss a man."

"Yeah. So."

"A lot more than kissing happened between us last night."

"I know."

"What exactly does that mean, Angie?"

"Oh, the hell with it. Fine. I'll tell you." Staring straight at him, she clutched the small book against her chest like a shield. "My friend Kimmie slept with her first boyfriend when we were in high school. The next day he broke up with her because he'd 'gotten what he wanted' and bragged about it all over school. Her reputation was totally ruined. I swore that the same thing wasn't going to happen to me. I'd wait for true love or die a virgin. People laugh at me. I'm the town joke. I've never slept with a man, never had a man touch me the way you did last night. Well, once Burt's son grabbed my breast and I punched him—I suppose Burt told you all about that too—but no one has ever..." She looked down.

Jared waited.

Angie sighed heavily, then looked back up at him. "No one has ever seen me nearly naked. No one has ever made me feel so..."

"Loved?"

"No, I wasn't going to say that. Damn it, Jared, I don't know how to explain it. This is really embarrassing."

"So, last night was the first time you ever had an—"

Angie put her fingers on his lips. “Don’t say it. The answer’s yes and before you ask, it was beyond anything I’ve ever experienced in my life. Are you happy now?”

Jared took her fingers from his mouth and kissed the palm of her hand. “Yes, I’d say you just made me very happy. Now what did you want to tell me that you thought was more important than this conversation.”

Angie smiled in spite of herself. “Yesterday, I was packing books in the library when I noticed one of the bookcase boards had slipped. Then I saw something sticking out. I pulled the board loose to find this book.” She held the volume out to him. “Jared, it’s Theodore Slayton’s personal journal.”

“Really?” Jared took the book from her and started flipping through the pages.

“I wondered if there were entries about Clyde and Ruby,” Angie babbled on. “And there sure are. From what I’ve read, Theodore knew about Ruby and Clyde before he found them together at Clyde’s house. Now, listen to this—Theodore thought Clyde was going to kill him and take over the homestead. It’s all right there, you can see for yourself. He also vowed if Clyde *did* murder him, he would haunt him forever.”

“Geez, you don’t take a breath do you?”

Angie laughed. “But there’s something else really strange. Theodore had an affair with Sally Mayfield before he married Mary. He writes all about it. He had a son named Theo with Sally before Mary got pregnant. So…Theo would have been blood heir to this homestead, although he couldn’t lay claim to the property.” Angie paced in front of Jared. “According to the journal, it was a sore spot with Sally. She swore vengeance on Theodore for breaking promises to her. Isn’t this so exciting?”

Jared read avidly. This was the proof he needed, right here in his hands.

Angie touched Jared’s arm. “So what do you think?”

"I think this is something better left alone."

Angie stared at him, eyes wide with shock. "You're kidding, right? If we could track down the current heir to the plantation it would be great for business. Just think of the advertising."

"I told you to leave it alone, Angie," Jared snapped, still turning pages.

"Don't you think this is a great find?" She fought hard to keep the annoyance out of her voice.

"Yes, it's an amazing find. It's just not worth worrying your pretty little head over." Jared started out of the barn with the journal. "I find it rather odd that you're forgetting this heir might interfere with our new business, not help it along."

"My pretty little head?" she repeated angrily, following him. "Give it back."

"I thought you wanted me to read it."

"I did. Now I don't. Give it back."

"Fine." He stopped, turned and held the book out to her.

Angie jerked it from his hand. "You're forgetting one thing Mr. Maxwell. The so-called heirs, if there are any, wouldn't have any more right to the property now then they did two hundred years ago. I just thought it would be fun to get them involved in the inn somehow."

A muscle twitched along Jared's jaw as he watched Angie storm back to the house.

ANGIE DECIDED SHE would get to the bottom of this one way or the other, with or without Jared Maxwell's help. Now it was her own personal quest to find out more.

She marched straight into the office, picked up the phone and dialed.

"Hello."

"Hi, Alan, it's Angie. Can you come over here? I need to speak with you. Alone."

"Is something wrong, dear?"

"I'm not sure. I have a hunch, but I need your help. This doesn't involve Jared. Can you come over?"

"When do you want me there?"

"Right now, okay? Jared will be busy on the grounds. I thought we could go over to my house where we can talk privately. We'll only be gone and hour or so."

"Is it that important to you?"

"Yes."

"Okay, walk up to the hard surface road. I'll pick you up there, then we'll go to your house."

"Okay, bye." Replacing the receiver, Angie watched Jared through the window. There was something wrong with this picture. Jared Maxwell was hiding something. She could feel it. It was time she discovered his secret.

"WOULD YOU LIKE some water, Alan, or a glass of wine? I'm afraid that's all I have since I cleaned out the fridge before going to the Slaytons'." Angie motioned for Alan to sit on the couch.

"I'm fine. Why don't you just tell me what's going on? You didn't say a word on the drive over here. That's not like you." Alan smiled, but he was worried. He knew he had to keep the conversation light. If experience told him anything about this woman, it was that she'd shut down in a minute if she felt pressed too hard.

Angie sat down on the loveseat. "Well, there are two things. I had a fight with Eddie but I'm not getting into the details of that now. I called you because yesterday I was working in the library and found a book hidden behind a slipped board." She held it out to him. "It's Theodore Slayton's journal."

"Are you serious?" He took the proffered tome from her hand.

"Of course. I've read it from cover to cover. I think there's a clue in this book that I'm missing."

"Clue to what?"

"I don't know. That's what I need to figure out. According to the journal, Theodore knew about Ruby and Clyde, but he didn't know they were married."

"Really? That's interesting."

"Here's something even more intriguing. Did you ever hear a rumor about Theodore Slayton and a Sally Mayfield?"

"No."

"It seems Theodore and Sally were an item before he married Mary. Sally gave birth to Theodore's son and named the child Theo."

"That's in here?"

"Yes. It also says Sally told Theodore she would have her revenge one day for all his broken promises. Her revenge would be wrought on his children and their children's children."

"What did Theodore promise Sally?" Alan thumbed through the pages, still listening.

"He was supposed to marry her, but fell in love with Mary instead. He broke up with Sally, then two weeks later he writes that he watched Ruby and Clyde from a window. Their body language led him to believe they were lovers. So he planned to follow them to see if he could catch them together, then confront them."

"Which leads us to the rumors that Theodore found them in bed together."

"Theodore's entries end without confirmation of that. There's one entry made after Theodore's death."

Alan leaned forward. "How do you know the entry was made after his death?"

"Because all of the entries are dated. Plus this entry is in a different handwriting and signed by Mary. Why don't you read it?"

Raising his eyebrows, Alan picked up the book and turned to the last written page.

My love, my life, my Theodore. I saw what Clyde and Ruby did to you with my own eyes. I heard you curse them before you died, so I made them pay for killing you. I had the gypsy witch curse everyone who ever hurt you. Now they are cursed to never find love in life and doomed to haunt the earth for two hundred years. Only three people will be able to break the curse. It was the gypsy witch who gave them the powers. The virgin dreams, the sister knows and the unknown one sees spirits. If the three find true love like ours and then become part of one family, the curse will be broken. If they don't, the tormented souls will have to walk the earth for eternity. I did this for you, my love, to carry out your last wishes and revenge your death.

When I finish this entry, I'm hiding your journal, Theodore, just like you asked me to when you came to me last night. Ruby will never know about you and Miss Sally or the baby. But our baby will know you are his father. I will help you, even in death, my love. Come to me again, Theodore, please, come to me again. I'll love you forever. Your wife, Mary

"Holy Mackerel! Angie, do you know what this means?" Alan could hardly contain his excitement.

"It means that it doesn't matter if I dream of Theodore or not, because you have age-old written proof that someone else saw his ghost."

"Yes, it does. This will be great for the inn. We couldn't have asked for a better marketing plan. What do you think about this curse?"

"People believed that witches and curses existed back then, just like some people believe in modern day witches now."

"So you're saying it could be true."

"I'm not sure. I think it's possible. But not probable. That's all."

"Angie, you're a virgin who has dreams that come true."

"Alan, I'm telling you, that entry could just be the babblings of a distraught pregnant woman who lost her new husband, the love of her life, in a traumatic way."

"What if this curse is true and you are one of the three? From the date of this entry, the two hundred years are up next August."

"Oh, yeah, I'm the dreamer, I have a sister who knows and there's an unknown sibling out there somewhere that will link the three of us together." Standing, Angie walked to the window. "Listen to what you're saying, Alan. I'm an only child."

"Don't be so skeptical. Maybe the curse isn't talking about your biological sister. Jared said his sister Terri has paranormal things happen to her too. If you and Jared fell in love and got married, then you and Terri would be linked within the same family as sister-in-laws."

Alan looked up when Angie burst out laughing.

"You know, Alan, you're a hopeless romantic."

"Think about it, Angie. It fits."

"Alan, Jared didn't say what kind of paranormal experiences his sister has. You're just assuming she's psychic."

"Yes, I am."

"Where would the unknown one who can see spirits come in?"

"Don't you see spirits in your dreams, Angie?"

TEN

"YOU'RE SERIOUS?" TAKING THE JOURNAL, ANGIE SAT ON the loveseat to read Mary's entry again.

After a few moments, she looked at Alan and said, "I'm not unknown, so I can't be the person Mary is talking about. If the curse was real and we both know it isn't, there would have to be a third person, an *unknown* relative who is visited by spirits and who would have to find true love too."

Alan took the book she held out to him. "I still think it's possible, Angie."

"Oh, Alan. *I'm* the one with psychic abilities. I don't agree. There's one major problem with your theory. Jared and I will never fall in love or get married. There's nothing between us now nor will it be in the future. One thing I do know…"

Alan, his eyes twinkling, leaned back in his seat. "What's that, my dear?"

"This book is more valuable to the inn than even Ruby's letter. I want you to put it in your vault for safekeeping."

"All right, I will. I'll have it authenticated too. Did you show it to Jared?"

Angie frowned. "That's the reason I want you to take it."

"I don't understand."

"I was so excited to share the journal with Jared. He and Burt were painting the house. Burt told him 'The Story' about me."

"Why would Burt gossip to Jared?"

"You know how Burt is, if he thinks someone's interested in me, he tells them about my virginity. He thinks it's funny, but sometimes it seems like he does it to warn them away from me. I don't pay any attention to him anymore."

"What did Jared say?"

"We're getting off the subject, Alan." Angie smiled at him. She knew by the look in his eye that he had matchmaking on his mind. You couldn't help but love such a romantic as Alan Harland.

"I know," he responded. "Sorry."

"It's okay. Now listen to this. When I tried to tell Jared about the journal I only told him about the affair with Sally and the resulting child."

"Why didn't you tell him everything?"

Standing, Angie started to pace. "Because he walked off with the journal. He had this weird gleam in his eyes, as if he had just won the lottery or something. He flipped through the pages and told me not to 'worry my pretty little head' about it."

"And that bothers you?"

"Damn straight it bothers me!" Angie said too quickly. Shoot. He just saw through me, she thought, glancing at Alan. "What I mean is, why would he blow off such an important discovery for the inn, unless he had another agenda besides our partnership. I think he's up to something, Alan and I don't trust him."

"But you love him."

"*What?* Good lord, man. You know, Alan, it really gets on my nerves when you do that." She plopped into the chair beside the coffee table. *Can't I hide anything from him?* "Maybe you're the one who *knows*."

"I can't be. I don't fit the description. Martha was my true love and she's gone." He paused for a moment, looking down. "So," he ventured at last, "how long have you been in love with Jared? Let me see…" he looked at his watch, "it was—what? Two minutes ago that you said there'd never be anything between the two of you?"

"Alan, please, can we forget about all that for a minute?" Angie tucked a loose strand of hair behind her ear. "Now listen, okay? Before Jared tried to walk away with the journal, I suggested to him that we try to find a descendant of Sally's. That's when he told me not to worry about it. Don't you think his reaction is strange?"

Alan shrugged. He knew Jared had made Sam Slayton a six-figure offer before he died. He couldn't help but wonder if Jared's reaction to the journal and that offer were somehow connected.

"You know what I think, Alan?"

"No, tell me." Alan raised his brows at her then leaned back further on the couch.

"I think Jared is related to Sally or Mary. Otherwise why wouldn't he want to look for the heirs?"

"I can't answer that, but what makes you say he's related to Sally or Mary?"

"It's just a hunch."

"Hmm, I know about those hunches of yours. Sometimes they come true, just like your dreams," Alan said softly. "Okay, Angie. I'm going to take this seriously. What else is that hunch of yours saying?"

"I think he's going to try to sabotage the inn's success as revenge for his family," Angie told him. "Look Alan, I know I'm not always right with my hunches, but he's hiding something. I just know it. Can't I get him out of the partnership?"

"No, that's impossible, the contract's solid. Let me do a little investigating. I'm interested in getting to the bottom of this myself." Alan turned the journal over in his hands. "Angie, what are you going to do if you're right?"

"Try to buy him out, of course. I don't want him to destroy the inn."

"I'm talking about your feelings for him."

"Oh. I don't know, Alan. I'm not even sure what my feelings are yet."

"Angie, you listen to an old man. Don't let the inn affect your feelings for Jared. If he has some secret agenda, we'll figure it out. I know from experience that Jared is a good man. I've watched him work and gotten to know him on a more personal level too. If I didn't think he was a good man, do you honestly believe I would let you two live together without a chaperone?"

"I knew you were playing matchmaker!" Angie sat down beside Alan, wrapping her arm around his shoulder. "Why are you always trying to fix me up?"

"Because I know I'll get it right one of these days."

"Well, Jared may have touched my heart but he's the wrong man for me."

"Are you so sure, Angie? You've never had your heart touched before, as far as I know."

"You're right, I've never felt like this about anyone before." Angie sighed. "Alan, I had an observer dream about Jared."

"You what? One of those dreams that come true?"

"Yes. I have very conflicting feelings about him because of the dream. Sometimes he scares me."

"Angie, tell me everything, right now. We're not leaving this house until you do. How long have you had this dream and how often?"

"Every night for the past six months."

"My God! Why didn't you mention this before?"

"There was no reason to. I realized the man in my dreams was a real person the day before we all met in your office. He came into the store, nearly scaring me to death." She didn't mention the way Jared stirred other feelings in her too.

"Did he hurt you?" Alan's concern was obvious in his voice.

"No. He was shopping. When he turned around, I recognized him as the man in my dream. It was a shock, that's all."

"I want to know about the dream."

"No, Alan. I'm not going to worry you with the details. I just wanted you to know how I feel. Jared's not trustworthy." Angie patted him on the knee. "Don't waste your breath telling me to move out of the Slayton house because I'm staying there. I'm in for the duration, regardless of what happens."

Alan's eyebrows knitted together and he reached out as though to dissuade Angie.

But she said, "Who was it that always taught me to face my fears? You did." Angie leaned over and kissed him on the cheek. "So I'm taking your advice. I'm finishing this job. It's become important to me."

Alan let out a long sigh. "You're just as frustrating as Martha."

Angie laughed, "Thank you."

"Just promise me you'll be careful. I don't know what I'd do if something happened to you."

"I'll be fine."

"I also know you've never dreamed about yourself before, either."

"And just how would you know that?"

"Martha loved to brag about her favorite niece. She always thought of you as her daughter."

"I always thought of her as my mother." Angie took his wrinkled hand in both of hers. "And of you as my father."

"You make an old man proud, Angelina."

"You should have forced Aunt Martha, you know."

"Forced her to do what?"

"To marry you."

Alan laughed dryly. "You can't force someone to marry you. You know that. I tried everything else I could think of, Angie.

Believe me. She was a stubborn woman, your aunt. She said she could never think of me as her husband."

"She thought of you as her lover, so why not her husband?"

His eyes widened, "You knew?"

"Of course I knew. The whole town knew. I think she was afraid of marriage because of what happened with my parents. I know my mother loved my father and he died during my infancy. I think Aunt Martha was afraid that if she married you, she'd lose you the same way."

"Maybe my being fifteen years older than her had something to do with it. She never really gave me a solid reason."

"Of course not. The woman had more pride than anyone I've ever known. She would never tell either of us about her fears. I guessed. That's the only reason I can tell you this now." Angie looked at Alan's tired old face and her heart broke for him. "Can I ask you something, Alan?"

"Anything."

"Did she ever tell you how much she loved you?"

Alan shook his head. "She said she loved me as a friend, that's all it could ever be. I've never loved another woman the way I loved Martha."

"I know, Alan and she never loved anyone the way she loved you."

Alan stared at Angie, his eyelids brimming with tears. "How can you be so sure? I always said I loved her and she'd just kiss me on the cheek."

"Oh, Alan, you silly man. Didn't you know that's how Aunt Martha said she loved you? She'd do the same thing to me. It was rare for the words 'I love you' to cross her lips. They were hard for her to say, regardless of how deeply she felt. But I always knew she loved me when she'd kiss me on the cheek. You should have known it too."

He smiled. "I guess I did, really. But it's not the same as

hearing it said. It would have been so nice to hear her say it just once before she died."

A grin tugged at the corners of Angie's mouth. She went to an antique rolltop desk, opened the bottom drawer then removed a shoebox.

She sat down beside Alan and put the box in his lap. "Aunt Martha told me to give this to you when the time was right. I argued with her, told her that she should give it to you herself because I wouldn't know the right time. She just laughed at me and said I'd know. Well, I guess she was right because I feel like I should give it to you now. Hurry up and open it, because I'm dying to see what's in there as much as you are."

Alan slowly lifted the lid.

Inside were a note, videotape and lots of envelopes. Picking up the note, he handed it to Angie.

"You have to read it, Alan."

"Okay." Hands trembling, he began reading aloud, "To my dear friend, Alan. I never had the guts to tell you exactly how I felt when I was alive, but I know Angelina will give this box to you one day. You deserve to know that I love you, Alan. I've loved you since the day that we met. I was a coward to never say the words to you. Please forgive me. I will always love you, even in death. Your favorite 'roll in the hay', Martha."

Tears streamed down Alan's cheeks. "You've made an old man very happy, Angie."

"You don't *look* very happy," Angie teased, then, "I love you too, Alan," she added and hugged the only father she'd ever really known while he wept.

DARKNESS HAD FALLEN by the time Angie walked into the kitchen at the Slayton homestead. The emotions of the day had drained her. Stopping at the sink, she washed her face, then dried her hands and face with a paper towel.

Alan should be almost home with the box full of letters. He would certainly stay up late reading them and watching the tape.

Angie was glad she'd decided to trust Alan with the journal. She'd given him something worth more than the guaranteed success of the inn. She'd given him her aunt's love.

And he gave her a lot to think about too. When he dropped her off at the barn, he'd said, "I hope Jared brings you as much happiness as Martha brought me. Don't let your stubbornness or fear keep you from the man you love the way Martha kept herself from me. It's not that I want to interfere in your life, Angie, I'm just adding my two cents worth."

All she'd thought about on the walk back to the house were her feelings for Jared. *Just his two cents worth indeed.* She'd never get to sleep now, not with his words running through her head.

The high-pitched laugh of a woman broke the silence. *What the heck?* Angie threw the paper towel in the trash and followed the sound.

Pasting on her brightest smile as she walked into the living room, she said, "I'm back from my walk, Jared." Her smile quickly faltered at the scene in front of her. "Oh, sorry. I didn't know you had company."

THE WOMAN ON the couch had curly blond hair that reached to her waist. Jared was grinning like a teenager. Angie guessed that blood red lips and doe eyes would do that to any man.

"You were gone quite a while," he said cheerfully to Angie.

She balled her hands into fists.

"Angie, let me introduce you to—"

"Oh, pleased to meet you," Angie interrupted. "I'm sorry for barging in. I'd better jump in the shower. I'm hot from the walk and all. I'll leave you two alone. Goodnight."

Jared laughed as Angie ran up the stairs.

"You know Jared, that was cruel," the blonde said.

"Serves her right. She should have told me where she was going. Besides, sis, what's wrong with making her a little jealous?"

Terri smacked Jared on the arm. "A lot. You wouldn't like it if she made you jealous, would you?"

Jared thought about Eddie's appearance at the house. "Probably not. I'll introduce you tomorrow. You'll like Angie."

"I think she was shocked to see me," teased Terri.

"I think so too." Jared stood. "I have something for you."

"A birthday present?" Terri grinned, rubbing her palms together.

"How'd you know?" Jared grabbed her hands, pulled her up. "Come on, kid."

Terri followed him into the office. "Let me run upstairs and check on the boys while you get it."

"Terri, you just put them to bed thirty minutes ago. They're sound asleep."

"Oh, all right then. Gimme, gimme, gimme, big brother!"

"You always were impatient," Jared laughed, handing her a manila envelope.

"I thought you said you were giving me a birthday present."

"I am."

"Well, where's the wrapping paper and bow?" Terri stuck out her bottom lip.

"Geez!" Jared jerked the envelope from her hand, drew a bow on the outside and handed it back. "Okay?"

"Okay." Terri smiled while she opened the tiny metal clasp and pulled out several sheets of paper stapled together.

"Damn you, Jared!" she blurted after looking them over quickly. "I'm not taking your charity, even if you are filthy rich."

"Happy Birthday!" Jared went to hug his sister but she pushed him away.

Tears welled in her eyes. “You lied about missing us. You just got me here to give me a farm that you know I can’t accept.”

“I didn’t lie about missing you and the kids.” Jared sat down in his office chair. “It’s not charity. It’s a gift. Why can’t you accept a gift?”

“You just expect me to move to this place, without any regards to my family?”

“I am your family, Terri.”

The brimming tears spilled over and began falling silently down Terri’s cheeks. Jared knew it had been hard on her raising the boys alone. Now he was offering her a chance to get out of Richmond and start over.

Jared took her hand, gave it a squeeze. “Happy Birthday, sis.”

Terri wiped her eyes with the back of her free hand. “Happy Birthday? Happy Birthday? I’ll show you Happy Birthday, you big, lying jerk!”

Throwing the papers on the desk, Terri jumped on Jared, almost flipping the chair over. She wrapped her hands around his neck, pretending to choke him.

Jared laughed so hard his eyes watered.

He’d won.

Playing along with her game, he sputtered, coughed and gagged.

“Oh, sorry.” Angie’s voice came from the doorway. “I needed a file, but I’ll get it later. I thought you two were in the living room. Sorry.”

Surprised, Terri loosened her grip on Jared’s neck then realized Angie couldn’t see she was strangling her brother and tightened it again. “Angie, wait,” Terri called.

Too late.

Terri released Jared’s neck and poked her index finger into his chest. “You’ve got some ’splaining to do.”

“About the farm? Listen, Terri, I wanted to have you and the kids closer to me. I've missed you. I mean that. You know you've wanted to move here ever since I did. Now you can. Besides, it has stables and a horse and two ponies."

"Stables? You mean you already bought the horses too? Oh geez!" She shook her head and then looked at her brother. "Ah, Jared, I just can't turn that down. You shouldn't have done it. You know you shouldn't. But—thanks!" She gave him a big hug then kissed his cheek. "I'm not the one who needs the explanation though, it's Angie. She really has the wrong idea."

"Tomorrow."

"You're going to let her think I'm your date until tomorrow?"

"Um-hum." He grinned.

"You are so bad, Jared Maxwell," she said. "You should be ashamed of yourself."

ANGIE DIDN'T FALL asleep until two in the morning and then the nightmare had woken her up repeatedly.

It was because of the note she'd found on her pillow.

She turned the torn paper over in the morning light and looked at it from all angles. If she told Jared about it now, he'd be furious. He'd want to know why she hadn't told him last night, when she found it.

What could she say? That she kept quiet because, when she came downstairs to show it to him, she'd found some woman with him?

Or that she thought maybe he'd put it there himself?

No way! He was never going to know that her heart had ripped open when she saw him laughing with another woman. Or that she was still wary of him, even though it was a different kind of fear. Now she was more worried that he saved her in the dream and being involved with her now might get him killed. That guilt and loss would be unbearable.

She unfolded the crinkled brown paper and, with trembling hands, read the note again.

Eleven

ANGIE, ANGIE, ANGIE. BEFORE LONG YOU WILL ONLY WISH for this world. I swear on your life that soon, very soon, you will die by my hand for what you did to me. But first I'll take what you denied me. How does it feel to know I've been in your room?

Folding the note, Angie slipped it into her dresser drawer, then looked at her reflection in the mirror.

She was plagued with huge black circles under her eyes.

I look like I've taken a couple of punches. That's what I get for staying up half the night, crying.

Maybe she could sneak by Jared, grab a cup of coffee and hide in her room until the furniture arrived.

That's exactly what I'll do.

Downstairs, she went into the office and dialed Trevor's number. Voicemail. Pressing the button that would take her to the operator, she asked the dispatcher to get him to come right over. Satisfied that she could resolve this note problem without Jared's knowledge, she went to the kitchen and put on a pot of coffee.

Waiting for the water to drip through the machine, she leaned against the counter and stared out the window. *Who wants me dead? The man from the fire...his voice...it was vaguely familiar. I wish I could place it.*

The gurgling of the coffee maker interrupted her thoughts. *Ah, good, the brew is ready.*

She was taking a cup from the shelf when she heard the sound of footsteps behind her. Her back stiffened.

"So how did you sleep?" Jared asked, playfully tugging the back of her hair.

Angie let her breath out in a little rush, then filled her cup. "Fine," she said. Adding milk and sugar, she stirred the liquid. "And you?"

"Like a baby."

"I'm sure you did." Keeping her back to Jared so he couldn't see her eyes, she added, "I'm going to start work. I'll see you later." She picked up her coffee cup and headed for the office.

Jared followed her. "Cat got your tongue this morning?"

"No, I'm just tired, that's all." She sat her cup down and started sorting through the file drawers.

"That's all, nothing else?" Jared pressed.

"Nope, nothing else." Angie pulled out a file, closed drawer, grabbed her coffee and headed for the door. Jared blocked her way.

"Excuse me," she said. "I need to go around you."

"Why aren't you looking at me?" Jared took her coffee cup away from her and sat it on the filing cabinet.

"Hey, give that back," she said, her head still tucked down.

"Not until you look at me." Jared lifted her chin, but she stubbornly kept her eyes closed.

"Look at me, Angie. Please?"

She raised her lids, staring defiantly into his eyes.

"What the hell? Who did this to you?"

"It's not what you think. When I don't sleep, I get dark circles under my eyes. That's all. My skin is so fair they look much worse than they really are. Now, if you've finished inspecting me, can I please get to work?"

"Why didn't you sleep well?"

"You wouldn't understand."

"But I would," said Terri.

Startled, Angie turned to see the blonde standing in the hallway, holding a coffee mug. *What was she still doing here?* "How could you possibly understand?"

"Did jealousy keep you awake?" Jared prodded eagerly.

The nerve of that man. "Don't be ridiculous," she said haughtily. "Jealous of what? Look, if the two of you will excuse me, I really need to get to work."

"Jared, that's enough already," said the blonde. "Angie, let me introduce myself. I'm Terri Logan, Jared's half sister. If you'll look through that window, you'll see two small boys trying to climb the tree. They're my twin sons, Kevin and Devin. Their father gave them rhyming names."

"Oh," she said, glaring angrily at Jared. *He tried to make me jealous on purpose.* "It's a pleasure to meet you, Mrs. Logan."

"Please, you're making me feel old. Call me Terri, okay? I'm only twenty-six, like you and that means we're both four years younger than old man Jared."

Angie smiled, but said quickly, "How do you know how old I am?"

"I didn't tell her," laughed Jared, his palms up. "Who are you calling an old man, sis?"

Terri grinned then picked up Angie's coffee cup. "I'll explain in a minute. Where are you working today?" she said to her.

"My room, until the materials get here around noon." Angie reached for the mug in Terri's hand, but she started up the steps with it.

"Jared, will you keep an eye on the boys for me?" Terri called, still climbing. "I'll be down later."

"Sure," he answered, walking to the front door.

As Jared went outside, Angie began following Terri up the stairs.

What's she up to? Angie wondered. *Does she have something to hide too?*

"After you, madam." Terri stood by the door, waiting for Angie.

Angie scrutinized the blonde in front of her, then turned the knob and pushed open the heavy oak door to her room. She laid the files she had brought with her on top of her chest of drawers, then went and sat on the edge of the bed.

Terri sat Angie's coffee on the nightstand. Approaching the window, she sipped from her mug. "You know, it's really nice here."

"Yes, I like it." *What does Jared's sister want with me? She seems to be a take-charge sort of person. Maybe that comes with having kids.* "Thanks for bringing up my coffee."

"Oh, no problem, sis." Terri sat down in the overstuffed winged back chair.

Angie raised her eyebrows. sis? That was a bit too familiar. She decided not to mention it since Terri obviously wasn't leaving yet. "What can I do for you, Terri?" she said formally.

"It's more like what I can do for you."

"I'm sorry, I don't follow."

"Tell me about the dream, Angie."

Angie's heart plunged against her ribs in surprise. Reaching for her coffee, she took a gulp, burning her mouth.

"What has Jared told you about me?" she blurted.

"Not much." Terri sat her mug on the end table. "He said you're single, stubborn and moody. The same kinds of things he says about me, actually. You know, we're a lot alike, you and I. Well, maybe you *don't* know, but you will."

Crossing her legs, Terri linked her fingers together around her knee. “So, if you don’t want to tell me about the dream, give me the scoop. What’s up with you and Jared?”

Angie cheeks burned. “There’s no scoop. We’re coworkers.”

“Um-hum.” Terri grinned, “Don’t you think he’s cute?”

Angie’s cheeks burned hotter. “He’s okay.” *Hot. Sexy. Built.*

Terri giggled. “Don’t you think he’s hot? Maybe even a little bit sexy?”

Okay, this is too weird. I just thought that. “Oh, I don’t know. I’ve never really looked at him that way.”

“Have you got a brother?” Terri asked, switching positions to tuck her legs under her.

“I’m an only child.” Angie took another sip of coffee before setting her mug down. “I always wanted a sister though.”

Terri grinned. “Maybe we’ll be sisters one day.”

“Oh yeah, right,” Angie laughed, but she was beginning to feel some kind of bond forming between them. “How old are your boys?”

“Five.” Standing again, Terri went to look out of the window.

“Is your husband coming here too?”

“I’m not married.”

“Oh.” Great, Angie! *Open mouth—insert foot.* “I’m sorry, I didn’t mean to pry.”

“That’s okay.” Terri sounded sad. “I was married, in case you’re wondering. Yesterday was the one-year anniversary of my divorce. It was also my birthday. Great combination, huh?” She sat down again. “It’s hard, raising the boys alone. I came to visit Jared hoping to take my mind off things for a while.”

“Happy belated birthday.”

“Thanks.”

Angie felt for her. “Do you want to talk about it?”

“Not now.” Grinning broadly, Terri slapped her hands on the arms of the overstuffed chair. “I came up here to ask you if you wanted to tell me about your dream. Now look, you’re comforting me. Hey, maybe we're soul sisters."

Their gazes locked. Somehow Angie knew Terri was dead serious even through that grin. So she wasn't alone in feeling a link between them. "Say there was a dream," she began cautiously, "how could you even know about it?"

"Clairvoyance."

Uh-oh. The curse.

"Now you think there's something wrong with me, right?"

"No way."

"Why not?" Terri scooted to the edge of her seat, leaned forward.

Angie sighed. Most of the town knew, so what could one more person hurt? Terri would understand because of her own abilities. "I have dreams that come true. Some people think I'm a freak because of it. That hurts. So I'm not about to hurt you the same way."

"Yeah, it sucks how people react sometimes, doesn't it?"

"You've got that right!" Angie laughed, then sipped her coffee again before replacing it on the nightstand.

Terri nodded. "I've seen parts of your dream," she said. "That's how I know about it. I didn't want to intrude. When I get a vision, I can't control the way it comes, but I can close my mind to it after it's started. That's what I did with your dream. I closed it off, ignored it. Do you want to talk about it?"

The dream was too personal to share. Angie shook her head. "No." For her, the lightness of the moment had darkened.

"Well, if you change your mind, I'm here until the end of the week. And, because of Jared, we'll be moving here in the fall."

"Because of Jared?" Angie gave her a puzzled look.

"Let's just say I received one heck of a birthday present last night."

Angie stared at her, still confused.

"Listen, Angie, it's fine if you don't want to talk about the dream."

Was Terri deliberately changing the subject?

"I understand, really I do. But you have to tell Jared about that note."

"How did—" Then Angie remembered. "Oh, clairvoyance again?"

"No, I was walking by the office and overheard your message for the sheriff."

"I can't tell Jared yet, Terri."

"What does the note say?"

"If I let you see it, will you promise to let me tell Jared when I'm ready?"

"I promise, sis."

Walking to the dresser, Angie took out the note, then handed it to Terri. "Here."

Accepting the note, Terri read in silence, then sighed as she handed it back.

"Can you use your clairvoyance to see who wrote it?" asked Angie.

"All I feel is angry confusion," Terri said, closing her eyes to concentrate. "There's a big man, but I can't see his face or name." She opened her eyes and smiled at Angie. "Being clairvoyant isn't all it's cracked up to be, you know. It works when it wants to, not always when you want it or need it."

Angie sat back on the bed. "Really? I thought you could see everything if you were clairvoyant."

"Nah. It's like your dreams. You can't help having them nor can you force them to come either. Most of the time my impressions are dead on the money and other times they're off a little, or I get bits and pieces over time that connect together. I've used my abilities to help friends and I've even used them in police cases. It's not easy and it is a responsibility." Picking up her coffee cup, Terri turned to go. "Angie, you should tell Jared about the note as soon as possible. The longer you wait the worse his reaction will be. Trust me, I know my brother."

"I'll think about it."

"All right, I'll let you get to work. I better make sure the boys haven't driven Jared crazy by now." She headed for the door.

"Terri?"

The blonde woman paused at the doorway. "Hmm?" she said, turning to Angie.

"Why do you call me sis?"

"Oh, I just feel like we're connected somehow." Terri smiled, then grabbed the doorknob. "I hope you don't mind if I call you that." When Angie shook her head, Terri grinned again, said, "See ya later," and went out of the bedroom.

"Okay." Angie watched as Terri closed the door. *Connected? How could that be?* Deciding that Terri was too complicated to figure out right now, Angie picked up her files and sat in the chair.

Ten minutes later, Angie was still looking at the same page. She couldn't concentrate, so she closed the file and went to the window.

In the yard below, Jared was chasing the twins around a tree while Terri led Thunder from the stable.

If Angie didn't know they were siblings, she'd think Terri and Jared were a married couple. The love between them was that evident.

Watching him with the twins, Angie wondered how Jared would behave with his own children.

Their children.

Oh Angie, cut it out, she admonished herself. But, try as she might, her heart ached. She could still feel Jared's hands on her body, the intensity of his kisses.

She could never give herself to Jared. The one institution she held sacred was marriage. That would never change.

She turned away. Go figure. The first and only time she could give her heart, she couldn't give her trust.

I have to find out, she thought to herself. *I'll have to tell Jared about the note, gauge his reaction. If he wrote it, surely he'll give himself away somehow.*

When she heard the crunch of tires on gravel, Angie glanced back through the window, hoping to see the delivery truck. It was the wrong vehicle. Sheriff Oakley had arrived much too fast.

Knowing she had to catch Trevor before Jared got to him, she stuffed the note in her pocket and ran down the stairs. She didn't see Jared until she bumped into him on the last step.

"In a hurry?" Smiling, he wrapped his arms around her.

"Yes, I heard a truck." She had to get to Trevor. "I'll talk to you later, I need to get outside.

"They can wait a few minutes."

Angie looked at him. Her stomach tightened. What was he up to? "Um…you can let me go now."

"Maybe I just like to hold you." Jared tucked a strand of hair behind her ear then caressed the lobe between his finger and thumb.

Angie flushed. "Don't do that."

"Why not?"

"Because for some reason I lose control around you." *And Sheriff Oakley is going to knock on the door any second.*

"There's nothing wrong with losing control sometimes."

"With you, there is. Let me go, Mr. Maxwell."

His eyes teased her. "So we're back to formalities?"

"Yes, it's for the best."

Jared ran the pads of his thumbs under the black circles that darkened her eyes. "You know, Angie, you have to get more rest."

"I'll try. Now please let me go." She tried to wriggle free of his arms.

"Wait," he said, his voice low and gravelly.

His tone made her go still and look up at him. "Why?"

"Because I need to ask you something."

"So ask then."

"I will," he breathed against her cheek.

Angie's heart pounded against her ribs. His closeness sent her senses reeling. Jared's maleness, the musky scent of him, even the softness of his lips caressing her cheek as they inched toward her mouth, excited her. She turned slightly, leading him into the kiss.

The tightness inside her liquefied. Her quest momentarily forgotten, she thrilled in the joy of connecting with the man she loved.

And lost another little piece of her heart.

The passion unleashed with the kiss shook her sanity. She'd thought she could control her emotions, but now even caution threatened to leave her. He'd never stay with her, let alone marry her, but she wanted this man like she'd never wanted any other.

Jared slowed the intensity with one small kiss after another, leaving her breathless. A thrill tingled through her when she heard his labored breathing.

"What did you want to ask me?" she whispered against his lips.

"Would you sell your share of the inn to me?"

"Huh?" Her brain was still clouded with passion. "Can you repeat that?"

"I'm offering to buy you out," he said softly.

"Why don't you two just go upstairs?" Terri giggled from the hallway.

Surely I'm going to die from embarrassment, thought Angie, pulling away from Jared's embrace. Her face burned like fire. *I must be blood red. How could I lose control and kiss Jared like some wild woman?*

"What do you think?" teased Jared. "Wanna go upstairs?"

"I think I better go check on…um…the delivery truck." Angie hurriedly walked by Terri, ignoring her broad grin and went out the front entrance.

"Quickest escape route," laughed Terri as the door closed a little too hard behind Angie. "So, things are back to normal?"

"What are you talking about?"

"Well, it looks like you two made up." Terri grinned slyly and punched him in the arm. "I was worried that your new lover was mad at you."

"I don't have a lover."

"Of course you do. I saw the passion in that kiss. Only lovers kiss each other like that!"

"Maybe so, but we're not."

"Then you will be soon."

"Highly unlikely."

"Okay, what's the deal?" Terri asked, crossing her arms and leaning against the banister.

"She's saving herself for true love."

"You mean she's still a virgin?"

"You hit that nail on the head."

Terri giggled. "I think I'll leave that one to you." Jared's shocked expression only made her laugh harder. "Oh, stop being such a prude. You've never been shocked by an innuendo before."

Jared walked to the door. "I'll catch you later, sis."

"Where are you going?"

"To work."

"Ah ha! Now I've got it!" Grabbing his arm, Terri spun him toward her. "You're in love with Angie, aren't you?"

He looked flustered for just a moment. "No. She's stubborn, controlling, has an unbelievable temper and…and…"

"And you love her."

Jared blew out a breath and ran his hands through his hair. "She's afraid of me."

"She didn't look afraid a few minutes ago."

"It's hard to explain, Terri," he said, looking into her eyes.

"Just leave it alone."

The pain she saw in his expression made Terri's heart ache for her brother. *He's really got it bad,* she thought. *It's about time! Maybe I'll just help the romance along a little.*

TWELVE

CLOSING THE FRONT DOOR, JARED NARROWED HIS EYES against the sun. Once he regained his focus, he saw Angie sitting in the sheriff's SUV, her back against the passenger window.

What's going on here? There isn't a delivery truck in sight.

He walked up to the vehicle and tapped on the window. Angie jumped and turned to look at him with a guilty expression on her face.

Sheriff Oakley waved to Jared, got out of the SUV and walked around the front of the vehicle to stand by Jared.

"Let me tell him, Trevor," Angie said as she closed the passenger door.

"I thought you looked guilty," said Jared, crossing his arms over his chest. "What's going on?" *So she was on a first name basis with the sheriff now?*

She touched Jared's arm. "I wanted to tell you last night. When I came downstairs, I didn't know Terri was your sister or I would have told you then."

She sighed deeply and looked into his eyes. "I found another note on my pillow last night. I called Trevor to come pick it up."

Jared gritted his teeth, working the muscles in his jaw.

"You might want to take a look at this," said Sheriff Oakley, holding out the paper.

Looking away from Angie, Jared took the brown scrap. It looked like it had been torn from a paper grocery bag. The dark script written in pencil spoke words that chilled him to the bone. His anger turned to shock as he read the note again.

"You will die by my hand for what you did to me." Jared handed the note back to Trevor. "That's it. Angie needs around the clock protection. I want someone with her at all times."

"No way!" Angie objected. "I will not have a bodyguard!"

"Obviously you're not grasping the seriousness of this situation," Jared growled through gritted teeth.

"This is probably just a practical joke."

"A joke? Are you insane, woman? Someone wants to kill you and you think it's a joke?"

"Hold on, you two!" Sheriff Oakley stepped between them. "The situation is bad enough without the two of you going at each other's throats."

She stalked away from the men, fuming.

"Listen, Angie" said the sheriff, "I have to agree with Jared. This is a direct threat on your life. Like I told you before, we can't take chances. We know he's going to come after you, it's just a matter of when."

"If you don't have the manpower, Sheriff, I'll up the daytime security I already have in place."

She whirled around. "What daytime security?

"I've had security in place since the hay barn was burned."

"You mean those extra construction workers you brought in are security guards?"

"Yes."

She didn't know whether to hit him or hug him. He'd protected her and she hadn't even known. Her heart swelled with love and pride. "Fine, but I don't see any reason to have security inside the house. What if I have to go to the bathroom in the middle of the night while I'm in my nightgown?"

"Okay. We'll keep security outside," Jared said. "Inside the house, I'll protect you whether you like it or not. Come on in, Sheriff. We need to make some plans."

ANGIE SWIVELED IN her office chair in front of her computer. The light clatter of her teeth against the plastic ink pen she twisted in her mouth was the only sound in the room.

She scrolled further down the page. There were so many descriptions of paranormal phenomenon, but none fit the glowing oval she'd seen the night of the fire. There must be some information to explain that blue light. She clicked on a link.

Trading the pen for a vanilla wafer, she typed Angel Manifestations in the address window then hit the enter key.

Alan was nagging her about the curse. During their phone conversation a few minutes ago, he'd asked if she thought the blue glow was connected to it. Now he had her curiosity piqued. What if they *were* connected?

"I'm coming in." Jared called, tapping on the doorjamb.

She stared at him. "Okay. But you don't have to make such a big deal about it."

"I thought I should announce myself since you're always so jumpy."

"I'm not jumpy. You just sneak up on people."

Jared sat at his desk and started rummaging through a box filled with paperwork. "What are you working on?"

"I'm not working right now."

"Looking for an online boyfriend?"

"Oh yeah…that's exactly what I'm doing. Tell you what—why don't you log on and meet me in a chat room. I'll pretend I don't know you." His laughter brought a smile to her face. "I'm doing research."

"For?" Jared inquired.

"For an explanation of the glow that appeared to me the night of the fire."

Jared laid down the papers. "Maybe that glow was just your imagination. You were in a life-and-death situation. Sometimes our minds can play tricks on us."

"I don't think that's it. This thing was so real. Besides it saved my life. I've already looked up ghosts, spirits, apparitions and angels. There's a lot of information but I haven't found anything exactly like what I saw."

"I bet you don't either."

"You're just a skeptic."

"No, I'm not. My sister has paranormal experiences. Remember? I could go get her. She might know something about this kind of thing."

"That's okay. I'm sure if I'm meant to find it, I will."

"Suit yourself."

Angie continued to search the internet, but her concentration was gone. Jared's nearness toyed with her focus, kept her glancing over at him too often. He had moved from the box to the computer screen.

Maybe I'll go work in the library. But he might think I'm leaving because of him. Nope, I'm going to stay right here, no matter how uncomfortable I feel.

Her mind drifted back to the night Jared cooked dinner for her and the feelings she experienced at the touch of his hand. Instantly, she became hot and damp. *Forget it. I need to get out of here.*

Clicking the X to close the browser window, she pushed her chair back and stood to leave. *Air, that's what I need, some fresh air.*

Jared stopped her. "Bring your chair around here for a minute."

"Why?"

"I found something you may be interested in."

Pulling the chair around to his desk, she sat down beside him.

"I searched for ghost hunters and this site with a lot of pictures came up. Look at this one."

"I can't believe you found this." Angie stared at the groups of pictures. "No, that's not really it. Can you scroll down some please?"

He moved down the page, pausing over each frame. "Any of these?"

"No."

At the bottom of the page a link in bold red lettering said, *Cursed Spirits—Enter At Your Own Risk.*

Jared put the cursor over the script. "Wanna see what they look like?"

"I don't think so." Angie shivered. "Why would it say enter at your own risk?"

"Probably someone was trying to make the site seem scary." He clicked the link.

"Jared, no wait— Oh my God!"

"What?"

Angie pointed at the screen.

"Is that it?" Jared looked from the screen to Angie. "That's what you saw?"

Staring at the web page, Angie could only nod. In the middle of one picture glowed a large oval of blue light. The brilliant edges faded to a center of white. The apparition was large, just like the one she'd seen the night of the fire.

"Well, say something." Jared stared at her, waiting.

Angie looked at him. "First of all, how someone could actually get a picture like this is beyond me. Do you think it's fake?" *It must be fake,* she reasoned, but in her heart she knew it was very real.

"I don't know. A lot of things on the internet are. If I can find a contact number, we'll call and talk to someone about it."

"Okay." Her mind whirled, trying to make sense of it all. *I saw a cursed spirit? Why would it help me escape?*

"Here we go…" Jared wrote down the number, picked up the telephone and punched the numbers on the dial pad. He made a connection and said, "Hello."

Angie had to move. Her nerves wouldn't let her just sit. She went into the kitchen, fixed two glasses of iced tea then grabbed a bag of chips.

Am I cursed too? Slow down Angie, she reprimanded herself. Her thoughts were getting worse by the moment. Returning to the office, she put the drinks on the desk, plopped down in her chair and ripped open the bag.

Jared smiled over at her. He talked for a few more minutes, said goodbye and hung up the phone. "Do you always crunch so loud?"

Angie smiled. "Only when I'm nervous. Who did you talk to? What did they say?"

"I talked to the head of the ghost hunter's society, Garrett Lloyd. He said there are two types of curses. One can be broken, the other can't. The research he's done on cursed spirits indicates that if a curse can be broken, the spirit must help the living in order to end it."

"This is too weird," Angie said between bites. "How did he come up with all of that? Did he just walk up and ask the cursed spirits?"

Jared laughed as he grabbed a few chips. "Are you hungry?"

She shook her head. "Very nervous, though. I've got to do something with my hands. I don't smoke, so I eat."

"I guess it's a good thing the bag isn't super sized then."

"Ha, ha, very funny. Even nervous, I couldn't eat that many chips."

"If it makes you feel any better, Garrett said it's a positive sign that you saw the apparition. It's trying to help break whatever curse has it captured."

"So, it's not following me around, watching me?"

"I didn't ask him that, but I doubt it."

"I guess I feel a little better then. I don't understand why I keep seeing strange things lately."

"What else have you seen?"

"Nothing really." *Whew, that was close. I almost revealed my dream.* Sticking her thumb in her mouth, she licked the salt off her fingers, watching Jared. "Did he say anything else?"

"He asked if I knew about a curse in this area. I told him no, but he said he'd like to come out to run some kind of tests."

"What'd you tell him?" She replaced her thumb with her pointer finger.

"That we'd keep him in mind if anything else happened."

"Okay." She took her finger from her mouth but before she could replace it with another, Jared grabbed her hand.

"Let me." His gaze locked with hers as he slipped her finger into his mouth. He sucked gently, removing the residue with his tongue.

She held her breath.

Jared leaned forward, threading the fingers of his free hand through the hair at the nape of her neck, slowly pulling her toward him.

He put her ring finger in his mouth, caressed the salt off and replaced it with her pinkie.

Breathing shallowly now, Angie's heart pounded in her chest. Her blood rushed through her veins, its heat making her dizzy.

Erotic. That's the only word that came to mind. The man had her sizzling. Thank God for the chair.

She could not, would not, lose control again.

His lips moved from her pinkie to lightly touch her mouth. Shivering, her heart swelled, then skipped a beat.

I love you so much, Jared.

His tongue traced the outline of her lips until she no longer had a choice. Her body defied her mind, as her lips parted. Jared ravished her mouth with a force that took her breath away.

She tilted her head back as Jared pulled her onto his lap. He held her face within his palms, whispered between kisses, "I want you, Angie", his breathing quickened.

He wanted her. She had affected him, stirred his desire.

Something in the back of her mind told her that she wasn't all he wanted. What was it?

I can't think when he touches me like this.

The inn. He wants to buy me out of the inn.

"Wait," she breathed against his mouth.

"Hmm…" Jared kissed her neck, then nibbled her shoulder.

"Jared. Stop."

Pulling back, he smiled at her, his dark eyes smoldering.

Angie slid from his lap, back into her chair. "I need to ask you something."

"Okay."

"Earlier today you asked me to sell my part of the inn to you. Why?"

Jared leaned back and ran his hands through his hair. "I thought you wanted to run The Variety Vine. If I buy you out then you're free to go back to your normal life."

"You want me to move out?"

"Well, no. Not yet."

"You mean not until you get me in your bed."

"That's not what I meant, Angie." Standing, then adjusting his pants, Jared moved away from her. "I just thought you wanted out of this deal."

"Not anymore." *Not until I figure out why you want me out.* "This wouldn't have anything to do with that journal I found, would it?"

He grabbed her arms before she even blinked. Shocked, Angie stared up at him.

"Why would that journal have anything to do with my offer?"

"Let go. You're hurting my arms," Angie said through clenched teeth.

He released her. "I'm sorry. I shouldn't have reacted that way. I don't know what got into me. What's in that journal that makes you think of me?"

"Nothing." She grabbed her drink and notepad. "I'm going to bed."

"Angie, wait. I'm sorry I overreacted. I was still affected by our kiss. Please, don't leave like this."

"You've made your intentions pretty clear, Mr. Maxwell. Goodnight."

"You're wrong, Angie," Jared called to her departing back. Then he sank into the chair. "Damn! I need to get my hands on that journal."

THIRTEEN

A SOFT TAP DREW ANGIE'S ATTENTION AWAY FROM THE robin perched on a tree branch outside her window to her door. She went over and pulled it open to find Devin and Kevin, Terri's children, standing shoulder-to-shoulder, giggling, their hands over their mouths.

Smiling brightly, Angie knelt to their eye level. "Good morning. You two sure are up early."

"We're going to see a surprise," they said in unison.

"You are?"

"We want you to come too," Kevin said, taking her hand.

"You do?" Angie giggled with the boys. "Why?"

"Cause Uncle Jared—" started Devin.

"Devin! Kevin!" Terri called from down the hall. "Did you two wake Angie?"

They nodded their heads, giggled again. "Yes, Mama."

"I'm sorry, Angie." Terri walked up and held each child by the shoulder. "I told them to wait. We're going to see our new farm and they want you to come along. Can you?"

"No, I'm sorry but I can't. I have too much work to do."

"I believe Mr. Harland, along with the entire country has

declared July Fourth a holiday."

"Well, yes, but I have some wallpaper I need to get up. I don't want to fall behind schedule."

"Tell you what—change into a pair of jeans, come with us to the farm, then we'll stop and check on your store. Besides, it gives me a good excuse to shop. Burt said you carry unusual merchandise."

"Yes, the store is unique." Angie shrugged her shoulders. "I don't know, Terri. I'll feel guilty if I get behind. Besides, I'll have to stop early as it is to get things going for the cookout."

"Okay. I'll make a deal with you. Come with us, then after the cookout, if you still want to put paper on that dumb wall, I'll help you do it."

"Have you ever hung wallpaper?" Angie eyed Terri suspiciously.

"How hard could it be? A little glue, a little paper."

Angie laughed. "I'll make you a deal. I'll come with you so you'll stop bugging me. But you have to promise that you'll stay far, far, away from the wallpaper and glue."

"Done. Now get out of those shorts and into some jeans. I'll meet you outside in five minutes." Terri grabbed the kids by the hands. "Come on, you two urchins." The boys giggled, pulling their mom down the hallway.

Angie changed her clothes, then met Terri and her kids beside the rental van. "I'm ready."

"Let's get this show on the road then. You can sit up front, Angie." Terri stood in between the seats, strapping the boys into the third row seat belts.

Jared opened the driver's door and sat inside.

"You know, I changed my mind," Angie said, her anger with Jared still fresh in her mind. "I better stay here and put up that wallpaper before the cookout." She reached for the door handle just as Jared pulled away. "Jared, can you stop so I can get out?"

"Nope."

Angie glared at him but he concentrated on the road.

Fine. I can handle this.

She sat back with a determined look on her face. The twins began asking so many questions that eventually their excitement rubbed off on Angie. She couldn't help but smile at their glowing faces and bright eyes as they chattered about someday having a pony of their very own.

Seeing the joy in those happy little faces, Angie started to think how wonderful it would be to have kids of her own.

Jared would be a great dad. Right then, he was in the middle of telling the twins a story about ponies, knights, enchanted forests and the fairies that lived deep within them.

Jared glanced her way, caught her staring at him and winked. Angie felt her aggravation with him soften. He was really enjoying himself, weaving his tale. The corners of her lips lifted into a smile as the children unsheathed invisible swords and held up pretend shields, then bravely rode their steeds into the shadows of the forest until the van stopped in front of a rustic ranch house made of brick.

While Terri unbuckled the boys, Angie laid her hand on Jared's arm. "You're really good with them."

Jared locked his eyes with hers. For Angie, time seemed to stop. They were the only people in the world. "Angie, I'm sorry about—"

She shushed him with her fingers to his lips. "Not now."

The slam of the van door shattered the moment. Jared grinned, quickly running his finger down her nose. "Come on, let's go see Terri's new home."

Angie followed the family through the four-bedroom house while Jared gave the grand tour. The children's laughter echoed off the empty walls as each chose his bedroom and planned where they would put their toys.

Suddenly Angie missed the joy of family she'd known with Aunt Martha. Her heart ached as tears burned behind her eyes.

I will not cry. Angie reprimanded herself as she turned away from the others.

The tears didn't listen.

Slipping away from the group, Angie made her way to the deck, which overlooked a beautiful lake. Leaning her elbows against the railing, she dried her eyes with her fingertips.

The lake looked like glass. Years ago she'd heard that Tom McNichols built it behind his house, but she'd never had the opportunity to see it until today. Gazing out over the water, determined to gain control of her emotions, she pushed the memories of Aunt Martha to the recesses of her mind.

And jumped sky-high when hands rested on her waist.

Angie quickly turned, right into Jared's arms and choked on her words. "I thought we agreed not to sneak up on each other."

"I didn't sneak." He tucked a stray strand of hair behind her ear and tilted her chin to look into her eyes.

At the sound of children's laughter, Angie moved out of his embrace.

Kevin and Devin ran around the corner of the house waving frantically. "We're going to the stables, Uncle Jared."

"Have fun. You might even find some surprises in there," he replied. Smiling, he gave his sister the thumbs up before turning back to Angie.

"I bought them ponies," he said.

"That's so sweet of you." Angie returned his smile, then turned away to lean against the railing again.

Closing in, he whispered in her ear. "There may be some surprises here too."

"What do you mean?" She continued to look out over the lake at the mix of pine and oak trees on the other side.

"Why are you standing out here alone?" he asked, turning her to him. "You look like you've been crying. Is something wrong?"

Angie looked up at him. "No, I'm fine." She heard the wobble in her voice and cleared her throat. "I just miss my aunt sometimes. It's still so new."

Angie's pain hit Jared in the pit of his stomach. No matter how much he wanted to pull her into his arms, he had to win her trust too. He'd kissed her too much lately. Way too much! "I wish there were something I could do for you."

"Sometimes it just hits me that she's really gone. That's all."

"Let me take your mind off it for awhile." Grasping her hand, he led her down the deck stairs. Walking in silence to the lake, holding hands, Jared held his free index finger to his mouth when they neared the water.

Angie motioned that her mouth was zipped shut. Jared grinned at her antics. When they approached a small weeping willow on the edge of the lake, Jared pulled her to him then moved a few branches to reveal a nest of ducklings.

"Oh my gosh! How cute!" Angie whispered in his ear, "Where's the mom?"

Jared pointed to the other side of the tree where the branches disappeared into the water. The mother duck's head was submerged, her tail in the air. He let the branches slip quietly back in place, slid his hand into hers then retreated from the willow.

When they were far enough away that they wouldn't disturb the ducks, Angie spoke. "How did you find them?"

"Mr. McNichols showed the nest to me when I listed the farm. I thought they might pick up your spirits."

"They did. Thank you."

Jared squeezed her hand. She felt his warmth radiate through her. If only she could do this every day, go walking with the man she loved.

If only.

"Penny for your thoughts."

She withdrew her hand. "Oh, I was just thinking that this is nice."

"Walking together and holding hands?"

"No," Angie lied and shoved her fists into her jean pockets. "This is a nice farm. Your sister will love it here."

"Maybe the two of you could become friends."

"Maybe." She'd like to be friends with Terri.

"Angie, I'm sorry about last night. I just hoped you'd sell your share of the inn."

"I'm not interested, Jared. What I would like to know is why you want me to sell so badly. Are you playing real estate agent again, Mr. Maxwell?"

"I guess." Walking slowly toward the barn, he looked up at the sky, then over at her. "Angie, I wanted to apologize for something else too."

"For what?" she asked without interest, kicking a little rock out of the way.

"For scaring you."

"Oh, it was nothing. I didn't hear you come up behind me. That's all."

"I'm not talking about on the deck. I'm sorry you're afraid of me. I don't know the reason, but I wish you'd tell me."

Damn! As hard as she'd tried to hide her feelings, he still figured it out.

"Angie?"

"Listen Jared." She turned suddenly to face him. "I'm not afraid of you."

"It seems like you are," he declared. "Did I do something wrong?"

"Yes… No… Oh, just forget it," she replied, staring intently into his face. "Besides, last night, we were getting along fine, weren't we? The project is ahead of schedule. That's what's really important right now."

"You *can* trust me, Angie," he said, his voice a low rumble.

This time Angie studied him, really scrutinized his face. He looked sincere, but looks could sometimes be deceiving. "I'll try," she said to appease him.

"Good," he sighed, "I know I was too short with you when you brought me Theodore's journal. I really do want to read it. Maybe I can get through it tonight."

"Impossible."

"Hey, I'm a fast reader," he said jokingly.

"The journal is being authenticated," Angie stated. "It's not in my possession right now."

His brows furrowed slightly. "And one last thing."

Angie laughed. Then in response to the serious look on his face, added, "What is this? Confession?"

"No. Maybe… Look, I end up kissing you every time I'm around you. I don't want you to take it the wrong way."

Stopping in her tracks, Angie stared at him, her interest piqued. "What way should I take it then?"

"I know you think I have a string of broken hearts behind me, you told me as much, but you're wrong. If you don't believe me, then feel free to ask Terri."

"Why are you telling me this? Let me guess. After the intense make-out sessions we shared and now that you know I'm a virgin, you either feel guilty or you want to make me trust you so you can get me into bed." She rolled her eyes, walking ahead of him. "I've heard it all before, Jared. Believe me your well-rehearsed lines will not affect me." Stopping she turned to confront him. "I'm waiting for true love, something you couldn't possibly understand and until then I'll remain as I am. The other night we went too far. I assure you, it will not happen again."

She sounded so calm, so disinterested. "I'm not convinced of that, Angie." He said with a half smile. "I don't want you to have the wrong impression of me, that's all."

"Hmm, it's interesting that you would worry about the impression I have of you. What are you up to, Jared Maxwell?"

"I'm not up to anything."

"Really?" Angie studied him, but he turned away, quickened his pace.

"Let's go see how the kids liked their new ponies," he said, striding ahead of her toward the barn.

ANGIE TOOK THE lettuce, tomatoes and onions out of the refrigerator and set them on the counter.

The outing had been interesting. She'd eventually realized the farm was Jared's birthday present to Terri, along with the horse and two ponies. What kind of brother would give his sister a farm with stock as a gift?

A wealthy one. She'd never thought of Jared as rich before, but maybe he was. At The Variety Vine, much to her amazement, he'd even spent a few hundred dollars on the children.

She'd secretly hoped to find that the store couldn't operate without her, but it was running as smooth as silk under Sharon Brady's management. Sales were even up a little. Although everyone told her they missed her, everything was under control.

Terri had purchased two matching antique floor lamps for her new home, proclaiming herself the newest regular customer.

Smiling while slicing through a tomato, Angie placed the red circle on the last empty lettuce leaf surrounding the condiment bowls centered on the platter. She'd cut the onions next, then the hamburger toppings would be complete.

The screened porch door slammed.

"Looks like we're outnumbered," said Terri as she washed the hamburger and hot dog tray. "How in the world do you work with so many guys?"

"They're a bunch of good old boys," Angie replied, getting the onions from the bottom cupboard. "I've known most of them since I was a child."

Terri ripped off a paper towel and dried the tray. "So who's the guy with the dark curly hair in the red baseball cap?"

"Sid McNichols."

"He's cute."

"He's available," Angie said. "I'll introduce you when I come out."

"No thanks. I'll just look. I'm not ready for the dating scene yet."

"Let me know if you change your mind."

"Okay." Reaching in the fridge, Terri put more hotdogs on the tray. "Where are the hamburgers?"

"Second shelf." Angie peeled the outer layer off the onion.

"Got 'em. Man these guys can sure eat," Terri grumbled. "Do you think I'll have to come back for thirds?"

"You might," she laughed.

"Okay, sis, see ya later."

"Later gator." Filling a glass with water, she set it beside the cutting board, then, taking the knife, she sliced the onion.

"Hey, stranger!" said Alan excitedly. Grabbing Angie from behind, he gave her a big squeeze, then released her. "You know that old glass of water trick doesn't always work."

Angie laughed, turning to him, tears streaming down her face. "Yeah I know, but Aunt Martha ingrained it in me. It usually works if the onion isn't too strong. This one's a doozie!"

"You look beautiful crying too," Alan said and wiped the tears from her cheeks.

"When did you get here?"

"Just a few minutes ago. I had to give my best girl a hug first, but now I better get out there and teach those boys how to cook those burgers and dogs."

"Don't burn them, chef," Angie laughed at Alan who gave her

a wink and two thumbs up on his way out of the door. She just adored that man.

A few minutes later, the door slammed again.

If any part of the house is Grand Central during a cookout, Angie decided, *it was the kitchen.* Putting the hamburger toppings aside, Angie started mixing milk, sugar and eggs she'd measured earlier.

"Are you back for thirds already, Terri?" she asked without looking behind her.

"I haven't had first or seconds yet," Jared said with a chuckle. "What are you making?"

"Dessert. How's it going out there?" Angie asked, glancing at him. "Are the hamburgers done?"

"No, Alan and Burt are arguing over how long to cook them."

"Those two," she laughed, "they'll argue about anything. Sometimes I think they just do it for kicks."

Jared closed the distance to stand directly behind her, crowding her work area. The smell of musk and soap was intoxicating. Leaning against her back, he whispered, "What do you do for kicks, Angelina?"

Thank goodness he can't see my face, thought Angie, feeling her cheeks flame. "None of your business, Mr. Maxwell." Her words were too breathy, her pulse too quick against her veins.

"Can we please go back to Jared?"

Angie hesitated before she poured in the vanilla flavoring. "It's none of your business, Jared."

"I'd like to make it my business," he said and then boldly caressed the dark tendrils of her ponytail. "Your hair's so soft."

You're making me crazy! "Thanks."

Sliding his hands down her back, then snaking his arms around her waist, Jared rested his chin on her shoulder. "What's for dessert? Anything hot, sweet and delicious? Something like…you?"

"No. Something cold. Homemade ice cream and if you don't let me go, someone's going to come in here and get the wrong idea."

"So?" He nipped at the nape of her neck, scraping his teeth along skin that was silky smooth.

"So," she said, a hint of desperation coloring her tone, "I don't want people thinking that we're interested in each other." Shrugging him from her neck, Angie removed his hands from her waist and turned to face him. "Jared, we are working here, doing a job. That's all."

"It could be more," he pointed out.

"It will never be more," she backed further away from him. Turning, she opened the refrigerator and stared inside. *I do want more. So much more, but until I know if you'll hurt me and why you want my part of the inn, I can't trust you completely.*

Her heart had jumped ship, betraying her by giving itself to Jared Maxwell.

"If that's the way you want it," Jared interrupted her thoughts, sounding wounded at her dismissal. Picking up the tray of condiments and toppings, Jared took them outside without another word.

Yes, that's exactly the way I want it. Don't I?

Two hours later, everyone had eaten and the cookout was cleared and cleaned up. Angie sat alone under the sycamore tree. She watched the men preparing fireworks in celebration of the holiday. She had always loved watching the fireworks with Aunt Martha and Alan when she was a child. Tonight would be almost like old times. She sensed Aunt Martha was there with her in spirit.

Still, she couldn't get Jared's words out of her mind. Could she vanquish her fear of him to have that something more she craved? No, he's too complicated. Maybe he seemed complex because her own feelings were so mixed up.

On the surface he seemed trustworthy enough. But her gut still said that Jared had a secret, something that he was deliberately hiding from her.

Was it a secret that could cost her life?

Drinking deeply from her wineglass, she decided to just get tipsy and forget about it. Then again, maybe that wasn't a good idea, considering what happened the last time she drank.

Angie's gaze drifted over to Jared. There was no question, no question at all that she liked the way he made her feel when he touched her. The way he made her become one with him in a kiss, the way her body warmed inside…

She liked it a lot. Maybe too much.

When those blue eyes turned angry and the villain from her dream reappeared, fear of him would rip through her, tearing her emotions to shreds.

Get a grip, Angie, she reprimanded herself, then downed the rest of the crimson liquid.

Jared hadn't spoken to her since he'd left the kitchen. No matter how much she had watched him, willed him to look her way, he just ignored her. It hurt that he couldn't even bring himself to look in her direction.

What else should I expect? she admonished herself. *I told him there would never be anything between us.*

The wine was warming her, lowering her inhibitions. Maybe she was being too hard on Jared, she mused. Should she give in to him just a little?

Burt tuned a battery-operated radio to a popular country music station. He and his wife did a lively dance and when the song ended, Burt swung her around, their laughter filling the air.

Angie smiled. After thirty years of marriage, you could still see the sparks between the two of them. Could she even hope to find that kind of love herself one day? Sighing, she picked up the wine bottle, tilted it to look inside. Half full. *So much for not getting tipsy,* she thought, pouring more into her glass.

Looking across the yard, Angie thought she saw Eddie standing near the edge of the woods. *What's he doing way over there? He must have just arrived.* She put the bottle down, waved and called to him but Eddie only stared at her. She wanted to try and make up with him. They'd been friends for too long to let a misunderstanding come between them.

"Look at all my lightning bugs, Angie!" Kevin said, running up to her and shoving the jar in her face.

Facing Kevin, she put her glass down and took the jar, twisting it side to side. "Those are spectacular, Kevin! Or is it Devin?" she teased.

The little boy giggled. "I'm Kevin." Taking the jar back, he ran off to catch more of the flashing insects. She turned back toward Eddie but he was gone.

Someone changed the station on the radio. A sultry slow song filled the night air. As she looked over the crowd for Eddie, Angie noticed several of the workers slow dancing with their wives. Maybe Eddie was talking to Alan. *No, Alan's talking to Jared. It's as if Eddie just disappeared.* Closing her eyes, Angie leaned her head back against the tree. Forgetting about Eddie, she let the night and music embrace her.

"May I have this dance?"

Her eyes flashed open to see her longtime friend, Sid McNichols, standing beside her. Lifting her hand to him, she grinned. "Sure."

Sid led her to the grass dance floor where Angie slipped her arms around his neck. "So how's my favorite football player tonight?"

"Good, but I could be doing better."

She laughed aloud. "What do you want, Sid?"

"I never could hide anything from you, could I?" Sid spun her around. "Who's that blonde?"

She glanced over at Terri, then pulled back a little from Sid's embrace, scrutinizing him. "Why, Sid McNichols, you're breaking my heart!" she said, mimicking a southern belle.

Sid laughed. "But you know I'll always love you, Scarlett," he said, bending to kiss her on the cheek.

"Yeah, I know." Out of the corner of her eye, she saw Jared watching, so she kissed Sid on the cheek too. "That's Jared's sister, Terri Logan."

"She's a looker."

"She's really sweet too. I think you'd like her. Why don't you go and talk to her?"

"I might." Sid looked around her at Terri.

Angie rolled her eyes at him. "Yeah, sure. What am I going to do with you, Sid? Marry you myself?"

"Yuck, marry you?" he teased. "I'd feel like I was marrying my sister."

"Then get your butt over there and talk to the woman!" she said, tugging his hair.

"Okay, okay," he conceded. "I will, after we dance."

She sighed dramatically. "Sid," she began, "we've known each other a long time. I know very well that you're thinking you don't have a chance in hell with Terri and you're not going to risk talking to her. Well, you don't know until you try. Maybe she's not as high maintenance as she looks."

"Oh, all right." Sid laughed and squeezed Angie tight.

"Mind if I cut in?"

Sid turned to the man beside him, then winked at her. "I guess you can have her." Kissing her on the cheek, he handed her over.

"Thanks." Jared's scowl said much more than words ever could. Her heart skipped a beat. *What the heck was his problem now?*

"Have fun with your little lover boy?" he growled.

"Sid's a friend from school, not a lover boy." Her tone was

firm. No way was he starting with her again.

"That's not what it looked like to me." Holding her tightly, Jared danced them apart from the crowd, where their conversation couldn't be heard. "From where I stood, there was a lot of kissing going on."

"Oh, for Pete's sake, Jared," she snapped. "I'll kiss whomever I feel like kissing. Besides, if you watched that closely you certainly noticed all the kisses were on the cheek."

She felt her back touch something hard. With a backward glance, she saw it was the sycamore tree. Jared had danced her to the other side of the yard, out of everyone's view.

And she hadn't even noticed.

The faint yellow glow from the garden torches flickered against his skin, casting shadows around his eyes and mouth.

He looked sinister.

And oh-so sexy.

Her stomach tightened. "Jared, I think we better go back."

"What's your hurry?" he whispered, holding her taut against the tree.

Her body screamed as blood sped through her veins. The temperature skyrocketed. With his chest pressed against hers, the scent of him was completely overpowering.

Oh yeah. I want him something fierce. "Jared, I…"

"You want a kiss, pretty lady? Is that what you were after back there?" he questioned.

"No, I…" *I can't breathe.* "Cut it out, Jared."

He caressed her cheek with his lips, then moved to her earlobe where he nibbled gently. "Is this what you were hoping for with Sid?"

Her whole body tingled, her breathing became ragged. "I told you. Sid and I are just friends, we grew up together." Angie knew she should make him stop, but his lips on her body just felt so good. So right. "What's the matter, Jared? Jealous?"

Jared kissed the length of her neck before looking her in the eyes. Nose to nose, the heat of him filled her senses.

"Me, jealous?" he said. A slow, grin spread across his face, yet something else blazed in his eyes. Something she couldn't quite grasp. "You're forgetting who you're talking to, Angie."

Danger? Mischievousness? Desire?

Danger! That's what had flashed in his eyes. As soon as she recognized it, the fear she'd nearly forgotten overrode her excitement.

"Let me go." Pushing against him, she wriggled and squirmed, but he didn't budge. She couldn't free herself.

"You said you weren't afraid of me," he said softly.

"I'm not," she lied. "Jared, we've had a nice day. For once, we got along. Please don't ruin it."

"I'm not going to ruin anything. We didn't even speak for most of the day," he said, quickly brushing his lips against her jawline. "Look me in the eyes and tell me that you don't want me to kiss you right now. If you really mean it, I'll let you go, no questions asked."

She opened her mouth to speak, but the words wouldn't come. Looking into his eyes, she realized she'd been wrong. It wasn't danger she'd seen—it was desire.

Please kiss me! her mind screamed. She could already taste him on her lips. *No. I must fight my feelings. If I lose myself to him I'll be in trouble. What am I thinking? I'm already lost.*

The closeness of his muscular male body weakened her knees. Forcing the words to her lips, she looked down. "I don't want you to kiss me."

"You're a liar, Angie. You couldn't look me in the eyes and say it." Tilting her chin, he lifted her face to his. "Now tell me the truth."

She searched his eyes and her heart. She wouldn't lie to herself. For all the pain it would cause, no matter how hard she tried to deny it, she loved him. Her emotions tore at her even as her fingers curled in his hair.

Just one taste.

She brought his face to hers. "This is absolutely, positively the last time this will ever happen, Jared Maxwell," she whispered against his lips before crushing them under her own.

Jared didn't kiss her back. Not until she deepened the kiss, did he release his own passion. Moments later, he freed himself from her mouth. "I want you, Angie."

Struggling to catch her breath, she brought herself back to the here and now. Her head reeled. She'd lost her heart to the wrong man. "You and every other man I've ever kissed," she said.

Jared placed his forehead against hers until his labored breathing steadied. "You really know how to kill the mood."

"I don't mean to sound like a tease."

"No?"

"I wanted to kiss you, Jared. But that's as far as we go. It ends here." She sighed deeply. "This can't happen again. I can't let it."

"Why?"

Because I've fallen in love with you! "I just can't. We have to keep our relationship strictly business from now on." *Geez! It was hard to talk with his face touching hers.*

"Promise me, Jared. Our relationship is professional after tonight."

Jared lifted his head to look at her. "All right. I promise. After tonight, there will be nothing but professionalism between us." He grinned wickedly. "Angie, tonight's not over yet."

The corners of her mouth turned up, "No, it's not." *Stop it, Angie,* she told herself. *Don't flirt this way.*

Jared kissed her—hard. If this was going to be the last kiss for a while, he was going to make it a damn good one. One they'd both remember and dream about. He eased the pressure and gently caressed her lips, savoring the taste of her, the feel of her tongue tangled with his.

Angie frenziedly returned his kiss. She'd remember every movement—Jared's taste, his musky scent, his hands on her flesh, everything—for all eternity. When he gave, she took and gave back to him. Their bodies molded to each other perfectly. Jared didn't stop and neither did she.

If only it could last forever.

And then, just then, when they connected like she'd never connected to anyone before, she heard the screech and bang of fireworks.

Hey, I must really be in love!

Lifting her lids slightly, she saw the sparkle of blues, greens and reds in the night sky. Perfect timing.

Jared broke off the kiss and looked at the sky too. The sound of their ragged breathing mixed with the burst of the fireworks. "Looks like they started without us," he said, his voice raspy with desire.

"I believe, Mr. Maxwell, that our fireworks started before the ones up there."

Jared snaked his arm around her waist, lifting her away from the tree, then spun her around until she giggled. "I believe you're right, Ms. Benton. I do believe you're right."

FOURTEEN

TAKING A NAIL FROM HIS MOUTH, JARED POUNDED IT into a shingle, securing it to the roof of Clyde Davis' house. The renovation was almost complete. Only three more weeks until he moved back home.

It had been three weeks since the party and he'd avoided Angie as much as possible. She wanted professionalism and that's what he'd given her.

It was killing him.

Even though he received a daily report from the security guards, who continued to pose as workers, he still couldn't figure out why she was so jittery and nervous around him. *You'd think she would be more afraid of her stalker.*

If Angie didn't hear him coming when he walked up behind her—well, the woman almost jumped out of her skin. It really didn't make any sense. She'd fight him like a pit bull to his face, but if he surprised her, she'd pull back in fear.

He wished Terri and the twins hadn't left the day after the barbeque. At least they would have provided a distraction to keep him from dwelling on Angie.

I'll miss her when this job is over, he thought, his heart sinking.

And I'll worry about her. Her stalker was still at large. Sheriff Oakley hadn't been able to trace him. Even Eddie Harland hadn't been found for questioning. It was as if a ghost moved unseen among them.

But there was something else on Jared's mind. He'd been sure Angie would have agreed to sell by now. Clenching his teeth, striking another nail into place, he decided to find a new way to convince her to sell.

At the whine of a motorcycle engine, Jared raised his head.

Would wonders never cease? Angie rode a dirt bike, her hair streaming behind her in the wind. She looked beautiful, wild and free.

As the bike zoomed closer, Angie waved, calling his name. Jared felt a tug in his stomach, a pull at his heart. If he didn't have her soon, lust was going to get the better of him. The thought troubled him.

"Hey, Jared!" she shouted when she reached the house. "Come down here!"

Waving his agreement, he climbed down from the roof.

"Is everything okay?" he asked, as he jumped from the third rung of the ladder to the ground.

"Everything's great," she said, a broad smile covered her face. "Hop on."

Jared took off his carpenter's belt and laid it on the front porch. Then, straddling the bike, he climbed on behind Angie.

She was busily knotting her hair into a makeshift bun with a scrunchie. "Don't want it flapping in your face," she laughed.

How thoughtful. "Are you going to tell me what's wrong? Why aren't you wearing a helmet?"

"There's nothing wrong, silly. Why do you always think something's wrong? I couldn't find the helmet." Turning the switch, she knocked the kickstand horizontal. "Alan's at the house. He wants to see us."

"Next time, wear a helmet."

"Okay." Angie took off so fast that Jared had to grab her waist to keep from falling off.

"Slow down, woman," he shouted over the engine, leaning into her.

The rush of tearing headlong into the wind sparked a fire in Jared's soul. The feeling of freedom was too overwhelming. Impulsively, he pulled off Angie's scrunchie, loosening her black hair. It flew all around him, filling him with exhilaration.

When they reached the main house, Angie killed the engine just as Burt came out of the front door, carrying a can of soda. "Thanks, for letting me borrow the bike, Burt," she said, as they climbed off the bike. "Can I leave it here? Alan needs to see us inside."

"Sure thing, Angie baby," he said, taking a drink.

Angie stopped in her tracks. "What did you say?"

"Sure thing. I'll move it in a few minutes." Burt's blue eyes twinkled. "Go on now."

Grabbing her scrunchie from Jared, Angie bolted up the stairs, pulling her hair back at the same time.

"What's going on, Burt?" Jared asked, staring after Angie.

"Beats me. Harland got here about a half hour ago. Bit after that, Angie ran out to the stables, whooping and hollering, jumped on my bike and took off. Now, here you are."

"Hmm." Frowning, Jared shoved his hands in his pockets, still staring at the house. "I didn't even know she could ride a motorcycle."

"There's probably a lot you don't know about her. You best get on inside now, Boss and find out what all the fuss is about," Burt said, straddling the bike.

"Guess I better," Jared muttered, climbing the steps.

Inside, he found Alan and Angie sitting in the living room.

"Good afternoon, Alan."

"Afternoon, Jared. Have a seat. I have some great news."

"Do you?" said Jared, sitting down on the arm of the sofa farthest away from Alan. "What is it?"

"I've already told Angie," Alan answered. "That journal she found? It's the genuine article—written by Theodore Slayton himself."

"Really?" *So she gave the journal to Alan.*

"And the section written by Mary is also authentic. There was a legal issue involving Mary and an incident on a neighbor's property and she gave a written testimony. I had a handwriting analyst compare the testimony to her journal entry. It matched."

Damn! This was too close for comfort. What had Mary said in that journal? "Meaning?"

"Meaning, we have written documentation that someone saw the ghost of Theodore Slayton in this house shortly after he died."

"You're kidding!" A surge of relief coursed through Jared and he slid down into the loveseat's cushion. "That's what she wrote?"

"It's amazing that those documents were still on file," Angie put in, leaning back in her chair.

"Well, the historian had to do some digging to find the paperwork," Alan said. "They also ran analyses on the journal, testing the paper and leather, the binding, those sorts of things, before the determination was made."

"That's wonderful, Alan." Angie said, "I'm so happy for the inn."

Jared got up and walked over to the fireplace, where he put one hand on the mantel and leaned forward to stare distractedly at the hearth. His mind was racing. *What else did Mary say? If Angie and Alan learn too much, it could ruin my plan.*

"This will benefit all of us," Alan was saying calmly. "I have some more good news, Jared. Can you handle all of this in one day?"

Angie laughed. "Of course he can. Lay it on us, Alan."

"I've already booked all the inn's bedrooms from September first through the second week in January. Clyde Davis' house is booked too for the weekend of the grand opening and from Halloween through Christmas. I'm still working on September."

Jared still stared into the fireplace. *How can I get my hands on that journal?*

"Isn't that right, Jared?"

"Hmm?" he mumbled, turning toward the voice that had interrupted his thoughts. "I'm sorry, what did you say?"

"I said it's good that we're a week ahead of schedule," She replied tartly. "Right, Jared?"

"Yeah, that's right." His tone was cool and he turned back again to the fireplace, but not before he saw Angie wink at Alan. *Something is wrong with this picture.*

"I have one more piece of good news and then I'll let you get back to work," Alan told them.

"There's more?" asked Angie, pleased.

"Uh-huh." Alan smiled. "Do you remember Kimmie Turner, Angie?"

"Yes, of course."

"Well, it seems she's marrying the Wiles boy."

"Really? Which one? Randall or Barry?"

"Barry."

"I can't believe Kimmie's getting married!" she exclaimed. "Time really does fly. I still think of her as my freckle-faced teenaged friend, I guess. It's been a long time since I've seen her."

"Well, I haven't got to the best part yet," Alan went on. "You know how Mrs. Turner has her nose into everything?" He chuckled. "Well, she heard about the renovation. Seems Kimmie wants an outside wedding and her mother thinks holding the ceremony under the big sycamore tree would be just about perfect. She's getting married on Saturday, August eighteenth. Do you think we can have the place ready in time?"

"It'll be ready, just you wait and see." Angie beamed. "If she wants me to, I can help Kimmie with some of the planning. Just for what we'll do here, of course. Mrs. Turner will love it since she's always pumping me for information."

"Great." Alan turned to Jared. "Jared, what do you think? Will you have your part of the project finished by then?"

Jared glanced between the two of them. "Yeah, sure."

"Then I'll call Kimmie when I get back to the office and let her know the wedding can be held here." Alan's gaze pierced Jared's. "Is everything okay, Jared? You seem distracted."

"Oh, I'm fine." Still looking at Alan's concerned face, he felt Angie's eyes on him. "I was just thinking about the work I still have to do." *I must be more careful.*

Reclaiming the loveseat, Jared shook off his darker feelings and smiled brightly. "I'm sorry. I got lost in my thoughts for a moment. Let's continue, please."

Alan took a notepad out of his briefcase. "I need to know, timewise, where each of you is in your part of the renovation. There are only three weeks until Kimmie's wedding. We have to make this as perfect as we can. It'll help the business if we set a high standard now."

"Ladies first." Nodding his head toward the only female in the room, Jared leaned back in the loveseat and smiled at her.

"I'm ahead of schedule," Angie retorted, wrinkling her nose at him rebelliously. "The upstairs is complete and I have a crew coming in next week to refinish the wood floors. Then I need to paint and put up wallpaper in the office. I'm doing the office last because we're still using it, but I'm moving it to a smaller room."

"Where are you putting it?" said Jared.

"In that closet beside the library." Angie held her palms six inches apart and giggled.

Just looking at the happy glow on her face made him feel warm, inside and out.

"I'm kidding, Jared. The room's bigger than a closet. The tricky part was wiring it for phones and internet access but the telephone company pulled it off." She addressed Alan again, "There's one more shipment coming in but I should be completely finished in two weeks. The last week, I'll do the Davis house and help Kimmie with her wedding."

Alan stopped taking notes to flip the page. "What about you, Jared?"

"We found some sections of termite-infested wood in the structure of the main house and a lot more in Clyde Davis' house," Jared said. "We replaced the wood, had both houses treated and contracted with a pest control company for monthly services. The main house is complete and about ten days are left on Clyde's house. The remaining time will be used to fix up the sites of interest along the riding trail."

"The additional horses are due for delivery on Saturday the eighteenth," Jared told them, "but I'll move that to Friday morning so it doesn't interfere with the wedding."

"Very good," Alan said, closing his notebook. "I have an antique hay baler at my place, Jared. If you want to use it on the trail, just let me know."

"I will," Jared agreed.

"I want both of you to know how pleased I am with the work and commitment you've put into this project. Both of you have done a great job." Alan stood up.

"Thanks, Alan." Angie got up to hug the older man.

"Thank you, Alan." Jared shook his hand. "I've got to get back to work. I'll call you about the hay baler. Oh and I'd like to see that journal sometime soon."

"Well, there's not much in it, you know." Alan broke the handshake and put both hands in his pockets. "I still haven't received the actual journal back. We can talk about it when I get it."

"Great." Without waiting for a reply, Jared left the house.

Damn it! If he couldn't read the journal, it might mess up his plans. He had to act fast before they dug too deep. *But what can I do?*

"You want me to saddle Thunder, Boss?" Burt yelled from the workbench.

"No, I'll walk," Jared shouted back. Glancing toward the house he saw Angie and Alan framed by the window, watching him.

Burt took off his cap and ran a red bandanna across his face. "You sure, Boss?"

"Yep," snapped Jared.

Shrugging his shoulders, Burt picked up the planer and went back to work on a board.

Inside the house, Angie turned away from the window. "Did you notice how he reacted when we talked about the journal?" she asked Alan.

"Yes, he seemed a bit uneasy didn't he?"

"Have you found out anything about the descendants of Sally or Mary?"

"The genealogist should have the reports back soon. I'll call you for a meeting when they arrive."

"Do you think Jared's related to them?"

"I don't know. Something is going on with him."

"The sooner we find out what he's hiding, the better," Angie said, taking his arm. "Come on. Let me give you the grand tour."

ANGIE STOOD IN the ballroom alone, tilting her head back for a better view of the domed ceiling. She found it enchanting. A brilliant idea if she did say so herself.

A moon glowed against a night sky. Stars twinkled down upon her. Thanks to an awesome electrician and modern technology this manmade sky made you want to dance.

She let her gaze trail down to the walls. The artist had created three-dimensional gardens on them that looked real. The lilac blossoms of wisteria hung like grapes from white archways. Illuminated by the full moon above, masses of multicolored flowers lined pathways of stone. A person could lose themselves in the atmosphere of the room. It was relaxing and so romantic.

Angie felt more relaxed too. She hadn't had the Jared nightmare in at least two weeks. It seemed to have gone away, even though nothing bad had happened in real life. She almost couldn't believe it. This had never happened with one of her observer dreams before. But this time… She breathed in deeply, slowly and then released the breath. Maybe this time was different.

Spreading her arms wide, she twirled around the floor. She hadn't felt this free in seven months. *This is wonderful,* she thought in delight.

"Nice dance."

Angie jerked to a standstill then turned toward the voice.

Jared lounged against the doorjamb.

How long has he been standing there watching me?

Her pulse quickened, looking at him. He'd torn the sleeves and collar from his t-shirt. The neckline was ripped in the shape of a vee. His hair was damp and a sheen of sweat covered his body.

"Why do you always sneak up on me?" she asked.

She looked around the floor for her briefcase, determined to leave before Jared ruined the happy feelings of the last few minutes, the first taste of freedom she'd had in ages.

Locating it, she retrieved both the case and some file folders scattered on the floor.

"Going somewhere?" Jared asked, fixing her with an intense gaze.

"Yes." *Damn!* His eyes always seemed to pierce right through her, making her feel so uncomfortable under his scrutiny.

"You looked so beautiful twirling around like a ballerina." A Cheshire cat grin lifted the corners of his mouth. "Can you do it again?"

"Not a chance. I told you that I don't like it when you sneak up on me." Angie tried to pass by him but he shifted his stance, effectively blocking her.

"Move out of the way, please."

"What if I don't want to?" he answered smugly. His eyes glinted as his gaze continued to bore into her. His eyes held the same darkness as they had in her dream. She shuddered at the memory even though her anger flared at his refusal. "Move over, Jared."

"Password."

"What?" she stared at him in wide-eyed disbelief. How could he look so dark and then make a joke? "Jared. I have work to do. You're in my way. *Now move!*"

A deep rumble started low in his chest, moved through him until he exploded in a full-blown, boisterous laugh.

Making her even madder.

"You big bully! Get out of my way right now!" She tried to push past his large body but he didn't even budge.

Grasping her upper arms, Jared, still smiling, moved her in front of him.

Sudden panic engulfed her, stealing her breath. Angie struggled even harder to break free.

"Angelina," he said, still holding her. "Calm down."

Oh God! I thought it was over, but it's not. She had to get away. The briefcase dropped to the floor, followed by the files. Pushing against Jared, Angie wrenched her body from side to side in a frantic flurry.

"Angelina!" he said forcefully, "hey! Calm down!"

Terrified, her gaze quickly shot up to his.

"What in the world? What's the matter with you? I was only

teasing."

Quaking with fear, her feet were glued to the floor. She tried to speak but her throat was so constricted she could barely breathe, must less scream for help. Her stomach tightened into a hard knot of fear as her pounding heart threatened to break through her ribs. Eyes locked with his, she continued to shake uncontrollably—completely engulfed in the panic attack.

The dream never went this far. Oh God, what happens next? Her legs buckled beneath her.

Bending down, Jared scooped her up and carried her into the living room. He sat on the couch, with her still in his arms and gently laid her head against his chest. Without a word he held her, slowly stroking her hair.

I don't believe it! The thought burst into Angie's mind. The enactment of the dream, the thing she'd feared for so long, had ended not in death—but in Jared's embrace.

A deep feeling of safety surrounded her. A feeling of being loved and protected. *Oh, this is so wonderful.* She let her guard down for just a moment and Jared's emotions came rushing in, overwhelming her.

She had blocked her empathic abilities with him since that day at Clyde Davis' house. As much as she wanted to know, she wouldn't use her gift to pry. In this brief, unexpected moment, her empathic abilities took over. Just as quickly, she closed the gateway within her.

But not before putting a name to the intense emotion she'd felt coming from him. Could it really be true? Did Jared *love* her?

She shook her head. She'd made a pact with herself never to trust her abilities until they proved themselves right. *Concern for a coworker? Yes, that's probably it. Love? No way!*

"I'm okay now," she said, squirming to escape his embrace.

"What happened back there?" Still holding her tightly, he pinned her with a look.

"I guess I had a little temper tantrum," she said slowly.

"You're not a very good liar."

She looked away.

"What I saw in your eyes, Angelina, that was fear, terror, not a temper tantrum."

"Fear? Terror?" *He's right. I'm a terrible liar.* "You're crazy, Jared. You just made me so mad! Look, I admit that I went a little ballistic for a minute. I'm sorry."

His eyes narrowed, scrutinizing her, as if he knew she was still lying. "Apology accepted under one condition."

"Which is?"

"Tell me why you're so afraid of me."

Sighing, Angie lowered her lids. "Let's just say some things are better left unsaid."

Jared kissed her on the forehead. "I will never hurt you, Angelina. Never."

She riveted her gaze to his. "Please, let me up now."

Immediately, he released her. "Angie, why don't you believe me?" he asked, as she stood up.

"I'm going back to work."

Jared sighed deeply. "It's already eight o'clock. Why don't you stop for the day?"

Angie studied him for a long moment, wondering just which side of this man was the true one. Then, deciding that she couldn't decide, she headed back to the ballroom for her belongings.

Fifteen

ANGIE'S HANDS SHOOK AS SHE PICKED UP HER scattered files and shoved them into her briefcase. Maybe Jared was right. A hot bath followed by bed sounded much more appealing than work.

Leaving the ballroom she went into the library to look for a book, but was distracted by flashbacks of the scene that had so recently played out between them…

The moment in the ballroom doorway could have been straight from my dream, she thought, staring at the book titles without really taking them in. *But the setting was different and I didn't run.*

That's when it hit her. She leaned against the bookcase and closed her eyes. *Oh no. What happened tonight wasn't my dream coming true. It couldn't be.*

Angie's shoulders sagged. She'd felt her nightmare was over at last but now she realized it hadn't even begun. *What an idiot I am!*

She rubbed her eyes with the heels of her hands. She knew from experience that her observer dreams *always* came true, exactly as she'd dreamt them. She'd been in such a blind panic and had felt so desperately relieved when she realized that Jared intended her no harm, that she hadn't paid any attention at all to the details of the situation.

Damn!

Grabbing a book at random from the shelves, she rushed to the staircase. Halfway up, she paused to glance down into the living room. Jared was still sitting on the couch, his head in his hands and didn't even look her way. He was probably suspicious of her now. It shouldn't matter, but guilt rushed through her all the same.

Because I'm a liar too.

No, you're not, her inner-self protested. *You have to protect yourself. Jared doesn't need to know that he's in your observer dream.*

Still troubled, she continued on to the bathroom, shutting the door behind her. The hinge squeaked. *I better get some oil on that later,* she mused, as she turned on the bath taps.

While the tub filled, she went to her bedroom and gathered her toiletries and clothes.

"This is absurd. I shouldn't feel guilty," she muttered, heading back with laden arms. "He's the one in the wrong, not me."

She sighed as she poured lavender-scented bubble bath into the running water, enjoying the scent even as her mind still turned over the evening's events. When she placed several jasmine scented candles around the room and lit them, the glow began to work its magic. She slid out of her clothes, then kicked them under the pedestal sink. Knotting her hair in a scrunchie, she lowered herself inch by inch into the steaming water.

Already, a thick froth of bubbles bobbled and danced on top. She took her time, letting her skin adjust to the wonderful heat before plunging deeper down. When at last the water completely closed over her up to her neck, she stuck one foot out and turned off the tap.

Oh yeah, perfection. She sank back dreamily into the soothing warmth.

A little while later, she dried her hand on the towel, reached for the book she'd placed near the tub and opened it.

Pictures of chickens? She turned the spine toward her and read the title. *Chicken Farming Made Easy.*

Rolling her eyes, she tossed the book back onto the floor and slipped deeper under the foam. *I'll just think about the beach on a hot afternoon,* she mused, imagining the cry of the seagulls.

It reminded her of that squeaky hinge.

JARED, THINKING ANGIE was in her bedroom, entered the bathroom and closed the door behind him.

When he turned to reach for the light switch, what met his eyes were shadows, steam and candlelight glimmering on Angie lying in the tub.

Taken completely by surprise he sat down on the toilet seat, realized the solid lid was up and stood slightly to lower it before sitting again.

She was completely immersed in bubbles, her eyes closed and as he watched, she raised one slender leg through the water, pointing her manicured toes toward the ceiling, so that bubbles ran like liquid silk back down to her thigh.

She was so beautiful. Tempting.

I love her.

Whoa, boy. Get that thought right out of your head.

"Angelina," he whispered, his voice husky.

Angie jumped, then sank lower under the water. "What are you doing in here?" she cried. "How did you get in?"

"The door was unlocked. I didn't know you were bathing."

"You should have knocked." She started swirling bubbles around to cover her body.

Her movements thinned them out, instead.

Heat rushed through Jared as he watched more and more of her smooth rosy skin becoming visible under the water. He could see almost all of her breasts and even the promise of her slender midriff… He felt himself stiffen with desire. *Thank God I'm sitting.*

"Got a camera?"

The words were challenging, but her voice was low and gentle and it spread through him, flaming the heat into a raging fire. "What?"

"A camera," she said softly, but now he could hear nervousness in her voice. "If you take a picture, it'll last longer." A slow smile spread across her face as she looked at him. "Is there something you want, Jared?"

Is she coming on to me?

"Ah, Angie, look," he said, still standing indecisively in the doorway. "We have to talk."

"*Now?*" she said, with a little laugh. "Isn't it obvious that I'm busy soaking?"

"I can see what you're doing." God help him but he wanted to see more. "Look, Angie, I don't know why I frighten you so much but your reactions are bothering me. Will you please tell me what I've done?" Cornered in the tub, maybe she would answer. He doubted if she would storm out of the room naked and dripping bubbles. Then again, this was Angie. He wouldn't put anything past her.

She released a long sigh. "Can't it wait, Jared?"

"I've waited a long time already."

She looked up into his serious face. "Well, okay, if it's bothering you that much." She sighed. Shook her head. "It's not you, Jared, it's me. You haven't done anything." *Yet.*

"Are you sure? If I've made you afraid of me somehow—I want to put it right if you'll give me a chance." He paused for a moment. "Angie. There's something else going on between us too, you know it as much as I do."

Angie scratched her nose then blew at the bubbles that remained.

The silence pounded in Jared's ears as he waited for her to answer.

"There's nothing to put right and there's nothing between us, Jared," she said at last. "I don't know what you're talking about." She raised one languid leg above the water again.

"Yes, you do. You're just lying to yourself." He made himself look away as the delicate foot and glorious, golden calf dipped down toward the bubbles. "Can you please stop doing that?"

She looked at him innocently. "Doing what?"

"The leg thing."

"What? This?" she said, raising her eyebrows and the offending limb at the same time. *Payback time! You shouldn't come in while I'm bathing.* "Does it bother you? If it's a problem for you, why don't you leave me alone so I can enjoy my bath?"

"It doesn't bother me," he said, his voice thick. "It excites me."

The water splashed when her leg hit it. "Oh."

"You excite me." Kneeling by the tub, Jared ran his knuckles along the line of her jaw.

"Don't," she breathed harshly.

When she didn't pull away, Jared forged ahead. "Why not? It's the truth. You really don't know how you affect a man do you?"

Her eyes, widening in surprise, answered him.

Inching his fingers down the front of her neck, to her collarbone, he watched her eyelids flutter. As she inhaled deeply, the swell of her full breasts rose to the top of the water.

With soapy fingertips he turned her head and pressed his lips against her mouth. Lips parted and he deepened the kiss. Her hand caressed his forearm, then she squeezed tightly when he moved from her mouth to the tender flesh of her neck. Biting, sucking and kissing her warm skin.

Jared's sigh was almost a moan as he slowly moved his hand toward the objects of his desire. He slipped his hand into the water and cupped her breast, squeezing its fullness, feeling it overflow from his palm. He kneaded her slowly then tweaked the taut nipple between his fingertip and thumb. Angie groaned against his mouth.

Pulling her forward and out of the water, Jared kissed her neck, the rise of her breast and then flicked his tongue over the rosy pink nipple. He suckled then lathed the flat roughness of his tongue over the sensitive flesh. Angie pulled him back to her mouth, kissing him passionately.

Jared broke the kiss to look into her eyes, which were heavy lidded with desire. He slid his hand deeper into the water and down her abdomen.

Her hand caught his. She pulled his arm out of the water and cleared her throat. "It's time you left me to my bath, Mr. Maxwell," she said on a breath, stilling him with a look. "Now." She gently pushed him away.

"Maybe I'll get in with you," he offered and dipped down to give her a quick kiss.

She laughed. "Nope. Bye-bye." She flipped froth and water at him until he moved to the door.

"Okay, I'm going," he said, shoving a hand into one pocket to disguise his state of arousal. "That doesn't change the fact that you excite me. And I excite you. There's definitely something between us whether you admit it or not."

When the door shut Angie sat up, turned on the cold water and stuck her head underneath the faucet.

LONG AFTER ANGIE went to bed Jared wandered around the yard gazing at the stars. He'd hoped the coolness of the night would calm him, but the air was muggy and hot.

It was bad enough that he'd been unable to sleep. After Angie finished in the tub he'd showered, but the lingering scent of lavender and jasmine only made him think of her more.

He never thought a woman could capture his heart this way. His body yearned for her, to feel her softness underneath him. He had wanted to lift her out of that tub and make love to her right there on the bathroom floor. Now he was paying dearly for keeping his cool and respecting her. *I wouldn't have it any other way.* The thought came unexpectedly, but he knew it was true.

A shooting star flashing across the night sky caught his eye. Instinctively, he wished that Angie would fall in love with him and they'd be married, then went back inside the house and climbed into bed.

Two hours later, he was still tossing and turning when a terrified scream pierced the silence.

"Run! Run!"

Racing down the hall, Jared twisted the handle of Angie's bedroom door. Locked. He tore back to his own room, grabbed the master key he kept there, raced down the hall again, unlocked the door and thrust himself into her room.

She was asleep.

In the moonlight cascading through the window, he could see sweat glistening on her forehead and arms. Strands of her dark hair stuck to her cheeks as she thrashed around in the throes of what could only be a nightmare.

"Run! Run!" she screamed again.

What should I do? If I wake her, I'll surely frighten her. Would it be worse than the nightmare?

He lowered himself carefully onto the edge of her bed. "Angie?"

Her breathing came harder, faster and the sheet was twisting tight around her throat as she tossed about.

"Angie!" Jared said louder. *I've got to wake her. She's going to hurt herself like this.*

Her body jerked violently as she clawed at the sheet, at the air. Tears rolled down her cheeks, but she still wasn't awake.

Jared couldn't take it anymore. Pulling the sheet from her neck, he caught her arms as they flailed about. He held them still.

"Angie!" he growled.

Her eyelids flew open. Instantly a bloodcurdling scream shrieked through the night.

And scared him half to death.

"Angie, it's a nightmare! You're having a nightmare!" he yelled over her screams.

She fought like a wildcat trapped in a corner, hitting him in the chest, pushing him away, hysterically sobbing then screaming for him to let her go.

Releasing her arms he tried to soothe her with words. "Baby, calm down, please, calm down. I'm here now. You're okay."

With all her strength she shoved him away from her, jumped out of the bed and ran to the furthest corner of the room. "Get away from me! Don't hurt me!"

"I'm not going to hurt you, Angie."

Her eyes were wild with fear. He dared not touch her again. "Angie, you have to calm down. It's just me—Jared."

"I know who you are," she cried. "And I know what you're going to do to me." Her voice rose into another scream. "Get the hell out of my room!"

"I'm not going to do anything to you, Angie. Truly I'm not." How could he get her to believe him? "I heard you screaming. I thought something was wrong so I unlocked your door. Angie, you just had one heck of a nightmare."

"Get out!" was all she answered, her voice now low and level.

"Angie, don't you know I'd never hurt you?" he said desperately.

"Get out!"

"Fine. I'm out. I just wanted to help you," he said coldly, striding from the room and shutting the door behind him with a bang.

Angie ran and turned the lock. She could hear Jared's footsteps pounding angrily down the hall, then the slam of his own door echoing through the house.

She leaned against the wall, shaking. Her ragged breathing filled the otherwise silent room. Waking from her nightmare to find Jared there in the flesh, gripping her arms, had been so terrifying.

She stumbled over to the bed and sat down. Only then did she realize that her thin nightgown was soaking wet and sticking to her skin like plastic wrap. Immediately she went to the mirror.

Not only does Jared know about my dream now, but I gave him a peepshow too.

She ripped the gown over her head, flung it across the room. "I knew that nightmare would come back. I just knew it!"

She thought again of Jared and realized she'd seen real torment in his eyes before he'd stormed out of her room. Did he deserve the kind of treatment she'd just given him? It was her nightmare, her problem. He said he'd only tried to help. Maybe he meant it.

She took a T-shirt out of one of her dresser drawers and pulled it over her head.

What am I going to do now? She knew very well what she should do, but didn't feel up to doing it. Still…

I really have no choice, she thought.

She climbed hastily into a pair of shorts and set off resolutely down the hall to Jared's room.

Before she could lose her nerve, she rapped twice on his door.

No answer.

"Jared, please let me in."

Silence.

Angie twisted the handle and pushed the door open.

Jared was standing in front of the open window, his back to her. At the click of the latch, he turned to face her, his eyebrows raised.

"Jared, I owe you an explanation."

Now only one eyebrow stayed lifted as he looked at her, still saying nothing.

Angie took a deep breath. "I have had the same nightmare every night for the past seven months, except for the last two weeks. I thought it had stopped, but tonight it came back worse than ever."

This was so hard to admit, especially to him.

Her feet planted firmly to the floor, knees locked for support, she continued, "A man chases me. I know that if he catches me, he'll hurt me, maybe even kill me. The dream stops when he grabs my arms."

"When I woke up, you were holding my arms, exactly like the man in the dream. I'm sorry, Jared. I had no right to yell at you the way I did. I transferred my fear from the dream to you. I…I know you were just trying to help." *I think.*

Jared's burning stare pinned her where she stood. She hadn't noticed before, but he was wearing only boxers. "I just wanted to apologize."

When he still said nothing, she slowly turned away from him and left.

She was halfway down the hall when the tears came. What was her problem today? She had to get off this emotional roller coaster one way or another.

Before she realized what was happening, Jared spun her around, right into his naked chest. He held her tightly, caressing her back, kissing the top of her head until her tears subsided.

"Angie, am I the man in your nightmare?" he whispered.

She froze.

"I knew it. That's why you're so afraid of me. Didn't I tell you earlier today I'd never hurt you?"

She nodded. "The dream is just hard on me. I'm really sorry."

Tilting her chin, Jared gazed down at her. "Do you remember the day when you sensed Ruby's feelings for Clyde?"

"Yes."

"Can't you sense what I feel for you? Please, Angie—allow yourself to feel my feelings."

Looking into his eyes, she let the gateway open and in an instant she felt overwhelmed by a deep love. She also felt a slight hesitation, as if he wasn't completely sure of his feelings. So she shook her head in denial.

"Maybe this will help."

Lowering his lips to hers, he gently showered light feathery kisses along the outside of her mouth. Then he kissed the tip of her nose and each eyelid. For a second, he captured her gaze with his before feasting on her mouth in a fury of passion.

As he clutched her against him until they molded together, Angie felt as if they were becoming one in body and spirit. She opened herself up to him, to his hunger and desire. All of her doubts melted away in the closeness of his embrace. She gave herself willingly, realizing just how much she had missed his kisses.

Nothing would ever be the same for her after this moment. He'd comforted her and she'd felt his love for her. With that little glimmer, she lost the one piece of her heart she had never given another, the one part of herself she'd held back from him before. She gave her whole heart and soul, unconditionally.

Her love would forever belong to him.

The kiss became greedy, frenzied. She couldn't get enough of him, nor him of her. Desire burned into each of them, branding them forever.

Jared slowly drew his mouth away from hers, then whispered against her cheek, "I need you, Angie."

"I need you too," she whispered back.

Jared groaned. Kissing her again, he swept her up and carried her to her bedroom.

Angie pulled him down onto the bed so that he lay on top of her. Their lovemaking intensified and Angie reached down to caress him.

"Angie…Angie…" he breathed between kisses. "We can't."

"Yes, we can. I want you, Jared. Right here, right now."

"No."

Angie stilled. She'd never been willing to give herself to any man before and now *he didn't want her*. The heart she had just given so completely, shattered. "But I thought…"

"You thought right. I need you, Angie. I've never needed anyone like this before. But I'm not going to take what you've held precious for twenty-six years when I'm not able to give everything you want and deserve in return."

Angie felt the tears burning the backs of her eyes. Nothing he could have said would have hurt her more, especially after she'd just confessed her own desire. She tried to speak, but the words caught in her throat.

"I broke my promise to you," Jared said in frustration. "I agreed we would keep our relationship professional. Once again, I couldn't keep my hands off you. We'll talk in the morning. For now, try to get some sleep."

Gently, he pulled the sheet over her. Stepping away from the bed, he stood watching her, running his hands through his hair, as if he couldn't quite make up his mind. Giving her one last look of deep longing, he left the room, closing the door softly behind him.

Angie stared at Jared's retreating back in utter confusion. She couldn't take any more of this. Burying her head in the pillow she cried, releasing all the emotions that had been building up for weeks. The fear, the desire and the love all poured from her, cleansing her.

Exhausted, she snuggled into her pillow, her sobs growing softer as she fell asleep.

Sixteen

ANGIE HUGGED WHISPER'S NECK BEFORE THROWING her right leg over the animal's broad back and headed her down the road toward the Davis house.

She'd woken up long before dawn, grumpy and tired and remembered almost immediately that Jared had wanted to talk to her this morning. Talking to him was the last thing *she* wanted to do, so she went down to the barn and bridled Whisper. She wasn't supposed to venture out alone because of the stalker but she needed some time away from Jared to think things through and hopefully improve her mood before work. She could escape a stalker on horseback, she reasoned.

Angie let Whisper pick up the pace. *Where to go?* she thought now. *I'll let Whisper choose the path.*

But she couldn't let Jared choose the path between them. How should she handle him? Her emotions were in turmoil. Now more than her physical safety was at risk. Her heart was in danger too.

She couldn't believe Jared loved her. Not after the night before. Not after that awful rejection. Something caught in her throat, just thinking about it. A man who shied away from the responsibility of taking her virginity was a man who didn't want any kind of commitment. Or so she reasoned as she rode through the morning mist that breezed lightly across her face while the sky turned a somber shade of gray.

I'll just mend my broken heart, then move on. I survived Aunt Martha's death and I'll survive this too.

Aunt Martha. The realization hit her hard.

I'm doing exactly what she did. I'm so afraid of losing the man I love that I'm not even willing to give him a chance. That's not exactly right. I did give him a chance last night and he ran. Still, I only offered him sex. Nothing more.

"I'll give him a chance with my love," she told Whisper, "and if he turns that down…well, then I'll know there will never be anything between us. How's that sound for a plan, girl?" she said, patting the horse's neck. The decision lifted her spirits, cleared the feelings left over from last night. She urged the mare into a canter, closed her eyes as the wind whipped around her face.

No sooner had Whisper began to canter, than the mare came to a sudden stop, almost throwing Angie from her back. She clutched the reins, tightened the grip of her thighs and righted herself as the horse scrambled backward, snorting and tossing her head.

"What's the matter, girl?" she whispered. Angie scanned the woods around her, looked quickly over her shoulder.

When she faced forward again she saw them.

A man and woman, strolling down the road, wearing outfits reminiscent of the early 1800s.

Angie could hear the woman, whose brown long-sleeved dress touched the ground, giggle as she looked at the man. The gathers of material below her waist swayed as she walked, but the line of black buttons up her back stayed straight. The man's trousers were navy and his matching coat hung well below the waist. His hands were clasped together behind him at the waist.

The hair on the back of Angie's neck prickled. "Hello!" she called to them.

They kept walking.

Angie urged Whisper forward but the horse snorted again and pranced in place.

The couple remained oblivious to the noises behind them, but they stopped, faced each other and spoke in hushed tones.

Angie couldn't look away. Something was wrong with this picture. Whisper never spooked.

"Mary, my love, you are my precious gem."

The man's voice carried to Angie and her eyes widened in shock. *Oh My God,* she thought, gripping the reins so tightly her knuckles turned white.

"Theodore, you make me so happy. I only wish I could touch you."

"You're still happy with me after all this time? Even with the curse?"

"You know you are everything to me."

They both turned to face Angie.

Whisper reared and tried to bolt. Angie held tight, angling the horse's head away from the couple, her heart pounding furiously in her chest. She didn't dare take her eyes off the apparitions while she fought to steady her mount.

Smiling, the couple stepped toward her.

Hesitantly, Angie smiled back, still fiercely gripping the reins.

"Angelina," said Theodore.

He knew her birth name? "Yes, sir?" She barely breathed the words.

"Thank you, my dear, for making my home beautiful again."

Angie gazed at him in silence for several moments. "You're welcome, Mr. Slayton," she finally answered, softly.

"I'm happy that you'll be part of my family, Angelina," said Mary. And the couple turned their backs to her and moved away down the path.

"Wait!" Angie called. "Theodore…Theodore Slayton?"

Theodore turned again to face her. "Yes?"

"Just making sure it was you."

"Yes, I can assure you," His voice was low and a little gravelly, "It is I."

Bowing slightly to Angie, Theodore turned and the couple walked further into the woods, slowly fading into the morning mist.

Whisper calmed down.

Angie freaked out. Her heart was still pounding so hard it affected her hearing. Was this some new ability? Seeing spirits? Aunt Martha's ghost had terrified her, but now her heart pounded with excitement, not fear. "How stupid of me. Why didn't I ask Mary why she welcomed me to her family?"

It had all happened too fast.

She had to tell Alan and Jared. Pulling the right rein and turning Whisper around, Angie dug her heels into the mare's sides then raced back to the house.

She brushed Whisper down so quickly the currycomb fairly flew over the mare's flanks and then she stalled her, gave her a cursory pat on her neck and rushed to the house.

Once inside, she telephoned Alan, waking him up.

"Angie? What's wrong?" he said frantically and groggily.

"Nothing's wrong, Alan," she answered, "but you have to come over here right now!"

"It's six-thirty," he said in a weary voice. "Can't it wait until later?"

Angie shook her head, for nobody's benefit but her own. "Uh-uh. You get out of bed and get over here. It's really important."

Alan sighed. "Give me half an hour."

"Okay," Angie responded and added a quick "Bye," before hanging up the phone.

The smell of coffee drew Angie from the office to the kitchen.

"Good morning." she almost sang, bounding into the room.

Jared raised his brows, filled two cups with coffee, added milk and sugar then handed one to her. "You sure are in a good mood. What's going on?"

"I'll tell you soon." Angie reached for the proffered mug. "I have to wait until Alan gets here."

"Alan? This early?"

"Yes." She sipped her drink. He'd made it just the way she liked it. A little milk and a lot of sugar. "How can you drink your coffee black?"

"I like things that are strong and untouched."

Angie ignored his innuendo. It wasn't hard. She was all keyed up about her news. How could she wait another twenty minutes for Alan? She was about to burst!

Maybe if she kept busy the time would go faster. "Are you hungry? I'm hungry. Want some eggs?" she didn't wait for an answer but grabbed them from the fridge and started cracking open the white shells into a bowl.

"Angelina?" he said hesitantly. "I don't want to pressure you but…"

"Hmm?"

"We need to talk about last night."

"I know, but not right now, okay?" she said, flashing him a nervous smile.

"Okay, later then," he said, walking up to the stove. "Sooo, are you feeding an army this morning?"

Looking down into the bowl, Angie felt her face flame. She'd used up at least eleven eggs. "Oops. You *are* hungry, aren't you?"

"Not that hungry." He laughed.

By the time she'd finished cooking the biggest mound of scrambled eggs she'd ever cooked in her life, Alan had arrived. Angie sat him down at the table and shoved a plate in front of him.

"I don't normally eat breakfast this early, Angie."

"Humor me, Alan. Please?"

He shrugged, looked disconsolately at the huge yellow heap in front of him and sighed. "Okay, I'll do my best. Now, what was so important that you got me out of bed?"

She sat down and leaned eagerly toward him. "Remember when you said that you hoped I had dreams about Theodore Slayton while living here?"

"Of course I do. Did you dream about him?" Alan had a gleam in his eye that was brightening his whole face.

"No," she said, darting a warning glance at Jared. "Something even more amazing happened, you guys."

Both men had their forks halfway to their mouths. "What happened, Angie?" asked Alan, as he stopped the utensil in midair.

Unable to contain her excitement, she got up and paced around the kitchen. "When I woke up this morning I just felt that I…um…needed some fresh air, so I took Whisper out for a ride."

"How'd you get past security?" Anger flared in Jared's eyes as he dropped his fork onto his plate.

"I just walked to the barn. I guess they didn't see me."

"Damn it, Angie! Someone wants to kill you and you're sneaking around by yourself?"

"I didn't sneak." Angie's voice rose as she glared at him. "You're not going to control my life just because someone tried to hurt me before. I'm not stupid and I was careful. I needed to get away from here for a while—alone. Now can I please finish my story?"

"Fine. Go ahead. What was so intriguing that you risked your life to see?"

She rolled her eyes at him. "I got down to the little road by the creek, on the way to Clyde's house and Whisper spooked, almost threw me over her head."

"And you said you were careful?" Jared snorted. "The horse

almost threw you! What if she had? What then, Angie? No one would have even known where you were!"

"Oh hush up, you old mother hen and let me finish. Now, where was I? Okay—After I got Whisper under control, I saw a man and woman walking on the road ahead of me. I said hello but they didn't answer. Then they called each other by name…" she paused for dramatic effect, "Theodore and Mary."

The shocked silence was gratifying.

"You really saw them?" Alan said at last, putting down his forkful of scrambled eggs.

Angie nodded eagerly. "They turned and looked straight at me. Whisper reared up, but I held on. I turned her head so she couldn't see them. Spirits spook animals when they look at them, you know."

It was Jared's turn to roll his eyes.

"Theodore called me Angelina. He thanked me for the renovation. When he started to walk away, I called out, 'Theodore Slayton.' He turned back to me and said 'yes' like a question. I told him I wanted to be sure that he was who I thought he was. He said, 'It is I,' bowed, then turned around and they left. Both of them evaporated into the mist."

Angie drew in a huge breath. "I was so excited. I saw Aunt Martha one time a little while ago and it must have prepared me for this. I was terrified when I saw Aunt Martha, even though I loved her so much. This time I was a little frightened but I understood what was going on so I wasn't as scared."

She plopped down in the chair, drained, "It was exhilarating. I saw him, Alan! I saw Theodore Slayton's ghost walking around with Mary on the farm. It was odd though, they never touched each other. I wonder if they can't? Maybe it's because of the curse, which Theodore mentioned by the way. He asked Mary if she was still happy with him even with the curse. What do you think?"

Neither Alan nor Jared said a word. They just stared at her, then looked at each other.

Jared, calmer now, spoke first, “Angie, are you sure you didn’t fall off that horse and hit your head?”

“Oh course, I’m sure. I didn’t think *you’d* believe me!” Annoyance flared in her eyes and she stood, pacing again. “You believe me, don’t you, Alan?”

“Yes, I do,” he said quietly.

“What’s wrong?” Angie stilled, looking deep into his eyes. The sadness she saw there surprised her. “I thought you’d be happy.”

“Why didn’t you tell me that you saw Martha?”

Oh no. I’m such an idiot. Going to him, Angie put her arms around his shoulders. “Alan, I’m so sorry. I just didn’t think about it. She told me something private. I never thought of sharing it with anyone. Please forgive me, I didn’t mean to hurt you.”

Alan patted her arm. “Don’t you fret now, dear. It was just a shock, that’s all.”

“She’s fine, Alan. She looked beautiful and happy.”

Alan smiled at her. Angie hugged him tight.

“I didn’t mean to doubt you, Angie,” Jared said, between sips of coffee.

Angie stood away from Alan. “It’s okay,” she began with a smile in Jared’s direction. Then…”Oh! Oh! I forgot something! This is really strange. Mary welcomed me to her family, but I didn’t ask what she meant. I was too concerned with Theodore’s identity.”

Jared sat his coffee cup down with a thud. “Why would a ghost welcome you to her family?” *Unless it’s a sign that we’re supposed to be married, just like I wished.*

“How am I supposed to know?”

“I’ve got to get to work.” Pushing his chair back, Jared headed for the door. Opening it, he turned back to Angie. “Thanks for breakfast. Your story is amazing, but you have to promise me that you will not go anywhere else alone.”

"Fine. I promise."

"I'm holding you to it." He left the room, closing the door behind him.

She stared after him for a long moment.

"Angie, I want you to promise me too."

"Promise what, Alan?" She turned from her contemplation of Jared's departure toward him.

"That you will keep security or someone else with you at all times. I don't want to lose you."

"Of course, Alan." She went and sat down with him at the table again.

"Have you been able to find out anything about that blue light you saw?" he said after a moment.

"I didn't find anything myself," she answered, "but Jared came across this website that had a section on cursed spirits. They had a picture of the same blue glow I saw."

"What did it say about it?"

"Not much that made sense, really, until Jared phoned the people who own the site. They're a ghost hunter's society. Jared spoke to the head honcho. He turned out to be the one who took that picture. He told Jared there are two kinds of curses. One can be broken, the other can't. From the research he's done, supposedly the cursed spirit has to help the living in order to break the curse."

"If that blue glow was a cursed spirit," Alan interjected, "then you have to consider the facts. It helped you escape from that fire unharmed."

"Yeah, you're right. Maybe the curse is true. I'm still not convinced even though Theodore did mention it this morning." Angie drank some coffee. "Alan," she said after she swallowed, "did you notice anything odd in Jared's reaction?"

"Just now? Yes, he seemed bothered by what Mary said."

She nodded and frowned. "How's that research coming?"

"We're almost finished, Angie, almost finished."

"LOOK WHAT YOU'VE done with this place!" squealed Mrs. Turner. "I swannie, it doesn't even look like the same house."

"Thank you." A grin tugged at the corners of Angie's mouth. She couldn't remember the last time she'd heard someone say "I swannie."

"It's just so homey and warm," Mrs. Turner exclaimed. "Angie, dear, could you redecorate my place? I want to make some changes now that Kimmie's moving out. Your work is excellent."

Kimmie broke in. "Angie, it looks wonderful. You've done the most amazing things! I can't believe you found the perfect antiques to make everything look authentic."

"That's all part of my job." Angie smiled, then said to Kimmie's mother, "When this project is complete, I'd love to discuss your home with you, Mrs. Turner." She paused, her smile growing into a giant grin. "Now, both of you, come with me. I have something very special that I want to show you. I know you want to have the ceremony under the sycamore tree, but I thought you might consider having the reception inside."

"Oh, I think outside will be fine for the reception too," Kimmie said.

As they walked through the house, Mrs. Turner trailed along behind, peeking inside decorative vases and pitchers, running her finger along railings as though looking for dust, feeling the quality of runners and curtains. "I wouldn't want the guests to ruin anything in here before the inn opens."

"Let me show you this room before you decide."

Angie opened the double doors leading into the ballroom. Her heart filled with pride when she heard the gasps of appreciation behind her. No one outside of the renovation team had seen this room until now.

"Wait, there's more." Angie touched a switch and the ceiling immediately blossomed into a clear night sky. Little stars twinkled as the moon beamed down its iridescent glow onto the painted gardens below.

Kimmie's hands flew to her mouth then to her cheeks. "Oh, Mama," she said on a whisper, "Isn't this beautiful?"

For once in her life, Mrs. Turner was speechless.

What a compliment, thought Angie. "Don't you think this would be a wonderful place for the reception?"

Running over, Kimmie hugged Angie, squeezing the breath out of her. "Can I have the reception in here? Pleeaaassseee?"

Angie laughed out loud. "Oh course you can, silly. That's why I showed it to you."

"You are so sweet, Angelina Benton." Mrs. Turner took Angie's hand. "Now you must tell me how you came up with such a wonderful idea for this room. I've never seen anything like this in all my born days!"

"I guess I was inspired."

A knock on the doorjamb turned three heads in that direction.

"Angie, the delivery you expected is here," said Jared. "The driver needs you to sign off on the paperwork. Hello, ladies."

"Hi," the Turners said in unison.

"Okay." Angie nodded. "Can you tell him I'll be right out?"

"Sure thing."

"Well, well," said Mrs. Turner, patting Angie's hand as Jared disappeared from view, "if he was your inspiration, my dear, no wonder this room is so exceptional."

"Mrs. Turner! Jared was not my inspiration."

"You go see that driver, dear. We want to look under the sycamore tree again but let's definitely move the reception to this room." Mrs. Turner rubbed Angie between the shoulder blades. "Martha would be so proud of you, dear."

"Thanks." Angie followed the Turners through the house and out of the front door. "I'll be in my office once I accept this delivery if you need me."

"We'll be fine, dear." Mrs. Turner wrapped Angie in a bear hug. "I know you're busy so I'll just call to make the rest of the arrangements."

"Then I'll see you later." Angie smiled and waved as she made her way to the large delivery truck.

A prickle on the back of her neck caused her to pause. She looked over her shoulder but only saw Mrs. Turner and Angie making their way to the sycamore tree. Still, something didn't feel right. It was as if someone was watching her. Maybe it was just the stress of the stalker situation that had her on alert. She tried to ignore the feeling and walked closer toward the truck but couldn't locate the driver.

"Hello!" She noticed that the truck was painted a dark grey and didn't contain any writing. This wasn't the usual way they received deliveries. "Driver, are you here?"

She glanced over her shoulder again. The sky darkened as the sun disappeared behind a cloud. She looked up. Storms hadn't been predicted for today.

"There you are, miss!"

Angie jumped and looked in front of her. A large man, at least six foot five, head shaved bald and in his late twenties or early thirties, stood directly in front of her. "You frightened me! Where did you come from?"

"I was around back. Didn't you hear me walk up?"

"No."

The man stepped closer and narrowed his gaze. Angie felt the hairs on her neck raise as goose bumps raised on her arms. His body rippled with muscles under a shirt that was a size too small. His small, beady eyes didn't fit the roundness of his face.

"I've been waiting for you. Watching and waiting. Do you

know the one thing most overlooked in crimes of passion? The pleasure the killer takes in stalking and hunting his prey." He took another step toward her. "The pleasure of the kill."

Angie felt as if her feet were glued to the floor. Terror ripped through her at his words. This was the stalker. She wanted to run but couldn't move, couldn't speak. She felt paralyzed.

Suddenly the man broke into gales of laughter. "Man, I should land that part for sure! You should see the expression on your face."

"W-What?" Angie managed to get the word out though her dry mouth.

The delivery guy smacked her on the shoulder. "Thanks for the reaction! I'm trying out for a part with the theatre group. It's a thriller and I'm auditioning for the part of the killer. Do you think I'll get it?"

The loud thumping of her heart and blood racing through her veins pounded in Angie's ears. Had she heard him right? "You're auditioning for Killer Instincts?"

"Yeah, that's the name of the play. You've heard about it?" His excitement radiated. A large smile made him look handsome instead of the intimidating threat he'd been moments before.

"Yes. That was very good. I'm sure you'll get the part. Where's my package?"

"I'll get it for you." He disappeared inside the back of the truck.

The front door slammed. Angie jumped and looked back. Jared was walking across the yard toward her.

"He pulled that audition crap on you didn't he?" He said, stopping beside her. "I can tell by the look on your face."

Angie nodded. "It's okay. He doesn't know what I've been dealing with. He just wants a part in a play."

The delivery man exited the truck with a clipboard on top of a box. "Here you go Miss Benton. Just sign here and she's all yours."

Angie signed and he handed her the box then removed the clipboard.

"Ya'll have a nice day now. Thanks again for the great reaction, Miss Benton! I hope I get the part. If I do you'll have to come see the play!"

She nodded and waved as he got back into the truck and started it up.

"Come on." Jared took the box from her. "Let's go inside."

SINKING INTO HER office chair, now located in the small room beside the library, Angie opened the box and removed the decorative accessories she'd ordered for the fireplace mantel. Slowly inspecting each marble figurine brought calmness and returned her heartbeat to a normal rhythm. She pulled out the Renobook, turned to the task list and checked off the delivery.

Glancing at the calendar she realized that in only six more nights she could sleep in her own bed, in her own home.

But—something she'd never thought possible before—she'd miss the Slayton Inn, she really would.

She'd miss Jared too.

We've never talked about the night he refused to make love to me. I wonder why he never brought it up again after the morning I saw Mary and Theodore. It probably wasn't important to him and he's forgotten all about it.

She turned a page in the Renobook.

Who am I kidding? In my heart, I understand that he did the right thing. If I'm being really honest with myself, I know he saved me from making a terrible mistake. If he's not going to bring it up first, I'll be damned if I will.

Still, she'd miss those boyish grins, that tanned muscular body and the way he teased her.

Stop it! You'll just make yourself crazy.

She closed the book. All done. She'd finished the Davis house yesterday. Now, she could just hang out for a few days in case Kimmie needed help with her wedding or if any last-minute emergencies came up.

Picking up the phone, she dialed Alan's number. "Hey stranger!"

"Hi, Angie." He laughed.

"What's so funny?"

"You did it again. I was going to call you."

"Did you find something?"

"Yes, I did. Can you meet me in an hour at the hard surface road? We'll go to your house again."

"You've got it." Hanging up the phone, she glanced at the clock on the computer. She had just enough time to ditch security.

Angie sighed deeply.

After all this time, she'd finally know Jared Maxwell's secret.

"OKAY, ALAN. SPILL IT!" Angie exclaimed, locking the front door of her home.

"Impatient are we?" he asked. "Let's at least sit down first?"

"Sure, if we must," Angie laughed, leading the way into her living room and plopping down on the sofa.

Alan chose a high-backed armchair with the beige upholstery. "Okay," he began the minute he sat down. "The genealogist traced the lines of both Sally Mayfield and Mary. Sally's lineage didn't reveal anything unusual. The grudge she'd had against the Slayton's didn't continue with her descendants. The last of the line were two daughters. One died five years ago and the other twenty-eight years ago. Both married, but neither were able to have children."

"A dead end then," Angie sighed. "Sorry, no pun intended."

"Mary's story is different."

"Really? Tell me."

"There are several living descendants who can claim Mary Slayton as their ancestor."

"Who are they?"

Alan took a deep breath. "You're not going to like this, Angie."

"Let me guess. Jared Maxwell is a descendant."

Alan nodded. "Yes. Jared, his mother and his grandmother. This doesn't include his half sister, Terri. Jared's mother was Mary's descendant. Jared's parents divorced when he was three and his father remarried and had Terri with his new wife."

"I knew it!" Angie smacked her hand down on the sofa's padded arm. "He was too damn eager to jump into this project."

"There's more."

"More?"

Alan rubbed his forehead with one hand. "After Theodore's death, Ruby took over and sent Mary away. Mary took any work she could find and told everyone her story. She swore revenge on the Slaytons for ousting the rightful heir to the estate. Mary ingrained the idea of revenge into her son and his children and they instilled it in the grandchildren. In the last generations, the story became more of a folktale than a reality to the family members."

"Except maybe to Jared Maxwell?" Angie could feel anger rising like a flame inside her. "You mean Jared still wants vengeance? That's why he was so quick to be part of the inn." Angie stared at Alan in horror.

"I can't believe this!" Angie stood and went to the window. "That's why he wanted to buy me out. He had an ulterior motive all along." The controlled anger in her voice stilted her speech. "Is that all?"

"Not quite."

The calm assurance of his tone caused Angie to whirl around.

"You mean there's even more?"

"I just wanted to tell you that Jared offered Sam Slayton a hefty sum for his property before he died."

"How much?"

"Does it matter?"

"How much, Alan?" Fighting hard for control, Angie clenched her fists together.

"Nine hundred and fifty thousand dollars."

The words had the same effect as a bucket of ice water. Knees collapsing, Angie sank to the edge of the couch. "What?"

"I don't need to repeat it, you heard me."

"You mean to tell me that Sam turned down almost a million dollars?"

"Yes. Obviously he didn't need it, based on the fund he set up for the inn."

"Jared could have paid that much?" She sank back against the couch.

"Jared Maxwell's a very wealthy man, Angie."

"Why didn't you tell me?"

"What would you have done if I had? Married him?"

A lightning strike couldn't have moved faster. Angie jumped off the couch to sit beside Alan. "I'm sorry—can you please repeat your last sentence."

"Would you have married him?"

"Why in the world would you think I'd marry Jared?" Angie softened her voice when she saw the worry lines crease Alan's forehead. "Alan, that doesn't make any sense. You know I'd never marry for money!"

"You do love him, don't you?"

"No."

"Angie, you've never been a good liar. I've seen the way the two of you look at each other."

"Alan," said Angie with a mock frown, "have you by any

chance been playing matchmaker?"

Alan gave a shamefaced grin. "You caught me. I promised Martha that I'd look after you, get you fixed up with a nice man."

"Oh, Alan." Angie's heart melted as she hugged him. "You silly old fool. I hate to disappoint you but I'm not marrying Jared. I don't think he knows the meaning of commitment. Besides, he's not interested in me."

"Don't be too sure, Angie."

"Well, it doesn't matter if he is. I'm not interested." She glanced at her watch. *Obviously Jared isn't interested in me either or he would have made love to me that night—or at least told me since then why he didn't. It doesn't matter now anyway. I've fallen completely in love with a liar that can't be trusted.* Sighing deeply, she stood. "Can you take me back to the inn now? It's getting late."

"What are you going to do?"

"I'm not sure yet," Angie said, standing to leave. "I do know that Jared Maxwell is going to get a piece of my mind."

AN OLD OIL lantern bounced flickers of light off the wooden walls of the tiny storage shack.

He sat on the floor, leaned back against the wall.

Sliding a fifth of whiskey out of the brown paper bag, he crumpled and tossed the bag into a corner, then held the bottle up to the light.

"Damn!" he cursed. "Half empty." Pressing the glass to his lips, he drank deeply. The brown liquid scorched his throat, burned his stomach.

And he liked it.

He wanted to have a good buzz going before he went after Miss Goody-Two-Shoes tonight. Otherwise, he just might not have the guts to do the deed.

Too bad she'd gotten out of that damn hay barn. He'd waited

at the edge of the woods to hear her screams as she burned. He would have taken great pleasure in those screams, the begging and pleading for help. But that *thing* had helped her escape.

"What in the hell was that blue glow?" he muttered, taking another gulp from the bottle, then rubbing his mouth slowly with his shirtsleeve. From where he'd stood, it had looked like a man floating in the air.

Then again, he'd been quite drunk. He could have imagined the whole thing. That must have been what happened. The bitch had just gotten lucky, that's all.

Gotten lucky. How ironic.

Scanning the pictures of Angie that filled the wall, he felt hatred for her welling up inside. It has been so easy getting into her bedroom today. Those security guards were a joke. He wondered who would find the note he'd left behind.

His low baritone rumble of laughter bounced off the walls. He had to admit it was a perfect plan. He had made her suffer the same way she'd made him suffer.

Bitch.

Nothing would stop him now.

This would be the night of all nights. Tonight she would suffer the most. Angie would give him what he wanted, what he deserved, then she'd die. Or maybe, he'd wait until morning, after he'd sobered a little so he could savor the experience more.

No, that might be a mistake.

Could he pull the trigger sober?

He turned up the bottle, guzzled it dry. Two down. He tossed the empty container into a different corner. He didn't care if the room was a mess. Brown paper bags littered one corner, glass whiskey bottles another, his sleeping bag was right in the middle.

He could wade through the junk. Besides, he'd never sleep in this hellhole again. Tomorrow, he was hightailing it out of this godforsaken town forever.

Finally, revenge would be his.

Standing, he took the remote control from the pocket of his blue jeans. He'd known this little gadget would come in handy when he'd seen it in the store. It activated the deadbolt inside the door. The device had paid off already, when someone had tried to get inside his hideout.

Reaching down he grabbed several red bandannas from the floor and shoved them in his pockets. He extinguished the lantern's flame before pressing a button on the remote. The lock popped. He went outside, shut the door and pressed another button to secure the red shack. Adjusting the .357 Magnum stuck inside his jeans, he turned to leave.

And froze.

It was in that twilight when dusk becomes night, when a person can barely see. The moment before darkness descends upon the earth.

Facing the back of the old shack, he saw a blue light glowing inside the kitchen. The same iridescent light he'd seen the night he'd burned the barn. It floated toward the back door, glided right through the screen, passed over the three steps and continued across the yard toward him.

He bolted into the forest, never looking back to see it following close behind.

SEVENTEEN

"HEY, BURT." ANGIE SAID, STORMING PAST HIM ON HER way to the stable. "Where's Jared?"

Burt scratched his head. "I haven't seen him in a while. He got upset when you snuck away. He took off in the truck a couple of hours ago."

She whirled around. "In the truck? Did he say where he was going?"

"He said he got a call to personally pick up a delivery."

"That's odd." *Wonder what Mr. Sneaky-Rich-Man's up to now?*

"I thought so too," Burt said, adjusting his cap. "I'm taking off now myself, Angie. You look like a ticking time bomb and I don't want to be around for the explosion. See ya tomorrow."

"Yeah, you're right, Burt. See you tomorrow."

Angie waved, then, feeling I'm-being-watched prickles on the back of her neck, turned around and stared at the security officer following a short distance behind her. When he didn't retreat, she rolled her eyes and headed for the barn.

Go away! she mentally said to him as she went inside.

Feeding and brushing down the horses helped calm her, but

the sound of tires crunching on gravel made her anger flare again.

"Here you go, girl." She grabbed some sugar cubes from a storage box and fed them to Whisper, stroking the mare's nose. "You'll have some new friends in a couple of days. Since I've got less than a week left with you it's good that you'll have company. I'll come for visits too. You never know, maybe I'll buy you from the inn."

A car door slammed, the barn door creaked and the sensation of being watched spread all through Angie again, that prickling feeling that caused a slight shudder. She knew exactly who was causing it.

Without turning to look, she said, "Spying on me again, Mr. Maxwell?"

"No, I just walked up." Jared put himself into her view. "Where did you go this time? How can you care so little for your safety?"

"Some things are more important than my safety." She hung the currycomb on a hook on the barn wall. "Where have *you* been?" Her voice dripped with sarcasm.

"I had to pick up a delivery in town."

"What delivery could be so special that you couldn't send one of the guys for it?"

"A personal delivery."

She turned to glare at him, purposefully shooting daggers from her eyes. "Is that a fact?"

Jared raised a brow. "What's your problem tonight?"

"I don't have a problem." Pent-up anger made her agitated. She had to move or she would do exactly as Burt had said she would—blow up. Storming past Jared, she ran to the house.

"Like hell you don't," Jared muttered, following her. "Angie!"

The porch door slammed behind her as she went inside the house. Jared ran to catch up but she'd made it to the living room doorway before he got to her.

“Angie!” he said again, seizing her arm. She flinched and he instantly loosened his grip. *Damn! He’d forgotten her dream!* Ashamed, he let his hands fall to his sides. “What is going on here?”

“Maybe I should ask you the same thing.” Her eyes flashed with the fury threatening to unleash itself on him.

“You lost me,” he said with a sigh. “Can we please start this conversation over?”

“No, we can’t start it over.” Pressing her fists against her hips, Angie widened her stance. “Unless you’re willing to be completely honest with me. Which I highly doubt that you even know how to do!”

She’s ready for a fight, thought Jared. *Fine.* “I had to go into town and pick this up,” he said, holding up a small flat box. “I’ve always been honest with you.”

“Humph! Yeah right!” Glaring at him, her toe started a tap, tap, tap on the floor.

“Listen, Angie, I don’t know what you’re so mad about. Why don’t you tell me so we can work this out?”

“I have nothing to discuss with the likes of you. I thought you were a playboy at first, but I never took you for the conniving, underhanded creep that you are.”

“Excuse me?”

“Don’t act like you don’t know what I’m talking about!”

“I honestly don’t have a clue,” he said, throwing his hands up in the air, then, angling away from her, he lowered them. “Your ranting isn’t making any sense.”

“Does the name Mary Henry Slayton mean anything to you?”

“Yes,” he said calmly, turning to face her. “She’s one of my ancestors.”

“Anything else?”

Jared studied Angie for a moment. Her toe tapped furiously now, even though the tone of her voice had become more measured. "Mary Henry," he began quietly, "was on my mother's side of the family. She married Theodore Slayton and was pregnant when he died. She vowed revenge on the Slayton's because Theodore's sister Ruby took control of the estate and sent Mary away. She had a rough life because of Ruby's actions."

"And exactly *when* were you planning on telling me about this?"

"I wasn't," he said with finality.

"See, I knew it! You're out for revenge, just like Mary."

"No, I'm not." Placing his package on the table, he studied her again. *She's getting madder,* he thought. *Can't stand that she's not making me lose my cool, I'll bet.*

"How could you let me tell you about Mary and Theodore's ghosts and never mention your connection to them?"

"Would it have mattered?"

"Yes, it matters. You came into this project under false pretenses. It matters because you offered Sam Slayton almost a million dollars for his property even before his death. It matters because you hid the truth from me and we're supposed to be partners! It matters because, even now, you want to buy me out."

Jared sighed and ran his hands through his hair. How she could say so much on one breath of air was beyond him. "When did Alan tell you?"

"He told me today but the problem is that you *didn't* tell me. You never had any intention to tell me."

"It didn't concern you."

"Didn't concern me? Are you out of your freakin' mind? I'm a partner in this inn. How can you stand there and say it didn't concern me?"

Damn if anger didn't make her more beautiful—her cheeks were tinged with rose, her eyes wide, round and sparkling. "Angie, let's get out of the hallway and sit down for a minute." He gestured to the living room couch.

"I don't want to sit down," she snapped. "You betrayed me, Jared. You were only out for revenge."

"No, Angie, you're wrong. I was never out for revenge. Yes, I offered to buy the estate from Sam and I wanted to buy you out. But that was before."

"Before what? Oh, never mind, I get it now. Were you going to offer me as much as you offered Sam, or more because of all the fooling around?"

"Angie..." He stepped toward her, hands held out in surrender. "You're misunderstanding."

"Don't touch me."

"Fine." He crossed his arms over his chest. He had grown tired of this argument. "You have to let me explain."

"Go ahead, I'm listening."

"In my family, I always heard the story of Mary Henry's need for revenge over and over again—how it was up to one of us—her descendants—to make everything right, so her spirit could rest in peace. When I became successful, I decided to put an end to it all as soon as I could. That's why I purchased my farm. It was part of the original Slayton estate. I talked to Sam Slayton and offered to buy his farm, but he refused. I even inquired about your property after your aunt died."

Angie stilled. "You did?"

Thank God her foot stopped its insane tapping. "Alan didn't tell you? I found out he was handling your aunt's estate and I asked him if you'd be willing to sell. He told me to give you time to grieve before I approached you. So I left you alone."

"Why do you want these five hundred acres so much that you're willing to hide the truth to get them?"

"Because, I've had it drilled into me that someone must avenge Mary. Preferably, me. It was a tremendous burden. I was never praised for my own success, just told that I was one step closer to buying the Slayton estate. I don't want my own children put under the same pressure I was."

"They wouldn't be unless you forced it on them."

"I would never treat my children that way, but unfortunately my family would. This thing has to stop with me."

"Why haven't you mentioned any of this to me before?"

"I changed my mind when we were forced to become partners after Sam's death."

"Changed your mind how?"

"Because you intrigued me," he said, closing the distance between them. "When you found the journal but still kept digging, I knew you'd find out the truth and my plan would be ruined."

"Oh, just great!" Angie spun away, throwing her hands up. "The rich boy hides the facts from the country girl because she intrigues him! Admit it. You thought I couldn't handle the truth." She narrowed her gaze, prowling around him like a cat preparing to pounce. "Do you really think I could ever trust a liar? I've never been so disappointed in anyone. How I ever convinced myself that you were an honest, trustworthy man is beyond me!" Walking away, she paused at the front door before facing him again. "You know what you can do with your interest and your millions of dollars, Jared Maxwell?"

"I expect you're going to tell me," he said in exasperation, shoving his hands into his pockets.

"You can take all of it—your money, your interest in me, everything—and go straight to hell! I'm not selling my part of the inn and I'll never, ever be involved with the likes of you." Angie set her chin, murdered him with her eyes, walked out the front door, slamming it behind her.

Jared let her go. There was no point trying to talk to her when she was that furious. Besides, security would keep an eye on her. He'd let her cool down a bit, then he'd go after her. If she were calm it would be easier to implement his other plan.

He picked up the box from the table and carried it to the

office. Removing the lid, he took out another box inside, opened that one, then picked up the cold object.

Sitting down in his chair he leaned back, turning the metal over in his hands. His lips lifted into a grin when the light reflected into his eyes. "I'll give you some time to cool off, my dear." He replaced the item and locked the box in the file cabinet. "One way or the other, Angelina Benton, you *will* be mine."

ANGIE KICKED THE gravel in the dirt road and sent the small rocks flying through the yard. How Jared could make her lose complete control of her emotions was beyond her.

How dare he! What a stupid, obnoxious, gorgeous hunk of a man!

Aw, geez. Angie covered her face with her hands and cursed herself. *How could I have lost my heart to that conniving jerk? How could I? More to the point, what am I going to do?*

She went and sat down at the picnic table on the lawn. He had hidden the truth. No doubt about it. But he also was acting out of love for children he didn't even have yet. If she were honest with herself, really honest, she had to admit she found this admirable. Loveable. Sexy, even.

The voice of the security guard caused her to look up. He was talking on his radio.

She shook her head to clear it. *Jared's a dishonest creep, Angie,* she admonished herself as she stood up and kicked a large white rock. *How could he flirt with me and set me up at the same time?*

A while later, still kicking the rock ahead of her, she came to a decision. Jared would never have what he wanted so badly—the original five hundred acre Slayton homestead. He'd lied to her. Not just once, but many times. He'd have to remain her partner until she died, but that couldn't be helped. Her share of the inn would then go to her relatives, forcing her family to always to be partners with his. That was unfortunate, but far better than the alternative.

She'd have Alan see to the legalities.

Suddenly she realized that she was in front of the Davis house. Had she been so lost in her thoughts of Jared that she'd just wandered off? She remembered the stalker, turned back toward the homestead, quickening her step.

A crunch behind her made Angie stop dead and listen intently to the night. *It's probably an animal. I won't let it scare me.*

Then she heard the footsteps.

Looking over her shoulder she thought she saw the outline of a large man in the moonlight. As soon as he started to laugh—a dark, evil laugh that pulled the pit of her stomach to her throat—she ducked into the bushes.

"You can't hide from me, Angie baby."

Oh God! No! It's the man from the barn fire! Jumping from behind her cover, Angie raced up the road. Panic made her feet fly faster and faster over the ground.

Not fast enough.

He grabbed her arms from behind, jerked her shoulder blades together. Her scream echoed though the forest, mixing with his diabolical laughter.

"Angie!" yelled Jared, from somewhere up the road. "Where are you? Angie!"

Angie bit the man's arm and he loosened his grip.

She bolted away from him, shouting, "I'm over here! Jared!"

A large arm wrapped around her neck, stopping her mid-flight. Something round, cold and hard dug into her back.

"Don't make another sound," the man growled.

"Jared, he's got a gun!" Angie screamed.

Her attacker pulled her hard up against him with his left arm, her back to his chest. The next thing she heard was a shot ringing out.

"Jared!"

Angie's heart ripped apart when she heard a moan, followed by a solid thump. *Oh, God, he's killed Jared!*

She screamed his name again, just as the metal butt of the gun slammed against her skull. Pain exploded through her head.

The last thing she remembered was the night turning to complete darkness as she hit the ground.

EIGHTEEN

"HELLO!" ALAN PUSHED OPEN THE UNLOCKED DOOR, yelling into the Slayton house. "Anybody in here?"

He had telephoned all morning, only to get the answering machine. He decided to drive over since he needed Angie's signature on some paperwork.

If only his matchmaking had worked. After Angie's reaction over Jared, the sooner he was out of this, the better. They could fight each other until they realized what he could already see.

Walking through the house, he found it empty. *They must be on the farm,* he thought, spying Burt through a window.

"Hello, Burt," Alan called, as he exited the porch and walked down toward the stables where Burt was working on a tractor.

"Howdy, Alan."

"Where are Jared and Angie working today?"

"I haven't seen them." He closed the hood and walked around the machine, wiping his hands on a blue bandanna.

"Neither of them? What time did you get here?"

"Around six this morning."

Alan glanced at his watch. One in the afternoon. "Are the horses here?"

"Yep, fed them both this morning."

"Wonder where they could be."

"Did you check the bedroom?" Burt grinned, rubbing his face with the bandana.

"No, why would I look there?" Alan studied him.

"There's some mighty big sparks flying between those two, if you ask me."

"Are you saying they're sleeping together?"

"Nah, they may be fooling around a bit, but that Angie, you know she's saving herself for marriage."

"Okay, I'll check the house again," Alan said, turning back to the inn. "Thanks, Burt."

Inside the house Alan searched for Angie and Jared. When he got to her room, he found a crinkled piece of paper on her bed. He picked it up and read the note. "Oh my God!"

Hurrying back outside he ran toward the barn, "Burt! Where are you, Burt?"

The other man exited the barn, leading Thunder. "I'm right here. What's wrong?"

The lines in Alan's face deepened as he frowned and held up the paper. "I found this note on Angie's pillow."

Burt winced. "What does it say?"

Alan read it aloud.

"This is the third and last of my messages Angie baby. I wonder if you'll get this before I get you? Tonight's the night your blood will spill."

"Damn!" said Burt.

"Has Angie received two other messages, Burt?"

"I…um…" he didn't look at Alan, instead busied himself with the horse.

Alan reached over, grabbed his forearm. "Burt, I'm seventy-seven years old. I think I can handle the truth. This is important—I need to know."

"Yeah, she did." Burt threw the reins over Thunder's neck. "Secrets always have a way of coming out, don't they?"

"What did the notes say?"

"Just threats to scare her. I don't remember the exact words."

"Let me guess. Angie didn't want me to worry so she asked everyone who knew to keep them a secret from me."

"That's about the size of it."

A muscle twitched in Alan's jaw. "Let's check Clyde Davis' house. Saddle up Whisper, Burt. We're going to look for them. It's not like Angie to disappear like this." Fear for Angie clenched at his heart as her dream pounded in his brain.

"Alan, maybe you're overreacting."

"If you won't saddle her, I will."

Burt didn't argue but handed Thunder's reins to Alan then headed back inside the stable.

Alan followed. "When I was in the house I called the security company Jared hired and told then to send extra men. Sheriff Oakley's sending deputies out to check both of their homes. We're to meet him here in an hour."

"Don't worry, Alan," Burt said as he readied Whisper. "We'll find them."

Back outside, they mounted and walked the horses, searching the ground for clues until they were almost to the old Davis house.

"Burt, look!" Alan urged Thunder forward then dismounted.

"What did you find?" Burt asked, stopping alongside Alan.

"This section of road is full of marks, as if people were scuffling here."

Burt looked down at the road and dismounted. "Alan, these marks were probably made by an animal."

"I don't think so. Look, there are shoe marks."

Burt walked around the marks, inspecting them. He bent down then sat back on his haunches, lifted his hat and scratched his head. "I just don't see it, Alan. It's hard to tell what made this."

Both men stood up and began looking in a wider area around the scuff marks.

"I think I found something," Burt said, his voice thick with concern. Burt pointed down at a tie-dyed scrunchie beside the ditch on the edge of the road.

Alan walked over. He drew in a sharp breath. "Angie was wearing that when I met with her yesterday."

"Let's take this to the house." Burt bent to pick up the piece of fabric.

"No, don't touch it." Alan grabbed his arm, stopping him. "We'll bring the deputies back here."

ANGIE LAY MOTIONLESS against the hard damp ground, listening for her attacker. Only birdsongs filled the air and the birds couldn't tell her where she was.

Her thoughts flew to Jared—he'd been shot. *Please let him be alive!* She'd been wrong about him all along. Who cared if he was a descendent of Mary and Theodore Slayton? It seemed so unimportant now.

She should have listened to Alan, taken his advice. She'd let her fear and suspicions keep her from the man she loved. If she got out of this one, Jared Maxwell would know how much she loved him. She'd give herself to him, body and soul, married or not.

Angie twisted against the ropes. *This must be how a hog feels when he's tied,* she thought. *Lucky for the hog that his legs are short.* Her arms and legs ached from being tied together behind her.

She felt the rope with her fingertips. She'd struggled with the knot near her feet for hours yet it still held tight. At least she'd gotten her shoes off and eased the pain in her ankles.

If only she could see.

Angie rolled to her stomach, then to her other side. Changing positions lessened the pain in her shoulder and hip, at least for a while. She could smell the earth underneath her. She supposed the gag was a blessing since every time she moved a fine layer of dust settled over her face and the gag kept it out of her mouth.

Stay strong, focused and above all remain calm, she told herself.

Wriggling her foot she tried to push the rope over her heel. If she could just get one foot loose, the knot would be easier to untie.

She'd been working at the rope for a while when she heard the footsteps outside and froze.

The bump of the door told her he was inside. The dust settling against her bare skin told her he stood right beside her.

When the coolness of water soaked the gag, she sucked desperately against the cloth. She hadn't realized she was so thirsty.

She tried to speak, to beg him to let her go. The cold steel of a gun barrel moving slowly down her cheek, then neck, silenced her. His breath, hot against her face, reeked of liquor.

"I'll be back to make love to you, Angie baby." His voice was low and raspy as a large hand cupped her breast and the steel of the gun slid between her legs. His sinister laughter echoed around her.

Another bump, wood scraping against wood and he was gone.

This is no time to panic, said a little voice in her mind.

Tell that to my heart. She could barely hear herself think with it pounding in her ears.

Think Angie! What makes that sound? It only took a minute to put the sound and smells together. *I'm in a tobacco barn!*

Since she couldn't see, she imagined the inside of the one-roomed barns. The two doors on opposite walls, rows of burners ran parallel to the doors between the door opening and the walls without doors. So…with her back to the door she needed to scoot in the direction of her head or feet.

Angie rocked her body until, at last, her hand touched one of the metal burners used to cure the leaves. *I'm right!*

Feeling along the metal, in search of a sharp edge, the man's laugh echoed through her thoughts.

She didn't recognize his voice from anywhere except the break-in and the hay barn, he had done both of those things. Something about his laugh was hauntingly familiar.

A sharp protrusion pricked at her finger. Yes!

Positioning her hands around the metal, she started to rub the ropes hard against it.

He might come back any minute. I have to hurry!

She thought back to the intruder in the house and the man at the hay barn as she worked.

Who wants me dead?

Searching through her memories for someone with blue eyes and an evil laugh, she'd almost given up again when a memory struck her.

She stilled.

Oh my God! her mind screamed, *it can't be! It just can't be!*

SHERIFF TREVOR OAKLEY leaned against the police SUV, radio in hand, waiting for a response from Deputy Langford. After bloodstains were discovered on Angie's scrunchie, Sheriff Oakley assigned more deputies to widen the search of the five hundred acre farm. He'd also called in Doc Martin because Alan wasn't looking very well.

Trevor shuddered. He'd known Angie her entire life. This was the worst part of his job. If anyone hurt her… He pushed the thought aside. Angie had to be alive.

The Sheriff heard the baying of the hounds in the distance. Pressing a button, he spoke into the radio. "Langford, what'd you find?"

"You'd better get over to the Davis place, Sheriff. I'm in the forest behind the house, down near the creek."

Trevor told Alan and Doc, who were sitting on the porch, to stay put, then got inside the patrol car and prepared himself for the worst.

JASPER LANGFORD PUT the radio back on his belt and called over his shoulder for Deputy Sims, "Keith, over here!"

Langford approached the medium-sized tree and the man tied to it. Jared Maxwell was sitting on the ground—his feet and arms were around the trunk, there was blood on his shirt. The ropes that tied his ankles and wrists together were soaked with blood from his apparent struggle to get free. A red bandanna gagged him.

"Hang on there, Mr. Maxwell." Langford bent down to untie the gag from Jared's mouth first.

"Where's Angie?" Jared choked out the words.

Langford lifted a piece of the torn blood-soaked fabric from Jared's upper arm. The long wound wasn't too deep where a bullet had grazed the flesh. "Aw man, you've been shot. Looks minor though."

"Hold still while I cut you loose," said Deputy Sims as he took a knife out of his pocket and flipped it open.

"Mr. Maxwell, what happened to you?" Langford asked while Sims cut the ropes holding Jared's hands and feet around the tree.

"Where's Angie?" Jared demanded, while Langford helped him stand.

"She's still missing," said Sims.

"Missing? She didn't go back to the house last night?"

"No," Langford held Jared's uninjured arm to steady him. "We thought the two of you were together until just now, when we found you."

A sound of a vehicle driving up drifted down the hill.

"There's the Sheriff now. Hang on to me, I'll help you up this hill."

"I can walk!" Jared snapped, jerking his arm away from the deputy. Wincing in pain, he stormed up the incline to the SUV. It was bad enough someone had shot him, knocked him out and tied him up to a damn tree. There was no way in hell he'd let that deputy help him walk!

"Trevor, where's Angie?" Jared exploded as he reached the Sheriff.

"Maybe that's a question I should ask you."

"Me? Damn man! I've been tied to a tree since last night and you think I did something with Angie?"

"Sheriff, he's telling the truth," interrupted Sims. "We just got him loose. He has a bullet graze on his arm that should be bandaged."

Jared glared at Sims.

"Sorry, Mr. Maxwell, just doing my job."

"Fine. I have to find Angie."

"Get in," stated Trevor, indicating the SUV.

"We have to look for her," Jared argued, standing his ground. "What if the lunatic who trapped her in the hay barn has her again?

"First, we need to take care of your arm. Second, I need a statement from you. And lastly, I've got a lot of men looking for Angie already. Maybe something you tell me will help us find her quicker."

Reluctantly Jared got inside the vehicle. As Trevor drove him back to the house, he stretched the muscles in his legs, easing out the cramps while listening to the details on the search for Angie.

When they entered the kitchen of the Slayton inn, Jared headed straight for the sink. His mouth was so dry it hurt to talk. He drank a glass of water while Trevor called out, "Doc! Alan! Get in here—we found Jared!"

Jared washed his face and hands hurriedly then sat down at the kitchen table. He was dead tired and weak but every fiber of his body still ached to act, to do something to find Angie.

I can't lose her. Not now. Not like this.

Sheriff Oakley sat beside Jared and took a notepad from his pocket. Alan and Doc Martin rushed into the room.

Alan immediately squeezed Jared's shoulder, shook his hand. "Thank God you're all right. We have to find her, Jared."

"We will," Jared replied, alarmed that Alan looked to have aged twenty years. "Are you okay, Alan?"

"I'll be fine when my Angie's back. She's like a daughter to me." Alan's brows knit together. He turned Jared's hand, twisting it to inspect the rope burns on his wrist. "Doc, you need to patch this boy up, he's got rope burns on his wrists and ripped flesh on his arm. My God, we must be dealing with a lunatic. How'd you get these injuries, son?"

"He shot at me then tied me to a damn tree."

Sheriff Oakley put pen to paper. "Okay Jared. Start from the last time you saw Angie." He said, beginning to write.

Jared looked at Alan and the sheriff then explained the events of the previous night.

He faced Alan. "She was mad because you told her about my connection to the Slaytons. She said I was out for revenge. I tried to explain, but she wouldn't listen and stormed out of the house. I knew security would watch her so I gave her some time to cool off." Jared paused to drink.

"The guard said she was by the picnic table. The other guard radioed him and the next time he looked over, she'd vanished. I immediately went to search for her."

"Jared, I thought she had a right to know." Alan said.

"Don't worry about it, Alan. I should have told her. I should have told both of you."

Jared clarified a few points for the sheriff's notes, then

continued. "I called out to her but she never answered me. Then I thought I heard her scream. The sound came from the road to the Davis house so I headed that way. She yelled that he had a gun just as he fired it."

He took another long draught of water. "I dropped my flashlight when the bullet hit my arm. He attacked me, hit me over the head with it and the next thing I remember is waking up in the dark, tied to the tree. I tried to get loose but it was impossible."

"Tell me about the man," asked Oakley. "Did you see him at all?"

"The only thing I know is that he's taller and bigger than me. He had on a long-sleeved shirt and gloves."

"Okay, here's what we're going to do," Oakley folded up his pad and stuck it back in his pocket. "I've got every available deputy out here already, so I'm putting out a request for community assistance to search these three farms. Based upon the tracks we found where he took Angie—"

"What do you mean?" Jared asked in a panic. "That crazed maniac has her?"

"After what you just told me, I think he might. Alan found this on her pillow." Sheriff Oakley handed Jared an evidence bag containing the note and addressed Alan. "Is there anyone who would want to hurt Angie?"

"No one I know of. I can't lose Angie, Trevor. Not after losing Martha such a short time ago. I don't think my old heart can take it. I'll go call some of Angie's friends. See what I can find out. Promise me you'll find her."

Throwing the bag on the table, Jared pushed his chair back. "I'll promise you, Alan. I'll never stop looking until we find her. Now, we need to quit talking and get back out there. Where's this place you found and why do you think she disappeared from there?"

"Mr. Maxwell, you don't need to go anywhere after what you

went through last night," said Doc Martin. "Just stay here and wait. I need to dress your wounds."

"Like hell I will!" he complained, then looked toward the officer in charge. "Unless you're going to arrest me, Sheriff, I'm going to look for her. Now where's the place?"

"We found the scrunchie she wore yesterday on the road to the old Davis place, right by the big fig tree." Sighing heavily, Trevor looked Jared in the eye. "The scrunchie was bloody, so we're assuming that Angie's been hurt. We won't know for sure until we get the lab analysis back. I'm making every effort to increase the size of the search party, we need to find her quickly."

Storming out of the house, Jared's long strides carried him down the road back to the Davis house.

The sheriff's words rang in his ears—the scrunchie was bloody. It was one thing to tie him up all night but to take Angie, to hurt her…

Jared remembered her scream. His stomach pitched when he realized she must have been unconscious while he was being attacked.

How could I fail her this way? The muscles in his jaw tightened, his steps grew further apart. *We haven't even had a chance to be together because I hid the truth from her. She vanished because she left the house, angry with me.*

And I let her go.

Regardless of the consequences, I'll find you, Angelina. That animal will pay for hurting you.

THE SWEAT RAN down Angie's arms, stinging her wrists. She knew they were bleeding. The warm stickiness of blood coated her palms.

She was almost free. She checked the thinness of the rope where she'd rubbed it against the burners. Just a little more…

She pushed hard against the metal and the rope snapped.

Hurry! Hurry! she thought, bringing her arms in front of her. She didn't expect the fiery-hot spasm that seared through her shoulders. She gasped then held her breath in case he had heard her.

She twisted to bring her legs forward. An equally excruciating sensation rushed up to her hips. Tears streaked down her face from the pain and she struggled fiercely to silence her sobs.

Ripping the gag and blindfold off her face, she looked in shock at the red bandannas. *It is Burt!* They were his—she knew it—she saw him with them every day. *How could he do this to me?* Throwing them onto the dirt floor of the barn, she thrust her feet into her sneakers and quickly stood.

Her legs crumpled beneath her.

Come on legs...work! She had to survive for herself and for Jared, if he was still alive. He had to know how much she loved him. Burt would *not* take her virginity.

Standing again, legs weak but functioning, Angie tried to open the door closest to her.

Locked.

Stumbling to the other door, she gently pushed. It moved a little. Hope lifting her heart, she quietly pushed harder and harder, ignoring the pains still surging through her body, until at last she fell through the door.

Blinded by the late-afternoon sunlight, she moved quietly away from the barn, not alerting her captor, then she started to run. Her body screamed in protest but she didn't stop to listen.

Laughter rang out through the forest. Terror ripped at her heart. She grabbed a tree for support, heard the crackle of snapped branches. No way would he catch her this time! Adrenaline pumped through her as she sprinted through the trees.

She fought the brush and bramble that tore at her clothes. She needed to find a safe place to hide. Her wounded legs wouldn't let her keep up this pace much longer.

She tripped over a tree root and slid face-first across the forest floor. A briar ripped into her jeans, tore the flesh underneath. She slipped on the damp forest leaves that caught in her clothes and hair as she struggled to get back on her feet.

The footsteps drew nearer, strong and deliberate. Angie looked over her shoulder but couldn't see any sign of her pursuer.

Running into a clearing, she spotted the shack on the other side.

This is it—I'm really living my dream!

She plowed ahead toward the house. It was her only hope. Maybe he'd trap her there. But what else could she do? Leaping onto the porch, she flung open the broken door. In the room on the left, she saw the same contents from her dream. I know what to do! She ran straight to the back door. No! He was headed across the yard toward the shack.

She ran to the antique hutch, crouched down behind it. If she went out of the back door he'd be there, just like in the dream. Maybe she could change the outcome if she went out through the front door.

The old pine floors creaked under his weight. Angie held her breath, listened to him move methodically through the shack, searching room by room.

At last, the footsteps left the house.

Cautiously she stood.

Front or back?

She glanced through the house for him, then moved toward the back door, looked out into the yard. She wouldn't relive her dream. No way.

Running down the hallway, she slammed out of the front door, jumped off the porch and ran toward a large tree.

I did it! I changed the dream! Still terrified, she ran behind the tree to hide.

And crashed right into him.

"Oh God! No!" she screamed, violently twisting her body. His fingers pushed into her flesh, pain seared through her arms. He growled her name…

"Angelina!"

She looked up into worried blue eyes and collapsed in his arms.

"Shhh. It's okay. I've got you now." Jared lowered her to the ground. "How badly are you hurt?"

She latched her arms around his neck. "I'm okay."

Jared kissed the top of her head. "Stay here. He's by the house. I've got a score to settle with him."

She angled her face from his chest to look at the house. Jared disengaged her arms and started to stand. She grabbed his hand. Bright red rope burns encircled his wrists. "Jared, what happened?" she whispered.

"I'll tell you later. Don't move."

"No, stay with me!" the words caught in her throat. She could only watch as he moved from tree to tree along the edge of the forest before crossing to the shack. When he disappeared behind the dilapidated building, she stood, supporting herself against the tree.

The blast of a gunshot rang through the air. Her heart stopped.

"No! No!" Screaming his name, she ran around the side of the shack into the backyard and stopped dead in her tracks.

Hank Emerson, Burt's son, lay unconscious on the ground with a bullet wound in his leg.

Running over to where Jared stood, Angie threw herself into his arms, holding him tight. "I thought I'd lost you!"

Picking her up, Jared carried her to the steps. "You scared me, Angie. When you disappeared last night I came after you." He took her hands in his, stared at the dried blood on her wrists. "I should kill him."

"No, Jared, I did this to myself, when I escaped. Let the police handle it," she said. Taking his face in her hands, she kissed him lightly. "I love you, Jared Maxwell."

Jared's lips crushed against hers. The emotions held in since last night poured from her. Possessing his mouth with the kiss, Angie knew she wanted him, forever. "Take me home, Jared. Take me home," she whispered against his lips.

Nineteen

"THANK GOD YOU'RE OKAY! I DON'T KNOW WHEN I'VE been more afraid." Alan gently rubbed the ends of Angie's wet hair in the towel.

She had insisted on a shower after Doc stitched her scalp, since he wouldn't agree to let her have one until the wound was thoroughly cleansed and sutured. The water had stung her rope burns but now she at least felt clean.

"It's over now." She turned slightly from her chair at the kitchen table to smile at him.

"Hold still, we're almost finished." Doc Martin said, wrapping the white gauze bandage around her wrist.

Jared, freshly showered, came into the room.

"You're next." Angie smiled up at him.

"I'm fine," he insisted, leaning down to kiss her. "How bad is she, Doc?"

"Three stitches in her scalp, rope burns, cuts and scratches. I want her to rest for the next twenty-four hours. Bring her to my office tomorrow afternoon so I can check these wounds and change the bandages."

"You've got it," Jared said, sitting beside Angie.

Alan continued towel drying her hair. "Angie, do you know why Hank would do this?"

"You know, I hate to admit it, but I thought it was Burt when I pulled off my gag and blindfold and saw the red bandannas. When I saw Hank lying on the ground…" her voice trailed off as she examined her bandages. "Lord only knows why he did this!" she said angrily. "I've been racking my brain trying to figure it out. The only thing I ever did that could have upset him was refusing to have sex with him. That was years ago. We only went out a few times and he sure didn't seem upset then." Angie glanced up at Doc. "Is Burt okay?"

Doc Martin took another roll of gauze out of his bag. "Honestly, I've never seen Burt this upset. He went to the hospital."

"Alan, what's going to happen to Hank?" she asked quietly.

Doc Martin gathered his medical supplies, stationing himself near Jared. Alan sat in Doc's place beside Angie and took her hand in his. "They'll do a psychological evaluation before they release him from the hospital. Then he'll go to jail until the trial."

"Where's Trevor?" she asked, accepting the glass of water Jared handed her.

"He took Hank to the hospital since he was in custody," replied Alan. "Hank confessed to living in that little storage shed near where Jared fought with him."

"Let me see your wrists, Jared," said Doc Martin.

"I'm fine Doc, really."

"Give me your arm."

Jared did as he was told. "That explains the noises I heard in that building at the beginning of summer. I meant to go back, but I never got around to it once the renovation started. Now I wish I had."

"You couldn't have known, Jared." Alan said, putting down the towel.

"How did you get those rope burns?" Angie gazed at Jared, her heart tightened. She'd almost lost him.

"He tied me to a tree."

"How did Hank get shot?" Doc Martin asked then started wrapping Jared's other wrist.

"We struggled. He pointed it down, pulled the trigger and shot himself in the leg right before I knocked him out."

"He could have killed you!" gasped Angie. "It serves him right!" she blurted out. "He ran that damn gun down the side of my face, trying to scare me."

The men stared at her for a moment, grasping the reality of what she had just said.

A thick silence lingered in the air. Doc Martin cleared his throat. "Well, now. I, for one, am glad it's over and you're safe. Angie, I want you to go up to bed right now. Stay there until you come to my office tomorrow." He turned to Jared. "You're done."

"I'll carry her up." Jared said, taking her hand.

"You're not going to carry me anywhere. I can walk." Angie stood but her knees gave way beneath her.

Jared scooped her into his arms. "Thank you, Doc. Please give any other instructions to Alan. I'm putting her in bed," he said, as he carried her across the room.

Doc Martin looked intently into Angie's pale face as Jared headed toward the stairs. "Call if you need me, Angie."

"I will, Doc. Thank you," she answered.

His brows furrowed with concern, Doc turned to Alan. "I didn't want to say anything in front of Angie, but you need to hire one of your buddies to prosecute Hank just to make sure he can never get to her again."

"Hank will be put away for a long time if I have anything to do with it," Alan told him as they made their way to the front door.

"Good." Doc picked up his bag. "I'm going home now. Make

sure she sleeps and call if her condition changes."

"I will. Thanks, Doc," Alan closed the front door behind the doctor, turned and looked upstairs. *Angie's safe,* he thought, as a wave of relief overcame him.

JARED SAT ON the edge of the bed, holding Angie's hand. The gauze bandages on her wrists filled him with guilt.

Her injuries were his fault. She ran out of the house and had nearly been killed because he lied. He had caused her emotional and physical pain.

Yet she had said she loved him.

"Angie, I'm sorry I hid the truth from you. It was stupid and wrong." He caressed her hand. "Can you forgive me?"

"You're forgiven," she whispered, her eyelids fluttering. "Lie down with me?"

"I don't know if that's a good idea."

Lifting her lids, she smiled at him. "I just want to fall asleep in your arms."

"You mean you're not going to attack me?" he said, then winced at the word, cursing himself for his carelessness.

"Not now," she laughed, "I'm too tired."

"Then I guess I can lie with you for a while." Kicking off his shoes, he slid under the covers. Angie snuggled into the crook of his arm, rested her head on his shoulder. Jared linked his fingers with hers. Snuggling, Angie molded her body against his.

Soon her breathing became rhythmic. Jared watched her sleep, wondering what it would be like to wake up with her every morning. Resting his cheek on the top of her head, he closed his eyes. A few more minutes and he'd go to his room.

When Jared didn't come back downstairs Alan went up to check on Angie. Peering through her open door, he smiled. Angie was cuddled against Jared in her bed. Both of them were sound asleep.

Alan closed the bedroom door. They'll be fine, he assured himself and maybe his matchmaking had worked after all.

ANGIE STIRRED AND pain shot through her stiff and sore body. Her pillow felt too hard so she snuggled into it and an arm tightened around her back.

Her eyelids flew open.

Jared lay beside her. Asleep, but still holding her. She sighed, *what a great way to wake up. I want to do this for the rest of my life.*

Watching him, she noticed his pulse beating against his neck and knew in her heart that she couldn't have him. *Savor the moment Angie,* she told herself, *because it will never happen again.*

He doesn't love you.

She'd said those three little words but he hadn't.

In the rush of the kiss that followed, she'd hoped they could be together. Now she knew he just wasn't one to settle down. If he was—if he loved her—wouldn't he have told her after all they'd both been through?

Jared shifted, blinking his eyelids, then rubbing them with his free hand.

The man is even sexy waking up, she thought. Leaning forward she kissed his neck, then his jaw before nibbling on his ear.

"Umm…" He grinned, wrapping his other arm around her, drawing her close. "Good morning, beautiful."

"Good morning." Smiling, she saw his blue eyes darken with desire. "I didn't know you were going to stay with me all night."

"Neither did I."

"Thank you, Jared." Laying her head across his chest she listened to the steady thump of his heartbeat and smiled when the pace quickened.

"You're welcome. How are you feeling?"

"Stiff. Sore. Safe."

"Come here, you." Jared pulled her on top of him, smiling as her dark tresses fell across his shoulders. "I was so worried, Angelina. I don't know what I would have done if I'd lost you."

"But you found me. You saved me."

"It wasn't enough. If I'd told you the truth from the beginning this wouldn't have happened."

"Don't talk about it right now. I want to enjoy waking up with you for just a little longer."

His eyes danced with happiness, a smile tugged at the corners of his mouth. "You are so amazing."

"Nah, you've just got sleep in your eyes."

"That's not what I have in my eyes and you know it."

"Jared Maxwell, what am I going to do with you?" Laughing, she tried to roll off him, but he held her tight.

"You're not going anywhere. Not until I give you a good morning kiss."

She laughed. "I need to brush my teeth first."

"Who says?"

Jared pressed his lips against hers, pulling her back down on top of him as he settled into the pillow. His kiss was slow, gentle. Nipping her bottom lip, he teased her mouth open and tangling his fingers in her hair he deepened the kiss.

Suddenly, Angie stopped the kiss.

"What's wrong? Did I hurt you?"

"My head. It's tender." *My heart, it's broken!*

"I'm sorry. I forgot." He moved his hands to her waist.

"I think we better get out of this bed now, don't you?" Wiggling off him, she lay on her stomach beside him.

"Nope, you're supposed to stay in bed all day."

"You don't really expect me to, do you?"

"Yes," he said, squeezing her butt. "You keep lying there like that and I might want you to do more."

Her eyes narrowed. Her heart plummeted even more. "Watch it buddy!" She forced a grin. "Kimmie's wedding is Saturday. I've got to help her."

Sitting up she flung her legs over the side of the bed, stood, wavered, sat down again.

"See why you need to stay in here?" Jared snaked his arm around her waist, gently pulling her back down beside him. "Why are you getting up anyway?"

"Bathroom."

"How about this way?" Getting out of bed with Angie in his arms he carried her to the bathroom, stood her in front of the toilet. "Can you manage from here or do I need to stay?"

The heat in her face told her she had flushed crimson. She gave him a little shove. "Thank you. Now go." *This is too comfortable,* she thought.

"Call me when you're done." He closed the door, leaving Angie alone.

The smell of bacon and coffee drifted up the stairs. Suddenly Jared realized they weren't the only two in the house. He put on his shoes and went down to the kitchen.

Alan stood at the stove leaning over the sizzling strips, pushing them around in the pan with a fork.

"Morning, Alan. You're here early."

"I slept here last night."

"You did? Where?"

"On the couch. Here, take this." He handed Jared a plate of sausage links.

"You should have slept in one of the bedrooms upstairs. This smells great—I'm famished. Want a cup of coffee?"

"Sure, black."

"Why'd you stay over?"

"I came upstairs to check on Angie and the two of you were asleep in her bed. I realized you were exhausted too, so I decided to stay here in case either of you needed anything." He lifted a slice of bacon out of the pan and placed it on a plate covered with two paper towels. "I checked in a couple of times during the night but you both were out cold. Is Angie up yet?"

"She woke up a little while ago. I left her in the bathroom." He put Alan's coffee on the counter beside the stove. "I hope you didn't get the wrong impression, Alan. Nothing happened."

"It's none of my business if it did."

"Angie's like a daughter to you. I want to assure you that I would never hurt her."

"Not intentionally. Angie wears her heart on her sleeve, if you haven't already noticed."

"I know, Alan. That's why I need your help and if you agree, you'll see exactly what my intentions are with Angie."

Alan narrowed his eyes. "What are you up too?"

The best way to keep the rest of his plan from being ruined would be to let Alan in on it. He looked down the hall to make sure Angie was still upstairs. "Can you keep a secret?" Jared grinned.

"You bet. Tell me."

DOC MARTIN UNWRAPPED the bandages from Angie's wrists and ankles. "How are you feeling today?"

"A lot better. I slept great last night." *No dreams.* She inspected her wrists. They looked better already.

"Your injuries are healing nicely. I want you to change these bandages in the morning and at night and keep ointment on the abrasions. It will speed the healing and help prevent scarring."

"Is Jared healing nicely too?" Doc had examined Jared first at her insistence.

"Don't worry, Jared will be fine."

"Do I have to come back?"

Ignoring the question he shone a light in her eyes. "Does your head hurt?"

"No, but the place you stitched is tender."

Moving her hair out of the way, he examined the cut. "There's no sign of infection. You're lucky you didn't get a concussion."

He sat down to write out a prescription, then, tearing the sheet from the pad he handed it to her. "This is for the ointment. Put some on each time you change the bandages. The stitches I gave you will dissolve on their own. I don't see any reason for you to come back to the office unless something changes."

"Please tell me I don't have to stay confined to bed."

"No more bed rest, but don't overdo it. If you feel tired, go lie down for a while."

"Good," she said softly, "Doc, can I ask you something?"

"Of course. What's on your mind?"

"Can you give me a prescription for birth control pills?"

Doc Martin pinned her with a look of concern. "What happened to your vow of celibacy until marriage?"

"I…might…" Her voice shook so she cleared her throat to steady it. *Yes, I love Jared completely,* she reasoned. "I might change my mind. If I do, I don't want to get pregnant the first time I have sex."

"That's a very responsible way to think." He looked in her chart, flipping a few pages, "You had your yearly physical six months ago. Okay, I'll be right back," he said leaving the room. Moments later, he came back with six sample packages of birth control pills.

He explained in depth how to take the medication and other preventive measures she should take during the first month. "Make sure you watch the expiration date on these, in case you don't start on them right away. If you need it, I'll give you a prescription at your next physical."

"Thank you for everything, Doc."

"You don't have to thank me. I'm just relieved your injuries were minimal. We were all very worried about you." He patted her shoulder. "I want you to give some serious thought to what you really want before starting those pills."

ANGIE WALKED IN the house with Jared to catch Alan and Mrs. Turner whispering in the living room.

Immediately suspicious, Angie put her fists on her hips and narrowed her eyes, "What's going on in here?"

"Oh, my! How are you dear?" Mrs. Turner chattered, "What did Doc Martin say? I'm so sorry to hear about the terrible nightmare you went through. Hank Emerson must be crazy to think he could get away with kidnapping you!" Grabbing Angie in a tight hug, she whispered, "I'm so glad you're okay."

"Thank you, Mrs. Turner. But I'm still a little sore."

"Oh silly me! And here I am hugging the living daylights out of you. Forgive me?"

"Of course." Angie smiled at her. "What's going on, Alan?"

"Nothing, honey. What did Doc say?"

"That I'll be fine. No more bed rest but I'm to take it easy."

"I'm so relieved," Alan said with a smile.

"I'm still waiting for one of you to tell me what's going on in here," Angie complained, darting her eyes from Alan to Mrs. Turner who burst out in giggles.

"Why don't I walk you upstairs?" Jared took her hand.

Angie continued to stare at Alan and Mrs. Turner, as Jared led her out of the room and up the steps. "Those two are up to something. I just know it."

"They're probably just discussing wedding plans."

"I don't think so. Something else is going on."

"I wouldn't worry too much about it. You know how Mrs. Turner gets." Stopping at her door, he leaned down to kiss her cheek. "Are you going to rest?"

"Yes. I might take Whisper out for a ride a little later."

"Are you sure you feel up to riding?"

"Positive." Angie went inside her room to put her purse on the bed.

"Then I'll go with you. I have to check on the Davis house first but we'll go for a ride before dinner."

"That sounds great," she said, returning to him.

"Get some rest." Jared gave her a quick kiss then closed the door.

Angie turned the knob to lock it. Removing the samples from her purse, she took them to her dresser, shoved them into one of her clean socks, buried it underneath the other socks and closed the dresser drawer. She went to the bedroom window and saw Jared crossing the yard. Now to find out what was going on between Alan and Mrs. Turner.

She hurried downstairs but couldn't find them inside. She went into the yard just in time to see both of their cars going up the dirt road.

"Angie!"

She whirled around. Burt was walking toward her. "Hi, Burt."

"Angie, how can I begin to say how sorry I am for what Hank did to you?" Taking her hands, he lowered his eyes. "I never thought I'd disown my son but I'm damn near close to it right now."

"Burt, you listen to me. It's not your fault. Hank's a grown man and responsible for his own actions."

"It's just…I…" Burt raised his eyes to hers, Angie saw they were filled with unshed tears. "You're like a daughter…" He choked on the words.

"It's okay, Burt." She hugged him, instantly regretting her previous suspicions. "Is Hank going to be all right?"

Burt pulled out of her embrace. "How can you even ask about

Hank after all the horrible things he did to you this summer?"

"Because he's your son. I care about you, Burt. I've known your family my whole life." Angie sat down on the picnic table bench. "Now, what did the doctors say?"

Burt sat beside her. "Hank had a high blood alcohol level. He's been ranting about you since they got him to the hospital."

"Why would he still be thinking about me after all these years?"

Burt blushed. "You're the only woman who ever told him no when he wanted to have sex."

"You're kidding, right?" Angie stared at him in wide-eyed amazement.

"That's what Hank said at the hospital. I thought he was still dating that girl he hooked up with after you. He's been distant lately, but I didn't think anything was wrong."

"Have they taken him to jail or is he still in the hospital?"

"He'll be in the hospital until his leg is better, then they're transferring him."

"Burt, I didn't want to press charges but Trevor didn't give me a choice because of the multiple attempts on my life. I'm insisting that Hank receives professional help too. I feel he'll get better results in a rehabilitation setting than a standard prison, but I don't know how much say I'll have in it."

He looked at her. "You amaze me, Angie. He's my son and I don't think I could be that generous. What he did to you is unforgivable."

"I saw it coming," she rubbed her eyes, "but I misinterpreted my dream and thought someone else was going to hurt me."

He shook his head. "I've heard about your premonition dreams. I'm sorry about all of this. I really am."

"You just help your son get better, okay?"

Burt nodded as the crunch of gravel drew their attention up the road. "Here comes Kimmie."

"There's something going on around here. Do you know what it is?" she asked, leaning back on the picnic table. "Oh, never mind, you wouldn't tell me if you did know."

He wiped his face with his red bandanna then stood, grinning at her. "You're right, I wouldn't tell if I knew anything, which I don't."

"Angie! Burt!" Kimmie shouted as she jogged toward the picnic table. "How are you feeling, girlfriend? I can't believe what that monster did to you. Oh man. Burt, that was mean of me. I'm sorry."

"Don't fret, Kimmie, it's your mama's genes, you can't help it. Angie, if Jared needs me, I'm going to check the landmarks on the trail. I'm taking Thunder."

"I'll let him know. See ya later, Burt."

Angie watched him stride away then turned her attention to Kimmie. "So what brings you way out here at this time of day?"

"My last fitting for my wedding dress is at noon and I wanted you to come with me."

"Oh, I don't know." *The last thing I want to do is watch a bubbling bride try on a wedding gown, but then again, it might be fun too.*

"Pleeaaassseee? You've helped me so much with the wedding—you have to go with me!"

"Fine, I'll go. Just let me leave a note so no one worries."

They went into the house, left a note for Jared and then called Alan before driving into town.

Kimmie pushed the glass door open and held it for Angie. Once inside the specialty store Angie gawked in amazement at the gown on display in the entryway.

"Oh my, Kimmie," Angie said, grabbing her friend by the elbow. "Have you ever seen such a gorgeous dress?"

"Want to try it on?" a salesperson asked.

"It's beautiful, but I'm not the one getting married," Angie said, pointing at Kimmie. "She is."

"It wouldn't hurt to try it on, Angie. You can try this one while I try mine. Come on, it'll be fun."

"That's okay, it's probably not my size anyway."

The salesperson was already taking the gown down. "Let's just see then. I think it will look beautiful on you."

"I tagged along to see Kimmie's dress on her. After she's done, maybe I'll try it on." They followed the saleslady to the dressing room where Kimmie's gown was already waiting. She placed the other dress in a different cubicle.

"I'll go first," Kimmie said with a wink to the saleslady. "You'll need to help me with the buttons."

"I'll look around over here while you change," Angie said, angling over to a pair of long lace gloves that caught her eye. They were a perfect match to the gown and veil.

A few minutes later Kimmie came out of the dressing room. "So, what do you think?" she purred, slowly turning around.

"Kimmie, you look beautiful!" Angie exclaimed. The scooped-necked gown glittered with white sequins. Puffed sleeves tapered to her wrists. The back buttoned from the waist to the neck and the mid-length train twisted around Kimmie as she turned. "Barry's going to be so surprised Saturday."

"I thought…" said the salesperson.

"Why don't you try on the other dress, Angie?" interrupted Kimmie.

When Angie didn't answer, Kimmie gently pushed her into the dressing room. "I want to see that dress on you, now try it on!"

"When'd you get so bossy?" Angie said with a laugh.

"I got it from my mama, girl," Kimmie giggled and then closed the door. "Now change!"

"Fine. I don't know why I'm letting you talk me into this."

"Wait until I'm done before you come out," Kimmie called from the other cubicle.

"Yeah, okay." Angie put on the gown then emerged from the dressing room a little while later.

"Oh my!" the saleslady whispered.

"What's wrong?" Angie looked from one woman to the other. Their eyes looked like they would pop from their sockets any minute.

"Nothing's wrong. You look absolutely stunning," Kimmie said, circling her. "This dress is beautiful on you."

The strapless satin dress did fit like a glove, hugging the curves of her body to just below her hips then flaring to the ground. She had latched the long train of gathered lace to her wrist and twisted her hair into a knot enclosed by the veil. The gloves finished the look.

Now the salesperson circled her too, a pair of white pumps in her hand. Angie narrowed her eyes at them and laughed. "You guys are like hawks!"

"It's a perfect fit. Here put these on." She stuck the shoes in front of Angie.

Stepping into the shoes, Angie turned from the women and looked at her reflection in the mirror. "Yes, it is a beautiful gown. Maybe one day…"

TWENTY

THE INN BUZZED WITH ACTIVITY AS THE LAST preparations were made for the wedding. Angie had collaborated with the caterer, musician and video guys because the Turners were missing in action. She'd even chosen the wedding cake.

Angie realized that she hadn't seen either woman since Wednesday nor had they returned her phone calls. *Where in the heck are they?*

Now she sat at her desk with the inn's reservation list and the wedding checklist, going over every little detail one last time.

"Hey, sis! Jared needs you to help him in the barn with the new horses," Terri said, entering the room.

"Hi!" Angie smiled at Terri. "I didn't know you were in town."

"I wouldn't miss this for the world."

"Are you invited to Kimmie's wedding?"

"Oh…yeah. Come on now, Jared needs you."

Angie pushed back from the chair and followed Terri to the kitchen. "Are you coming?"

"No, you go ahead. I've got to make lunch for the boys."

"All right. I'll see you in a little while," Angie said, giving Terri a quick hug before walking down to the stable.

Jared was latching a stall when Angie walked through the big double doors. “Aren’t they beautiful?” he said, stroking a roan on the nose.

Angie quickly took inventory. Twelve new horses filled the stalls. “Where are Whisper and Thunder?”

“Follow me,” he said, his long strides carrying him through the building and out the opposite side. “Here they are.”

Both horses were tethered to a post. “There’s no room for them inside?” Angie grumbled, rubbing Whisper’s neck.

“Nope. You see, I’ve owned Thunder for years. He goes home today. Alan bought Whisper for the inn. Now she belongs to you.”

“What?” Surprised, Angie stared over the horse’s back at him.

“She’s yours.” Loosening the reins, he handed them to Angie. “Alan called and told me to give Whisper to you.”

A broad smile quickly spread across her face. “She’s really mine?”

“Yep.”

Angie hugged the horse’s neck. “Did you hear that, girl? You’re mine!”

“Burt’s taking them to the stables later. Do you still feel up to that ride?”

“More than ever.” Angie mounted a bareback Whisper in a single move. “Wanna race to the creek?”

Jared was in his saddle in a second. “You bet!”

The pounding hooves echoed though the forest as they ran side by side down the dirt road. Angie nudged Whisper harder, beating Jared by a nose.

“I beat you again!” Laughing happily, Angie jumped off Whisper and let her graze near the water. “You need to learn how to ride, Mr. Maxwell.”

Jared twisted Thunder’s reins to a tree limb. “I ride just fine, thank you.” Reaching in the saddlebag, he took out the box he’d kept locked in his file cabinet. “Aren’t you going to tether her?”

Angie washed her hands in the cool water of the stream.

"She's not going anywhere."

Glancing up at him, standing beside her with his hands in his pockets, Angie twisted away from the creek to flick her wet fingers at Jared, sending droplets of the cool liquid over his face.

Quickly snaking his arm around her waist, he wrestled her away from the rocks and pulled her down to the grass. "Think it's funny that you beat me, huh?"

"Actually, I do," she said smugly. Jared's fingers were tickling her sides in an instant. "Mercy!" she cried out, laughing so hard that her eyes watered.

"Okay, mercy it is." Jared said, letting her go and lying back beside her. The sunlight filtered through the trees, splattered light on his face. Angie knew she'd never seen a more handsome man in her life.

"Do you remember the last time we were here together?"

"Um-hum."

"It was after you said you loved me at the Davis house."

"I told you, those were Ruby's feelings for Clyde." Her heartbeat quickened. *This is it! We've never talked about my declaration of love when he rescued me from Hank.*

He turned on his side, propped up on an elbow so he could see her face. Angie quickly closed her eyes.

"Angelina, look at me."

She did as he asked. Studying her for a moment, Jared rubbed a palm against his jeans and sat up. "I want to ask you something."

He pulled her to a sitting position in front of him. "When we were on the steps after Hank had been shot, do you remember what you said to me?"

"Yes." She tried to clear her mind. If she wished for it, then it would never happen.

"Did you mean it—" His words caught in his throat and he looked down. "Or did you say it out of relief that the ordeal was over?"

"Your turn to look at me," she said. When he met her gaze, she continued. "Yes, I meant it, Jared. I struggled with my feelings for a long time because you were the man who hurt me in the dream and I thought you were just a player. When Hank kidnapped me, I realized I'd misunderstood the dream and your actions. I've finally accepted the truth in my heart." *Even though I'm still not sure how you feel about me.*

She ran her fingertips through his bangs. "You're what kept me going while I was tied up in that barn. I had to escape so I could tell you that I love you more than my own life. I'll always love you, Jared. Always."

There. It was out.

"You're sure?"

"I've never been surer of anything in my life."

Jared took her in his arms, kissing her deeply before whispering against her lips, "You make me so happy."

Reaching into his pocket, he took out a small black box. "Angelina Benton, will you marry me?"

Paralyzed, she didn't move, but watched as he lifted the lid to reveal a two-carat square diamond flanked by six smaller diamonds, three on each side. The sunlight caught in the stones, reflecting into her eyes.

Breathe, Angie, breathe, she told herself.

Jared grasped the cool metal of the golden band, then laid the box on the ground beside them. Holding her left hand, he waited for her answer.

After a few minutes of silence, he asked again, "Angelina Benton. Will you be my wife?"

"Why do you want to marry me?"

"Because you make me happy."

Angie's stomach clenched as disappointment coursed through her. Her eyes welling with tears, she tilted her head down, away from his gaze. He hadn't said he loved her.

"I'm sorry, I can't," she whispered as a tear dropped to her leg. Jerking her hand away, she jumped up from the grass and mounted Whisper. Urging the animal into a gallop, they sped off toward the house.

"Angie!" Jared called after them. "Wait!"

"SO HOW ARE the horses?" Terri asked, as Angie stormed into the house.

Angie didn't answer, instead she ran upstairs, taking the steps two at a time.

"Boys, I want you to finish your snack, then go play on the porch until I come back, okay? I need to talk with Angie."

"Okay, Mama," the twins said in unison.

Angie slammed the bedroom door. Grabbing her suitcase from underneath the bed she flung it open then started throwing her clothes inside. When it was full, she pushed the lid down.

"Close, dammit." The latches wouldn't snap shut.

Dumping everything out, she folded the clothes and started repacking.

Terri entered the room, shut and locked the door behind her.

"I don't feel like talking, Terri, so don't ask."

"Want me to help you pack?"

She lifted her head in surprise. "Um…well…sure, there are some more clothes in the dresser."

Terri took the folded clothes from the drawer then laid them in the suitcase. She picked up a shirt from the bed and folded it.

"Why are you helping me?"

"Because my brother can be a big jerk sometimes and because I like you."

She plopped down on the edge of the bed. "He asked me to marry him."

"I expected as much," Terri said, placing the shirt in the

suitcase and picking up another. “So what did he do? Forget to tell you that he loves you?”

She stared up at Terri. “How do you do that?”

“I know my brother. He’s not very good at sharing his feelings.” Terri sat on the bed beside her. “He told me that you think he leaves a string of broken hearts behind him.”

“Doesn’t he?”

“It’s more like women throw themselves at him. He’s dated his share, but most women chase him for his money. Jared’s never given his heart before, until you came along. You’re the first one who has really loved him for himself and the first woman he has ever loved.”

“I find that hard to believe.” She hung her head, crumpled the shorts she held in her lap. “I don’t know what to do.”

“You have to follow your heart.”

“Angelina!” Jared shouted, pounding on the door.

Terri smiled and gave her a quick hug. “Here’s my darling brother now.” She crossed the room and paused as she grasped the doorknob. “Look in your heart, sis and you’ll know what to do.”

Unlocking and opening the door, Terri jumped out of the way as Jared bolted into the room. She quietly closed it behind her, leaving them alone.

“Where do you think you’re going?”

She slammed the top of her suitcase. “Home.”

“Why?” he demanded.

“Because it’s time.” Picking up the suitcase, she angled toward the door.

Jared blocked her by grasping her shoulders. “Angie, you didn’t let me finish before you ran off.” After a brief struggle, he took the suitcase out of her hand and placed it on the floor. Maneuvering her to the edge of the bed, he asked, “Will you please sit down and hear me out?”

She stood in beside the bed, arms crossed in front of her. “I’m listening."

"You're too damn hotheaded, you know that?" he blurted out in frustration and walked several paces away.

"I thought you wanted to finish, not insult me."

"Angie, I want to marry you." He faced her again. "Tomorrow. Right here at the inn."

"Kimmie is getting married here tomorrow."

"Haven't you noticed Kimmie and Mrs. Turner haven't been around much lately? Didn't you think it odd that you've been planning this wedding for the last couple of weeks?"

"Well, yes, but I thought they were busy with other stuff."

"Angie, Kimmie is getting married here on September first, opening day. We're getting married tomorrow, that is if you'll agree to marry me."

"What!" she shouted. "Why would Kimmie trick me?"

"She didn't trick you, I did," he admitted. "I wanted this whole thing to be a surprise. Kimmie only agreed because I begged her…and paid for her invitation corrections."

Jared moved toward her. "She's your friend, Angie. She wants you to be happy."

She stood her ground. *The nerve! The gall! How dare he!* "You were so sure I'd say yes that you've had me secretly plan my own wedding?"

"Yes, I wanted it to be a surprise—a romantic story we could tell our kids."

But the ticking time bomb that was Angie's temper exploded.

"Just who in the hell do you think you are? You cannot control a person's life! You think that because you have money you can buy someone's love? I said I loved you. Wasn't it enough?" She poked him in the chest with her finger. "Couldn't you have trusted me to plan my own wedding? You want our kids to think their mother is a pushover? I don't think so, buddy."

Frantically, she paced the room. *Calm down! Get hold of*

yourself, girl. A deep breath and she turned, picked up the suitcase, reached for the door handle.

Jared picked her up, suitcase and all, then tossed her in the middle of the bed. The suitcase bounced off and landed on the floor, bursting open, its contents spilling out. “Not this time, you little spitfire. You’re going to hear me out, not run away.”

She slammed her fists into his chest as he leaned over her. He caught them, held her arms high over her head. “I only did all of this secretly because I wanted it to be a romantic surprise. Damn it, Angelina, I did all of this because I love you. I thought it would make you happy.”

Immediately, Angie stilled. She stared up at him. “What did you say?”

“I said, I did all of this because I love you. I’ve never said those words to anyone, ever. Please Angie, don’t be upset.”

“Say it again.” The rage gave way to the intense happiness only Jared could give her.

Smiling, he stood and pulled her off the bed. Reaching in his pocket, he took out the ring box and bent on one knee, then took her hand in his. “Angelina Benton, I love you with all my heart and soul. It would be my greatest honor if you would agree to be my wife. Will you marry me here at the inn, tomorrow afternoon?”

“I love you too, Jared and yes, I’ll marry you.”

“You just made my wish come true.”

“What wish?”

“I wished on a shooting star that you would fall in love with me and we’d get married. When Mary’s spirit welcomed you to the family, I took that as a sign and decided that we were supposed to be together—forever.”

Taking the ring from the box, he slipped it on her finger. Kissing her hand, his lips traveled up her arm to her neck as he stood, then across her chin to her lips. “I love you, Angelina

Benton," he whispered, and kissed her soundly.

When he drew back Angie raised her hand behind his back and looked at the ring. "Oh my God, Jared!" She giggled. "It's a rock!"

He laughed. "There's no point in having money if you can't spend it on the people you love."

SIX O'CLOCK SATURDAY morning found Angie astride Whisper in front of The Variety Vine. A little over two months ago, she'd seen Aunt Martha's spirit on the front porch. Would she see her again?

Tethering Whisper to a tree on the side of the house, she went to the front porch.

With a stick in hand, she took a deep breath then started up the steps. This time she removed the spider web before it hit her in the face. She waited at the front door but nothing happened.

More than a little disappointed, Angie tossed the stick away. "Aunt Martha, I need to talk to you." She sat in her Aunt's rocking chair.

Silence.

"I'm getting married today, Aunt Martha. I wish you could be here with me, but I'll have you in my heart. I hoped that by coming here you might appear to me again."

Angie waited, just in case.

A cricket chirped.

"I gave Alan the letters. You were right, you know. I knew when the time was right, just like you said I would."

Angie waited for several more minutes but nothing happened. "Oh well," she said, walking to the bottom of the steps and looking around. "I love you, Aunt Martha. You'll always be my mother in my heart."

A burst of cool wind swept around her. She could feel Aunt

Martha's love. The breeze whispered to her. *I love you too, Angelina.*

Angie smiled. Aunt Martha would always be with her, of that she was sure.

ANGIE LOOKED OUT her bedroom window, watching the guests take their seats.

Jared had indeed arranged it all. The Turners helped prepare the guest list, even Alan was in on the surprise.

Taking a shaky breath, she smoothed the satin fabric across her stomach and smiled. Terri had special ordered the gown, then Kimmie had been slick in covering up the fitting so she didn't even guess she had tried on her own wedding dress. It was indeed a perfect fit.

A soft tap on the door brought Angie out of her thoughts. "Come in."

She turned to see Alan smiling brightly at her. Then the smile faded.

"What's wrong, Alan?"

Alan reached for her gloved hands and smiled, his eyes full of emotion. He kissed her on the cheek. "You are so beautiful you take my breath away. I swear if I were fifty years younger…"

"I'd marry you in a heartbeat!" She smiled, hugging him tightly. "Don't make me cry, Alan. My makeup will run."

"Are you ready for this?"

"Yes," she whispered, linking her arm in his.

"You know, sweetheart, after the wedding, you're going to have to get Terri fixed up with someone. Help her find true love so the curse can be broken."

"You're still stuck on that?" she wrinkled her nose up at him. "You're forgetting about the unknown one."

Alan smiled and kissed her on the cheek, "The unknown will

appear when the time is right."

She laughed. "You sound so mystical."

The music started and Alan led her down the stairs then out to the sycamore tree. She kept her eyes glued to Jared's. Her smile was only for him.

Surely, my heart will burst with love, she thought as Alan gave her to Jared and then took his seat.

Jared's eyes were dark with emotion. Grinning, he squeezed her fingers. With the words "You may kiss your bride," he drew her into his arms, dipped her back and kissed her with an intensity she'd known only with him.

The whoops from the guests egged them on until he finally ended the kiss by showering her face with many small kisses.

They were introduced as Mr. and Mrs. Jared Maxwell, then everyone moved into the ballroom for the reception. She winked at Jared when Terri caught her bouquet and elbowed Terri when Sid caught the garter.

Then she whispered in Jared's ear.

The ring of a silver utensil against crystal did nothing to quiet the quests. A long, loud whistle did the trick.

"Thanks, Burt," Jared said with a laugh before addressing the crowd. "I'd like to thank everyone for coming out today. You've made my surprise to Angelina very special. But now we are *out—of—here!*"

More whoops and whistles followed.

"Hang on everyone," Angie interrupted. "I want you all to write this on your calendar…the day Dansburg's oldest virgin got married. I'm really anxious to see what all the fuss is about, so if you'll please excuse us…"

Laughter erupted. The guests cheered when Jared lifted Angie and carried her outside into the night. Whisper, illuminated by the porch light, was draped in white flowers.

"Oh Jared," Angie exclaimed, "she's beautiful."

"Not half as beautiful as you, my love." he said, lifting her onto the horse and pulling himself up behind her. Waving to the guests, they galloped down the road.

"Where are we going?" she asked and leaned back against his chest as he slowed Whisper to a walk.

He didn't answer but brushed his lips across her cheek. Soon they stopped in front of the Davis house. Dismounting, he pulled her from the animal and carried her to the doorway.

"I thought we decided to market this as a lover's getaway, not a honeymoon suite," she said, her arms wrapped around his neck.

Turning the handle, he carried her inside. Candles illuminated the house. The scent of lavender and jasmine filled the air. "Jared, you did this for me?"

"Just for you," he said, still holding her.

"Look!" she whispered, then pointed into the living room. "Do you see them?"

Turning his head in that direction, Jared gasped.

"You *do* see them, don't you?"

Jared nodded. She smiled at the apparitions.

Theodore and Mary smiled back then faded away.

She turned Jared's face back toward her and kissed him lightly on the lips. "Are you taking me upstairs?"

"Huh, oh yeah," he said, starting toward the steps.

"Angelina."

A figure appeared in the doorway.

Jared stopped dead in his tracks. "What the—?"

Looking over his shoulder, Angie exclaimed, "Aunt Martha!"

Jared turned toward the voice.

"Angelina, my darling, you've married a wonderful young man," Aunt Martha smiled at them.

"I sure have, haven't I? Aunt Martha, I'd like you to meet, Jared Maxwell."

"You take good care of my niece."

Jared's eyes widened. "I...will..."

She grinned at her aunt. "He's in shock."

"I know, dear." Martha glided closer to them. "Angelina, I'm moving on. We will not see each other again. Your part of the curse is broken." She folded her hands in front of her. "Oh and sweetie, will you please speak to Alan? I appeared to him tonight to tell him that I love him, but that silly old coot thinks he imagined me."

"I will, Aunt Martha."

"I love you, Angelina."

She smiled. "I love you too, Aunt Martha."

In an instant, the apparition disappeared.

Jared stared at the now empty space. "Okaaay, we market it as a lover's getaway with a haunted twist. What's this about a curse?"

She laughed. Kissing him, she teased his lips with her teeth. "I'll tell you all about it later. Right now, all I want to know is if you're taking me upstairs or are you going to stand here holding me all night?"

Jared answered by carrying her up the steps and into the bedroom. The floor was covered in white rose petals, the bed in red petals.

"Oh, Jared."

"White roses for your purity," he whispered. "Red roses for our love."

"Don't forget that red is for passion too. Now put me down, Mr. Maxwell."

Jared stood her in front of him. He took the veil from her hair, causing it to cascade in long dark locks around her bare shoulders and down her back.

Softly, their lips met. "I'll love you forever, Angelina," he said against her lips. Without giving her a chance to answer, he kissed her deeply.

Then sweet, slow and seductively he moved from her mouth,

to her shoulder and around to the nape of her neck. Holding the clasp of her zipper he slowly inched it down to her waist, kissing the skin underneath as it became exposed.

The gown fell to her ankles.

She gasped, shivered with anticipation.

Jared hooked his fingers in the sides of her lace panties, slid them down, ever-so slowly. He followed with his mouth, covering her back with hot, wet kisses.

When he reached her knees, he turned her around. Looking up at her, his gaze ravaged her body. "My God, Angelina, you're exquisite."

His hands skimmed her thighs, hips and sides as he stood and scooped her in his arms, carrying her to the bed.

I must have died and gone straight to heaven, she thought as the sound of her heart pounded loudly in her ears.

She watched Jared unbutton his shirt, tug it out of his pants and throw it aside.

His eyes blazed, burning into her. She had to have her hands on him now.

"Jared, wait." Sitting up, she scooted to the edge of the bed, reached for the waistband of his pants. "I want…"

What do I want?

To help. To do something other than lie here. To touch.

Fumbling with the button, then the zipper, she pushed the pants down, leaving just his tented boxers. He stepped out of his pants and then slipping the boxers off he stepped out of them too.

Angie's eyes widened. "Oh my God!"

Jared chuckled. "Whatever you say, my dear."

He laid her back on the bed and dropped a kiss on the rise of her breasts. Taking one in each hand, he kneaded, tweaked and pinched until she was taut and tight.

"Jared… I'm so hot."

He took a nipple into his mouth. Arching into him, Angie

held on to his shoulders. She lifted his head with her hands, crashed her mouth against his.

The hot fire intensified.

She wanted…no needed…all of him.

The soft caress of his chest hair against her nipples, the hardness pressing low against her, set her ablaze.

Reaching down she took him in her hand, slowly caressing the length of him. His body was like silken heat.

"Ah… Angelina…" he groaned against her neck.

Moving his hand down her stomach to the slickness that waited for him he slipped a finger inside, capturing her gasp with his mouth.

She was consumed with him, with what he made her feel. She arched against his hand.

I'm beginning to understand what all the fuss is about. I'm so glad I waited. Jared is the only one for me.

Then his thumb stroked her, just there.

Hot ecstasy plunged through her. Her body rocked with the spasms, quaked until she was so tender she pulled his hand away.

Still she wanted more.

"Jared…"

"Baby… The first time might hurt," he whispered, gazing at her, his eyes burning with desire.

"It can't be worse than this wanting." She nipped his arm with her teeth, ran her tongue along the inside of his elbow. "I love you, Jared. My body's burning for you. Don't worry, you aren't going to hurt me."

Splaying her legs, Jared lowered his mouth to her breasts. His tongue teased her until she moaned with pleasure. She grabbed his hips and pulled him to her. Pausing at her center, he locked his gaze with hers.

"Yes…Jared…now."

Without waiting for him to move, Angie pulled his hips again, pushing him inside her. Jared, thrusting once, filled her, then held very still.

Blinding heat seared though her core, branding her as his. A few moments later the pain passed.

Angie pushed his hips away with her hands, pulled him back into her. “More, Jared. I want all of you.”

Jared took over, thrusting deeply as she rocked against him, meeting each thrust with one of her own.

So this is the big deal! she thought. *I like it.*

Moving faster, he pressed against her. Her body tightened. Something built, grew within her. Like a wild animal she pulled at him, wanting him closer, needing him deeper.

Until she went over the edge in release, rocketing skyward, exploding in some other dimension.

“Jared!” she moaned, still spiraling out of control.

Holding her tightly, Jared murmured her name, then followed her into the abyss.

Lost in each other, they didn’t notice as a glowing light appeared in the room. Swirling around them, it enveloped them in mist.

Suddenly a brilliant radiance flashed from their bodies, streaming out of the bedroom windows, streaking through the darkness of night until it found the souls of the cursed and plunged into them.

Holding her in his arms, Jared rested his forehead against hers until their ragged breathing slowed.

“I’ll love you until the end of time, Angelina.”

She lifted his head, her eyes molten with desire, “I’ll love you until the end of time and beyond.”

Teasing her lips with his mouth, Jared rolled over, pulling Angie onto his chest, whispering against her lips. “And beyond, my love…and beyond.

Epilogue

A SUMMER BREEZE GENTLY SWAYED THE TREETOPS AS an early morning mist rose from the forest floor. The flurry of feathers rode on the wings of silence.

Large oaks, planted in a circle two centuries earlier, dominated this section of woods. In the center of the sphere, a huge boulder jutted out of the earth, stretching five feet toward the sky.

An iridescent glow hovered above the flat top of the large rock, waiting.

Eight sheer forms appeared outside the circle of oaks, moving in from all sides. Each encircled the gigantic stone once, their bodies becoming denser when they stopped side by side in front of the glowing form.

A quick fierce wind blew into the circle, white sparks flitted through the air as the glowing orb slowly floated down to the rock. In a flash of light the orb transformed into the gypsy witch. His smoky eyes reflected the surrounding mist. Nodding, he quietly acknowledged each spirit form in turn, before moving to the next, until all were greeted.

Standing atop the boulder, he opened his arms up to the sky. As he lowered them back to his sides, the wind calmed to stillness.

"The time has drawn near," the gypsy witch said, sitting down on the stone.

"What can we do?" Mary Slayton asked.

"We have done enough, you and I," he said, the strength of his voice filling the air. "The curse I cast for you is near its end. In one year's time, we shall all be set free or doomed to walk these lands for eternity. The virgin who dreams has found true love. Now two more must do the same."

Stepping closer, Mary gazed up at the gorgeous young man whose eyes were now black. "Why are we trapped too? And Theodore? I don't understand why we can't touch each other or be together on this plane."

The gypsy witch gazed down at Mary. "Theodore cursed himself to haunt Ruby and Clyde with his dying words. The curse I cast for you came back on us threefold. By cursing others, we cursed ourselves."

"I didn't know…" Mary said, stumbling over the words.

"Nor did I at the time." He let his gaze linger on Mary for a moment. "Thus," he said on a sigh, "because of our actions, we are bound to these lands as those we have cursed."

"Will the other two find true love?" Mary asked, stronger now.

"That is blocked from my sight. I can see that the task the sister faces is great. Yet, she is strong and has the gift of clairvoyance. The outcome I cannot see."

Mary stepped back into the line with the other cursed souls. "Gypsy witch," she whispered, "will we see you again before the year's end?"

The gypsy witch spread his hands, palms outward in front of

him.

You are eight from families four,
Bound by death at its door.
I as one who can decree,
By my hand, I do agree.
We meet here once more to see,
Should true love stay or shall it flee.
When twice you look upon this face,
Then we each shall know our fate.

Placing his hands back in his lap, a blue glow surrounded the gypsy witch until he dissolved into a brilliant whiteness in the center of an iridescent blue oval.

Eight returned the way that they had entered, once around the boulder, the denseness of their bodies becoming more translucent with each step. One by one, they left the circle, disappearing into the mist.

Songbirds began their morning melody as a breeze played gently within the leaves. Flickering toward the forest floor, the sun evaporated the mist, warming the earth.

The blue glow faded, shrinking in size until, alone on top of the boulder, sat a single gray cat.

Keep reading for an excerpt from another paranormal romantic suspense novel by Melissa Alvarez writing as Ariana Dupré

TALGORIAN PROPHECY

Now available in print from Adrema Press

ONE

"WOULD *YOU* GO HOME IF A SERIAL KILLER ABDUCTED your child?" Megan Cassidy slammed her fists hard against the desk. "Would you?" Her angry stare bore into the steel gray eyes of the officer, emotions raging past better judgment. "How dare you dismiss me. You have no idea what I'm going through."

Lieutenant Randal rose from his chair and walked around the desk. He grabbed Megan's elbow, propelling her toward the door. "We'll call if there are any developments."

"I'm not going anywhere, you coldhearted—" She yanked her arm free from the tight, uncomfortable grip and faced him. She searched his eyes for some shred of understanding, any emotion she could connect with. His features were like a brick wall, cold and rough. "Don't you understand? I *need* to help you find my son."

A mangled, bloody scene flashed through her mind. The glint of a knife, the pitching roar of maniacal laughter rang in her ears. A hooded man stabbed a lifeless body again and again.

The killer's emotions radiated from him. The spark in his eyes reflected joy in the kill, yet the snarl of his lips held contempt for the victim. He looked up. His evil glare slammed into her.

Megan shrank back in terror, her pulse raced.

Anger. Pure and uncontrollable fury. His rage coursed through her. She trembled but couldn't pull her gaze away. She tried to see his face but the hood covered his features. Red crazed eyes stared at her from the darkness.

Locked within his hypnotic trance, Megan waited for some clue to the maniac's identity.

The scene vanished.

Megan dug her fingers into the hard flesh of Randal's arms. Her voice lowered, straining with emotion. "We have to find my son *now*!"

"Ms. Cassidy!" Randal jerked his arm away.

"I saw…" Her heart pounded. Fear rose up her spine at the thought of the Mangler with her son. She stepped between Randal and the door. "I can help you. We must search now before it's too late."

"What do you mean we?" Lieutenant Randal laughed. "I've told you I won't have some half-cocked celebrity in the middle of my investigation, especially one who claims to be psychic."

"I can use my abilities to find Robbie. I've assisted other police departments throughout the country in missing persons cases." She'd encountered resistance before but Randal had closed his mind to anything he couldn't see or prove with facts.

"Do you think I give a damn about what you've done with other departments?" Randal snorted.

"I'll stay behind the scenes. The media will never know I'm around. The Clarkston Police Department and West Virginia State Police can take all the credit." Despite her bravado, her voice cracked. Tears stung her eyes. "It's how I always work."

She braced her hands against the doorframe to keep Randal from pushing her out of the office. "This is my son we're talking about, Randal," she said, blinking back the tears. "Put yourself in my shoes. I'm begging you."

Randal sized up the woman blocking the door. Straight hair hung below narrow shoulders. Its honey color shimmered in the sunlight streaming through the window beside them. If the Mangler had abducted his son he wouldn't leave the station either but damn if he'd act like this. Maybe he was too hard on her but he didn't like her type.

"I understand your feelings. In abduction cases, hysterical mothers often exhibit your type of behavior. Raving like a lunatic about psychic powers doesn't do anything for you, your son, or our investigation."

"In each of the previous abductions the Mountain Mangler took the child first and then its parent, who had psychic abilities, like I do." She clung to the doorframe. "An hour after he killed the kid, he murdered the parent. The bodies were all found in the West Virginia portion of the Allegheny Mountains. He's going to come after me now that he has Robbie."

"I know his MO. As we agreed, when the time comes, we'll use you as bait to lure him to us if we can ensure your safety. If not, we'll try a different approach. We have men looking for your son." Randal rubbed the stubble on his cheek and blew out a heavy breath. "Until that time comes, you can wait over there if you'll stay out of the way." He pointed toward a navy blue chair sitting near the wall beside his office.

"When that time comes?" Her voice raised an octave. "We can't sit around and wait for something to happen. We need to find him now! Your men are looking in town, not in the mountains. Why won't you let me help?"

"Ms. Cassidy, I can't investigate your son's disappearance if you keep antagonizing me. We're working as fast as possible. Now please, have a seat."

Megan frowned. He wasn't going to give in. A new thought crossed her mind. What if he let her secret about Robbie slip? She couldn't deal with any more stress. She fought against the panicky anger Randal fueled in her. "You haven't told the press, right? I've worked hard to keep Robbie's existence a secret in my public life. I don't want them to find out about him now, in the middle of a serial killer investigation, or have the paparazzi coming after me to get a story."

"I promised not to release names unless it was necessary. You don't have to keep asking me. Regardless of what you think of my integrity, my word is my bond. Now, Ms. Cassidy, please, will you go sit down?"

Megan dropped her hands from the doorframe and stepped aside. "What are you going to do first?"

"Let me handle the investigation." Randal grabbed some papers off the fax machine, returned to his office and shut the door.

"Six people are dead, Randal." Megan yelled at him through the window. "My child isn't going to be next!"

She stared as the Lieutenant closed the blinds on the office door.

His word better be his bond.

One slip from Randal and her secret would be national news. Only a handful of people knew of Robbie's existence. She kept it that way to protect him. It had been difficult to go out in public together but they'd managed with Carmela's assistance. A lot of good it did.

She'd been lucky to find Carmela, Robbie's babysitter since birth. She was loyal and, as far as Megan knew, had never told anyone about him. A couple of times, they'd even pretended Robbie was Carmela's son when the paparazzi got too close.

She even chose the private school he attended because of the strict code of silence it maintained. Several other celebrities' children attended Cross Meadows. She'd always thought it was a necessary expense, until today when the serial killer abducted him from the school grounds.

This is my fault. If I hadn't chosen to use my abilities to support us, this never would have happened.

Working the television talk show circuit had thrown her into the limelight because her readings were so accurate and now, Megan Cassidy was a household name.

It had gotten to the point where she couldn't keep up with the hundreds of reading requests she received every day. Once she hit the talk shows the numbers increased. She spent her days conducting readings on the phone or in person and she was booked seven months in advance. Granted, she now made enough money to afford everything she and Robbie needed but why had success come at such a high price?

If only she could control the way she received the information maybe Robbie would be with her right now instead of in the clutches of a killer.

Wandering over to the chair, she couldn't keep the Mangler's vileness from her thoughts. That madman had her only child. She dropped into the seat. Leaning forward, she rested her elbows on her knees and held her head with cold hands.

Hours ago she'd seen Robbie's abduction in a vision while waiting in the school's car line to pick him up. Anger ripped through her at the memory.

"Your mom called and asked if someone could bring you home today. She's sick with the flu," the man had said, walking Robbie toward the front doors. Robbie saw the school's volunteer badge stuck to his shirt and believed him.

Upon receiving the impression, she'd thrown the car door open and run to the school's entrance, pleading, *Not my child—not Robbie. Oh God, please don't let this happen to my son.* Panic wound around her making it difficult to breathe. Her stomach clenched into a knot of sick desperation. Her heart beat at a frantic pace.

"Robbie!" Megan started, realizing she'd screamed his name

out loud, as she had when she ordered the teachers to search for him before racing to the parking lot.

"Ms. Cassidy, are you all right?" Gentle fingers moved her hands away from her face.

Megan looked into the soft green eyes of a female officer with short brown hair.

"I was too late," she whispered, "I didn't save my son."

The officer's expression melted into one of deep sympathy. "We're doing all we can to find him."

"What damn good are psychic abilities if I couldn't use them to protect my child? I ran as fast as I could but I wasn't fast enough. If only I'd sensed the abduction sooner."

"You can't blame yourself." The officer gave Megan's hands a squeeze. "I've seen you advise so many people on television. Don't you always say if you're meant to have a vision you will?"

Megan withdrew her hands. "Yes. Only this time it came too late."

Why can't I be right all the time? Why don't I see the visions far enough in advance to do the most good? No, I'm not doing this to myself again. It's out of my hands.

She always worried about her accuracy. There wasn't any point in doing readings if the accuracy wasn't there. Then she wouldn't be any different from the frauds that gave real psychics a bad name. Long ago she'd realized no psychic was ever one hundred percent. *It is a gift, not something I can control.*

A vague vision had destroyed her impending marriage to Brody. Now this one came too late and Robbie could lose his life.

The horrible, violent vision wouldn't undermine her determination. Megan straightened in the seat. He would not win. She'd use all the psychic abilities at her disposal to find Robbie alive.

"I've been a fan for years," the officer said. "Your secret is safe with me. I'm sure your abilities would be invaluable to us if only

Lieutenant Randal wasn't so stuck in his ways." She stood. "We have a couch in the lunchroom. You're welcome to sleep there."

Megan nodded. "Thank you."

"Anytime. I've got to go back to work."

As the officer strode away the memory of a dream flashed through Megan's mind. Robbie was in a cave, crying for her while she fought with an unknown assailant, the previous victim's bodies lay around a clearing. She hadn't understood at first but she'd

had violent, struggling dreams about each of the murders the night before. She froze in place—the dreams were like her recent visions.

A nauseous feeling rose in her throat, sweat broke out on her forehead as a chill trembled through her body. She tried to tamp it down by taking deep breaths but the shaking wouldn't stop. Her stomach pitched and rolled.

The Clarkston and State Police assured her the killer would hold Robbie captive while he stalked and terrorized the second victim—her.

Please, God, she prayed, *don't let the Mangler change his MO.* This time, it was personal.

She scanned the large open police station bustling with activity. Desks filled the main room while individual offices lined the walls. Phones rang, the water cooler gurgled and the copier clicked and hummed along with the low drone of people talking. There must be something she could do. Her nerves were too on edge to sit in a stupid chair.

She glanced at Randal's office, stood and took a casual stroll along the narrow outside corridor, which followed the four walls of the station's main room. She pretended to inspect the different posters on the walls while she listened to the conversations behind her, hoping to overhear any discussions about Robbie.

Halfway around she paused beside an open door. The plaque

underneath its window read Detective Paul Archer. She peeked inside. One of the officers who had responded to Cross Meadows emergency call sat behind a wooden desk reading a file.

Even sitting he looked tall, with black hair and tanned olive skin. When he glanced up, she moved away from the open door and feigned interest in a wanted poster.

"Brody Phelps is on line two," a voice said over Archer's intercom.

Brody? He'd been on her mind since the abduction.

Archer lifted the receiver. "Archer here."

She stepped closer to the doorframe, listening intently.

"What conflict of interest?"

Another long pause.

"You're the best tracker in West Virginia. If we have any hopes of finding this boy alive, you're it. Let me know if things change."

Anger ran through her like fire. Was Brody refusing to participate in the rescue because of their past? Well, it was time he got over it. She stormed into Archer's office. "Let me talk to him."

"Sure. Bye." The detective laid the receiver in its cradle. "I'm sorry, Ms. Cassidy. Can I help you?"

"I wanted to talk to Brody."

"He's gone."

Just like my son. She frowned and spun around. Facing the loud buzz of activity coming from the central room, she strode out of Archer's office.

A dark shadow moved through her peripheral vision. She looked toward it and found herself staring at people walking around. They were carrying files, talking on the phone, speaking in hushed tones. None of them was the person she'd seen. She realized it hadn't been a person at all but a spirit.

The shadow spirit triggered a deeper connection. The buzzing softened, sounding distant. Her vision darkened as if a tunnel was closing in around her. She waited for the psychic scenes to play out in her mind.

The tunnel's black walls led to a pinprick of light at the end. The white circle grew closer as the walls sped by. She traveled through its brilliance and into a forest clearing.

Megan glanced behind her. The police station had disappeared. Instead tall evergreens surrounded her. The smell of pine hung heavily in the air. The forest was strangely silent. She looked up at the sky through an opening in the forest canopy. It appeared to be early afternoon.

She stood in a clearing. The mouth of a cave was on the rockiest side and an old miner's cabin on the other.

Why am I here? she thought as she waited. Her heartbeat raced. She held her breath in anticipation.

A man exited the old wooden shack. He stepped over a dead tree as he crossed the yard, stopping several feet in front of her. She sensed danger and death around him. His dark hair hung in limp dirty strands past his shoulders. He wore a flannel shirt with black jeans and boots. His face was bony, his eyes bulging.

He laughed. The maniacal sound echoed through the silence. His lips curled back in a snarl.

Megan recognized his laugh. *He's the serial killer who abducted my son! The Mountain Mangler.*

Which meant, if the dream was right, she'd find Robbie in the cave.

She stepped sideways in sync with the man in front of her, matching his stride, watching his every move. She imagined a brick wall blocking him from getting into the cave where Robbie hid.

Small rocks, from the boulders surrounding the mouth of the cave, crunched beneath her feet until she stepped onto a small grassy area. She positioned herself so the cave and Robbie were behind her and the shack was behind him. She planned to keep it that way.

Bright sunlight streamed into the small clearing through the forest canopy. The Mangler intentionally slanted the knife in his hand against the sunlight and reflected it into her eyes, blinding her in an instant.

She looked down, blinking against the yellow spots left in her vision and saw a large branch lying on the ground near the forest's edge. She returned her gaze to the thin man.

A sword hilt stuck out of a scabbard secured to his back and there was a knife casing strapped around his leg. The antique weapons looked out of place with the red flannel shirt and black jeans. Had they been there a moment ago?

He lunged forward.

She ducked and rolled, sprang to her feet and ran for the stick. Grabbing it, she whirled to face him but faltered. She wasn't prepared for the pure evil in his eyes.

She couldn't wimp out now. She had to fight him. Robbie's life depended on using every skill she'd learned from her teacher, Zangar, in martial arts class.

His lips curled and a low growl rumbled from his chest. Her stomach lurched. A shudder of fear rocked her body. She'd seen that look before in her nightmares.

Robbie emerged from the mouth of the cave.

"Get back inside!" She lunged forward putting her body between the killer and her son. "Robbie! Go now!"

"Mommy!" Robbie cried, before darting back into the cave's depths. She turned back to the Mangler.

He shifted his weight and tapped the knife blade against his open palm. The leer on his angular face made him look gaunt. His lips curled in a smile, revealing yellow, rotting teeth.

She couldn't think about her actions. She rushed him swinging the stick. He twisted away and took the blow on the scapula. The impact sent a bone-jarring tremor up her arm. The sword rattled in the scabbard. Despite the pain from the last blow, she pivoted for momentum, swinging the stick full force at his head. It cracked when she connected.

He fell back a step.

Her confidence surged as he moved further from the cave and her son. She would not let him kill Robbie like he had the others.

He grabbed at the stick, missed and lost his balance. He retreated under her assault. She landed blows to limbs and head, driving him away further and further away.

Laughter rumbled deep within his chest. He rotated. She swung the stick but he blocked it with his forearm and slashed the knife down, gashing her hand.

She cried out as hot searing pain shot up her arm.

He pinned her with a stare. Yanking the stick from her grasp he slung it away. "Did you really think I'd let you win this little game?"

She stumbled backward searching frantically for another weapon. Blood flowed down her hand, dripping off numb fingers.

He grabbed her shoulders. Cold steel ripped into her skin right below the rib cage. He pushed the sharp blade down, slicing through the flesh to her hip. The burning hot

pain seared through her abdomen. Her shrieks of pain echoed through the forest. She couldn't breathe, her body shook and she gasped for air. She screamed again as he slowly pulled it from her body, laughing at her agony.

Megan clutched at the wound, a gush of warm blood filled her hands. Gurgling sounds rumbled in her throat and sweat broke out across her forehead. Wrapping around her, Death prepared to take her soul.

She looked at the killer.

She stared into dark brown eyes filled with concern, not evil intent. Detective Archer held her by the shoulders, not the Mangler. She was bent forward clutching her abdomen. She glanced down but blood didn't stain her stomach or hands. The vision had ended.

She straightened, dropped her hands and peered past Archer. Everyone in the police station had stopped working to stare at her. Lieutenant Randal watched her from his office doorway. Tall, muscular, black hair in a crew cut, Randal's wide stance and intimidating stature made him look more like a military commander than a policeman.

"Are you okay, Ms. Cassidy?" Archer asked, releasing her.

"Yes… I'm fine." She rubbed her eyes, pressing against the lids, trying to clear the scene from her mind without being obvious that this was a routine process.

"Come. Sit down," Archer said.

"No, really, I'm fine," Megan said.

"I insist." Archer guided her inside his office, shutting the door behind them.

Megan collapsed into a chair. The intense fight during the vision had exhausted her. Which was weird. Normally, she saw the scene play out. Visions took some energy but not a lot. They never affected her like this one had. Tired as she was, she could have been an active participant in the fight.

She looked up. Archer's stare bore into her.

"What happened out there?" he asked.

"You don't want to know." *You won't believe me any more than Randal did.*

"Yes, I do." Archer slid a chair over to sit beside her. "Why were you pressing on your eyes?"

He'd noticed? "To release a violent vision. I press my lids to clear my psychic third eye. If I clear it and project a calm happy scene I can let go of any negativity left from the vision."

"Very interesting. What was the premonition?"

"Does it make any difference? No one in this department will listen to anything I have to say, even when it's my son who's missing."

"I'll listen."

She studied him for a moment. He seemed sincere. "I saw where the killer is holding my son. It's in the mountains. There's a clearing with an old miner's shack and a cave. I fought with the Mountain Mangler. I'd die before I let him hurt my child."

Detective Archer studied her. "Are your visions always this intense?"

"What do you mean?"

"It's as if you weren't here. You moved, screamed even but I couldn't get you to respond to me."

"I'm connecting deeply because he has my child, so yes, the visions are more intense." She stood and walked to the door.

"Will you tell me the details?"

"Why?" Megan scrutinized Archer.

"I know Randal is giving you a hard time about the psychic stuff. I, on the other hand, have had some experiences of my own. I'm more open to things of a psychic or paranormal nature than anyone else in this department."

He might have some pull with Randal. Megan returned to the empty chair. She gave Archer all the details of every metaphysical incident she'd had about the case up to this point. He'd stopped her at the beginning to get a pad and pen for notes. When she got to the latest vision, she held back.

"I fought with the Mangler but he won the round." She wouldn't tell him she'd seen her own death.

"You're not going to give me the specifics of this latest vision are you?"

Megan shook her head. "Speaking words give them the power to manifest. I know I'm being superstitious but it's my belief. Let me use my abilities with the search teams."

"That's out of my control. Randal gave specific orders that you aren't allowed to work with them."

"Why not? What has he got against psychics anyway?"

"He's never said so I don't know," Archer laid the notepad on the desk.

"If we're done here, may I leave?"

"Where are you going?"

To find my son if I can get out of here. She pointed to the chair Randal had indicated earlier. "Right over there."

Archer nodded. "If you change your mind I'd like to hear about the vision."

"If I change my mind. Thanks for listening, Detective Archer. It's more than anyone else in this station would do." She strode across the room and plopped down in the chair. Archer watched her from the open doorway, Randal from another desk in the middle of the room. After a few moments both men went back inside their offices.

Hours later, there wasn't any more news. Randal and Archer had managed to keep her in their sights but now they joined several officers in a conference room. Megan glanced at the wall clock. Five a.m.

An officer shut the door to the meeting. Megan grasped the opportunity and headed for the exit. When Randal realized she'd left town, instead of going home as he'd instructed, he'd be furious. He'd probably want to kill her too. If the Mangler didn't do it first.

TWO

"MOMMY!" ROBBIE SCREAMED.

"Oh no!" Megan slammed on the car brakes and swerved onto the grassy shoulder. She threw the car into park. At least she'd gotten off the road this time before the vision hit her full force.

She gripped the steering wheel and laid her head against her hands. Behind closed lids, the blackness turned gray. Its fuzziness resembled a television station off the air. Suddenly, full color images filled the screen.

Looking down, Megan gasped at her blood-soaked hands and a wide gaping wound in her abdomen. Weakness wobbled her legs. Nausea rose in her throat, the taste of bile gagged her. She fell to her knees.

The killer stood over her. Horrible images of mangled bodies flashed through her mind. His burning anger at the previous victims overwhelmed her. He despised them, thought they were weak, useless, just because they were not the one he sought. Fury consumed his deranged thoughts. He spun away to stalk toward Robbie who stood at the cave's entrance.

Megan screamed, "Run, Robbie! Hide!"

Robbie fled into the darkness. The Mangler stopped. Turning around he settled an enraged gaze on Megan. "Now, you die."

Plunging the hunting knife into its sheath he yanked the sword from the scabbard on his back. The slick grating of metal on metal sent a shiver down her spine.

I must keep him from the cave.

The panicked thought drove her forward. Her eyes rolled upward with the pain and she almost passed out. Weak from the loss of blood, she clawed the ground, frantic to reach her son, to save him. Excruciating pain pierced her with every movement. She crawled forward, pushing her body to the limit.

A hard kick in the side knocked the breath out of her. Gasping for air she lost her balance and landed face first on the ground. He dug the toe of his boot under her rib cage and in one powerful movement flipped her onto her back. He pressed a booted foot against her chest.

Holding her down, he raised lanky arms high above his head, both hands clutching the sword's hilt. Muttering foreign words, he moved his foot from her chest to straddle her. She scooted backward on her elbows, pushing with her feet to escape. In two swift strokes he drew the sword down.

Her screams ripped from her. Intense pain racked her body under the slicing blade. He cut an X across her torso from shoulders to hips. Jerking her onto weak knees, he pushed her head forward and raised the sword high in the air to decapitate her.

If he kills me, I can't protect Robbie.

I won't let him hurt my only child.

Love and protectiveness for Robbie washed over her, pushing away the pain, filling her until she thought her heart would explode. Anger at the serial killer for abducting Robbie deepened, fought for a place in her heart.

Her eyesight expanded. Colors became more vibrant. Something shifted inside. Suddenly, she was floating above her assailant and could see everything around her.

This must be what death feels like.

Dark wings beat the air, giant talons dug into her assailant's shoulders, lion's claws ripped his chest. The flurry of motion spun her out of control. Her anger surged into a furious rage. Moments later the man disappeared beneath the animals' combined attack.

The scene changed to a fuzzy screen.

Megan jerked away from the steering wheel. Wave after wave of nausea churned her stomach.

Air. I need fresh air. When did it get so hot in here?

Her stomach heaved.

She popped the latches on the convertible top. Holding down the release button the motor whirred, the top lifted and bent back. The fresh chilly air cooled her skin.

Death waited within that madman.

She sensed an evil presence and twisted in the seat, peering over her shoulder, seeking the unknown. Only an empty road lay behind her. She looked into the trees. She couldn't shake the feeling that someone, or something, watched her.

Megan faced forward. Her imagination was working overtime, that's all it was. She rubbed her eyelids. The coldness of her fingertips took her mind from the murderous scene. She pressed down until she saw blackness. Moments later the lights in fuzzy shapes appeared. Darkness wiped her mind clean of the horrible scene.

She projected a new scene on the psychic screen within her third eye, one where she held Robbie in her arms, comforting him. She envisioned a glowing blanket of white light wrapping around his tiny body, protecting him, wherever he was. When it surrounded both of them she imagined it turning into a strong shield that could deflect any vibrations from entities wishing them harm. When the process was complete, she removed her fingers.

She'd never get used to violent premonitions but clearing the screen in her mind's eye grounded her. She didn't know if Robbie would feel her or not. She hadn't been able to connect telepathically with him since the abduction. It gave her hope to know that she'd tried to connect with him while erasing the negative images.

She opened her eyes. A large white wooden sign announced the entrance to town. She hadn't noticed it when she'd pulled over. Squinting against the early morning sun, she read the faded words.

Flatrock Creek.
Where Man Meets The Mountains.
Population 239
Home of the Talgorian Shifters
State Basketball Champions

They'd changed the name of the high-school mascot? The new name sent shivers down her spine. She couldn't think about that now, saving Robbie was the only reason she'd ever return here. Flatrock Creek had been her birthplace, her home and her heartbreak. Now it must be her salvation.

She looked into the valley at the sleepy little town. Old buildings lined Main Street. The forest butted up to their back doors. Its proximity was a little too close for comfort with a killer running free. She knew from experience how easy it was to slip in and out of the woods unnoticed.

A couple of city blocks outside town sat the ranger station. Wildcat Mountain's rounded peak rose into the sky. It was small compared to the other dominating peaks filling the skyline.

Megan needed the best search and rescue ranger in the state, someone with instincts bordering on psychic, even though he'd never admit it.

Brody Phelps.

I'm taking one hell of a chance.

He probably still blamed her. Otherwise why would he have refused Detective Archer's request? Even though the accident wasn't her fault, after all these years she still couldn't shake the remorseful feelings. She dreaded facing Brody. Since she'd left she'd tried to get up the courage to call, or write a letter. She'd been a coward and now it was time to face the consequences.

She wouldn't let Brody walk away from her again. Not this time, not when Robbie's life was at stake. And her own.

Shaky hands held the wheel. The sun warmed the leather but the chill of the premonition lingered. Slipping the car into gear, she eased it on the paved road and drove down the hill toward Flatrock Creek.

The breeze blew her ponytail, the pure scent of pine rode the crisp air, yet she grew even tenser. The clock on the dashboard said seven a.m. as she entered Main Street.

Everything looked the same. Frye's Pharmacy where she'd bought bubble gum, the malt shop that made the best chocolate shakes she'd ever tasted and the old farmers' hangout, Harvey's Hardware.

The dual lane road split on either side of the Town Hall, which sat on an island of land between the north and sound bound lanes. Recent construction had created a one-

way circle around the old white building. The black sections of new pavement were in sharp contrast to the faded gray street. Flowers bloomed in decorative designs on either side of the wrought iron railings leading up the stairs to the front door. Megan glanced up at the bell tower on the Town Hall's roof, only to find a clock in its place.

Her heart sank. As a teenager she'd loved the bell tower. She remembered the first time she'd snuck up there. Brody had to convince her to be adventurous, playfully tugging when she resisted. They'd shared their first kiss beside the tarnished, old bell.

Life had been fun and carefree. She hadn't had any worries. In the seven years since she'd left Flatrock Creek, she'd struggled to make a good life for Robbie. It had been hard work but she'd succeeded, alone. Her thoughts drifted back to the police station.

Randal would be furious when he found out she'd heeded her visions and snuck away to the Allegheny Mountains to find Robbie instead of waiting in Clarkston as bait. Archer might take her side though. She hoped he could make Randal understand why she'd left. That is, if Archer even got it.

I couldn't sit there, wasting time, any longer.

If only she didn't need a tracker she could find Robbie by herself. She couldn't find the clearing alone. She no longer knew these woods by memory. A lot of landmarks would have changed in seven years.

She glanced at the Town Hall in the rearview mirror. Turning her attention forward, Wildcat Mountain loomed on the horizon. The ranger station was a short distance away. Brody would be at work. She knew calling first would destroy any chance she had of gaining his assistance.

That was the problem. She knew. The police wouldn't listen to her. No one believed her.

Sadness washed over her. A good mother would never let anything bad happen to her child. She couldn't connect to Robbie and that worried her even more.

"Oh, Robbie. I love you, baby. Mommy's coming, you're not alone," Megan whispered.

Her stomach tightened and tears stung her eyes. *How could I fail my child?* She was strong in the face of adversity but this was the worst crisis she'd ever faced. When Brody broke off their engagement she'd gone into hysterics. Losing control hadn't gotten him back and it wouldn't save Robbie now.

Brody's words still hurt. *I hate you, Megan. Don't come near me again.* If she revealed the secret she'd kept from him the hatred would only deepen. She had to avoid that at any cost.

She wiped away an escaping tear, yawned and stretched her arm across toward the passenger seat. Her body ached from hours of high tension and lack of sleep. Even a catnap would lose valuable time. She had to force her body to stay awake.

The ranger station came into view beside a long narrow sign announcing the entryway into Edgewood National Forest. It reminded her of a ranch entrance. She turned into the building's parking lot, choosing a space away from the town-owned vehicles. She noticed the building sported new signage. It was now called Flatrock Creek Police and Ranger Station. She turned off the car, glanced at the clear sky and decided to leave the top down. She grabbed her brown purse from the passenger seat, exited the car and hurried toward the building.

BRODY PHELPS SIPPED coffee, which had gone cold long ago, while he flipped through the file lying open on the desk. The only excitement all week had been Owen Henderson's regular Friday night binge at Sheridan's Bar. He set the cup down to jot a final detail in Henderson's report and took the folder to the records room, filing it the tan cabinet labeled H-J. The bell over the front door jingled.

"Be right out." He slid the drawer closed and walked down the dimly lit hallway into the main office. Saturday morning sunlight poured through three large windows overlooking the mountains.

He blinked, waiting for his eyes to adjust to the brilliant light. A faint, fresh scent drifted to his nostrils, triggering a sliver of memory he couldn't place. It reminded him of springtime.

A slender woman stood with her back to him, looking out the windows. Tight jeans hugged curvaceous hips and a narrow waist. Her straight honey-colored hair with golden highlights was pulled back in low ponytail.

"What can I do for you, ma'am?" Brody asked, stopping a few feet behind her.

Instead of turning, she stiffened. Slender shoulders squared and her head lifted slightly. Brody frowned. Something about her was vaguely familiar.

Realization shot through him. *No, it couldn't be.* His heartbeat lurched and scorching heat seared through him.

"Megan?"

The woman cleared her throat and turned to face him.

"Megan!" Stunned, his jaw dropped but he quickly clamped it shut. Brody stared at her. The memories flooded back, making love, their engagement, the accident and the breakup. She didn't say a word but watched him with those brilliant blue eyes as if she had the power to penetrate him and see into his soul.

There was little resemblance to the glamorous psychic who appeared on television talk shows. Dark circles shadowed doe eyes and worry lines marred her classic beauty.

Brody shoved his hands into his pants pockets. "It's been a long time, Megan."

"How are you, Brody?"

Her voice sounded tense, not the carefree silky tone he remembered. Hearing the husky way she said his name made him think of the past and the desire they'd shared. Desire he buried years ago, that he'd rather not remember now. Her body was no longer the slim tomboyish figure of a teenager. Her curves begged to be touched.

Megan smiled softly.

Can she read minds? "I never expected to see you again. What brings you back to Flatrock Creek?" he asked.

"I need you, Brody."

"You need me?" He crossed his arms over his chest. "What the hell for?"

"It's Robbie. My son."

A son? So she had moved on, married and had a family. She'd been able to forget him so easily? She'd told him they'd be together forever, yet she'd wasted no time in finding someone else to love and have a family with. Resentment and jealousy stabbed at him. It was a feeling he hadn't experienced in years. "You have children?"

"Robbie..." She choked on the name. Her eyes filled with tears but she blinked them away. "I've kept him a secret from the media. I didn't want people to know about him because I was afraid someone would try to hurt him because of my job."

Brody stepped back. He had to distance himself from the memories, yet he couldn't stop staring at her.

"Why did you refuse Detective Archer's request?"

He frowned. "Robbie Cassidy is your son?"

Despite their past, or maybe because of it, her pain washed over him, clenching at his heart. He'd never forgotten how Megan had stood by him when his cousin, Arial, disappeared. When the police discovered the body he'd been devastated and angry. People shouldn't hurt little kids. He'd sworn to help children in danger and, as an adult, had become a ranger and a police officer. Arial's disappearance had upset Megan but she'd stayed strong for him.

Now her son was missing. He fought the unexpected longing to hold her the same way she'd held him back then.

He couldn't get involved with Megan again—not even to comfort her. Even though he'd sent her away, she'd always possessed his heart in a way he could never escape. Getting involved with her on any level would only bring pain back into his life. The accident had been Megan's fault because she'd misinterpreted her vision. If she'd been accurate he would have been able to repair the car and prevent the accident. His parents would still be alive.

He remembered the car's twisted metal. His heartbeat pounded harder thinking about the day his parents wrecked and the sadness of losing them both at the same time. His breathing quickened.

Megan's tired gaze held his. She wet her lips with the tip of her tongue. The feelings they'd shared had been nothing more than first love. It didn't matter how soft her skin looked now or how much her full lips begged to be kissed. She'd betrayed him and he wasn't ready to deal with Megan or her visions again. "Archer didn't tell me about you."

Megan stepped forward and grasped his wrist. The look in her eyes held a plea for help. "Brody, I need you. I'll even pay you to be my guide."

His skin burned under her touch. He wanted to pull her into his arms, plunge his tongue into her mouth and reclaim what had once been his. He should send her away and keep his sanity. "Archer will find someone to search for your son. I'm afraid you've wasted your time. Now, if you'll excuse me, I have to get back to work."

It took all of his self-control not to change his mind. He was acting like a jerk and couldn't stop. He tried to justify his actions by thinking of the wedding he had to attend this weekend. He really couldn't miss it. Besides, he never took time off work.

"Please don't send me away until you hear me out. Give me a chance to explain why you're my only hope."

Brody looked down at the slim fingers squeezing his wrist. She death-gripped his skin, her hold so tight the tips of her fingers had turned white. He looked into her eyes. The fear and pain he saw there pulled at his heart. His resolve slipped. How could he not lend a hand?

He pried her fingers from his wrist and then held her hand, caressing its softness. Looking up he examined her face. Something in her eyes captured his attention. Why did she have to stare at him as if he were the only person she could count on?

God help him, he was about to make the worst mistake of his life.

THREE

"OKAY, MEGAN," BRODY NODDED TOWARD THE LOUNGE area, "sit down and tell me why you're here."

She entered the room. An overstuffed brown couch with two matching chairs, a plank coffee table and end tables added a sense of coziness to the police station. She sat on the couch clutching the purse against her abdomen.

What was Brody thinking? Had he wondered about Robbie's father? Or what her life was like now? Maybe he felt indifferent about seeing her again. She took a deep breath to calm her nerves.

Brody lowered all six foot two inches of his toned physique into a chair. She let her gaze move over his broad chest and down strong arms as the shirtsleeves tightened around muscles bunching beneath the fabric. A utility belt holding a two-way radio and other items clung to his narrow waist. *Man, he sure fills out that ranger uniform.*

Her heartbeat increased watching him settle into the chair. She fought the urge to go to him, bury her head against his neck and let him comfort her. It was all she could do to keep her seat. She wanted to lean on him, to feel his strength protecting her. She hadn't realized seeing him again would be this difficult.

Years ago he had wanted her love and she'd willingly given it. She remembered the time he'd playfully tickled her at the community barbecue, chasing her into the forest until they'd both tumbled onto the grass and into each other's arms. The day he'd asked her to marry him had been the happiest of her life, a joy eclipsed only by Robbie's birth. Brody had been her most trusted confidant until that fateful morning when the accident ripped their world apart.

She'd tried to get over Brody by dating other men but none had compared. She'd even convinced herself she didn't need a man in her life and Robbie's love was enough. Now she realized she'd only kidded herself. A love like theirs was rare. For a moment she allowed herself to wish for love again.

Brody watched her.

Instead of the baby-faced teenager who caused her to spin out of control, the man staring at her with such intensity was a stranger. His features were more sculpted and laugh lines creased the outer corners of his eyes. She knew she'd never be able to deny her feelings, even after all this time or the pain she'd experienced when he'd broken her heart. How much had he changed after his parents' deaths?

She searched for any softness in his eyes, an unclenching of his jaw, anything to indicate he'd forgiven her. She saw nothing to offer even a shred of hope.

Not that she'd expected forgiveness.

"I'm waiting, Megan."

She stared at Brody and twisted the purse strap. "It started eight months ago. A girl was kidnapped and two weeks later her mother was taken. They found both of them murdered in the Allegheny Mountains about twenty miles north of Clarkston. Two months later, a man and his teenage son disappeared. When, again two months later, a woman and her daughter were abducted, the Clarkston police realized they had a serial killer on their hands.

They called in the State Police but neither department is saying much. The victims are always a parent and child, with the parent having some type of psychic ability and the killer cuts an X across their chest and decapitates them."

"The Mountain Mangler?" Brody crossed his arms over his chest.

"You have heard of him?"

"Archer wanted me on the search and rescue team with this case but you know that don't you? You came back to Flatrock Creek to see me because…"

"Yeah, I knew Archer wanted you on the team." She rubbed her face with her hands. "Brody, you're the best Forest Ranger in West Virginia and a trained police officer. You've been tracking these mountains your whole life. You know this area better than anyone and have proven it by finding eight missing people. If anyone can find Robbie, it's you."

"Have you been keeping tabs on me, Megan?" His eyes narrowed and the muscles in his jaw twitched.

Megan jerked her gaze from him. Heat rose into her cheeks under his scrutiny. She couldn't admit that was exactly what she'd done. "I saw you on television when you found the Anderson boy in the Allegheny's."

She met his stare but his expression remained cold. "You were quite a hero."

"This is out of my jurisdiction."

"Not as a ranger."

"What does Robbie's father say about your coming to me?"

"I'm not married so there isn't anyone else to consider. Please help me."

Brody stood and paced over to the desk.

Megan waited. She knew better than to pressure him. And because this concerned her, it wouldn't be anything less than monumental for him to agree.

He turned to face her. Indecision and something else flitted in his eyes. Images from their youth flashed through her mind, the accident, his anger.

Crap. I'm reading him. Megan tried to break the connection by imagining a brick wall between them. It didn't work. She looked away and thought of the serial killer taking Robbie. Anger took over and broke her psychic link to Brody.

"I'm sorry, Megan." He frowned. "I'm going out of town tomorrow. I can give you the names of other rangers who are good trackers. I hope you find your son."

"What? You must be kidding!" She wouldn't settle for a ranger who wasn't a natural tracker and didn't have the intuitive ability, instincts and dogged determination that Brody had. "This is unacceptable. Couldn't you cancel your trip?" Megan rubbed her temple. "You still resent me, don't you? I did not kill your parents."

"I don't want to talk about it."

"No." Megan stood. "We will talk about it."

She moved to stand in front of him, in case he decided to walk out on her—again. "My son's life is in danger. He may die. What about your promise to Arial? When she was murdered you swore you'd always find a way to help a child in danger."

"There's too much in our past. You'll be better off with someone who doesn't have our history."

"I don't want any other ranger. I want you. You're the best. You've got an instinct about this sort of thing—intuitiveness—even if you don't agree. Please, Brody. I haven't bothered you in all these years. The one time I ask for your professional expertise, not for myself but for my child—how can you refuse?"

"Because I have other commitments. I can recommend Ranger Thompson in Calgory. He's an excellent tracker." Brody reached for a pen and wrote something on a notepad. He ripped the page from the pad and held it out to her. "Here's his number.

Tell him I referred you." He tossed the pen on the desk.

Dark brooding eyes bore into her. "Dammit Brody, Robbie needs you." Her anger swelled.

Brody turned away. When Detective Archer asked him to work this case it had been a hard decision to choose his cousin's wedding over work. He'd let her complaints influence him.

Now Megan needed him.

He wanted to be there for her, he really did but the risk to his heart was too great. Megan had torn his world apart once. He couldn't let history repeat itself. Not now, not ever again. "You only want to use me for my tracking skills just like everyone else. You only came to me because I know these mountains. You said so yourself."

Tracking was his job and he loved it. He didn't mind being used for work but with Megan it was different. He'd always hoped if he ever saw her again it wouldn't be work related.

"Brody, there's something—"

He threw up his hands. "I don't want to know, Megan. Whatever it is, it won't influence my decision. For once, why don't you accept you've made a mistake?"

"A mistake?" Megan stared into his eyes as she stepped toward him. So these were his true feelings. "I'm not too proud to admit when I'm wrong. But there's not a psychic on this planet who is right one hundred percent of the time."

For a moment he watched her. Megan hoped he was reconsidering his decision. Maybe he'd change his mind and search for Robbie.

"I know you're under a lot of stress. I'm not going to put myself in a position to be hurt by your *visions* again." He took her hand and pressed the piece of paper with the phone number into her palm. "I'm sorry."

"I don't want your sympathy, Brody." Megan backed toward the door, crushing the paper in her fist. "You told me how you felt seven years ago. I should have believed you. I don't know why I ever thought you would feel differently now. I'll handle this situation like every other one in my life—alone."

Megan jerked the front door open and slammed it behind her. She ran down the steps, fumbling with her keys. They slipped through her fingers, clattering onto the sidewalk. She scooped them up but dropped them again.

Anger boiled in her stomach, mixing with the ever-present fear. Tears clouded her vision. She snatched up the keys. Her heart beat so furiously she thought a heart attack was imminent. She paused to take a deep breath while visualizing her heartbeat decreasing. Once the rapid pounding and her breathing slowed, she continued down the porch.

And stopped dead in her tracks a few feet away from the car.

Her gaze narrowed on the child-sized, blue baseball cap lying on the Mustang's dashboard. The letters NY were stitched above the brim.

Oh God! Panic tore at her, catching her breath and shattering her. She ran to the driver's side door and leaned into the car for a better look.

Robbie, in capital letters, was embroidered in white above the adjustable clasp.

The killer's here!

"Give me my son!" Megan screamed and spun around, looking for him. "Damn it, show yourself, coward! Give Robbie back to me!"

Fear rose along her spine. The Mangler had followed her to Flatrock Creek! It was too soon. This meant his MO had changed. He wasn't waiting to come after her, which meant he could have already harmed Robbie.

Megan halted her frantic circling. Only a few feet separated the station from the trees. The Mangler must have disappeared into the forest.

She willed herself to slip into a semitrance and tapped into the psychic part of herself. She stood immobile, allowing her physical vision to go out of focus as she searched the woods behind the buildings across the street psychically, setting her mind free. In her third eye she moved quickly through the trees, watching them speed by in a colorful blur in her peripheral vision while she focused on the clear view directly in front of her. She searched everywhere for any trace of the killer's darkness or the sight of him fleeing through the forest.

She dropped the invisible wall she kept around her own emotions, making her vulnerable to others' feelings. She tried to connect with the killer's emotions. Apprehension and uncertainty immediately enveloped her, jerking her back into the ranger station and Brody. She imagined a wall around him to keep his emotions at bay. She'd deal with him later.

Megan traveled back into the forest, searching for any other negative emotions that might belong to the killer. If he were nearby, she'd be able to sense him.

Nothing! She turned and performed the same search in the forest behind the station. Projecting her mind forward again, she found an eagle feasting on a kill in a clearing, while a rabbit hid beneath a nearby bush—he'd narrowly escaped being the bird's breakfast. A little farther away, a large black and gold iguana peered at her from the top of a boulder. Her mind sped past the animals but the feeling of being watched caused her to backtrack in her mind's eye to the iguana's rock. The odd-colored reptile had disappeared. How did an iguana get out of its natural tropical habitat and into the Allegheny Mountains anyway? It probably escaped from the pet owner's cage. Megan scanned past the rock and further into the forest.

Megan's frustration melded with fear in her mind. How had the killer disappeared without a trace? At every turn she hit a dead end. It was as if he'd somehow blocked her psychic attempts to find him. She'd sensed this before, from other psychics. She did it herself to keep other psychics from reading her. If the Mangler could block her that meant…

The mental connection severed. She slipped from the semitrance to full consciousness. Refocusing her vision she examined the cap.

She fought the deep knowing filled with unthinkable possibilities. Was the killer psychic too? Moisture beaded her forehead, her body started to shake. The taste of bile filled her mouth, her stomach pitched and rolled. She pushed the feelings back down. She wouldn't throw up.

Megan slid down the side of the car and collapsed on the gravel beside the wheel. She covered her face with her hand. It was wet from tears. *When did I cry?*

The weight of the past hours—worrying about Robbie, arguing with the police and facing Brody had been tough. The Mangler had followed her, changing his MO. The possibility of a psychic killer—it was overwhelming. She grabbed her knees. She couldn't take any more. What had she done to deserve such a horrible fate? Pain and loss took control of her emotions. Tears poured down her face. She couldn't hold back anymore.

"My baby, my poor baby," she cried, rocking her body like she rocked him to sleep. "Someone, please, anyone! Help me find my son!"

To be continued…

Photo by Isabel Barney

Melissa Alvarez is a multi-published, award-winning author. She writes nonfiction under her real name and paranormal romantic suspense as Ariana Dupré. She owns Friesian horses, Barock Pinto horses and German Shepherd dogs with her husband and together they are successful breeders of champions. She enjoys reading, spending time with her family and horses, and designing book covers when she's not writing. Melissa lives in sunny South Florida. Visit her online at MelissaA.com for updates on new releases or at BookCovers.Us or BookCoversGalore.com if you're an author in need of a cover designer.

www.ingramcontent.com/pod-product-compliance
Lightning Source LLC
LaVergne TN
LVHW020532100826
845148LV00010B/1433
* 9 7 8 1 5 9 6 1 1 1 0 7 3 *